The Daunting Canvas

The Rise Of Kendra Blake

J. Alexander Paine

Contents

Preface

This started a few years back, when I was invited to be in an Indy film (still in post production). After being on set for a few days, and attaining my own scene, I was hooked.

It was not long after that, I met my good friend, Actress Linzi Gray. Together we wrote the screenplay that this story is based on, 'A Portrait of Evil'. For two years we wrote many screenplays together and did our best to get this on the big screen. Sad to say, it hasn't happened, yet.

After taking a long break from writing and creating, I decided to shift gears and attempt to write a novel, as all of my scripts are just sitting there collecting dust. After all, how difficult can it be? Right?

That being said, I got in touch with another great friend of mine, Laurie Leigh, who had just published her first novel, as well as my long time friend Ron Arold, who has published two so far. Now, I had some coaching and guidance, as well as two people to read as I wrote. And boy did I learn a lot!

Needless to say, this has been, and continues to be a great adventure as I never know what my characters are going to do next! I guess we will all have to have to find out. On a serious note, I do hope that whoever reads this, will consider the message behind it, and realize the issues of child abuse that happens everyday, often right under our noses. Many are plagued by this trauma in their lives, with a feeling of having nobody to turn to for help, out of sheer fear. I will tell you, this is one of the reasons I created such horrific scenes and gave a worst case scenario in this story.

"Be carefull how you raise your children, you
don't know what demon you could be creating."

J. Alexander Paine

Prologue

Kendra stood in front of a blank white canvas, inside of her studio. She stared deep into the vast emptiness of it, letting her mind drift far into her past to a time that she would rather forget. She saw the child she used to be, sitting quietly in the sitting room, afraid to speak for fear that her mother's wrath would pour out upon her, and once again, be taken down into the basement by her father, William. The dark room, lined with what would become her future, her profession and her greatest coping tool.

As she sat quietly, her mother Francine rambled on about how wealthy and better off they were than most people. The air was filled with the smell of vodka and what had become the incoherent nonsense that she had no way of understanding. Kendra listened intently, trying to understand what they spoke about. She understood none of it. Only that her misbehavior would bring pain and suffering.

The longer time went on, drink after drink, the more dangerous it had become. Please, let me just make it to bed tonight. Other plans had been made unknown to her. Francine stood at her normal post, in front of the fireplace, while William stood across from her, his arm perched on the mantle, and the other holding a Martini.

"Did she tell you what she did today William?" Francine looked over at Kendra with a harsh grin chiseled into her aging face.

"No my dear, tell me, what did the little unsightly child do this time?"

Kendra started shaking. She knew very well what this was going to lead to. Tears formed in the young girl's eyes, and rolled down her cheeks. "No! I didn't mean it! It was an accident I swear!" Francine scowled at her. "Silent! You will keep your mouth shut while your father and I are speaking! What would you know anyway?! You're only ten years old! You know nothing!"

William approached Kendra with his fists clenched. "What have you done to upset your mother this time? Let's have it! Tell me now!" Kendra bawled uncontrollably. "It was the vase that was on the table. I moved my book, and it fell. It broke on the floor! I didn't mean it! Please!"

William grabbed her up by her arm and started for the door. She knew what was coming next. He turned on the light in the basement and dragged her down into it. Opening the door to that room, he put her in and closed the door, locking it.

Keep quiet, just keep quiet and they will go to sleep. She reached up and flipped the switch on the wall, turning on the light. She wiped her eyes with the sleeve of her dress and looked around, trying to ignore the chair in the middle, laden with rope. There, in the corner sat a blank canvas. She picked it up and looked at it, setting it on an easel. She stood in front of it, looking deep into its empty face. Nothing, nothing was there at all. Just an empty white void, waiting for someone to come and give it purpose.

She grabbed a bottle of red paint off of the shelf and opened it. Looking around, Kendra saw a brush laying among others, untouched. Grabbing the brush, she dipped it into the paint and swung it through the air. The paint sprayed and splattered the canvas. Her eyes lit up, and she did it again. There were small red dots now covering areas of the canvas and some larger ones that had run. Kendra stepped back and admired what she had done, forgetting all about William and Francine upstairs. She dipped her finger into the paint and signed the bottom, Kendra Blake.

While Kendra sat admiring her work, she heard the door unlock. Quickly she tried to hide it, but it was too late. William walked in and saw what she had done. With a quick grab, he tore her dress almost completely off. She screamed. "Daddy no! Please! I just wanted to—" Before she could finish, she felt his hand strike hard against her cheek. Kendra fell to the ground, trying her best to cover her body up with her torn dress. William reached down grabbing the rope, and pointed to the chair.

As Kendra looked into the canvas in her studio, her mind came back to the present. She was safe. All that mattered was right here and right now. She grabbed a brush and red paint and started covering the canvas with red splatter. She screamed as the paint flew off the end of the brush and found its mark, turning white into red.

"Fuck you! You filthy mother fucker! I'll kill you! You and that bitch!" She screamed, throwing the paint brush across her studio. She dipped her finger into the paint, signing her name on the canvas, Kendra Blake.

She stepped back, hoping it would somehow all make sense, hoping she could find a reason. But there was none to be found. Frustrated and enraged, she flew out of her studio and upstairs to her apartment. She opened a drawer in the kitchen, pulling out a large chef's knife.

That's it Kendra. This only ends one way. You know what to do!

Kendra ran back downstairs screaming at the voice in her head. "Shut up! Leave me alone!"

Never! I will never leave you. You're nothing without me!

She stormed back into her studio and again, stood in front of the canvas.

Come now Kendra, you certainly can do better than that. After all, you are Daddy's favorite little girl!

Kendra screamed and started slashing the canvas with the blade, knocking it onto the floor. She cried unmercifully, and sat on the floor next to it, putting her head on her knees, and covering her head with her arms.

"One day." She sniffed. "One day you son of a bitch. I am going to kill you, both."

Chapter 1

The Daunting Canvas

One by one, sometimes two by two, clients walked through the door of the Daunting Canvas. The semi-quiet street outside lay wet with rain. Not a soaking rain, but the rain that comes down to refresh the dryness of the ground and everything upon it. The street lights shimmered through the light shower as the night pressed on. Kendra had positioned herself in a corner just across from the entrance, keeping watch on those coming and going. For a small room, the floor space was filling up rather quickly. Three rows of Kendra's artwork divided the room into sections. Dimly lit, with melodic stringed instruments being played over the speakers, the ambience enhanced the name of Kendra's gallery, The Daunting Canvas.

To Kendra, a self-made artist, her studio was the world, her escape, her haven away from all the dark things that walked through her mind and tried to split her very soul in two and devour it, and her artwork resembled the weapons that she used to fight off those dark entities. Now the world could see what she had felt, see her victory in battle, and bring those victories home with them for a price. Not all who viewed her work were fans, however.

An older couple, standing but a few mere feet away, was looking up into the removed eyes of one of Kendra's pieces. A King and Queen, portrayed on the canvas as being d·

in all of their royal attire, sitting upon a throne made of decomposing corpses, looked back at the elderly couple. The Queen's mouth, sewn shut carelessly, but tight as the King's eyes were removed. All that remained were two black holes adorned in crimson red around them. The man grasped his wife's hand.

"What goes through the mind of a person to create such a barbaric scene?"

The woman buried her head in her husband's chest, "Can we please just go? This is disgusting!"

He wrapped his arm around his wife and made their way towards Kendra, and to the exit. She watched them walk by as they both looked at her with disdain and horror written on their faces. Kendra responded, grinning with an evil glare. "Well, fuck you very much..." under her breath.

The couple exited the gallery and vanished into the rain, which was now coming down harder than before. After they left, Kendra walked over to a table, not an enormous table, but big enough to hold some wine, glasses, and some caviar for the guests to consume and enjoy. She grabbed a clean glass and filled it halfway with a red Chardonnay. After taking a sip, she made her way down the aisles slowly, speaking to various guests. She was extremely happy to see some guests actually admiring her work without the consumption of mind-altering substances and thanked them kindly as she departed their company. At the end of the next aisle, she noticed a middle-aged man staring at one of her sculptures. The sculpture was of a man, bound in chains, with his hands bound behind him. His head hung low, looking at his naked body and an erect stub that had once been his penis.

As the man in black stared at the piece, Kendra watched him, intrigued by his attire, black shoes, socks, suit and shirt with a red tie. He was clean cut, hair done nicely and gave the appearance of someone who is refined, dignified and well rounded in worldly matters. Drinking a glass of champagne, he could not seem to take his eyes off of the figure that was before him. After a few moments, he finished his glass and retrieved a card from the inside of his suit jacket. Making his way to the front of the gallery, he placed his empty glass on the table next to the others and propped his card against the glass. He caught Kendra looking at him, gave a slight smile, and left the gallery.

Kendra walked to the table and picked up the man's card. "The Great Bastille," she read aloud. "Who in the hell calls himself that?"

She flipped it over, and there was a phone number and an email on the back. Flipping the card over once more, she looked at it again. It impressed her how the red lettering shined against the matte black background. Kendra smiled and shook her head. "Even matches his card."

She walked to the door and looked left and right to see if she could catch another glimpse of him, but he had gone. The rain had stopped and the glow from the streetlights shined brightly on the wet streets below. The smell of a fresh summer rain was in the air and everything seemed calm and peaceful. In her heart, Kendra felt happy and accomplished.

The hour was getting late, and people were leaving. A few stayed behind to speak with Kendra and purchase some of her art pieces. As she dealt with the customers and admirers, the image of "The Great Bastille" stuck in her mind to the point of distraction. She stared at the statue the Great Bastille was standing in front of.

"I'm sorry, Mrs. Kendra?"

An older gentleman's voice shattered her wandering mind for the moment.

"Oh, yes, I'm sorry. It's been a bit of a long day." She played it off politely, laughing, "These premiers make for an endless day indeed."

He smiled and shook his head in agreement. "Oh, I can only imagine. And to do this all by yourself, that makes for an endless day. Quite impressive."

Smiling, she extended her hand to him. "Oh, you're too kind. Was there something I could do for you?" He shook her hand gently with a smile and inquired about a painting she had on display.

"Yes, I am very interested in the piece you have right over here."

The man let go of her hand and started walking down the second aisle, stopping in front of a painting of a woman. She was fully clothed, with her headless body draped over an old stone well. When one looked at the painting, one could only imagine that the head belonging to the body was down, deep inside the well. He stared up at the painting, rubbing his hands together with a look of almost ecstasy in his eyes. "How much for this one?"

Kendra stood next to him and gazed at the painting. "Ah, 'The Well of Heads'. This is one of my favorite pieces. I really enjoyed painting this."

"Oh, I bet you did. It is so lifelike, it seems like I could wipe the blood off with my finger."

She giggled, "I assure you it is dry, but thank you. This one is five hundred dollars." She had expected that to be the end of her conversation with him, but the man reached into his jacket pocket and retrieved a checkbook.

"Do you take checks? Or would you like me to use a credit card?"

She smiled gratefully at him. "Whatever is easiest for you."

Kendra took the painting down from the wall and walked with the man to the back of the studio where her office was. She sat in her chair in front of the computer and opened it up.

"Now if you like, I can have this wrapped and delivered to your house by, let's say tomorrow if you like? That ensures a safe delivery, so the painting remains undamaged. Or you can take it this evening after I have wrapped it up. Delivery is free."

He thought for a second as he wrote out the check. He handed it to her.

"I think I would not mind it being delivered. Can you make it tomorrow afternoon? I don't want my wife seeing this. She will be off to play bridge after four. Is that too late?"

"No, four will be just fine. I don't want you to get in trouble with the wife now."

He scowled,

"Oh, she will see it tomorrow night, gonna piss the old bitch off good this time!"

Kendra laughed in a shocked manner, "Well, I don't give refunds for divorces."

"If she does, I'll buy every painting you have!" They both laughed for a moment.

"Kendra, it has been a pleasure, and thank you. I'll see you tomorrow at four."

He shook her hand and turned. "Four o'clock sharp." she replied.

She stood up and followed the man out into the almost empty studio. Another half hour passed and another two sales, and it was over. Tired from the evening, she walked to the front door and locked it. Turning around, she glanced at the table that held mostly empty glasses now. "Fuck it. I'll clean up in the morning."

She shut off the lights except for a few over the paintings, and set the door alarm. Walking to a door in the back of the studio, she opened it, and ascended up the stairs; on top of the stairs was the door to her apartment. Not an immense place, but certainly not too small for one person. As she got undressed, she reached into the pocket of her leather jacket she was wearing and retrieved the black card the man had left for her. "The Great Bastille," she exclaimed as she placed it on her nightstand. She walked to the bathroom across from her bed and shut the door, then turned on the water for a shower.

After Kendra had dried off, she put on only a nightshirt, and looked at herself in the mirror. The shirt didn't display the body that was beneath it. Her body looked toned, slim, with dark hair that flowed past her shoulders. A very attractive woman, self made and twenty-seven years of age. She was beautiful, but she was the only one who could not see it. Blah!" She exclaimed and looked away from the mirror. She made her way to her bed, climbed in under the covers, and closed her eyes.

"Who in the fuck names themselves Bastille, anyway?" she said, yawning and fell fast asleep.

The morning came too early, as far as Kendra was concerned. It let her know of its arrival with a ray of sunlight beaming in through her window. Opening her eyes, Kendra stretched, and reached over to grab her phone and see what she may have missed the night before. She opened the app she used for sales.

"Whoa! Last night went better than I thought!"

She sprang out of bed, throwing her phone down onto it. Quickly, she opened her dresser and retrieved a pair of black jeans, a t-shirt, socks and panties, and threw them onto the bed as well.

"Fuck, I need coffee! Too early for this."

Hurrying into her kitchen, she started a pot, and returned to her bedroom to get dressed. After a few moments her clothes were on, the phone was in her back pocket, boots on and perfume applied. She went into the bathroom to run a brush through her hair. After she finished, she looked in the mirror closely at her eyes. "Well, good morning bitch." She smiled at herself. "Oh, good morning bitch."

This was her normal ritual, greeting herself every morning. Putting on lipstick and a small amount of eye shadow, she stepped back to get an overall look. "That will have to do." Turning out the bathroom light, Kendra went to the kitchen to get her coffee. Her day had officially started.

Turning on the light in her office, she sat at her desk and opened up her laptop. Scrolling through emails and looking at the bids and orders that were placed the night before.

"I can't believe this!" One particular bid stood out from the rest. "This can't be right." They had submitted a bid online for "The Bound Man". This was nothing new. Frequently receiving bids was a normal occurrence, but not for twenty-five thousand dollars. She was used to people low balling her work, $50.00 here, $100.00 there, never really putting in a seriously high bid, until now.

Wrapped up in her excitement, she marked the item as sold. Kendra leaped from her chair and ran into the studio, turning on the lights, unlocking the door and turning off the alarm.

Heading back to her office, she stopped in front of "The Bound Man", placing her hands behind her back and leaning into him she whispers,

"Finally rid of you. See you soon you old bastard." Standing up straight, she gave a quick smile at the sculpture and returned to her office. She took notice of the clock on the wall that let her know it was 9:30 AM. Sitting back in her chair, she reached for her phone. No sooner did she pick it up than a notification rang out that she had a message.

"Who is messaging me this early on a Sunday?"

The number was vague in her memory, but nevertheless, familiar. She opened up the message.

Thank you for securing my bid. Should we discuss the transaction, let's say, over tea? Two Brothers Tea House at 1:00pm. The Bastille.

She sat back in her chair, breathless for a moment and still in disbelief. After a moment of collecting her thoughts, she responded.

Yes, that sounds like it would be a lovely idea.

A few moments later, her phone went off. Again receiving yet another message from him, she quickly opened it, and read.

Splendid, I will see you then.

Kendra's eyes lit up and then darkened a bit. She opened up the drawer to her desk and pulled out an envelope, retrieving its contents. She pulled out an American Express Card that her parents had given to her when she moved out and went on her own. They loaded it up with $20,000, and to this day, never did she use it, not once. "Think I'll just bring this back to you today. I don't need your guilt money." she said, placing the card back into the envelope and putting it in her bag that lay next to her on the floor. "Time to call a taxi."

Chapter 2

Mommy and Daddy

Kendra set the alarm and locked the door behind her, stepping out into the daylight on the sidewalk. It was getting close to 10:30AM and her taxi was only a few blocks away. Looking down the street, she noticed that for a Sunday the streets were a little busy. This kind of surprised her, as over half of the stores were closed on Sundays because of the religious groups that populated the area.

Religion was not prevalent in her life, nor did she have an interest or question, rather or not a supreme being existed or was in control of her and her surroundings. She didn't care. She had spent most of her time trying to escape vile memories of her childhood, and she found painting and sculpting the mutilated works just fine for her.

A few moments passed, and a yellow taxi pulled up to the curb. Kendra opened the back door and got in.

"Where am I taking you, miss?" The driver asked.

She could see the driver's face in his rear-view mirror. He was a middle-aged man, but his eyes told a story of an uneasy past.

"I'm going to 167 Mockingbird Lane."

As the driver pulled away from her studio, he looked at her through the mirror.

"Ah, the old silk stocking district."

"If you want to call it that." she answered, with an unimpressed look on her face.

"I don't get many calls to go out there. Usually those people have their own drivers."

Kendra was staring out of the window, watching the buildings go by, people here and there, walking down the sidewalks and relishing the thought of what she was about to do.

"No, my 'parents' live out there."

"I have to ask, why a taxi? Most people use Uber these days. Driving a taxi is a dying trade, I tell ya."

"I like the nostalgia of it, I guess."

Glancing back at her, he added a tone of excitement to his voice.

"Sunday lunch with mom and dad, eh?"

Pursing her lips, she replied, annoyed, "Do you always ask this many questions? And they are not my actual parents. I'm adopted."

The driver's smile faded. "Sorry, just making conversation. It's a bit of a drive. I'm Mike, by the way." he responded in a friendly, kind voice, attempting to soothe her seemingly irate disposition.

Kendra relaxed and sighed. "No, I'm sorry. Didn't mean to go off like that. I just hate seeing them."

"So no lunch then?"

That got a lugh out of her, and she started to relax. "No, no lunch. But if you would be a doll and wait for me outside, I won't be long."

Mike shrugged. "As you wish, but the meter stays running."

Turning her head, she went back to looking out the window. "No, that's fine. I don't foresee this taking long at all. I'm Kendra. Kendra Blake."

Mike was making a turn to enter the interstate, "Well, it's my pleasure Miss Kendra Blake, we will get you there and squared away." He pressed down on the gas pedal and exited the on-ramp and entered the interstate.

The cab pulled up in front of her parent's house. A very large white house, with two stories, green kept up lawn, with flower beds, and a cobblestone driveway and walkway to the front door.

"Wow, it must have been nice growing up here." Mike said as he looked at the house.

As Kendra got out of his cab, she faced Mike, looking in through the driver's window.

"Yeah, a rancid dream," she replied sarcastically, "Just wait here. I won't be long."

She turned and started walking towards the house, leaving Mike in his cab.

"I'll be here." Mike turned on the stereo, leaving the motor running, and lighting a cigarette.

Kendra's insides turned as she approached the front door. For a moment, she pondered on just returning to the cab and forgetting about it. *After all, twenty-five grand is twenty-five grand.* She thought to herself for a moment, *But shoving this card up their ass? Priceless!* She regained her composure and opened the front door and walked inside.

Entering the foyer, she could already could hear the incoherent babbling of her Mom, Francine.

"William, did you hear something? It sounded like the front door."

The woman's voice was shrill, mumbled by the effects of what Kendra surmised to be too many morning martinis already.

"No, I didn't hear a thing, but as I was saying, El Greco was nothing more than a hack! I never could see why anyone would want to put such rubbish on display-"

Kendra's voice cut William off from his rambling. He stood surprised at her appearance as she entered the well displayed and large sitting room. There were paintings, statues and fine furnishings that were carefully placed and remained clean throughout. It gave the feeling of walking into a museum, except for the rancid smell of vodka that seemed to fill the air, permeating one's nose upon entering.

Francine and William were in the sitting room. Both of them

were well into their sixties, with their skin pale and thin looking. Their hair grayed from age and alcohol abuse. It didn't matter to Kendra how much wealth they had. They were still the worst thing she could imagine in the universe, and no amount of money could fix that.

"Well, I see that you have not lost your talents of completely talking out of your ass!" Kendra announced as she placed her bag on a small table next to her.

As she set her bag down, she noted the statue on the table, A Grecian piece, of a naked man, with missing arms. *Not a poor reproduction.* She thought to herself, *But still fake as hell.* She looked up to see Francine's eyes widen.

"William! Why is she here?!" she belted out, then turned her head towards Kendra. "You can't just walk in here whenever you wish, and remove that bag at once! The piece is priceless!"

She rolled her eyes at them, and shook her head, pointing at the statue on the table next to her bag. "That 'piece' is a cheap knockoff, and for your information, William, El Greco was not a hack! Why don't you actually learn some shit about what you're talking about instead of opening your-"

"You will shut your mouth this instant! You-you are nothing more than a hack yourself! What? You ran broke and needed more of our money? Is that it?" William waved his hand through the air, almost spilling his Martini. "You think you can come here, into our home, unannounced, and insult the very people who took you in?"

William set his glass down and straightened his leisure jacket. "This insolence will not do, and certainly will not go unpunished!"

He started walking towards Kendra. She thought to herself, *And here is the reason I haven't seen them in years.* But there was no way she could keep silent as they would have her be, a good little well-behaved young lady that does what she is told.

"You just stop where you are, old man. I didn't come here for this."

She reached into the bag and took out the envelope that was

holding the card. "I came by to give you this." She extended the envelope to William. Francine stood by the fireplace, holding the bridge of her nose with her thumb and forefinger.

"Oh William, this... this child is giving me a migraine again!" Francine wailed.

The tension in the air was getting thick. Kendra could feel her heart racing and noticed her hand trembling as she handed the envelope over to William.

"Shut up Francine, before I give you a real headache." Kendra exclaimed.

William's face grimaced as he walked over and snatched the envelope from Kendra's hand. "Just what is this?" He snapped as he glared at Kendra.

"Why don't you open it and see, ya lush?" she asked with a nasty tone in her voice.

William opened the envelope and pulled out the credit card. This was the moment Kendra had been waiting for, to see the look on his face, when he realized that she never needed their money at all.

William's bloodshot eyes grew wide, and he trembled. "Do you know what I have in mind to do to you, Kendra?!"

He handed the card towards Francine, who stumbled over and took it from him. She eyed the American Express and threw it to the floor.

"Well, well. It seems the little miss princess is all grown up." Her voice lowered and dropped in pitch, "William dear, why don't you remind our little girl what Daddy does to young ladies who cannot seem to behave?"

Kendra knew that look all too well, and remembered all the countless times that she had seen it before, just like it was yesterday.

"What?! Just what in the fuck are you gonna do?! Ya gonna, what, drag me down to the basement again? Lock me away in a room? Or I know," she said, as she kept her eyes fixed on Francine and William, lowering her head with an evil grin, "tie me up and give me that special bad girl treatment you used to give me? Come on Daddy, I'm sure you have a little blue pill somewhere--"

Francine dropped her martini from her hands. The glass shattered on the tile floor and scattered. Clutching her chest, she sat down on the couch and bent over, hyperventilating.

"Oh look Daddy! She is having one of her famous panic attacks. Better do something Daddy." Kendra exclaimed, pointing at Francine and laughing.

She kept her grin and felt something dark, filling her from her feet all the way to the top of her head. She blinked a few times and huffed.

"You little slut! I will not tolerate this at all!" William snarled, lunging at Kendra, throwing his drink to the ground, letting it smash on the floor below. The glass shattered, and Martini splashed onto the furniture. With arms stretched out, he advanced towards her, enraged. Without thinking, Kendra reached down and grabbed the statue next to her bag off of the table, by its upper half, and swung.

The impact to William's head sent him flying back, falling over a coffee table and landing on the floor. His body lay still, blood running from the opened wound on the side of his head, and starting a small pool on the floor. Francine stood up and screamed.

"William!"

She ran over and knelt down next to him, placing her hand on his head. He was breathing shallow breaths, but still alive. She then looked up at Kendra, who stood there, half in shock at what she had done.

"You're going to pay for this you-you disgusting harlot!"

She went to stand up, but could not. Kendra bent down and grabbed Francine by the hair, lifting her face up to her own.

"This has been a long time coming, bitch!" Kendra yelled.

Drawing Francine's head back, with a handfull of hair, she slammed it onto the coffee table, knocking her unconscious, with her body slumping over next to William's on the floor.

"I never needed your money! Never! I did it all on my own!"

Kendra stepped back and moved her hair from her face with her hands. "Fuck me!" She looked around for a moment and then looked back towards the front door. "Shit, the cab."

She ran outside to see Mike standing outside of his cab, having a cigarette. He was looking at the ground, and then looked up at her as she approached.

"Jesus, man, are you okay in there?"

Doing her best to play it off, she gave a nervous smile and laugh. "Yeah, um, you know how brothers can be."

Mike looked at her hand that had fresh blood splatter on them. "Yeah, sibs can be a bitch for sure. Still want me to wait?"

She reached into her back pocket and pulled out a wad of folded bills. "Yeah, how much do I owe ya so far?"

Mike turned and looked at the meter in his car. "About $45.00 so far, miss." He turned back around and looked at her concerned, "Are you sure you are alright?"

Kendra smiled and flipped out two fifty-dollar bills and handed them to him. "Never better." she said, as she turned and went to head back inside. "Keep the meter running!" Mike just shook his head. "It's your nickel, honey."

Re-entering the house, she closed the door behind her and walked up to her parents, who were still laying on the floor. Francine was stirring, and groaned as she tried to move. Kendra crossed her arms and looked down at them.

"Tsk, tsk. What to do with you two now?" She knelt down close to them, squatting and looking over them. "Now I just can't have you two running to the phone now, can I? I think it's time you both had a well-needed time out."

Grabbing Francine by the hair again, Kendra dragged her towards a door that led straight to the basement. Francine wailed and tried to struggle, but it was to no avail. Kendra opened the door and yanked hard on Francine's head, looking down at her.

"You shut your mouth or so help me God, I will throw you down those fucking stairs!"

She wrestled to get the women down the steps, but she managed. Being five foot six had its advantages and disadvantages. But the adrenaline was still flowing, and she knew exactly what she was going to do with them.

The basement, being dimly lit, contained shelves that lined the walls that were littered with old jars, things collected for years, and a lot of terrible memories for Kendra.

She dragged Francine to a door and opened it up. Inside, it was just as she had remembered. A single light on the ceiling, old art supplies and paintings stacked against the wall and on shelves. And in the middle of the floor sat a single chair, with rope still gathered around it.

After looking at the chair for a few moments, her thoughts went deep into her past. Memories came flooding back to when she was a little girl. The endless days, weeks and months she had spent, tied up in that chair, and the late night visits she would get from a drunken William to deliver his own method of punishment. Her eyes welled up for a moment, until she heard Francine's voice, that had now turned frail.

"What... What are you doing, Kendra?"

Kendra cleared away the rope and picked Francine up and placed her in the chair. "Damn, you're heavy for an old broad." she said, struggling to get her up. She grabbed up the rope and tied Francine up to the chair and turned towards the door, glancing back. "Now you are a good little girl and stay put." Francine watched the door shut, heard the lock latch, and Kendra running up the stairs.

She stood over William, still catching her breath from dragging her mother down the stairs. "Now for you, oh Daddy dearest."

William, still unconscious, proved to be a bit more of a struggle than his wife. She dragged him by his arms to the top of the stairs, and walked down slowly backwards, causing his heels to thump on every step. After a few moments of a battle, she could get his limp body to the bottom, and then to the room. She unlocked the door and opened it to see Francine sulked over in the chair. She looked around and then down at William.

"Well, I can't have this. We have to get you a chair, Daddy. We don't want Mother dearest all by herself. Why, that would be just rude!" she exclaimed, placing her fists on her hips.

Kendra walked to the room next to the one where Francine and William were in and retrieved a chair and another piece of rope. With a bit of trouble, she got William's body to sit up in the chair.

"We have to hurry. The cab is outside waiting." She stopped a moment and looked over at Francine. "You know, you could help instead of just sitting there looking pathetic!"

Reaching out, she slapped Francine in the face, hard enough to make William's body nearly fell out of the chair. "Now look at what you made me do!" Kendra exclaimed, sitting William back up in the chair.

She got busy tying William up. "I am so glad you taught me about Shibari Daddy, it really has come in useful." She tied the last knot and stood back to look at her work.

"Damn! I may just have to make you both my masterpiece!"

She laughed, shaking her head at the insanity that has transpired, and turned for the door. "Now you two behave, and um, don't go anywhere." she whispered as she shut the door.

She latched the deadbolt and turned off the light. "Okay, time to head back." Running up the stairs and into the kitchen and looking at the wall, where William kept his keys, she grabbed them and threw them into her bag as she scooped it up, and left.

Mike was still standing against his cab as he saw the door to the house open up, and Kendra emerged. She locked the door, turned around, and headed for the cab.

"Sorry, that took longer than I expected."

Kendra opened up the door and started getting into the back of the cab. Mike crushed out his cigarette and got into the driver's seat. He looked in the rear-view mirror and noticed a smear of blood on her head. He put the car in drive, went a few yards, and stopped.

"What are you doing? Did you forget something?" She asked, with a worried look on her face. Mike put the car in park and turned around with his arm draped over the passenger seat.

"Look miss," He glanced back at the house as it was still in view, "I don't know exactly what just went on in there, and really it's none of my business, but um-"

"I told ya, my brothers are a handful." As she fidgeted inside of her bag.

"Yeah and I wasn't born yesterday. You need to check your look in the mirror." Mike said, looking at her through the mirror.

He moved the mirror so she could see better. Kendra looked up and leaned in so she could get a good look, and saw the blood smear across her forehead. He reached into his glove compartment and pulled out a napkin from a fast food place, and handed it to her.

"I always keep some around, ya never know."

Kendra took the napkin and sat back in the seat. "Fuck!" she exclaimed,and started frantically trying to wipe off the blood. Mike turned back around, put the car in drive, and continued.

"You're welcome."

She leaned forward and looked in the mirror again. "Sorry, thank you."

Satisfied all of it was gone, she returned to sitting back in the seat. A few minutes of silence went by as Mike once again was on the interstate.

"So I'm not gonna get a call later asking if I know where to bury bodies, am I?" he asked, and looked in the mirror to see her reaction.

"I don't know Mike, would you?"

Her face did not change expression. Instead, she looked straight into his eyes. A chill went up his spine for a brief second. Reaching down under the seat, he took the safety off of his 45, and placed it on the seat where she could not see, and did his best to put a grin on his face.

"Oh, I don't know, it may cost you more than a cab ride." Laughing it off, trying to lighten the mood.

"Some things are worth the cost." she said, in a serious tone.

"So, ya want to tell me what happened? For real?"

Kendra stared blankly out of the window. "Just take me back to the gallery." Mike put his turn signal on and exited the interstate.

"Sure thing, miss."

They were a few blocks down the street from Kendra's gallery. The streets were still semi-busy, and the sun was glaring. Already it had burned off the rain from the night before. Kendra looked up towards the mirror.

"Mike?"

"Yeah, what's up?"

He was getting nervous every time she spoke.

"Do you know where the Two Brothers Tea House is?"

"Sure, it's about six blocks north of here, on six and Main, on the left-hand side. You can't miss it."

She kept her eyes on him through the mirror. "I have to meet someone there at 1:00 this afternoon. Do you think you could come and get me and bring me there?" Mike laughed. "Should I just clear my schedule for you?"

Kendra, who had calmed down by now, got an actual laugh out of Mike's response, "Why yes Michael, you shall be my personal driver from here on out."

They both started laughing at the tone she had used. "Sure, I can make sure you're there. Have to make sure my boss knows though. He is a real bastard, but it pays the bills."

Mike pulled up in front of The Daunting Canvas and put the car in park. "Okay, here you go."

She then gathered up her bag. "How much do I owe ya, Mike?"

He looked at the meter. It read that she owed him $110.15. He relaxed back into his seat, looking into the mirror. "It's $110.15 Miss. You already gave me $100.00."

Opening the door, she got out and shut it, and leaned into Mike's window, handing him another $50.00. "Just keep it. We will consider it hush money." she whispered to him, giving him a wink.

Mike smiled at her and whispered back, "OK, lips sealed".

Kendra looked over Mike's lap and saw the gun sitting next to him on the seat. "Nice touch, cowboy." She smiled and walked around the front of the cab and up to her door.

Mike shook his head. "Nice ass, bat shit crazy, but nice ass." he said, putting the car in drive, "Now that's a moneymaker." And drove away, down the street and out of sight.

Chapter 3

Great Bastille

Kendra had just finished up wrapping the paintings she had sold the night before to get them ready for delivery. All were due to deliver later that week, except for the "Well Of Heads" that she was to have delivered that day.

"Dammit, I am running out of time."

Looking at her phone to see if she had missed a call, she was disappointed to realize that nobody had called at all. "Why hasn't she called?"

Just then, the door opened to the gallery. A blonde lady walked in, just a few inches taller than Kendra, wearing tight jeans, and a button-up shirt, worn loosely at the top, to accentuate her cleavage. She proceeded straight to the back, joining Kendra.

"What's going on, Chicky?"

Kendra looked exclaiming, "Oh damn, I was about to call you. I just have this one for this afternoon to be delivered to the address I texted you."

The lady looked at her funny, "Um, what text?"

Kendra looked aggravated. "The one I sent you last night after the premier? Come on Michelle, get it together."

Michelle shook her head as she scrolled through her phone, "Sorry baby cakes, you never texted me last night." She put her phone back into her back pocket. "I just figured since last night was busy and you never called or messaged, I had better stop in and check."

Kendra looked at her phone again, scrolling through sent messages. "Shit, sorry, I thought sure I texted you. Anyway, can you get this delivered by four this afternoon? I'll send you the addy."

Michelle giggled, "Damn girl, you really need to get some. You're losing your shit. But I got ya babe. I'll get it over there safe and sound."

Kendra sighed in relief, "Thanks, I have to go out and meet a client in about 20 minutes. Do you have this?"

"Does a hooker have crabs?"

Kendra shrunk her face up, "Ew! Damn girl, you're nasty!"

Michelle grabbed the painting and chuckled, "I'm not the one with crabs." She picked it up and started carrying it to the front door.

"I don't have crabs either! Ya bitch." Kendra exclaimed laughing, "Thanks Doll!"

Michelle opened the door and left. "Yeah, whatever."

Minutes were ticking away, and Kendra was rushing and getting nervous. "Okay, you got this," she said to herself. She looked in the mirror and heard a beep outside. "Shit! He is here already." She grabbed her bag and shut out the lights, set the alarm and walked out the front door, locking it behind her.

She closed the door to the cab and settled in for the brief trip to meet The Great Bastille. Mike seemed a little off from the Mike that she had met earlier that day.

"You alright up there Mike?"

"Yeah, I'm fine. Excuse my French, but my fucking boss is a complete ass!"

"Yeah, no apology needed. I completely get it. Not to be a pain in the ass, but will you be able to pick me up later from the tea place?"

"I can try. I really can't say. He is riding my ass about not getting this piece of shit in the shop, then when I try, he is riding my ass about the meter not being on. Kinda screwed either way, and there isn't even a fucking shop open today!" Slamming a hand on the steering wheel.

"Wow, what the hell? Sounds like a real Dick." Kendra said as she reached into her bag and pulled out some cash and handed it up front to Mike.

"Here, this is for this trip, and for picking me up later when I call."

Mike grabbed the cash. "You're overpaying me girl." he said, as he placed it in his shirt pocket.

Kendra smiled. "Yeah, maybe, or it's an investment." Mike looked in his mirror at the smiling Kendra in the back. He shook his head a bit and pulled up in front of the Two Brothers.

"Here we are. Do you know when your meeting will be over?"

"No, I actually do not. Either way, maybe I'll see you a little later this afternoon, yeah?" Kendra asked hopefully.

"Um, yeah, I mean, if you have somewhere to get to, just call."

"Or I might have you stop by the gallery for a drink after you are off?"

"That sounds like it could be a plan in the making." Mike said, giving her a smile.

Kendra opened the door and started getting out of the cab. "You got that right." She gave Mike a wave and a wink and walked to the front door of the teahouse.

He pulled away with a grin on his face, putting on his shades and draping his arm out of the window, "Oh yeah. Mike still has it."

Kendra took notice of the front of the teahouse for a moment. The building was covered in red brick, with no windows, and the door, constructed of wood, wore a black iron handle on it with matching hinges. A sign had been placed out front, next to the door that read, *The Two Brothers* on top, and on the bottom, a grieving passage:

Rest in Peace Frits, my beloved Brother.

The sign seemed to be made of bronze, weathered and old in

appearance. "Well, that's curious." Kendra said as she opened the door and entered.

Inside was much like the outside, dark, dimly lit with red brick walls. Jazz played low, through the speakers mounted on the walls. There was a small bar and some assorted tables, mostly for two people, in front of a stage, with a single microphone that remained lit up from lights above. The place was empty except for a gentleman behind the bar that greeted her.

"Good afternoon miss, welcome to the Two Brothers. You must be Kendra, the artist Gustav told me about."

This caught her by surprise, and off gaurd. "Yes, thank you, I am." She extended her hand and shook his as he led her to a table. As she sat down, she looked up at him. "You said Gustav?"

"Ah yes, he is the owner. He shall be here shortly. In the meantime, I am Dante, and would love to get whatever you would like to drink. Would you like to see what we have on our list of teas? We have a very extensive assortment."

Kendra, feeling out of place, shifted in her seat. She was not much of a tea person. "I'll just have whatever you recommend."

"How about I surprise you?"

"That sounds like fun, I love surprises!" clapping her hands as a child would after hearing they were going out for ice cream.

"Excellent, I will be back in just a moment." Dante left her and went behind the bar, getting busy making Kendra her tea.

Taking a mirror from her bag, she looked herself over to make sure she was presentable. After being satisfied, she replaced it and opened her phone. No new messages. She stared off towards the stage, briefly admiring its simplicity, until an all too familiar voice taunted her.

Kendra, you idiot, you just met him. He will not help you get rid of your parents. Who are you kidding? You're fucked! You should've just stayed at the gallery and took care of your business!

She sat trying to hide the war that was going on inside of her head. *Don't you fucking start! I am not dealing with you today!* She thought to herself, but the voice was relentless, still trying to antagonize her and ruin whatever chance she was about to have in this meeting.

Fine, but don't come crying to me later when this all goes to shit.

Kendra shook her head for a moment, trying to shake the voice that haunted her from inside her head. She looked over to the bar to see Dante coming around to bring her the surprise tea. He approached the table and set it down in front of her.

"Oh, thank you! So what is it?" She asked, giving a friendly smile.

"This is one of Gustav's favorites. It is an oolong tea from Wuyishan, China, and one of the most expensive teas in the world."

"Expensive?" she asked, with a perplexed look.

"Oh yes, this tea goes for around $10,000 a pot."

"What in hell? I never heard of such a thing!"

Dante laughed, "Few have, only true tea connoisseurs drink this, mostly because of its price, but it has a very exquisite taste as you shall see." Kendra picked the cup up and took a small sip and set it back down on the saucer.

"Wow, not bad at all, actually very nice. I guess ya learn something every day."

"One would hope, and do not worry, this is on Gustav, who should arrive any moment. He is very precise with timing and is never late."

"Well, thank you Dante, you are wonderful."

Dante gave a slight bow, turned, and went back to the bar. Kendra picked up her phone again and looked at it. Still no messages. She noted the time, 12:59. "Let's see how punctual this Gustav really is."

No sooner did she put her phone down, Gustav walked in through the front door. She looked back at her phone. 1:00pm, exactly.

Gustav walked straight to the bar and greeted Dante. They exchanged a few words and pleasantries, then Gustav walked towards Kendra, who was trying not to be obvious in studying him and his manor. Gustav was a few years older than her, from what she could tell, mid-thirties, handsome with well kept short hair, a nice build on a 5'9" frame, give or take an inch. As he sat down at the table, she noticed the Rolex watch attached to his wrist. Now she was really feeling very out of place. *What have I gotten myself into?* She thought to herself.

"So you are Kendra, the woman behind all the artwork. I have to say, your work is very impressive." he said, as he placed himself across from her at the table as Dante brought him his tea.

"Will that be all, Gus?"

"Yes, thank you Dante. I think we will be fine for now." Gustav smiled as Dante turned and left their table.

"So you are the Great Bastille, huh?" Kendra grinned while sipping her tea.

"Yes, the one and only Great Bastille," Gustav replied, raising his hands outward and stretching his arms, laughing. "My name, as you already have heard, I imagine, is Gustav, Gustav Olsen." He reached across the table to shake Kendra's hand.

"Kendra Blake, I own and run the Daunting Canvas a few blocks away." Right after she said it, she felt her face blush, and the voice in her head harassed her.

Oh way to go, why don't you tell him what he is wearing or something else that he already knows? I swear I don't know why I bother with you. You are so pathetic!

Kendra tried to ignore the voice and keep her composure. Gustav sat back in his chair. "Yes, I am glad I went to your premier last night. I look forward to acquiring more of your work."

"Oh well, I am sure that can be arranged. All that was on display last night was just my latest. I should have another show in about six months, where I will show off, and hopefully sell, my newest pieces."

"I will definitely have to attend. So let me ask you, where did you attend?"

"Excuse me?"

"School, where did you study?"

"I didn't, why?"

"My apologies," he said, "I just assumed that you had gone to college to study the arts. Don't worry, it is a compliment, I assure you."

"Thank you, no, I taught myself. I had a lot of time as a child with no lack of supplies, so actually, I guess I am fortunate."

"Your parents must be proud."

Kendra smiled a bit. "Something like that." she replied as she brought the tea to her lips, taking a drink, and setting it back down. "So Dante tells me you're really into tea?"

"Yes, I love tea for sure, among many other things."

"And who is Frits? If you don't mind me asking. Noticed the sign out-front."

"Ah, Frits is, was, my brother. He passed away some time ago while in Egypt. We always said we would open up a specialty tea shop, so in his memory, I opened up the Two Brothers."

"Egypt? I don't mean to be personal, but how did it happen?"

"No, no, it's fine. Frits was always the adventurous type. He loved exotic things, animals, reptiles and such. So he went with a small group in search of a Pitted Horned Viper. He was half a day away from civilization when he found it. He made one slight error in judgment, and didn't make it back in time for treatment."

"Oh my God, that is horrible!" she exclaimed.

"Yes, but I had warned him frequently to hire a professional to go on these ventures with him. He always laughed, saying I worried too much."

Gustav sipped his tea for a moment and looked at his watch. "Anyway, enough about that. Let's talk about where Kendra Blake is going in the future."

"Yeah, okay. I suppose that could be an interesting topic."

"Yes, I thought so. So where do you see yourself in, let's say, ten years?"

Kendra laughed, "Ten years? I have no clue. I would definitely love to be in Europe, though."

"There are a lot of wonderful things to see there, but I am referring to you as an artist. Where do you see that going?"

Kendra sat back and thought for a moment, "I don't know, never really set any goals. I just take it as it comes. If people like it, they buy it and then on to the next. I guess." She replied with a shrug.

Pausing for a moment, she looked up to the ceiling, and then back at Gustav. "I guess I really don't know. Never really gave it much of a thought. I know nobody ever paid what you did for one of my pieces, though. Way to give a girl a fucking heart attack." She laughed as she expressed her shock at his purchase.

Gustav leaned in. "Would you like to know a little secret?"

She leaned in as well, so close she could smell the light scent of his cologne. "Yes, I love secrets." she whispered.

"That piece I bought from you earlier has already sold to another buyer."

Kendra sat back, her brow tightening in slight disappointment.

"Really, I thought you had bid on it for yourself."

"No. No, I love the sculpture." Gustav said, sitting back in his chair. "But $200,000 seemed to be a fair enough trade for me to part with it."

Kendra spit her tea out when she heard the number, "For fuck sakes, you're joking me, right?!"

"No, I never joke about business."

Kendra started getting angry. Her mind was spinning. *I did all of that work, and he makes $175,000 off of it! This is bullshit! What a dick!*

Gustav could see that she was getting upset and not at all impressed with what he had told her.

"Kendra, relax. I had you come here for business reasons. I am very intrigued by your work and equally intrigued by the mind behind it."

"I'm listening."

"Let me ask you this, How much did you take in last year from your work?"

"Take in?"

"Yes, how much did you make money-wise?"

"Oh, I don't know, overall I guess around 75k, before expenses and all of that." she replied.

"As a relatively new artist, I would say that is impressive. And, that you're self made is even more impressive. Let me ask you, have you ever done any commission work?"

"No, not that I recall."

"I see, the people I know, let's take, for instance, the one that has purchased The Bound Man. Well, let's just say that their pockets have no end. They are very wealthy and love the darker things in life. I have a friend in Finland, the man that just purchased your sculpture, who would like to have more of your work. How does that sound?"

"Um, wow!" she exclaimed. Her face turned blank with the idea of someone wanting her work that will pay real money for it. "I am not sure what to say, like what are we talking about here? Paintings? Sculptures? What?"

"Well, he definitely has an extreme taste for the dark and morbid, and after speaking with him, he would love to see some more sculptures for sure."

"Well, I can do that, but they take time and inspiration. But let me ask you something now, why didn't he just bid on it himself and buy it straight from me? Are you like a broker or something?" she asked, trying to get a feel for what he did exactly.

"No, Nirro is, let's say, more family to me, and he is very private. He does not like to deal with many at all outside of his circle. So when I purchase something, I show him. If he wants it, he buys it at a very generous price. If not, I have another piece to add to my collection. Really, it is a win-win for me. But no, I am no broker, just an entrepreneur. One could say that has a vast interest in many things."

"Well, this is quite interesting I admit, but to dedicate my work to one customer, that is not something I think I can do career-wise."

"Yes, I thought you may say that, so I wrote this out for you." Gustav reached into his jacket pocket and pulled out a check and slid it across the table to her, face down.

Kendra picked it up, flipped it over and gasped, "Are you fucking kidding me right now?!"

Gustav sipped his tea and placed it back down. "Is it not enough?"

"No! I mean no, it's more than enough! Um-" Kendra's knees were shaking, her head was spinning, and she started feeling light-headed.

"Are you feeling alright?"

"Yeah, just give me a second to collect my thoughts, um, wow!"

Kendra stared at the check for a few moments, pulled her hair back with her hands, then rested her elbows on the table, looking directly at Gustav in his eyes. "This is for real, right? I mean, you're not just fucking around trying to get laid, right?"

Gustav laughed, "No, I assure you this is very real, and hopefully the start of something very good between us. And as far as the getting laid thing goes, I never once considered you as someone with a lack of morals. Rough on etiquette, yes, but not what they would call promiscuous."

"Okay, well, sorry I'm just a little um-"

"Shocked?"

"Yes, I mean two million is a, um-"

Gustav crossed his arms and smiled. "A lot of money, and just the start. I assure you."

"Yes! That! Well, it seems I have a lot of work to do. I shall start tomorrow early on my next piece."

"Absolutely not." he demanded, "There is no timeline on this.

The finest of wines come with age. Nothing good comes from rushing. So, take this tomorrow, and deposit it." Gustav looked towards the door. "I noticed there was no vehicle outside. Tell me you didn't walk."

"Oh, uh no, I took a cab. I have an SUV I bought on a whim, but to tell you the truth, I don't know how to drive. I don't even have a license."

"Interesting. You are definitely a very intriguing young lady, Kendra. Perhaps, maybe you would care to join me for dinner this evening?"

"Dinner? Okay, look, if you are as rich as I think you are, me and nice places don't really go over that well, ya know? I'm not, nor wish to be 'refined'."

He smiled, "Yes, I gathered that. No, we do not have to go to a gourmet restaurant."

"Yeah, I'm not a 'go out and eat' type of girl. I know, how about you come by the gallery, let's say round six this evening and we will have a drink?"

"I know I would regret it if I said no. 6PM then."

"Nice! It will be fun. I will show the Grotto. You have seen the gallery, but there is much more in that building of mine."

"Oh, you own the entire building?"

"Well, the bank does. I should have it paid off in a few-maybe tomorrow!" she exclaimed with a bright look on her face as the idea came to mind.

"There you go. How much do you have left to pay on it, if you do not mind me asking?"

"Let's see, as of last month, another hundred and twenty-five thousand and some change. So ya, I guess if all goes well, I should just pay it off, right?"

"Assets are good to have. I would definitely pay it off if I were you. Listen, this check is not just to commission work, you were everything I had expected you being. That is why I wanted to meet with you. In my years, I have gained a very, let's say, large bank account. So really, what I am doing is investing in you. You make the pieces, I make my money on the ones I sell, a match made in heaven if you ask me."

"Of course, of course, I will still get paid for my work though, correct?"

"Oh, absolutely, and more. I promise you will not regret this."

Kendra looked at her phone. "Shit, I'm sorry I have to get going soon, um thank you! Oh my God, this is amazing!"

"Yes, I also have some things to attend to. So, six pm tonight at the Canvas?"

"You bet!" She gave hima hug. Surprised, he gave her a friendly hug back.

"Sorry, I'm just a little excited at the moment."

"No need to apologize. I will see you this evening."

Gustav smiled and walked to the bar, sitting down in front of Dante as Kendra exited the front door.

"Well, what do you think?" Dante looked at the front door and then back at Gustav. "I think she will be perfect."

Kendra waited outside for Mike to pick her up. A few minutes went by and the yellow cab appeared and pulled up in front of her. Kendra climbed into the back seat. "To the Daunting Canvas, James!"

Mike giggled, "Well, I guess that went well?"

She was glowing, happy and excited. "Yes! Yes, it did. Mike? How much of a dick is your boss, anyway?"

Mike looked in the mirror replying, "On a scale of one to ten? A solid twenty," Kendra smiled, "Good!"

Chapter 4

The Driver

A s the cab pulled up in front of Kendra's gallery, she leaned up towards the back of Mike's head. "This is where you shut your car off and come in and talk to me for a bit."

"Shit, I would love to, but I can't. I have to keep driving until ten tonight, otherwise I would."

Kendra sat back in her seat. "Mike, how much do you make a week doing this?"

"After everything, I clear about eight-hundred on a strong week. Why?"

"I think you really need to come inside with me, leave the meter running and the car on. I'll pay the fare."

Mike put the car in park. "If you say so."

"I say so." she said, as she opened the door and skipped to the front door of her gallery, unlocking it and opening it, motioning to Mike to follow.

"I am going to regret this." Mike said, as he got out of his cab and followed her inside. The door closed behind him as he entered and looked around for a moment. "So this is what you do, huh?"

Kendra was walking towards the back of her gallery. "Well, don't just stand there. Come on, the meter is running." she demanded, motioning him to follow her.

Mike did as she asked as she led him into her office, then sitting in the chair she pulled out for him.

"So, Mike, your boss is a dick and you don't even clear a grand a week, correct?"

"Yeah, that is pretty close to what it is."

Sitting back she crossed her arms, looking very confident. "Stand up for me a second, let me get a good look at you."

He looked at her, confused, and stood up. She motioned him to turn around. "What am I modeling now?" Mike laughed as he slowly turned around.

"What are you? About 6'1", 6'2"? Kendra asked as Mike sat back down. "Yeah, about, weigh about 190. I try to stay in shape."

"Perfect. How good are you at keeping your mouth shut about shit, Mike? Are you the kiss and tell type of guy? Or can you keep quiet under pressure?"

"Look, I don't know what you want, but this is kinda weird, okay?"

"*This*? *Weird*?" Kendra waved her hand around in a circle. "No, *this* is me seeing if I want *you* working for *me* personally. That is what *this* is."

Mike started laughing, "Doing what? Girl, I am a cab driver. I don't know shit about no art or any of that."

"Yes, you were a cab driver. Now you are my driver and security."

"Wait, what? I can't just quit driving a cab and hang out all day sticking to your heels." he explained, "There is a plan I need to stick to. I plan on having my own company one day in the next couple of years."

"$200,000 a year."

"Huh?!"

Kendra sighed, "Good looks, but not too bright. I will give you a $200,000 salary a year, plus pay expenses." She smiled and gave him a demanding look.

Mike let his jaw drop upon hearing her offer, and from what he gathered, she would not take 'no' for an answer.

"Well fuck, um, I guess I could do that." he replied in a skeptical voice,"When am I supposed to start this?"

"Mike, what is your boss's name?"

"Bixby, why?"

Picking up her phone, she dialed the cab company.

"What are you doing?" he asked, worried.

Kendra motioned for him to be quiet, then a voice answered on the other end.

"Bixby Cabs."

"Yes, is this Bixby?

"Yes, this is Bixby. Where do you need to go?"

"I don't need to go anywhere. This concerns your driver, Mike. You know the tall, good-looking one?"

"Yes Mike, he had better not have messed anything up! I do not pay him to-"

"That's right! You don't pay him anymore, I pay him! He no longer works for you, you nasty son of a bitch. Come get your fucking cab at The Daunting Canvas!"

Mike grabbed his forehead. "Oh, fuck-"

"Who is this-?" He was cut off as Kendra hung up the phone.

"Oh my God, what in the hell did you just do?"

"Nothing that you didn't want to do yourself." Kendra got up and walked to a safe in the corner, unlocked it and pulled out some cash, and handed it over to Mike. "There is $5,000 here, take this, and tomorrow I want to see you with new clothes, because you're not gonna be seen with me wearing that, and get yourself a new phone as well."

Mike held the money, counting it and realizing that she was not playing around. "Jesus!" he exclaimed.

Stabding still, arms crossed, she watched him and giggled, "He ain't got a damned thing to do with it, baby. Now follow me."

She then led him out of the office and through another doorway into the back of the gallery. There was a good size room with a bar and a few couches with a table as a centerpiece. She turned on the lights.

"This is where I entertain. Sometimes, like tonight, when I have guests." she said, walking to another door. She turned her head and smiled as she unlocked and opened it. Mike followed her into a garage that was in the back of her building. In it was a black SUV, brand new with a light coat of dust on it.

"Damn, is this yours?"

"Yeah, I bought it last year after a sale, but never drove it. I have a friend come and make sure it all runs and all, but I don't drive. So, that's where you come in. Ya like it?"

"Hell yeah, I like it." he said as he ran his hand along the truck's side and looked at the dust, now on his fingers.

"Yeah, it needs a bath. You can take it and get it washed this afternoon," she said, "it has less than fifty miles on it, so you should have no problems."

"If you say so, then what do you want me to do?"

"Do you have anything nice to wear? Preferably black?"

"Yeah, I may not be rich, but I know how to dress." Mike was laughing, "Damn girl, you move quick!"

"I have to at the moment. There is a lot of work I have to do. I need you back here at 5:30PM. I have a guest coming at 6:00pm and I don't want things getting weird."

"Weird?"

"Yes, weird. Look, he just dumped $2,000,000 into me and I am not sure what this guy's angle is yet. So I need you here."

"Holy shit! You're fucking loaded!"

"Not yet. I have to deposit it in my bank tomorrow morning, then I will breathe better."

"Yeah, I hope it's good, seeing how you just quit my fucking job for me!" Mike exclaimed, a little irritated.

"Calm down, it will be fine. I got you either way." She started walking back out to the gallery, with Mike following. "Okay, well, that's part of the tour. I will show you the rest soon."

"The rest?"

"Yes, my studio and the upstairs."

"What's up there?"

"My apartment and two more that remain empty."

"Shit, really? And you own all of this?"

Kendra looked around at her gallery, "I will in the morning. Till then, go take the truck and get it cleaned and waxed. That place down the street is open seven days a week."

"Cool, and um, I think the phone place is open as well. Want me to go take care of that also?"

"Good man. Yes, do it. Just be back here at 5:30, sharp."

"You're the boss." he said, and started walking to the back and stopped. "Hey um, I need keys."

"Keys are in it," she replied, "and the garage door opens with the controller on the dash."

"Oh, alright, awesome." Mike walked again back to the garage. "Oh, and Mike?" she said, before he could leave.

"Yeah?" he turned around to look at her.

"Nice ass!"

"Hey that's sexual harassment!" he laughed jokingly.

"Yeah, it sure is."

Mike disappeared through the door and left. Kendra headed back into her office and looked at the clock on the wall. 3:16 PM. "That should give him enough time." Kendra lifted her arm and sniffed her armpit. "Shit, girl, you need a shower." She made her way back into the gallery, locked it up, and went upstairs to her apartment. She shut her door behind her and placed her bag on the counter.

You are going to fuck all of this up. You can't honestly believe anyone would invest in you, do you?

Kendra held her hands to her ears. "Shut the fuck up!" she yelled as she walked into the bathroom and rested her hands on the counter in front of the mirror. "This is your big Fuck you! This is how I show them who I am!" she said aloud in the mirror.

No, this is where you get completely fucked and lose everything! replied the voice in her head. *I will never let you win Kendra, I own you*!

She turned away from the mirror, opened a cabinet, and pulled out a bottle of pills. She put a few into her hand and glanced at them.

Go ahead, take your pills. It won't work because I am never leaving!

Putting the pills back into the bottle, she hurled them against the wall, screaming, "I'll get rid of you if it's the last thing I do!"

Chapter 5

A New Mike

K endra sat at her desk in her office, looking at her computer and scrolling through her emails. As she was looking, her phone went off. There was a new message.

Hey Kendra, this is Mike, phone is taken care of. Now to get the truck washed. C U soon.

"Good boy Mikee, good boy." She sighed and looked to see what time it was. 4:36PM. "Perfect." she said aloud, then she realized-Michelle. Rushing to grab her phone, she picked up her phone and called her.

"Yes, my love!?"

"Hey Chicky, did ya get it all dropped off and taken care of?"

"I did. What a trip! That guy really hates his wife. She must be a real bitch because he is cute as all get out."

"Yeah, he said this should really piss her off. Maybe I should send him flowers with perfume sprayed all over."

Michelle started laughing, "Yeah, that will get her going for sure."

"So, do you have plans tonight?"

"Yeah, I do, I have a date!"

"Oh, you trollop! With who?" Kendra asked.

"Oh, a bottle of wine and this sexy artist I know, you may know her." she giggled.

"Oh stop. I actually have a date, well, sort of. We have a lot to catch up on, girl."

"What, since this morning?"

"Oh yes, and I mean a lot."

"Want me to come by?"

"I don't know. Well yeah, come by around eight pm if you can."

"Sure girly, Still want that bottle of wine?" she asked, in a promiscuous voice.

Kendra started laughing, "Sure babes, whatever you want."

"Ooh, whatever?"

"Stop!" Kendra replied, laughing, "I have to go. See you tonight."

"Alright party pooper, see then."

She hung the phone up and went into her gallery to unlock the door and turning all the lights on, she started looking at all of her work she had done. The gallery was quiet. Not a sound, except for her feet crushing the carpet fibers beneath her footsteps, and that sound was faint. She strolled up and down the aisles, looking and admiring her work, stopping in front of one of her paintings. A woman bound in knots with rope, naked with a smile cut across her face. Her eyes were bleeding and sewn open, with a heavy cord.

You can't do this without me, can you?

Kendra sighed in frustration, "Stop it! You're not real!"

Oh, but I am real, I am very real.

"No you are not, you're just some fucked up thing in my head!"

Yes, fucked up indeed, but you will never make it without me.

The voice grated on her nerves, the raspy whispering that had nothing good to say at all, the mischievous and demonic entity that lurked deep within her mind, waiting, stalking and finding just the right moment to strike.

Her fists clenched, as she wanted to rip the painting down and smash it, just to show whatever the entity that lived inside her, that it had no power. But she restrained herself. After all, time was ticking away, and Mike would be back soon, then Gustav coming for drinks. No, she had to keep her wits about her and keep it together. Now was not the time for one of her breakdowns.

Do it! Go ahead, I will just make another one. You will never win Kendra, you're too weak!

Kendra's anger was building, and just then, Mike opened the front door. Kendra looked in his direction, startled. Mike was all cleaned up, hair pulled back into a tail, Black dress shoes with pants and button-up shirt to match with a black leather blazer. To top it all off, he turned his rough looking facial hair into a groomed mustache and goatee.

Mike glanced at Kendra and noticed the look on her face. He was expecting a bit of a unique response.

"You uh, you okay there girl?"

Kendra looked away for a second, not wanting him to see her on the edge of snapping.

"I'm fine, just a nerve-wracking day. Good, but nerve-wracking." she explained.

"Yeah, I get it. So what's the deal with tonight?"

"Just hang and be the strong silent type, you know, the strong bad ass bodyguard thing."

"I can do that."

"Good, now follow me. I want to show you something."

Kendra led Mike to the stairs that led up to the apartments above. When they reached the top, there was Kendra's door on the right, and a hallway with two other doors, both on the right.

They walked down to the last door. As she was opening it, Mike was looking out the window in the hallway. "Nice view of the alley from here. Really picturesque." he said, trying to be funny.

Kendra laughed slightly, "Smart ass." and opened the door. "This is what I wanted to show you."

He followed Kendra through the door and into a large studio apartment. It was quite immense, with a full kitchen, bathroom, and a small separate room that was used for a bedroom at one point.

They had positioned the windows over the street below, with a good view of part of the Delaware River. Mike drew open the curtain and looked out. "Damn, looks nice from up here. Good view of the bridge."

"Yeah, I almost took this one instead of the one I am in. I like mine being close to the top of the stairs, so this one and the one next to it remained empty."

"Why didn't you just rent them out then?"

"I like my privacy, and when I need to create, I can blast whatever music I want, as loud as I want, and not worry about people bitching and whining."

"Yeah, I guess. That's a good point, actually. So why are you showing this to me?"

"Well, you are going to be around a lot, so I figured I would give you the option of taking this one."

He walked around the apartment for a minute, looking in the bathroom and the bedroom. "It is bigger than mine, that's for sure." he said, as he walked back over to the window, rested his hands on the sill, and looked at the bridge again. "There are a lot of people who disappeared under that bridge."

"Excuse me, what?" she asked, shocked.

"Oh, you never heard about it? People being killed and thrown into the river? Supposedly mob hits, way back a while ago, no convictions."

"Shit, no, I never heard about it. But I watch very little t.v. Anyway."

"Ah, yeah, if you were here, you would have noticed, but you were probably still with your parents."

"Ya, for sure. So, do ya want it or not?"

He turned and looked at her, "I have a pretty good deal where I am. How much do you want for a month?"

Kendra shook her head, "All expenses Mike, I told you that when I hired you earlier, remember?"

Mike froze, shocked at what she had told him. "Damn, you were not playing around were you? Alright." he said, nodding his head in agreement. "Yeah, I can do this. Besides, being in charge of security I can have a good view of who is coming and going from up here. It gives me a good vantage point."

"Vantage point?"

"Yeah, it's when you, oh-nothing. Nevermind, it's not really important."

"Good, then it's settled. I'll get hold of someone this week to have your stuff moved in."

"You move fast girl. Better slow down before you run yourself over."

"I know, but life hands you a diamond only once if you're lucky, and mine is going to be here in-" Kendra looked at her phone. "Fuck, fifteen minutes. Okay, let's go back downstairs, and remember, strong silent type."

"Yeah, I got it."

Kendra started walking down the hall as Mike closed the door and followed.

They entered the entertaining room, and Mike stopped. "I need to move the truck. Should I just park it in the garage?"

"Yes, that will do nicely. I like to keep the front clear and open for visitors and customers. You know, because I'm so fucking busy all the time." Kendra started laughing.

"Seems to me you are, really."

"No, not usually. Usually I have a pretty laid back pace. Just a crazy time right now, that's all."

"I get that." Mike said, as he put his hands in his pockets. "Well, I better go get the truck parked. Be back in a second."

He walked out through the gallery and got into the shiny black SUV. After pulling it around back and parking it in the garage, he reached into the center console and opened the lid. He grabbed his forty-five and looked at it for a moment. "Ya never know." he said, before getting out and closing the door. After tucking his pistol into the lower back of his waistband, he went inside to the entertaining room.

There was a large mirror on the wall, and Mike could get a good view of himself. "Jesus," he said, "just like the old days." He looked for a moment longer and turned away. *That was a long time ago, Mike.* He thought to himself.

He headed out to the gallery to see Kendra, who was not there, but in her office. She was looking in her mirror, putting on lipstick and checking herself over. "You're looking bomb hot, boss lady." She turned quickly and smiled at Mike.

"Are you flirting with me?" she asked.

"Nah, I'm on the clock. Besides, the boss might get pissed and fire me on my first day." He replied, grinning.

"Well, I suppose it is better to be safe than sorry." She walked past him, heading to the studio, "But you should loosen up a bit," smacking him on his rear end.

"What in the fuck?"

Mike laughed it off, but his head had thoughts and questions. The thoughts that should be best forgotten, for now.

He followed Kendra into the entertaining room. She had dimmed the lights slightly, giving it a bit of an eerie feeling. Standing at the bar, she was pouring a couple of drinks on the rocks. "Ya like bourbon, Mike?" she asked, as she poured.

"I really am not much of a drinker. But I guess I could use just one. Have to stay alert, ya know."

"Just one won't kill ya."

"I guess not."

She handed him the glass and raised her glass to him toasting, "To a new Mike!" The glasses clinked together and they drank down the bourbon, not taking their eyes off of each other.

Setting his glass on the bar, his mind was still processing the moment. *More like the Mike I'd like to forget,* he thought to himself. Glancing one more time into the mirror on the wall, he shook his head slightly, and turned away.

"Everything alright?"

"Just getting my head into the game, ya know, getting into the 'strong silent type'."

"You will be fine. Just watch my back and listen closely to anything you might find strange."

"I got you, better head out front. It's just about six." They walked out to the gallery, and at 6:00PM sharp, Gustav walked in.

Gustav let the door close behind him, adjusted his jacket, and addressed Kendra.

"There she is, and may I say you look stunning."

She wore a solid one-piece black tight dress that ended mid-thigh. Her hair had been pulled back with a few strands hanging in the front, with black high heels.

"Why thank you!" Kendra smiled and extended her hand. Gustav gave her the handshake of a gentleman to a lady, as he looked over and noticed Mike.

"Oh, I didn't know this was going to be a party. I am Gustav." He reached out and shook Mike's hand.

Mike responded introducing himself, "Mike…"

Kendra interrupted, "I thought about what you said, and since I have a new SUV and don't drive, I thought I could use a driver."

"Well, it looks like money well spent. Glad to see you are doing good things for yourself."

"Well, I am off to a start. Mike here also serves as my security. I figured, with a sudden influx of income, I might be better off safe."

"Always a good idea. You just cannot be too careful these days. There are many wolves that prowl these cities."

"Indeed, shall we go into the Grotto?"

"Grotto?"

"Yes, it is where I entertain guests. Come, this way."

She motioned for Gustav to follow. Mike walked slowly

behind, watching Gustav. *Fuck, I know him. But from where?* As a sick feeling formed in his gut, he cleared his throat and dismissed it as nerves.

Kendra stepped to the bar. "What's your pleasure, Gustav? I have wine, red and white, Bourbon, Scotch and I believe some very good vodka. What shall it be?"

"Scotch will be fine, straight up."

"Oh, would you like it in a dirty glass as well?" Kendra looked over and winked at him.

"No, no, a clean glass will do just fine, thank you." Gustav grinned at her humorous tone and took the glass as she walked it over to him. Mike stood by the doorway, against the wall with his arms folded to his back. Kendra sat on the couch and Gustav joined her, sitting his drink on the table before them and leaning back to get comfortable. He looked over at her and put his finger up to his temple.

"So, Favor me. Why the dark and menacing style of art?"

Kendra took a drink and set her glass down. She turned her head towards Gustav and sat back, "It's a long story. Let's just say that my childhood was less than satisfactory."

"I see, so this work you do, this form of art. This is your way of dealing with the past?"

"It is what I see. Plain and simple. So, when what I see becomes what I feel, then the magic happens. I can't really explain it better than that."

"Pardon my saying so, but that is kinda sad. I mean, to have such a dark outlook on life."

"Oh, I don't have a dark outlook on life, just certain aspects of it."

"Like parental aspects?" Gustav asked, raising an eyebrow.

Kendra's face turned blank as she reached down and grabbed her drink. She lifted it up and finished it.

"Are you ready for another?" she asked plainly.

"No, not I, as you know, I am mostly a tea person. I find alcohol to make me unreasonable and dimwitted. But knock yourself out if you wish. I am not here to judge."

She got up, adjusting her dress, and went to the bar, pouring herself a three-fingered glass and returning to the couch.

"I'm sorry. My parents are a very touchy subject with me. But-" she paused and drank half of the glass's content, "since you have invested so much in my work, I guess I can be honest and tell you about it."

"That is really unnecessary Kendra, we all have something in our past that haunts us." He stopped for a moment and looked over at Mike. "Isn't that right, Mike?"

Mike tried hard to keep a straight face. *He is pressing his luck.* He thought to himself before responding, "Yeah, Gustav, I couldn't agree more." *Goddamned it, where do I know him from?*

He looked over at Kendra and gave her a reassuring nod, letting her know he was going to keep her safe.

"I was adopted. When I was two, I think. My parents, well, adopted parents, took me home to their house in Cherry Hill. You know the place, Mike." She explained, looking over to Mike, still by the door.

"Please come over here and sit down? You need to hear this."

"As you wish."

Mike walked over and sat in a chair across the table from them. Gustav folded his hands on his knee with one leg crossed over the other, giving her his full attention, "Few children get the chance to grow up in such a wealthy neighborhood. Seems to me you were fortunate."

"Fortunate? No. They were fucking monsters. Rich beyond anyone's wildest dreams, but evil to the very core."

"How so?"

Kendra sighed and took another drink before finishing the glass. Mike, standing up, could see that she was starting to get worked up. "Here, I got it." he said, taking her empty glass from her.

Kendra looked up at him. "Thank you, you're such a doll."

As he went to the bar he thought, *Damn, this could get out of hand, real quick.* But poured another for her as she continued.

"It started, well at least I remember it starting when I was five. They always taught me to be proper, use good grammar, no elbows on the table--blah, blah, blah. Then, one evening, they were having drinks by the fireplace, like they did every night, day, morning, basically all the time. I don't know how they ever adopted, they always reeked of booze. Anyway, I came in from the kitchen with a cup and saucer. I had juice in it, I think, from what I remember, I wanted to have a drink with mommy and daddy. So I did. I went to take a sip of juice, and then it happened..." her voice trailed off as she started to stare off at the wall.

"What happened?" asked Gustav. Mike gave Kendra her drink and sat back down, leaning in, as he was curious as well.

Snapping out of the stare, she continued, "Francine slapped me across my face and I dropped the cup and saucer. It broke on the floor making a big mess."

"Why would she slap you? I mean, what did you do to deserve such a thing?" Gustav asked.

"Because I didn't put out my little finger, Gus. Because I didn't act like a perfect, proper little lady."

Mike, disturbed at her horrifying experience, sat back in his chair. "Jesus Christ."

"Yeah, and it got worse from there. She got so irate at the red juice on the floor, she made William, my dad, take me down to the basement, to this room. They filled it with art supplies, canvases, brushes, oils and paints, tons of it. And that is where I stayed most of my childhood. That's where they would take me for punishment."

"Well, now I can see you definitely had time to learn your craft. At least that came from it." Gustav reached down and grabbed his glass.

"Do you think they just put me in there? Oh no, when I was around 8, Daddy would come down there late at night. I remember the first time it happened." Kendra's eyes welled up. As she went on describing what her dad had done, looks of horror came over Mike's face, turning to rage.

Gustav sat and watched as tears flowed down her cheeks. He

remained calm, motionless, and held seemingly no emotion from hearing what she had endured.

On and on she went, the more she told, the more she let go of herself, until she was sobbing uncontrollably. Mike finally stood up, not being able to see anymore, and went over and wrapped his arm around Kendra and knelt down to her. She buried her head in his chest. "I think she has had enough, Gustav. Maybe it is better if we just call this one a night." Mike said, cautioning Gustav that it was enough.

Kendra sniffed a few times and sat up. "No, no, it's alright, sorry, I have told no one any of that before."

Gustav finished his drink and sat it back on the table. "I bet you feel a lot better now."

"Actually, yes, I do really."

"Well, to tell you the truth, I already knew. I just wanted to hear it from you."

Mike's ears perked up. "Already knew?"

"Yes, just like I know you have a loaded forty-five on your lower back, Mike." Mike remained silent, and didn't take his eyes off of Gustav.

"Relax, I am glad you are here protecting my investment." Gustav said, "We don't need her disappearing under a bridge or anything like that." Gustav winked at Mike with his eye and stood up. I think it is time, though, that I must be going."

Kendra stood up along with Mike, looking at the clock, 7:30PM. "Wow, man, time really flies. Oh shit! And I have Michelle coming by tonight, too." she groaned.

They all went out into the gallery. Gustav gave Kendra a hug goodbye.

"The bank opens sharply at nine am. By tomorrow afternoon, I want you to own this building."

She smiled, with her eyeliner and mascara running. "Alright, sorry, I must look like a mess."

"Nothing to be sorry about. Everything is going to be okay, trust me. You have a bright future ahead of you, Kendra."

"Thank you, Gustav, really, thank you."

Gustav smiled, looking at Mike, "Take good care of her tonight, make sure she is alright before you leave."

"I'm not going anywhere tonight. Think I will just crash in the Grotto."

"Bullshit." Kendra exclaimed, "You can come upstairs with me until we get your stuff from your place. Besides, I don't want to be alone tonight."

"Well, I bid you both a good evening. I will see you tomorrow." Gustav said, then turning around and leaving.

Kendra looked up at Mike, as he stood there looking at her with a look of pity for her on his face. She wrapped her arms around his waist and hugged him tightly. "Thank you Mike." Then she giggled.

"What in the world could you have found so funny right now?"

She pulled back and looked up at him with a smile. "Hell of a first date, huh?"

Mike started laughing, "Yeah, I guess so. Am I off the clock yet?"

Letting go of him, she walked to the stairwell. "Come on, I have to call Michelle and cancel. I can't deal with her tonight. Plus, I have to get cleaned up." She started walking and looked back. "Come on, I'll show you my apartment."

Mike followed her up the stairs and into her apartment, which was a little smaller than his.

"This is a nice little place you got up here. Actually, very nice."

"Awe, you're too kind. I got a good deal on the furniture and an even better deal on the deco." she said, and started laughing. Mike looked around as she headed to the bathroom. The walls had a few of her paintings here and there, lit up by a single lamp over each one of them. A few potted plants, a large entertainment system, with a huge T.V. on the wall.

"I thought you didn't watch T.V."

"Midget Porn Mike! A girl has to have it!" she hollered from the bathroom.

Mike started laughing loudly, "Oh my fucking God, you

didn't!"

She popped her head out of the bathroom. "I sure did, and you loved it!" She closed the door, laughing, leaving Mike out in her bedroom.

"Good Lord, what have I gotten myself into?" Mike said, letting his hair down.

Kendra looked into the mirror. Her face was a mess of black smudges. "Oh, Jesus, you look like shit, girl." She grabbed a cloth and wet it, applying soap, and washed her face. After she rinsed off, she looked again. "Now that is better." Then it returned.

Is it really better? Does the little K.K. feel better now that she had a good cry?

"Stop it!"

Oh, don't be so dramatic. They know now. Now you know what you have to do.

"No!"

Yes, yes Kendra. You must deal with them. Tonight!

Kendra stood straight up, with a look of amazement. For once, the voice made sense. Besides, she could not leave them down in that room for too long, not until she figured out what to do with them. Kendra grabbed her phone and called Michelle. The phone rang a few times, then she answered,

"Hey love! I'm about to come on over." Michelle exclaimed.

"Yeah, sorry, I have to take a rain check on that baby cake." Kendra replied.

"Oh, are you kidding me?"

"No, I am afraid not. I'll catch up with you tomorrow, okay?"

"You better, you little witch!"

Kendra laughed, "I swear I will. Alright?"

"Fine." Michelle sighed, "I'll come by tomorrow."

Kendra hung up the phone and left the bathroom, turning

out the light. Mike was sitting on the edge of her bed. "Mike?" she asked in a flirty manner, "How much do you love me?"

He seemed baffled by the question, inquiring, "Well, let's see, I just met you today, you quit my job for me, hired me and now I am sitting on your bed in your apartment. I have no earthly clue what in the fuck is going on, but I guess my answer is, a bunch?"

She started laughing and sat in his lap, putting her arm around his neck. "Be a doll and drive me to my parents." as she ran her fingers through his hair.

Mike looked at her, "Are you sure that's a good idea?"

Kendra got up and stood in front of him, "Remember that whole not kissing and telling thing?"

Suspiciously, Mike answered, "Yes."

She smiled and leaned down. "Let's go to Mommy and Daddy's, I'll kiss, and you won't tell."

"Okay, well, now I am officially confused." he said, standing up, "Let's go."

"I promise you will be well rewarded if you're good."

Mike opened the door to her apartment. "Oh, I can hardly wait." with a tone of sarcasm in his voice.

There was not a lot of traffic on the interstate. Mike was driving and remaining silent with an uneasy feeling about what he was going to get into when they got there. Kendra was humming some old song and looking out of the window. "Kendra?" he asked.

"Yeah, what?", she replied, turning her head, looking at him with wonder.

"Just what am I going to see when I get there? Or am I just sitting outside again?"

Kendra looked back out of the window. "I have Mom and Dad

tied up in the basement, Mike. They are both bleeding, and I need to make sure that they are not dead. Good enough?"

Her voice had taken a turn for the serious suddenly. Mike was back on the clock and he knew it. "Good enough. We will handle it."

Kendra glanced back over at him. "I knew I was right about you."

Chapter 6

For The Long Haul

I t was getting very close to midnight as they approached her parent's house. As they got closer, Mike turned off the headlights and pulled into the driveway. Kendra directed him to the drive that led to the back of the house, where they could park and not be seen. "This is good. Doesn't really matter, I don't think anyone is around here anyway. It's not like they have any neighbors right next door." Kendra said, getting out of the truck and shutting the door. Mike turned the motor off and got out. "Pretty smooth move, turning out the lights," she added.

"Yeah, believe it or not, this isn't my first rodeo."

"So, what do you think of Gustav?"

"Oh, boy." he sighed, taking a deep breath.

"What do you mean 'Oh Boy'?"

As they reached the back door, Mike stopped, and confronted her about his thoughts on Gustav. "Look, I don't know, but I got a strange feeling about him. It's like, I know him from somewhere, but I don't remember where."

"Do you think I can trust him?"

"What? With this shit? Kendra, I think you trust too easily."

"Well, I trust you, don't I?"

"And that right there is my point. You didn't know me from shit this morning, and now I am about to be a part of God knows what, and you're telling me shit you told no one." He said to her, "See what I mean? You can't go around trusting people, thinking money buys silence. Trust me, that does not always work out in the end."

Kendra opened the back door and entered. "You're trying to bum me out, Mike. I told you I had a feeling about you."

"Well, you lucked out with me. Besides, I had nothing better to do, and you're cute, so."

"Oh ha ha, flattery will get you everywhere. Now come on."

She led them inside to the kitchen and turned on the lights and placed her bag on the table and walked into the room with the fireplace. As Mike entered, he turned on a switch that was on the wall. The room lit up, exposing the mess that Kendra made earlier. "Holy shit! What in the fuck did you do?" Mike asked, as he knelt down and looked at the blood on the floor and table, and the broken glass scattered on the floor.

"They weren't too happy to see me."

"Oh, well Okay." He shrugged, rolling his eyes, "Makes all the sense in the world now."

"Sorry, things got a little tense. Apparently Daddy dearest didn't realize I am not the little girl I used to be. He went for me, I went for the statue, Daddy got knocked out. End of round one."

Mike picked up the statue from the floor, looking at the dried red stains on the white figure, "Jesus, that's fucking brutal. Lucky you didn't kill him."

"His luck, not mine."

"I guess I don't blame you. Honestly, I want to kill them both myself."

Kendra grinned. "Come on, I'll take you downstairs. That's where they are."

They opened the door and turned the lights on to the basement. They could hear moaning, mixed with weakened words coming out of the room where she had left them. "Doesn't sound like they are dead." Mike said.

"No, it does not." Kendra stopped just short of the door. She took a place in front of Mike and faced him, looking him dead in his eyes. "Mike, when I open this door, that's it. Up till now, you have been amazing. How do I know you will not flip out and run when you see what I have done to them?"

He grabbed Kendra by the hand and walked her back to the foot of the stairs, sitting her down next to him. He sat, staring at the floor for a moment, reaching around and rubbing the back of his neck. Kendra looked at him, reached out and gently grabbed his chin, turning his head towards her. Their eyes locked intently for what seemed an eternity, then he broke the silence.

"I wasn't always a cabby, Kendra." he said, as he held his hands out and looked them over, front and back. "There was a time when I wasn't who I am now."

"Yeah, well, that is a part of growing older. They make these pills, ya know." She replied, trying to break the now awkward moment they were in.

"Come on, I am being serious."

"Okay, what's on your mind, Mike?"

He looked back over at her, removing a few strands of her hair that had fallen onto her forehead and hanging down in her face. "You have entrusted me with a lot. Especially your past." He paused for a moment, looking away again.

"Look, whatever it is, it's alright. I like you. I'm sure it is not as bad as you think."

He turned looking back at her, "I used to clean."

"What? Like windows? Cars or houses?"

"No, I used to clean. People, Kendra."

"Like medical shit?"

He was getting frustrated. "No god dammit, like take care of problem people for other problem people."

"You mean like a hit man?"

"Now we are getting somewhere. Yes, something like a hit man."

"Holy shit!" Kendra stood up and walked back and forth, pacing. "So you actually killed people for money?"

"Yeah, I'm not proud of it, but yes, that is what I used to do before I went upstate for a 5 year bid."

"You have been to prison too?" Kendra started laughing with excitement, and walking in circles. "Oh, this is better than I thought! What did you go to prison for?"

"They wanted to nail me on murder, but in order to do that, I would have had to testify. I didn't, so they got me on some possession charges for firearms. And, since I didn't rat, I didn't have to clean anymore. There is more to it, but that is the short story."

"Fuck!" Kendra ran up to him and got on her knees, looking up and smiling excitedly. "So, how many did you kill?"

"What the fuck, man? I mean, this doesn't freak you out?"

Kendra stood back up. "No, not at all. Actually, I think it's kinda hot."

Mike smirked, "You are one fucked up chick Kendra, hot, and pretty cool, but fucked up."

"And you love it."

"Yeah, it is growing on me. So anyway, I guess what I am telling you is, I am in this for the long haul with you, you can't shock me. Trust me, there is nothing behind that door I have not seen before."

Kendra stepped to the door and unlatched it. "Good. See, I told you I had a feeling about you. Now I present it to you, the thing I call Mom and Dad!"

She swung the door open and turned on the light. Francine and William looked up, squinting their eyes, being blinded by the sudden flash of light. Mike walked up behind Kendra and scrunched his nose. "Fuck, it stinks in here, like old booze."

Sweat was beading on their foreheads. They were soaked in sweat and urine, and the blood from their wounds had dried.

"You two are a filthy mess!" Kendra put her hand on her hip and shook her finger at them. "I swear I can't leave you two alone for a second, and just look at this mess you made."

Francine was the first to speak, looking up at Mike. "Please, you have got to stop her. She is insane. Mr. Please-"

Mike stepped around Kendra and bent down to look at Francine. "You want me to help you?"

She nodded her head as William spoke, "We did everything for her, we gave her everything, and you see what she does."

Mike turns his head towards William, then looks up at Kendra. "They, um, they did everything for you." Looking back at William, Mike asked, "So, I guess you could say she owes you then?"

William responded, yelling, "You're damned right she does! Now get us out of here so we can call the police! Can't you see she is crazy?"

Mike stood up and stretched his shoulders and looked back down at William. "Those are, those are some interesting knots." he said, pointing at the knots Kendra used to tie them up. "Those particular knots are used in bondage. I wonder where she learned that?"

"She is a sick little freak! That is where she learned it! She will ruin you, young man! Ruin you!" William wailed.

Mike put his hands behind his back and leaned down again towards Francine, looking into her eyes, and addressing William calmly, "William, is that right? William, it's your name, correct?"

"Yes, that's my name!"

"And this is your wife, Francine, I believe."

"God dammit, yes!"

Kendra stood behind Mike, arms folded, scowling at William. Mike reached around with one hand and put it in his front pocket, pulling out a lock-blade knife and opening it with a flick of his wrist, not breaking his eye contact with Francine.

"Yes! Now cut us loose!" William ordered.

Mike looked over at him again. "How much do you love your wife, William?"

"What? What kind of nonsense is that? I demand you cut us loose now!"

William struggled, veins were appearing to pop out of his head that were growing purple, making his wound bleed again.

Mike put the knife up to Francine's face and slowly slid the blade down her frail skin. "How much do you love your wife, William?" He asked louder. "Do you love her enough to tell the truth, William?"

"Yes, I love my wife! Please, just stop! I, I won't tell, I won't call the police! Just untie us!" William begged.

Francine was crying and sobbing. "Why Kendra? Why are you doing this?"

"William!" Mike screamed. "Where did Kendra learn to tie these fucking knots?!" He positioned the blade longways on her face and applied pressure, making a shallow cut on her face. She screamed in pain as Mike looked at William and kept slowly making the incision.

"I will keep going, William. I have all night. Now where did she learn the goddamn knots!?"

Kendra was getting furious,and screamed, "Tell him you sick mother fucker! Tell him what you did!"

William's body went limp and his head hung low. "I showed her." He sobbed.

"I'm sorry. Did you say you showed her? I mean, I am a little confused here." Mike stood up and dramatically waved the knife around in the air. "I mean, was it like a girl-scout thing? Or were you teaching her how to sail?" Grabbing Francine by the hair and jerking her head back, he put the blade to her throat. "How in the fuck did you show her sex knots, William?" he yelled.

"I tied her up! Please let her go!"

"Did anyone let Kendra go?"

Mike, enraged, threw Francine's head back down, causing her to howl. He stood up, putting away his knife and looking down at William. "I just wanted to hear you admit it, you son of a bitch."

Looking at Kendra, he walked out of the room. "I need a breath of fresh air." he said as he passed her.

Kendra gave him room to get by and looked at Francine and William, both pathetic, tied up, bleeding and begging. She stood before them. "This is just the beginning." Turning off the light and shutting the door behind her.

Kendra went back upstairs and found Mike resting his hands on the counter in the kitchen. He was looking down and huffing.

"That was fucking amazing!" she exclaimed.

He raised his hand up to silence her. "Just give me a minute, alright?"

"Okay, okay. Really was awesome, though. Seeing them squirm in fear that way."

Mike sighed heavily and turned around. He grew flushed, and his eyes had become bloodshot.

"Jesus baby, you look horrible." Kendra said, looking concerned.

She grabbed a glass from the cupboard and filled it with water from the sink. "Here, drink this."

Mike grabbed the glass and drank it down, then set it on the counter.

"Fuck!"

"Are you going to live?"

"Yeah, I'll survive. That's just someone I thought I had left in the past, that's all. Been a long time since I had to be 'That Guy'."

"So, what should we do now?"

Mike looked up at her and broke his gaze from the floor. "I guess that's up to you. I can tell you this, though. We better get them cleaned up if you want them to live much longer. They will get infected down there and quickly."

"Ew! I say let them rot. That is the least that they deserve."

"I agree, but not until you have it sorted out. We need to clean them up and give them some water at least. I take it we are going back to your place tonight, correct?"

"Yeah, I need to leave soon. We have a big day tomorrow at the bank."

"Alright, do you have a first aid kit? Or something I can use to bandage them up and clean the wounds?"

"Yeah, I think there is one in the bathroom. I'll go get it." Kendra said, turning and walking out of the kitchen.

Mike pulled the knife back out and turned on the water to the sink, washing off the blade, cleaning the knife well with soap, getting rid of all the blood.

"This should work." Kendra announced as she walked back into the kitchen. She was carrying a woven basket filled with bandages and other things like peroxide and rubbing alcohol.

"Yeah, looks like there is enough in here to do the trick." Mike grabbed the basket and looked through it. "Get a bucket or something and a rag, and some soap."

"I think there is one in the washroom." She left the kitchen again, quickly returning with the bucket.

"There is a spigot downstairs and a hose. Daddy used to wash me with it."

"Good God! What a fuck?" Mike exclaimed, with a disgusted look on his face. "Alright, now all we need is some water for them to drink and that should be good."

"Yeah, I will let them eat tomorrow." she said, with a determined look.

"I doubt they will. From the looks of it, they will have the dry heaves soon from detox. If they drink as bad as they smell, it will last for a few days."

"Good, I hope they suffer!"

"It may kill them. Better get some booze to put in them. Don't want them dying of a heart attack."

"How did you learn all of this stuff?" she asked.

"I told you, this isn't my first walk in the park. Now let's go take care of this and get the fuck outta here."

"You're the boss!"

"No, you're the boss. I'm just in charge at the moment."

Kendra started giggling, "Yes, sir!" and followed him back down to the basement.

∞∞∞

They got back to Kendra's apartment just before 3 AM. Kendra got to her bed and fell onto it, and bounced slightly. "Oh, my God! I am wrecked."

Mike took off his coat and laid it across a chair. "Yeah, this has been too long of a day. Where is the couch?"

Smiling at him she patted the bed. "Oh no, you're sleeping right here with me."

Mike started taking his shoes off. "Is that a fact? Kendra, I really am exhausted, I think I-"

"Relax Cowboy, I said sleep."

He shook his head, with a feeling of relief, and laid down next to her on the bed. She nestled up to him and he put his arm around her. He went to tell her goodnight, but her body was already twitching as she was fast asleep. He kissed her on top of her head, "Good night Boss," and closed his eyes.

Kendra awoke a few hours later, got up, and went into the bathroom. She washed her face and undressed, putting on her favorite night shirt.

I can't wait to see how you fuck this up. What are you going to do with him, Kendra?

"Shut up!" She whispered.

Oh come now, they damaged you. You don't think that man in there would ever want you, do you? Your garbage Kendra! Go back and make them pay!

"Damn you, damn you! Why won't you just leave me alone?" Kendra turned away from the mirror and shut the light.

Mike was sleeping soundly and had not moved. She stood at

the foot of her bed and stared at him. "She is right. You never would want me. Nobody ever will." Climbing back into bed, she curled up with Mike again.

Tears were forming in her eyes as sadness took her over. She wiped the tears away and closed her eyes, falling back into a deep sleep.

Chapter 7

Millionaire Status

Mike awoke to see Kendra walking out of the kitchen with two cups of coffee. She placed one on the nightstand next to him. "Good morning Mikee." She smiled, patted him on his head and turned around and went to her dresser.

"Good morning. What time is it?"

Kendra looked at her phone. "7:20 AM baby. Time to rise and shine."

He sat up and wiped the sleep from his eyes. Kendra stood at her dresser, looking for something to wear. Still wearing only a nightshirt, she bent over to open a drawer, exposing the back half of her lower body.

"Well, that will wake me up for sure. Jesus, girl."

Kendra turned around and grinned. "Oh, it's nothing you haven't seen before. I'm gonna hop in the shower real quick. Hurry and get up. We've got a lot to do this morning."

"Yeah, thanks for the coffee." He sat up and planted his feet on the floor, reaching over and grabbing the cup and smelling the coffee through the steam. "Damn, this smells good. You make it strong."

She stood in the bathroom. She had left the door open and had the shower running. "Have to have it strong! That's the way I like it!"

She poked her head out of the open doorway. "I'll only be a

minute if you want to take a shower. I have a towel out for you."

"Sure, thanks, I could use one." He stood up and stretched. "Mind if I smoke in here?"

"Knock yourself out, just don't burn anything." she replied, as the shower quieted her voice.

Mike grabbed a smoke from his pack and lit it, walking to the window. He looked out, gazing at Philly in the distance. Taking a sip of his coffee, he turned back around. Kendra was already out of the shower and drying off, making no effort to hide her being naked.

"I guess you're not the shy type at all, are you?"

"Nope! No time for that." she replied, stopping and looking over at him, staring at her. "You're not embarrassed, are you?"

Mike laughed, "I don't think you would call the word 'embarrassed'. I'm good."

"Good. Don't want to scare you away just yet." she exclaimed, as she wrapped a towel around herself.

"No, I don't think you're going to do that. Distract me maybe, but definitely not scare me."

"Oh? And just how am I distracting?" she asked, walking towards him slowly and seductively.

He grinned and got up, trying to ignore the fact that he was starting to want her. "I need to get a shower. We have things to do." Mike walked past her and stopped. "You're a tease, ya know that?" he asked, and continued to the bathroom, shutting the door.

"Who said anything about teasing?"

Kendra's face grimaced with disappointment as she grabbed her phone and looked at her messages. There was a new message from Gustav.

Plans have changed. I will meet you at your gallery at 8:30 this morning.

"Fuck!" she yelled.

He was in the shower already, and could hear her through the noise of the shower. "What's going on?"

"Gustav said plans changed. He wants to meet me here at 8:30 this morning."

"I fucking knew it!" He yelled as he was washing his hair.

Kendra heard him and walked into the bathroom, leaning against the counter. "Knew what?"

"Not sure. I am telling you I have a bad feeling about this guy. I know I know him from somewhere. Just can't place it."

"Maybe you're just being paranoid."

"No, I don't get paranoid. Remember how he said he knew I had a gun in my back? That is what I call a tell."

"A what?"

Mike poked his head around the curtain. "A tell. It's what I call it, anyway. He was telling me he knows me."

"That makes little sense. Why would he do that? Why not just say, 'long time no see'?"

Being finished with his shower, he turned off the water. "Can you hand me a towel while you're there, please?"

She handed him the towel, and he started drying off, still behind the curtain.

"Kendra, there is a whole different world out there that you are not used to, that you don't know. I consider it part of my job for you, making sure that you don't find out."

"I can handle myself Mike, you don't need to worry about that."

He opened the curtain, with the towel wrapped around his waist. "I'm not doubting that, but you have enough problems. I just don't really want to see anything happen to you, that's all."

"Awe, big brother, looking out for the little sister?"

He looked down at her, not really seeing a playful outlook on the matter. "I have to get dressed."

She eyed him up and down. "I'm not stopping you." She said, and stayed where she was.

Mike turned around and dropped the towel, inciting Kendra to bite her lower lip. Then her eyes caught sight of a round scar on his upper back. "What happened to your back? Mr. Modest."

"Gunshot, a long time ago."

"What happened?"

"He made the mistake of not killing me. That's what happened." he replied, turning his head to look at her.

"Damn! You really are a cowboy, aren't you?"

He turned completely around after putting on his briefs. "Far from it, Kendra, far from it."

Kendra spun around and walked out. "Great, well, thanks for the show!"

Mike was brushing his hair and getting dressed. "Seems all I ever get, a fucking show." she muddled under her breath.

"Yup, happy to be of service." He grinned as he looked in the mirror. "Yup Mike, said it once. I'll say it again. Ya still got it."

"What was that?" Kendra was in the kitchen, pouring another cup of coffee.

"I said time's ticking. We need to rock it," Mike replied, speaking loud and clear.

"Oh, sure." She walked back to the bathroom, "Because I could have sworn you said 'I still got it'."

Mike turned to her, buttoning up his shirt. "Well, do I?"

Kendra grinned, looking at him up and down again. "We shall see."

Fully dressed, and ready to go downstairs Kendra exclaimed, "We better hurry. I don't know what he has planned this morning, but we don't need added headaches right now."

"Yeah, I'm coming."

He turned out the light, walked to the nightstand and grabbed his pistol, placing it on his lower back once more. He put on his jacket and shoes and was ready to go.

Gustav showed up at the gallery at exactly 8:30. Kendra was looking out the front window and saw his Jaguar parked, and him getting out, carrying a briefcase.

"Damn Mike! Gustav drives a new Jag."

"Well, yeah, I imagine he can drive whatever he wants."

Gustav opened the door and walked in. "Good morning to the

both of you."

"Morning, Gustav. So what is the change of plans? We are ready to head to the bank."

"Yes, about that."

"Oh God, are you having second thoughts?" Kendra asked, showing a look of disappointment on her face.

Gustav laughed, "Oh, of course not. I am a man of my word. But I will need that check back. It will take a few days for it to clear, unless you want to open an account at my bank, which will make this easier. So I figure we have a few options. One, I can go with you to the bank, and have the money transferred into your account directly, or I can give you straight cash, and you can deposit that way. I recommend the first, but the choice is yours."

"Well, I think having you deposit from your account is a better way, actually. What do you think, Mike?"

He stood motionless. "I am not a financial advisor, but it seems like a good idea to me. Pretty solid of you, Gustav."

Gustav smiled. "Good, then let us go. If you wish Kendra, you can ride with me, or follow in your own vehicle. It is up to you."

Kendra looked over at Mike. "I think I will just ride with Mike. That is what I pay him for."

"Good enough."

Gustav walked out to his car and got in, starting it up. A few moments later, Mike and Kendra pulled out of the alley and onto the street, heading towards her bank.

"You really think he had all of that cash on him, Mike?"

"Yeah, He is trying to show you how wealthy he is. It's a cheap flex move, but a good one for you."

"Flex move?" she asked, laughing. "Where do you invent these terms? I swear I am going to need a dictionary."

He smiled. "Well, I guess I'll have to write a list with definitions."

Gustav was tailing close behind, making sure he didn't lose them in the morning traffic. He pressed a button on his stereo console. "Call Archie." The phone rang and Archie answered quickly.

"Ah Gustav, my friend! What can Archie do for you this morning?" he asked. The Russian accent was heavy, but audible.

"We are heading to the bank now. Everything is going accordingly."

"Ah good! Good! My friend Gustav, you always deliver!"

"Always. I will contact you later and let you know how this turns out. I should need you, maybe in a few days or sooner, for that delivery to Finland."

"Yes, of course, of course. Whenever you need, call Archie. Archie always takes good care of his friends."

"Thank you, Archie, I got to go."

"Okay Gustav, I talk to you soon, no?"

"Count on it."

It was 2:00 PM after they had finished with the bank and signing papers at the real estate office. They were all standing on the sidewalk by their vehicles.

"Well, Miss Kendra Blake, how does it feel?"

Kendra looked at Gustav. "How does **it** feel?" she asked.

"Success. We must celebrate."

"Oh, I like to celebrate!" Kendra exclaimed, clapping her hands. "You have got to meet my friend Michelle. She is coming by the gallery this afternoon. Maybe we can meet up there around five-ish?"

Gustav, looking down at his phone replied, "Yes, actually make it six if you can. I have a thing I have to do."

Mike cocked an eye. A thing. Mike thought to himself. *I know you, you son of a bitch, but where? Come on, Mike, think!*

"Six it is! Michelle is just going to love you both!"

"I'm sure she is wonderful." Gustav gave a shallow smile and nodded his head to Mike. "Mike, I'll see you this evening."

"I'm sure you will."

Gustav got into his car and drove off. "Well, that is that." Kendra said.

"Yes, that is that, and thanks for the deposit. I can breathe better now."

"I told you I would take care of you."

"That you did. Hey look, I have a chest at my apartment. I need to get out before people move my things into your building. Mind if we swing by and grab it?"

"No, that's cool. What do you have in there? Dead bodies?" She asked, trying to get a rise out of him.

"No, just some old stuff I need to go through, pictures, a few odds and ends. Nothing big, just personal stuff."

"Sure, if you want to go now, we can."

"Great, thanks. I appreciate it."

As Mike was driving, Kendra was playing with the stereo, until she found something she wanted to listen to.

"Oh, my God! I love this song!" she exclaimed, turning it up. The heavy music was blaring out of the speakers. She rolled down her window and started singing loudly.

"Welcome to my padded cell, where the sky is always clear! I'm so sure it's so nice outside, but I'd rather stay in here! Augh!!!"

"What in the fuck are we listening to?" he asked, "Sounds good and all, but I don't think I have ever heard it."

Kendra laughed, "It's called Asylumized. It's from an old band I used to listen to a while ago. I can't believe they are playing it."

Kendra was invested in banging her head while she listened to the song. Then she paused looking at Mike and turned the stereo down. "Mike?"

"Yeah what?"

"This is going to sound corny, and please don't take this the wrong way, but…"

Oh God, what now? I swear! This chick is spun. Seriously spun. Mike thought to himself.

"Take what the wrong way? What's up?"

"I don't know. It just feels like I have known you forever. I know, how cliché, right?"

"Yeah, if that's a pickup line, that's pretty cheesy."

Kendra crossed her arms and pressed back into her seat. "I'm being serious. You don't have to be mean."

Glancing over at her, he could see that he seriously upset her. "Sorry, I wasn't trying to be mean, just never know when you're serious or not. But yeah, I guess it feels like we have. We have known each other for some twenty-seven hours and already we are a felony in progress." he said, trying to smile and lighten up her quickly turned mood.

She didn't respond, just sat and looked out the window. Mike sighed and put his hand on her leg.

"Look, really, I am sorry. I wasn't trying to be a dick."

Kendra looked back at him and started laughing. "Oh! You ought to see the look on your face, cowboy! Oh, this is priceless! Hook, line and sinker!"

"Are you fucking kidding me?" he asked, agitated at being made a fool of.

"No, I am not kidding. I really got you." She stopped laughing and took on a more serious tone. "I am telling the truth, though. It really feels like I have known you forever. I hope I am not making a mistake."

"Mistake?" He asked, glancing over.

"Yeah, a mistake. You're right, I trust too easily, and it fucks me every-time."

"Yeah, I gathered that. Just keep your wits about you, Kendra. This world is fucked at best. Trust me, there are things you would rather not know about."

Kendra smiled. "That's what I have you for. My knight in black clad armor!"

Mike laughed, "Yeah, something like that."

They pulled up to Mike's apartment building. There were several units combined in a white cinder block structure. Mike pulled up in front of his apartment and parked.. "I will only be a minute."

Kendra looked at him walking to the door of his apartment. She sighed and rested her head in her hand. "My knight in black clad armor."

Chapter 8

Cats Out of The Bag

Mike set the chest down inside the bedroom of his new apartment. Kendra was carrying a duffel-bag of his that had some clothes in it, along with some personal care items. "Where do you want this?"

"You can just set it on the floor."

"Or I can put it in my apartment. I can't have you sleeping on the floor, at least until we get your stuff here." Kendra suggested, looking at him with hopeful eyes.

"About that. I have everything I need right here. I got some money now. You may be able to help me pick out new stuff. If you don't mind. But until then, go ahead. I don't mind staying with you."

"Well, well, look at you getting all spruced up. Of course! I would love to go shopping! I haven't been in like, forever!" Kendra exclaimed with a look of excited anticipation of her face. With the bag in hand, she ran out of the apartment.

After watching her run off, he returned his focus to his trunk. "Alright, Mr. Gustav, I know I have you in here somewhere."

After he unlocked and opened his trunk, he pulled out a large case and set it on the floor,along with a few other smaller cases, and put them carefully beside the large one.

"Ah, here we go." he said, holding up a manilla envelope.

He opened it up, removing its contents. Most of it was pictures he had taken, with some paperwork mixed in between. Everything, in perfect order. Carefully looking at the pictures, one by one, he placed them face down on the envelope that he set on top of the large black case.

"Bingo! I fucking knew it!"

"Knew what?" asked Kendra, standing behind him.

"Shit!" He put the picture down and gathered up the rest, placing them back in the bag. "Sorry I didn't hear you come in again."

"What did you know, Mike?" Standing with her arms crossed, and leaning against the doorway.

"Fuck it, I might as well show you." he sighed, pulling out the pictures, and showing her the one he was looking for. It was black and white, with two men talking outside of a building. He handed the photo to Kendra. "See anyone familiar in this picture?"

Kendra looked closely. "That looks like Gustav. Who is he with?"

"Who is he with? A Russian named Stepan."

"Okay, so he knows a Russian named Stepan. So what?"

"Stepan was a smuggler. Mostly in small arms, but also into human trafficking. High-level ties with some terrible fucking people." He explained.

"Was?"

"Yeah, 'was'."

"Did you, um, you know--" she asked, putting her hand up like a gun, "Shoot him?"

"No, it wasn't my doing, but I know whose doing it was. Good riddance, I say."

"Well, what is Gustav doing with him?"

"That I don't know. I was tracking Stepan. I had never seen Gustav before, or even heard of him." he replied, "Whatever he was doing, I am sure it wasn't good. Stepan and his people were into some really nasty shit."

"Just my luck. So what's the deal with the cases?"

"Stuff, I hope I don't have to use." He replied, putting the pictures and cases away, closing the trunk and locking it.

"So what now? What are we going to do about Gustav?"

"We? No, I am going to make a few phone calls and see what I can find out. You need to play it cool with one eye open. Just pretend you didn't see this. Can you do that?"

"I won't say anything. You didn't have to hide it from me, ya know? I know that's what you were doing."

"I know, some things are just best left unknown. Now I have to be on point. No more parties for me, no booze or anything." he said, pulling out a cigarette and lighting it.

"Oh, come on! We are celebrating tonight! Don't be a downer." she begged, reaching up and rubbing his chest, "I need you to have fun with me too, you know?"

"We will see. Just know, I am uneasy about this cat."

"So you will have fun tonight?" she asked, smiling and pulling at his shirt, batting her eyes.

"Yeah, I guess, but not too much." he replied, with a slight laugh.

"Yay! Goody for me! I have to call Michelle!" She exclaimed, dashing out of the room and out of the apartment, dialing on her phone.

"Hey girl! Party at the Canvas tonight!" Her voice trailed off as she closed the door to her place.

Mike walked out into the living room of his apartment, looking around. "Damn, this is really fucking empty. I need some shit for sure." He pulled his phone out and went through his contacts. "Ah, yes! Glad they all transferred. Okay, time to call Lucky."

After Mike had finished his phone call, he went back to Kendra's apartment, to find her lying on her bed and talking on the phone. "Oh, speaking of tall, dark and handsome, hold on, he just walked in." she said, putting the phone down for a second. "It's Michelle. She is dying to meet you."

"Spreading rumors about me already?"

"No, just facts." Kendra winked and put the phone back up to her ear. "So anyway, be here at 6."

"Well, what did he say?" asked Michelle.

"Nothing. He thinks I am spreading rumors about him."

"It was a joke, Kendra." Mike hollered from the kitchen.

"Well, I heard that. What is he doing?" Asked Michelle.

"Getting something to drink, I think."

"So are you two, ya know, an item?"

"No, I wish. Don't think it's, um, ya know, up his alley." Kendra replied, sounding disappointed.

Mike walked around the corner. "What's not up my alley?"

"Champagne, she wanted to know if you wanted her to bring some."

He replied with a disgusted look on his face. "Yeah, um no thanks. I'd rather drink panther piss."

"Okay girl, I got to run, so I will see you tonight?"

"Oh, for sure! Can't wait to meet this mysterious man, and Mike, of course. Sounds hot."

"Mine!" Kendra exclaimed.

"Alright! I got it, hands off the merch. Love ya, lady, see ya tonight." Michelle said, laughing.

Kendra hung the phone up and sat up. "So, got any ideas on what you want to do with your place?" she asked, as she watched him standing at the window.

"Not really. I am a sort of 'I'll know it when I see it' type of guy."

"Ah, I got ya. Maybe tomorrow we can go do some shopping."

"Yeah, that would be cool. I need some new threads as well."

Kendra started laughing, and bouncing on the bed. "Threads, what the fuck are you in the 70s?"

"Yeah, let's go to a disco." Mike replied, laughing.

She got up from the bed and walked over to him, slowly, like she was in contemplation. "So, we have an hour and a half till they get here." Mike was still standing at the window, facing her. "Got any ideas of what to do with the time?" she asked.

"Yeah, actually I do." Looking back out of the window, he could only wonder what Gustav was really up to with her. He knew that no matter what, he was not going to let anything happen to her, come what may.

As he turned his head away from her, the voice came to her again, invading her mind with suggestions she would rather not hear.

I told you he would not want you, silly girl. You need to get rid of him.

Kendra closed her eyes and forced the voice from her head. "And what's your idea, Mike?" she sighed.

"I am waiting for a call. I called an old contact of mine about our friend Gustav. He is looking into it to see what he can dig up."

"Man, he really has you shook up, doesn't he?"

"Me? No, I'm just being careful. And you should be too. Stick close to me tonight. I don't trust him."

Kendra walked up behind him and wrapped her arms around his waist.

"Is this close enough?" She asked.

Mike smiled. "I guess that will do." And continued looking out the window at the street below.

She kept her arms around him and rested her head on his back. "Can I keep you?"

"Keep? What, am I a dog now?"

"Yeah, a big Rottweiler! One big cuddly Rottweiler." she replied, squeezing harder with her arms around his waist.

"I can accept that, if you would have said poodle, you may have gotten thrown through the window."

She slapped him on the back of the head. "Behave!" She laughed as Mike grabbed his head with his hand.

"Ouch ya little shit! Careful, I'm old and brittle." He exclaimed, as they both started laughing hysterically.

"Oh yeah, you're older than fucking dirt! I bet when you were a kid, you had to change the channel on the T.V. with a hammer and a chisel." She did her best to egg him on and get a rise out of him, anything to get his attention focussed on her and her alone.

"Oh, you're asking for it!"

She laughed and held up her fists exclaiming, "Yeah? Bring it, big boy! Show lil' ole me what you got!"

Just then Mike's phone went off. "Hold on," Mike looked at his phone. "I got to take this. It's Lucky." He said, answering his phone.

Kendra let her arms drop and thought to herself. *What am I going to have to do? He isn't gay is he? Fuck! I never thought of that. Oh shit.*

"Yeah man." Mike answered the call.

"Ya Mike, I did some digging on that Gustav character like you asked."

"And? What did ya find out?"

"Well, he has ties to some pretty nasty shit alright, but nothing I can find that is solid so far. Apparently, he is not allowed back in Egypt, though. I don't know what happened there, but he is a dead man walking as far as they are concerned. Made some dangerous enemies." Lucky explained.

"Egypt?"

Kendra's ears perked up. "Mike, he said his brother died in Egypt, I think from like a snakebite. His name was Fritz."

Mike got a surprised look and asked Lucky, "Did you hear that?"

"Yeah, I heard it. I'll see what I can find out about his brother. Look, if you are dealing with this guy, be careful. Lemme know if you need anything, and in the meantime, I'll see what I can do to help. Besides, Reggie is still in the game. You know we can count on him if things get crazy."

"For sure, is he still bouncing at clubs?"

"Sure is, a real shit hole this time, called *The Slab.* But he is still all about business."

"Text me the club address. I may just have to pop in and say 'hi'. Make sure you keep me in the loop, alright?"

"Sure thing Mike, I'll call you as soon as I know anything. Later."

"Later."

He hung the phone up and put it back in his coat. "Looks like your friend Gustav has some pretty bad associates, Kendra."

"Well, maybe he is a bad guy, and just likes art and to make money. Ever think of that?"

"Oh, I thought of it alright. Just covering the bases. It is kinda my job with you."

"True." She agreed, as Mike walked into the bathroom.

"Mike?"

"Yeah, what's up?" Mike was looking in the mirror and brushing his teeth, trying to get ready for the evening.

"Are you gay?"

Mike stood over the sink and spit toothpaste foam all over the mirror. "What in hell? Fuck no, I'm not gay. I mean, I have had gay friends and shit, but that's not my deal. Why in the hell would you ask me that?" He asked, confused by her question.

"Then maybe you are just dense."

He spit into the sink and rinsed, then cleaned the mess off of the mirror. "I would like to think I have some intelligence. Fuck, what are you trying to say here?"

"Well, let's look at the facts," She started to reply, "you slept next to me, nothing. You saw me mostly naked, nothing. I have thrown every hint and signal at you, and still nothing. See my point? Or maybe you're just not into me."

After he dried off his hands and turned off the bathroom light, he approached her, taking her by her hands.

"Look Kendra," he said, "I do like you. But the truth is, I haven't been that way with anyone for a very long time. People that get close to me either wind up hurt, or dead. So I got into the habit of just being alone. You are awesome. Really, you are. So don't think it is you. You are bat shit nuts, but awesome. Alright?"

Kendra broke away from him. "So that's it then, just business?" She had gotten a golem look about her, and seemed to instantly decline emotionally.

"I didn't say that. Let's just see how things go. I try to be a very careful person. Especially if I care about someone." He replied, kissing her on her head.

Kendra smiled. "Okay, if you say so." She turned back and faced Mike, and looked up at him. "Just remember," she said, reaching down and grabbing his crotch, "I own you." She giggled, let go, and walked into the kitchen.

"Guess so." He responded, then thinking to himself. *Why didn't I just stay driving the fucking cab?*

∞∞∞

Michelle showed up at a quarter of. She walked in as usual and went upstairs to Kendra's apartment, reaching the door and knocking.

"Come in!" She heard Kendra yell from inside.

Michelle opened the door and found them sitting at a table, buried in their phones. "Oh looks like the party started without me!"

"Hey baby!" Kendra exclaimed, getting up and giving her a hug, with Mike standing up, and putting away his phone.

"So this must be Mike?" Michelle asked.

"The one and only." Mike stood up and walked over to greet Michelle. "You must be Michelle."

"I am, yes." She glanced over at Kendra. "Damn girl, you weren't lying!" She exclaimed, looking back at him and eyeing him up and down, undressing him with her eyes.

"Behave, Michelle." Kendra laughed.

"I am, I am, just damn. So when is this guy Gustav supposed to be here?"

"In about fifteen minutes." She looked at her phone and slid it into the back pocket of her jeans. "We can go downstairs now and I'll fix us all a few drinks."

Michelle was glad to see Kendra happy and not stressed for once. "Lead the way, baby doll, lead the way." She said, as Mike locked the door behind him, and they headed to the Grotto.

Chapter 9

A Night In The Grotto

The evening events were well underway, while Gustav sat on the couch, where he had sat on his previous visit, with Michelle sitting next to him. Mike and Kendra had taken seating in the chairs across from them. Everyone was drinking, except for Mike, who was taking part in the laughter and telling tall tales, but more focused on studying Gustav and his reactions to things said.

"Mike, You're not drinking. Want me to fix you one?" Kendra asked.

He looked over at Kendra, noticing that she seemed to be glowing. Her whole personality was shining and he didn't want anything taking that away. "No, I will get it. Do you have coke?"

"Yeah, there should be some under the bar."

"Nice. I feel like a mixed drink." He said, getting up and going behind the bar. He opened the mini fridge and pulled out a coke, setting it on the bar. After putting some ice in a glass, he poured the coke in, then went to the front of the bar and grabbed the bottle of whiskey. Mike turned his back to everyone, so what he was doing was out of view of everyone else. They saw the bottle lift, but they could not see the pour itself. Replacing the bottle to the bar, he returned to his seat.

Whiskey and coke, minus the whiskey, perfect. He thought to himself.

Michelle was over twirling her hair with her finger and looking at Gustav. "So that's a pretty new Jag I saw you pull up in."

"Yes, I just picked that one up last month. I always loved the Jaguars. Really nothing like them." said Gustav, with a matter-of-fact tone in his voice.

"I have never ridden in one before. I bet it's nice and comfortable."

"Yes, very. Go with me sometime, and you can ride along and see for yourself. Perhaps dinner?"

"That sounds like a good idea. I really would love that. Always busy running this girl's things around for her." Motioning to Kendra with her foot, as her legs were crossed.

"Maybe all of us could go, my treat." Gustav suggested.

"That sounds like a nice evening," Kendra said, looking at Mike and putting her hand on his arm. "What do you think? Think that would be something we would like to do?"

"Sure, Kendra, you're the boss." Mike took a drink and tried to fake a smile, knowing well he wanted nothing to do with Gustav, much less spend any social time with him.

"And that's why he is amazing. He never argues with me." Kendra added with a smile.

Gustav raised his glass. "Well, it seems we will have to plan an evening. I will check my schedule and let you know."

Mike looked at him and tried to get a read on what was behind Gustav's smile. "Yeah, maybe we could go into Philly one night. They have some places there. Lots of history in that city as well."

"Yes, a lot of history, history that has never been written about, as well."

"As in?" Michelle asked.

Gustav glanced at her and thought he could elaborate on the matter. "Well, that's not entirely true. Newspapers have tried to stab at the stories, but nobody that knows anything truly, has written about any of it."

"About what?" Kendra asked, getting curious.

"Well, there is a lot of rumor that went around years ago about a crime syndicate working in the area. Bodies being found, murders under the bridge, that sort of thing-"

Kendra's eyes lit up. "Oh, Mike was just telling me about that the other day! Sounds like some exciting times."

Gustav took a drink and set it back down onto the table, and crossed his legs. "So you were around when all of that happened, Mike?" He asked, smugly.

Shit, this mother fucker knows exactly who I am. Play it cool, man, play it cool. Mike thought to himself. "Yeah, I was around. I remember hearing about it on the radio, and of course, like you said, articles in the paper. Pretty violent piece of the past. From what I remember. I think they mentioned some Russian organization. Is that right?"

"Yes, supposedly. I think it was all hype, and just some local crime groups, wanna be wise guys trying to make a name for themselves." Gustav replied, as he tried to keep silent the little cat and mouse game he and Mike were playing.

Michelle finished her drink and set in on the table, chiming in, "Well, I must have been a little girl when that happened. Besides, I was probably still in New York back then."

Gustav grabbed his drink again. "Well, this was about fifteen years ago, so I imagine you were quite young."

"I suppose I was." Michelle said, standing up. "Kendra, can I go use your bathroom?"

"Yeah, sure girly, Mike locked it, so you will have to use your key."

"No problem, be back in a minute."

Michelle left the Grotto and went upstairs. Gustav got up and poured himself another drink. "So, Kendra, I was thinking about your work."

"Sure, what were you thinking?"

"Well, after hearing your story, it became very apparent that you are using your talents to cope with the trauma." Gustav explained with authoritative conviction, "This happens a lot to artists, musicians, actors. They try to keep the demons at bay by bringing them out in their craft. Get what I mean?"

"Yeah, it actually makes perfect sense."

"Have you ever thought that perhaps you could kill those demons once and for all?"

"Like how?"

Leaning forward, Gustav started to explain what he had meant. "Living art. Making your work feel the pain you went through, there are a lot of twisted people in these cities, many who like being tortured."

"I don't know about all that," Kendra stated, "kinda sounds like something that could wind me up in a lot of trouble, to tell you the truth."

"Well, that is a strong possibility. Just keep it in mind, and see where your mind takes you."

Kendra looked into her glass and took another drink, and thought to herself. *You wanted to make your mom and dad your masterpiece, carve out their brains. That seems more like art to me.*

"So, Gustav. Other than tea, Kendra tells me you have invested in tea, and artist, what else do you dabble in?" Mike asked, trying to change the subject.

Gustav looked over at Mike taking notice that he was purposely changing the subject. "All kinds of things. For instance, I have an associate who was into concrete for a long time. He manufactured a way to spray it in liquid form, almost like paint. But here is the interesting part: it fits perfectly to form, so there is no finishing, and also, when it hardens, it expands, making it a little over a quarter inch thick."

"Wow, that actually seems pretty cool. What are the applications of it?" asked Mike, pretending to take interest in what Gustav had to say.

"Well, endless really. Let's say you wanted to spray this couch. After it was all said and done with, it would appear to be a concrete couch, a stone statue of one, really. In a hundred years, if you could break it open, it would be perfectly preserved, and still intact. But you would have a rough time breaking it open to see. He sprayed an entire vehicle with it," he continued to explain, "hoisted it up with a crane, and dropped it from nearly 22 feet. No damage, and no leaks from the fluids. It has a special sealant in it, and you can also add pigment."

"Has anyone ever sprayed anything down, like, say, food? And see how long it would last?" Mike asked.

Gustav laughed. "Well, I am not sure I would want to eat it, but in theory, yes, it would stay perfectly preserved. And if not, you would never smell the rot of it. Pretty high-tech ingenuity. I don't even pretend to understand the science of it."

"So you invested in this concrete spray?"

"Yes indeed. And I am still getting income from my investment. I find a mark, and I make it. Winners only." Gutav said, raising his glass.

Kendra interjected, "Has anyone ever sprayed a human body with it?"

"No, not that I know of." Gustav looked up at Mike while lifting the glass to his lips. "Bet that stuff would have come in handy back in the day." He added.

Okay, Now I know he knows me. What in the fuck? Kendra is not looking so good. I have to end this soon. Mike thought to himself, trying to keep his composure. "Yeah, well, I guess there could have been a lot of uses for it."

Michelle came prancing into the room. "I'm back, party animals, what did I miss? Anything juicy?" She took her seat back, next to Gustav and sat back, crossing her legs again.

Kendra looked up at her as she was sitting down. "No, Gustav was just telling us of a few of his investments that he has been successful with." She said, looking over at him and raising her glass. "Only winners, right?"

He raised his glass to her again. "Winners only." Finishing his drink and looking at his watch, he set the empty glass back down on the table.

"Well, I hate to cut out so early, but I have a very early appointment in New York City I have to be at." He looked over at Michelle. "Dinner soon?" He asked her with a smile.

Michelle smiled. "Absolutely. I am looking forward to it."

"Good, as I am as well."

Gustav picked the empty glass back up, stood up and walked over to the bar, and set it down. As he walked past Mike, he stopped and grabbed his shoulder, tighter than needed. "We must get together soon, Mike. I have a feeling we will have lots to talk about concerning my investment."

He wasn't too keen on Gustav being behind him, and stood up, offering his hand in a shake. Gustav reciprocated, with Mike power-shaking his hand, slightly bringing him in. "I'll be looking forward to it." He said, looking Gustav in his eyes.

"Good," He said, pulling his hand back, "Good grip, that comes in handy as you know." Gustav looked at Kendra and Michelle, smiling and nodding 'goodbye'. "Ladies." Turning and walking out of the Grotto. Mike trailed behind and watched him walk out of the gallery and into his car. After making sure he left, he went back, joining the girls.

"Michelle, I think we are going to call this thing a night."

"Really? Not much of a party animal, are you?"

Kendra looked at her phone. "He is right. We have another long day tomorrow." She was looking over at Mike and smiling at him, full of positive thoughts about where they were going to wind up. "Mike and I are going to go shopping for his new apartment."

Michelle stood up, grabbing her purse. "How nice. I bet you are excited. I love that apartment she has on the end."

"That's the one she gave me alright. Got to love the view for sure."

"You are so lucky." She looked at Kendra, cocking her head and giving her a huge smile. "Well, Chicky, guess I'll come by tomorrow and make those deliveries for you."

"Yes, that would be great. I'll have some money for you as well, oh yeah, speaking of which--" Michelle was standing next to her as Kendra looked up. "You got a raise."

"Ah baby cakes, you're the best" Michelle leaned down and gave Kendra a hug. "I love ya lady."

"Yeah I know, love you too."

Michelle walked out of the Grotto, with thoughts of Gustav flying through her head. "See you both tomorrow, nice meeting you Mike."

"Yeah, you too."

Mike sat down in the chair next to Kendra, leaning into her. "Want to tell me what's going on?"

"With what?"

"You're like a million miles away, your whole being changed. What's going on?" he asked, with a look of genuine concern in his eyes.

"Just thinking of my parent's. I wonder if they will sit until morning."

"Yeah, they won't feel too good, but they will sit. Not like they have a choice in the matter anyway, right?"

"No, they have no choice. But I do." Kendra said, standing up, "Come on, let's close up and go to bed. I am tired. They can wait till morning. Besides, you have had a few drinks."

Mike grabbed his glass from the table and handed it to Kendra. "Taste it." He grinned and chuckled as she took it from him.

Taking a drink from his glass, she gasped, "You motherfucker, it's just coke."

"Yeah, I told you I had to keep watch. It's an old trick, but effective."

"Dammit Mike! I wanted to get you drunk and take advantage of you! Now you have fucked it all up." She ranted, crossing her arms as she pouted.

"Foiled again, Kiddo."

"Yeah, thanks!"

"Or maybe not." he giggled.

"And how's that?" Kendra asked with a grin.

He bent down and scooped her up. Kendra screamed, laughing, "Oh, my knight is carrying me off?"

He held her up, looking at her face to face. "Better watch what you wish for."

Kendra wriggled. "Put me down," she demanded, "I have to

lock up, then you can carry me off."

Putting her down, Kendra locked up her gallery and turned out the lights. She walked back to him with her arms raised in the air. He picked her up, and she looked at him. "Home James!" she ordered.

He started laughing. "Home it is my dear." He carried her up the stairs, enjoying the fact that she was happy, but knowing also, what he had planned for her when they got up there.

When he had reached the top, and her apartment, he opened the door. As he entered, he closed the door with his foot, before walking her to the bed, and gently lay her down.

Kendra did not let go of him. With her arms still around his neck, she pulled him in close, on top of her, bringing his lips to hers.

As they embraced, with their tongues reaching for each other, and testing the boundaries of their inner desires, Kendra still had thoughts run through her mind.

God, I hope I am not fucking this up. It has been too long since anyone has touched me. Please stay with me Mike, please.

He backed away, momentarily, and got off of the bed, standing up, and taking off his jacket, placing his gun on the nightstand.

Kendra got up and started to unbutton his shirt, kissing his chest as she went, one button at a time, slowly and methodically. His cologne filled her nostrils as she pressed her lips to his skin.

As she reached the front of his black jeans, she unfastened the button and unzipped his fly. As she took them down, Mike reached down and lifted her up, again kissing her and hoping that she felt the desire that he had for her.

"Why did you stop me?" She whispered.

"I didn't stop you. I just want all of you." He replied, lifting her tight dress up, and unpeeling it from her body.

The passion between them escalated as their bodies became free of the clothing that separated the two.

As the final articles of clothing gathered on the floor, he picked her up, with her legs wrapping around his waist. "I want you inside of me." she whispered in his ear.

He lay on the bed, with her on top of him, their tongues locked together as their breathing deepened with every pounding heartbeat.

She reached down, grabbing ahold of him, feeling every throb and every inch of him. As she guided him in, they both let out moans of pleasure.

"Kendra, it's been a long time since I've been with anyone." he said to her as she lowered herself down, taking him in, little by little.

"I know. That's what round two is for. Don't worry, you have nothing to prove to me."

As she moved her hips, she looked down at his face and thought to herself. *No matter what, I am going to make him stay with me. He has to be the one.*

She found herself falling for him, and now that he was inside of her, she wanted him even more.

She lowered herself down, taking him all the way in and burying her face beside his head. As he grabbed hold of her hips, he thrust harder. She ground herself into him, making sure he was hitting just the right spot, to send her over the edge. "Perfect," she whispered, "not yet. I want you to come with me."

He held on, fighting the release until it started getting to be too much to handle. "I can't hold off anymore." he panted.

"Go ahead baby, I'm there." she moaned as her hips became frantic, driving him and herself past the point of no return. As their orgasms overtook them, they gripped each other tightly, with moans of pleasure and intensity filling the air, until she collapsed on top of him.

Both lay there, out of breath, and covered in perspiration and each other's fluids.

"I'm sorry, it's been a while, like I said." Mike said, catching his breath.

She looked over at him and smiled. Wiping the sweat from his brow. "It's been too long for me too. Round two won't be so quick."

"Just give me a second. I'm definitely wanting round two." he exclaimed with a shallow laugh.

"Can I ask you something?"

"Yeah, as long as you let me have a smoke, what's up?" he said, moving her off of him and sitting up.

"Was, um, this just a fuck for you?"

Mike looked over at her, laying on her side, with her head propped up on her hand. Her naked body glistened with perspiration and it suddenly sank deep into him. He was falling for her as well.

"No. Not at all. You may be bat shit crazy at times, and we just met, but I truly want to see where this goes with us. You are such a beautiful woman Kendra, talented, driven and becoming very special to me already. So, no. This was not just a fuck." he said, reaching over and caressing the side of her face.

"That makes me happy. I think I want to keep you."

He started laughing as he grabbed a smoke from his pack. "Well, I guess that is a good thing."

"Yeah, I think it is." she said with a smile on her face, gazing at him with still hungry eyes. "Now hurry and smoke that. I'm ready for you to fuck my brains out now."

"Yes, ma'am!" Mike exclaimed, crushing out his cigarette and climbing back into bed, and into Kendra's awaiting arms.

Chapter 10

An Old Friend

When the morning came, Kendra opened her eyes. Rolling over to put her arm around Mike, she sat up, startled, realizing he was not there. She jumped from the bed, undressed, and ran to the kitchen. "Mike?" She called, but there was no answer. She grabbed her phone from her nightstand and looked for messages, only to find none. "Oh no. Come on, tell me this didn't happen." she begged aloud. Panic rose within her as her mind raced and imagined the worst.

Just then, her apartment door opened. Mike was carrying a to-go bag and quietly whistling a tune. She ran up to him and threw her arms around him. "Oh my God, I thought..." Her eyes were already welling with tears.

Mike hugged her with one arm. "What's wrong? What happened?"

Kendra let him go and sank her forehead into his chest, holding onto his arms. "I thought you left and weren't coming back."

He looked down at her and kissed her on top of the head. "No, not at all." he said with a kind smile, and laughed a little. "I went and got you breakfast, complete with a cafe latte."

She let go and went and put on a robe that was hanging in her bathroom. Coming out, she stopped, leaning against the wall. "You really got me breakfast?"

"Yeah, I wanted to get back before you woke up, but I guess I fucked that part up."

"Oh my God." She wore a look of amazement on her face and shook her head.

"What?"

She looked at him in disbelief. "Where in the world did you come from?"

As he started walking to the kitchen with the bag, he answered, "Well, I was driving a cab one day, and the funniest thing happened; this crazy bitch got into the back."

"Shut up!" Kendra replied, laughing.

They sat down at the kitchen table and Mike took out their breakfast. Kendra got up and grabbed two plates, placing them on the table with knives and forks. After sitting back down, she looked out the window, then back at Mike. "Thank you for staying."

"Nah, you're not getting rid of me that easily."

"So, you don't regret last night?"

"Regret?" he asked, "No. I thought about it last night. Maybe it is time to take a chance. Have to admit, the last few days have been pretty wild. Crazy, but very cool."

"You really think so?"

Mike chewed his food and sipped his coffee. "Definitely."

They sat and ate in silence. Kendra had a smile on her face, and for once, that menacing voice had nothing to say.

When they finished, Mike stood up and gathered the plates and utensils.

"Hate to rush this morning, but we need to head back to your parents. If anything, to see if they are still alive."

"I know." Kendra agreed, getting up from the table, "But I keep thinking they are still fucking me."

"How so?"

"Because there are things I'd rather stay here and do." She replied walking up, smiling, and kissing him deeply. Then his phone rang.

"Fuck me." she moaned, egregiously.

Mike looked at his phone. "It will have to be later, it's Lucky." Mike answered his phone. "Tell me stories, bro."

"Well, I don't have any good ones to tell you Mike." Lucky said.

"Yeah, I kinda figured. Hey, do you mind if I put this on speaker so Kendra can hear?"

"No, that's fine. It is just the two of you, right?"

"Yeah bro, just us." Mike switched his phone to the speaker. "Okay Lucky, what ya find out?"

"Does he ride around with a guy named Dante?"

Kendra's eyes widened when she heard Dante's name. "Is he gay?"

"How in hell should I know? Have you seen him?"

"I think so," she answered, "he works for Gustav at his tea place. About six feet or so, slim build with black hair and dark skin? Not black, but ya know, kinda dark?"

"Yeah, that sounds like him alright."

Mike's brow lowered. "What's with this, Dante, Lucky? Why sound so worried?"

"Well, he has not been in the states too long. He is from across seas and heavily involved in this Satanic cult thing in Europe. Him and Gustav used to run very close back a few years ago."

"Any ties to Russians?" asked Mike.

"Don't know," Lucky replied, "but I am going to keep looking and see what else I can find. I have a feeling I am about to go down a rabbit hole with this."

"Find out what you can, bro. I appreciate it."

"Yeah, no problem Mike."

"Hey, would you have Reggie's number? I haven't had time to see him yet."

"Reggie doesn't keep a phone." Replied Lucky, "He keeps things real small and tight, if ya know what I mean."

"Yeah, same old Reggie. Good to see some things never change. Hey, you still have my old gear, right?"

"Safe and sound, man."

"Good, thanks. I'm going to go into Philly tonight and see Reggie. It is the address you sent me, right?"

"Yeah, that's it, be careful, that place is nasty."

"Yeah, that's what you said before. I'm good. Gotta go brother. Talk to ya soon."

"Okay Mike, you take care."

Mike put his phone in his back pocket, looking at Kendra. "So, ya want to go to a club tonight?"

Kendra smiled and yelled, "Hell yes!"

She walked to the bathroom to get dressed, but Mike stopped her, grabbing her arm. "Look, no drinking tonight. This place is not that great of a club. I just have to see my old friend, Reggie."

"That's fine. It's not like I have to drink, baby."

"Good." He said, letting her go.

"Are we going to my parents' this morning, then?" She asked, putting on her jeans.

"Yeah, for a few anyway. Then maybe do that shopping we were talking about."

"Sweet!" She popped her head around the doorway. "I may even let you off the clock today."

Mike laughed. "Why is it I have the feeling I am always on the clock with you?"

"Because I'm awesome!" She exclaimed, walking out of the bathroom and sitting on the bed. She had on an old band t-shirt and black ripped jeans. Reaching under the bed, she pulled out her favorite Chuck Taylor's converse. Mike looked and grinned.

"What? They are my favorite shoes."

"Nothing, that's cool," He replied, "just never know what I am going to get with you. I kinda like it."

Kendra stood up and kissed him on his cheek. "Try to keep up." She said as she walked over and grabbed her bag. "Ready to go?"

He checked and made sure he had everything, and lit a cigarette. "Yeah, let's get this over with."

∞∞∞

They had reached the exit to pull off, and Mike turned on his blinker. Kendra had her foot up on the dash and was trying to find a song she wanted to listen to on the radio. "So, this Reggie guy, how long have you known him?"

"Since we were in high school."

"Really? Did he, you know, clean with you?"

"Who Reggie? Some, but we were into some other things."

"Like what?"

"Well, I can tell you this. There are a few things to know about Reggie. One, if he says he has your back, he has your back. Second, Nobody, and I mean nobody, can crack a safe or pick a lock better or faster than him."

"Wow really?" she asked, "So you guys did like robberies and stuff?"

Mike looked over at her. "Yeah, if the price was right."

"Holy shit, that's insane! So what's the third thing?"

"Never, ever get punched by him. He seriously only needs one punch, and that's it. He almost made golden gloves."

"Why didn't he?" She had a curious look as she was getting invested in learning more about Mike's best friend, she wanted to know it all. ABout his past, his friends, and their future.

Turning his head towards her, with a serious look on his face, he answered her question. "The guy didn't get back up."

Kendra's jaw dropped. "Shit! So we are going to meet him tonight?" she asked, shocked.

"Yup. Been a few years, too. I'm sure it will be cool."

"Awesome! I have never met a boxer before."

"Yeah, he doesn't like to talk about it, so, ya know, mum's the word."

"Don't worry, I'll be cool."

After changing channels several times, Kendra got irritated

and turned off the radio. "I need to get a fucking like, **thingy** for this. I need music." Irritated, she turned it off and looked at mike as if to say, "Please fix this stupid thing!"

"I'll take care of it soon. We will get you Sirius in here. Till then, though, are you ready?"

"Yeah baby. Ready as I'll ever be." she exclaimed, rubbing her hands together in an excited fashion.

They pulled into the driveway and into the back. They went inside after Kendra unlocked the door. The house remained undisturbed. It was all just as they left it.

"Look, just in case, I need to clean this mess up in the sitting room." said Mike, as he started to walk out of the kitchen, but was stopped briefly by Kendra, who didn't think it was that necessary.

"Why? Nobody wants to see them."

"I imagine, but it is bugging me."

"Fine, clean it up if you must. But I am telling you, there is no need." She started to leave, and continued downstairs, as Mike headed into the sitting room.

"Yeah, no need until the cops show up and we all go to prison." he said, as he looked at the wreckage she had left behind.

After Mike finished with cleaning up the mess, he joined Kendra downstairs. She was standing in the doorway looking at them, still tied to the chairs. They were still sweating out alcohol. The room still reeked of urine,sweat, and rancid booze. She didn't say a word, just kept looking at them. Mike walked up behind her, placing his hand on her lower back. "You alright?" He put his hand on her back, and lightly rubbed it, letting her know that he was there for her in any capacity needed.

"Yeah, just look at them."

"Yeah, they are a mess alright. We need to check their hearts and make sure the detox won't kill them. We may need to give them a few shots, and definitely make them drink some water."

"I'll go get a bottle." Kendra said, leaving and going back upstairs.

Mike leaned down and checked William's pulse. His heart was pumping hard. Looking over at Francine, he could see her carotid artery pulsing. "Yeah, you guys are in rough shape."

William picked his head up from being slumped over and looked over and asked Mike, "Are you here to get us out?"

Mike stood up, looking at William and tempted to slap him. "What? You don't remember why you are here?"

"Kendra."

His voice was weak and feeble as he was shaking with the tremors of detox.

"Yes, that's right, Kendra." Mike checked the knots, they were solid and unmoved. He checked the bandages and cleaned the wounds again, and gave them fresh dressings. As he was finishing it up, Kendra came back in with a gallon jug of water and a bottle of vodka. "Here baby, is this enough?" she asked, handing him the bottle.

Mike grabbed the bottle. "Yeah, we are not gonna give them enough to get drunk. Really, they should have a shot an hour, but that will not happen."

After taking the cap off of the bottle, he put it up to William's mouth. Putting the bottle up to Williams mouth, so he could drink, didn't work out so well. William coughed and spit it out at Mike, spraying him down. Jerking the bottle away, Mike yelled, "You fuck! Now I smell like this shit! Dammit!" He grabbed William by the back of his head and pulled it back, putting the bottle up to his mouth again. "Now drink you fucker!"

Kendra watched, then closed her eyes, turning around and walking to the stairs to sit down.

Mike put down the bottle of vodka and held up the water. William took a few heavy gulps from it, then he went over to Francine, picking the bottle back up. "If you spray this on me, I'll let her kill you right now."

Francine remained silent and leaned her head back. To Mike's surprise, she took it down rather well. Enough to put most men to shame. After a few gulps, he pulled it away and replaced it with water.

When he finished, he placed the water and the vodka on the floor in front of them. They both looked down at the containers. Francine looked up at Mike with her eyes. "Just a little more,"she begged.

"No, I don't think so. You are going to be here for a while, so you better just get used to it."

"You're going to pay for this, mister. You're going to pay dearly. I swear I will end you!." threatened Francine.

Just then, Kendra came rushing through the door screaming in rage and jumping on Francine, digging her thumbs deep into her eyes while grabbing her head.

"Don't you ever threaten him! I'll fucking kill you! You fucking bitch!"

Francine and Kendra fell onto the floor with Francine's head hitting hard. Mike Grabbed her. "Kendra, stop!" He pulled her off of Francine and wrapped his arms around her so she couldn't move. "Kendra! Dammit, calm down! Not like this!"

"Let me go! I'll kill her!" screamed Kendra, as her temper took over, making her want to cause them unimaginable pain and suffering.

William, looking over in shock, strained at the ropes, but it was no use. Kendra stopped kicking and squirming and Mike let her go. She stood looking over Francine, breathing heavily. William was looking over at his wife on the floor. "Kendra! Look what you did!" He yelled.

Kendra's head snapped towards William with her eyes narrowed and breathing heavier.

Mike stepped back. "These fucking people just don't have a clue. Do they?" He was so focused on her parents, he didn't notice that something was coming over Kendra. Kendra was changing.

"No baby! They don't!" She knelt down and tried to sit Francine back up, but it was no use. Kendra's small frame could not lift the dead weight of Francine in that position.

Mike stepped around and grabbed the back of the chair, standing it back upright. He lowered himself down, getting closer to Francine's face.

"If I were you, I would not test the laws of gravity again. They are not on your side at the moment."

William started screaming at Kendra again. "You little bitch! Don't you know who you are dealing with here? I am William Blake! You will let us go right now!"

Kendra snapped her head back at William. And then it came.

Go ahead Kendra, you know what he wants. Give it to him. You know you miss Daddy's love. Don't you, sweet little girl?

Kendra lowered her head, not taking her eyes from his. Taking a few slow steps towards him, she started running her fingers up his barren chest.

"What's the matter Daddy?" she asked, "You don't like this?"

She walked slowly behind him, running her fingers through his gray hair, and taunted him even more asking, "You don't miss me Daddy? Our late nights in this room? With me all to yourself?"

"I wish you had never been born!" William yelled.

Kendra walked back around so she was facing him. "Now Daddy, that's not a delightful way to talk to your little girl." she said, in a seductive manner. Kendra started moving her hips, dragging her shirt up as William looked on, with disdain writing on his face.

Mike stood behind her. His eyes were fixed on the situation and standing in disbelief as to what he was seeing. "Kendra, I think we better go for today."

"No baby, Daddy misses his little girl."

"Kendra-" he started to say, but she was beyond the point of reason. For her, there was no turning back.

"What's the matter Daddy? Upset, this man behind me gets to fuck Daddy's little girl instead of you?" She continued to torture William with her seductive, harsh words.

Mike, shaking his head, spoke under his breath, "Jesus Christ."

"Looks like you're all tied up in knots, Daddy," Kendra said, giggling for a moment, then grabbing the sides of her head and closing her eyes tightly.

"Knots... those knots! Those fucking knots!" Kendra screamed, as she jumped onto William's lap before Mike could stop her.

She grabbed one of his shoulders and reached down between his legs, and grabbed his testicles in her hand. screaming, "Is this what you want, Daddy!?"

She squeezed hard and William yelled out in pain. Mike went to grab her, but she turned her head around and he stopped dead in his tracks.

"Jesus, Kendra! Your eyes!" He exclaimed, breathless. His heart raced at the sight of her, as her pupils had turned black as night.

She turned back and looked at William, still squeezing, and applied more pressure. William wailed in pain as his testicles ruptured in her hand. "Oh, I hit a home run with that one! Didn't I, Daddy?" she yelled, "You're going to feel that in the morning!" She bounced up and down on his lap, laughing hysterically with her head laid back, looking to the ceiling.

Mike couldn't handle seeing Kendra act like this any longer. Grabbing her again, he pulled her off William. This time, she did not struggle, but kept her eyes locked on William as she laughed, pointing at him in pain.

"Baby, that's enough! Come on!" he yelled, as he picked her up from the back and carried her out of the room, leaving William screaming and Francine bawling, with her eyes bleeding, and yelling for William.

As he sat her down at the bottom of the stairs, Kendra bent over, holding her stomach psychotically laughing and riding the emotional roller coaster she was on.

"Kendra." Mike said calmly, putting his arm around her.

She sat up and looked at him. The laughter had turned to tears, and the tears turned to waterfalls cascading down her makeup smudged face. She wrapped her arms around Mike and sank her head into his arms, sobbing.

∞∞∞

After Kendra had calmed down and cleaned up, they locked the house up and left her parent's once again. It was getting well into noon as their day pressed forward. She didn't say a word for some time as she watched the scenery go by.

"So what now?" Mike asked, looking over at her with a look of concern.

She looked over at Mike, saddened, asking, "What now? I imagine you never want to see me again. Not after that. I can't really blame you. I'm a mess." she continued as she looked back out the window. "Daddy is right. I'm just going to ruin your life. You don't deserve this, Mike."

"Will you shut the fuck up? Seriously, shut the fuck up!"

He pulled over to the side of the road and put the truck in park, turning and facing her. "You better understand something and understand something right now! Mike Langley doesn't do a fucking thing Mike Langley doesn't want to do!" he yelled with intensity, "Mike Langley also doesn't get scared! If I say I got you, I mean I fucking got you! I don't disappear like a bitch, and I don't run off! My circle is very small, and if you are in it, which you are, then no matter what, I have your back! Get it? Got it? Good!"

Putting the truck in drive, he stomped on the gas, spraying gravel from the tires as they got back onto the road. Kendra stared at him with a blank look, unsure of how to react.

"Goddamn it! I don't know if I want to let you kill him, or I just want to kill him myself for fucking you up so bad. But whatever you are thinking about running me off, just do us both a favor and stop." he continued, looking back over at her. "Okay?"

"Okay baby." she replied quietly.

She put her hand on his, and he wrapped his fingers through hers. "Didn't mean to make you mad. I just feel shitty. I mean, it seems to me a few days ago, you only had to worry about a bitchy boss. Now you have one that is a homicidal maniac that hears voices in her head."

But the voice inside of her, had something much different to say.

Instantly, she closed her eyes tightly as the voice resurfaced within her.

Well, way to go, you stupid little bitch. Now he is going to know all about me. How much more do you think he will take from you? Oh, you're going to lose him alright.

"Voices in Your Head?"

"Oh, that just slipped out. I didn't really mean voices like crazy voices." She tried her best to cover up what she had let slip out of her mouth.

"Yeah, I think that is exactly what you meant. Guess what?"

"What?"

"Still ain't shook." Mike said with a smile on his face, looking over at her to reassure her, that he was not going to be scared off.

She leaned over and kissed him on his cheek. Mike kept his eyes on the road. "Just be you, whatever or whoever that may be. I'll worry about what Mike can handle and can't."

"Deal." she said, sitting back in the seat, and started calming down. She looked out the window at the buildings passing by. Some of them were new, some old, but they all passed by, all the same.

"I guess you don't feel up to shopping now, huh?" She asked, after endless moments of silence.

Looking back at him, she had an idea run through her

mind."You want to just stay with me a while? Until we figure some things out?"

"You want me to move in with you?"

"I mean, you don't have to, but I wouldn't mind. I like not being alone." The look on her face begged him to say yes as she squeezed his hand a little tighter.

Mike pulled into the back of The Daunting Canvas and into the garage, closing the door.

"We can try that. I mean, I don't think you can have much more to surprise me with. Right?" Mike asked, laughing.

Kendra giggled, "It's been a crazy few days, huh?"

"Yes, I can definitely say 'it has'."

"Well, I have to make sure Michelle does what I need her to do this afternoon." she exclaimed, "Then I guess we will go to Philly?"

Mike stepped out of the truck along with Kendra.

"Yeah, that's the plan."

"Then let's do that. I need a shower anyway."

"Yeah, I can use one myself."

"So you joining me?" Kendra asked in the flirtatious way she always asked, when she wanted him.

"I am still on the clock." Mike said, winking at her.

"Yeah, and I am the boss, so your point?"

"Well, wouldn't that make me a prostitute? Or like escorts or something?"

Kendra opened the door and walked through. "Get upstairs and get your fucking clothes off, Mike."

He laughed and followed her in, smacking her on her rear end. "Goddamn I love this fucking job!"

That evening, Kendra and Mike pulled up to *The Slab* and parked in the parking lot across the street. Mike looked out the window as he was rolling it up. "Hey, see that black guy by the door?" he asked Kendra, pointing to Reggie.

She looked over at Mike so she could see. "Is that your friend Reggie?"

"Yes, it is! Now you're gonna meet my family."

"Jesus, he is huge!" She was surprised to see just how big Reggie was.

"Yeah, he is a big boy alright. But trust me, you're going to love him."

"I don't judge. Besides, everybody is bigger to me."

Mike started laughing. "Well, I guess that's a major plus for my ass now, isn't it?"

She got a big laugh and smacked him on the arm. "Shut up."

They got out of the truck and locked it. As they headed over to see Reggie, two guys walked up to him. Reggie stepped in front of the door.

"I don't think so. You know you're 86'd from here." his voice boomed deeply.

One guy stepped up to him and reasoned, "Come on, man, that was weeks ago. Just let us in, bro."

"Bro? Who the fuck you callin your bro? I ain't your bro!" Reggie replied, bowing up to the man.

"Look, I'll give you a hundy if ya let us in." the guy said, pulling out a $100 bill from his pocket.

"I'll give you a left hook if you don't leave." Reggie threatened.

The man got angry and yelled, "Man, what the fuck?!"

Just then, Mike and Kendra walked up and Reggie looked over at them. "Oh shit! Look what the cat dragged in." Reggie exclaimed, taking his attention away from the two unwanted men.

As he walked towards Mike and Kendra, the man yelled some more saying, "Boy, don't you walk away from me!"

Reggie looked at Kendra. "Excuse me, miss." Turning back towards the guy, he quickened his pace, approaching him. "I warned ya, bitch!" Reggie exclaimed loudly, then landed a hook directly on the man's jaw, knocking him down and making his body go limp. The other man started backing away and turned, running off.

Reggie turned back around, opening his arms. "My brotha from anotha motha! Bring it in, ya ol bastard!" Mike and Reggie hugged for a moment, then backed up. Reggie looked over at Kendra. "Damn bro. Who is this fine little vixen you got all up on you?" he asked.

As Kendra smiled at his question, Mike introduced her to Reggie saying, "Reggie, this is Kendra, my um, boss."

"Oh, so you an escort now?" Reggie inquired, giggling.

Mike and Kendra looked at each other and started laughing. "Long story, bro. Long story." Mike explained.

She reached out to Reggie and shook his hand. "Nice to meet you." she said, smiling, "Mike started driving for me the other day, and kinda being my bodyguard?"

"Oh damn, so it's like that with y'all then. Okay. I can dig it. Well Kendra, I am Reggie and if you're with Mike, in whatever capacity that may be, you're in excellent hands." Reggie said, looking at Mike and winking.

"Thanks Reg. Hey, I talked to Lucky. That's how I found you." informed Mike, hoping that Reggie would be willing to help if needed.

"Mike, if you talking to Lucky, something ain't right." he said, with his voice much quieter now.

"Yeah, no, there's just some rich guy that dropped a few mil on her. She is an artist, so he is 'investing'." Mike explained, "I knew I had recognized him, so I did some digging. Found a picture I had taken of him once, and guess who he was with?"

Reggie, seemingly intrigued by the story, asked, "Who? Lay it on me."

"Remember that Russian named Stepan?" Mike asked, reminding Reggie of the 'old days'.

"Oh, hell." he replied, looking over at Kendra, "What in the fuck you doing messing round with that?"

"Nah, bro. Not like that. She didn't know." Mike interjected.

"You need me to suit up?" Reggie asked, cracking his

knuckles.

"I don't know. Be nice if I could get hold of you, though."

"Alright, this is what I'm gonna do." Reggie said as he reached into his pocket and pulled out a phone.

"Bang!" Reggie exclaimed, holding up his phone.

"Holy shit, I never thought I would see the day." Mike said, shocked.

"Me either. Hit me with your digits." Reggie exclaimed, handing Mike the phone.

As they exchanged numbers, Kendra pulled out her phone asking, "Want mine to, just in case?"

"Fuck it. Lemme have it lil sista."

Reggie finished and texted them both. "Now you got my digits. So what's up? You guys want to come in for a drink?"

"No bro, not tonight." Mike replied, "It has been a long day. When are you out of here tonight?"

"Shit, not until 3 am, man." exclaimed Reggie with a disappointed look.

"Alright. Well, I will hit you up tomorrow and I will fill you in on the whole deal, alright?"

"Hell yeah. Sounds good. And it was great seeing you again, Mike, and nice meeting you Kendra."

Kendra shook his hand again and told him, "Oh, I have a feeling we will see each other again soon."

Reggie laughed. "Alright, bet!"

Mike and Kendra started walking off together. "You're right, I like him," said Kendra.

"Yeah, he is definitely a great guy. You can always trust Reggie."

They made it to the truck, got in, and drove off. The city lights were shimmering outside and the lights on the bridge were lit up brightly. Kendra looked over at Mike. "You know what?"

"What baby?"

Kendra put her hand in the wind out of the window as they drove. "I don't have a worry in the entire world right now."

Mike was glad to see her at ease, and told her, "That's good baby, that's good."

A few minutes went by, of them enjoying the cool air of the evening, until Kendra's phone went off, with a new message from Gustav.

We have a field trip tomorrow morning. I need to show you something. See you at the Canvas at 9AM.

Chapter 11

Now We Shall See

Gustav arrived, right at 9AM. Kendra and Mike were ready and waiting. As he entered, Kendra immediately noticed a change in his entire persona. He didn't seem laid back this morning. Something was off.

"Good morning, Gustav. How is everything?" She asked, putting on a smile and trying to ignore the red flags that were flying in her mind.

"Everything is wonderful this morning, but I am afraid it is all about business at the moment." he replied, "Our friend in Finland is hungry for another piece. A lot of money is on the line here."

Catching on to the urgency, she thought it best to put on her best professional demeanor. The last thing she wanted to do was risk losing an investor of this magnitude.

"Well, that is what you invested in. What is it? I shall get started right away."

"I am afraid your work is elsewhere this morning. You can take your SUV if you wish, but your subject sits at a warehouse I own. It is about an hour away, so we shall have to get going."

Kendra was ill-prepared for this. There was always a concept, a feeling or a thought that drove her creations. Now, she was going into it blindly. "Well, I need to know what I am doing. I have to have my materials, my tools."

"We have everything you need."

Mike interjected, "Well, now wait a minute. She is an artist. I mean, you invested in what she is good at. Shouldn't she get some sort of clue what is going on?"

Gustav stood still and smiled,Keeping his composure. "Fair question. I would like this to be a surprise. If this all works out, your bank account will double by the end of the day."

Kendra grabbed Mike's arm with both hands. "I'll paint the fucking Taj Mahal for that and then some!" she exclaimed, with thoughts of a future appearing before her eyes.

"We shall see soon enough. Now we must go. Follow me when I leave." In Gustav's mind, the conversation was over, as he turned away and left the gallery to get in his car.

Mike and Kendra headed to her SUV, then met Gustav out front. After he pulled out onto the street, they followed.

"I don't like this, Kendra. Not one bit."

"I am sure it is fine. Don't worry about it. Besides, we will roll in money, baby!"

"Money isn't everything, ya know."

"No, you're right, but it's a damned good start!" she exclaimed, smiling at him and grabbing his hand.

They followed Gustav out of town and finally turned into a place that had several warehouses. The property was by itself, and had a tall fence around it, topped with razor wire, and required a code to enter the gate at the entrance. After he punched in the code, the gate opened, and the two vehicles entered with the gate closing behind. They drove to the building at the end, and parked next to Gustav.

As he parked the SUV, Mike still had a bad feeling about what they were about to get into with Gustav. "Something about this whole deal seems off, just saying."

"I know. I'd be lying if I said I wasn't nervous, because I don't work like this."

"Well, I guess you do now. Let's see what's up." Mike said, opening the door and getting out.

They got out of the SUV and met Gustav in front of a steel door. Next to it was a large bay door for delivery trucks to come and go. Gustav opened the door and motioned them inside. There were two other men standing next to a shipping container in the middle of the large floor. They stacked several crates along the walls with various marks and shipping labels on them. The building was immaculate and well kept. Next to the shipping container was a large box truck. One man walked to the truck and opened the door, pulling out some keys, then shut it and returned.

He was a larger guy, heavyset, with a bald head and a cigar in between his fingers and greeted Gustav saying, "Ah Gustav! My friend! This must be the artist I have heard so much about!"

Gustav walked over and shook the man's hand, introducing Mike and Kendra. "Yes, this is Kendra, and her driver Mike." Motioning them to come and make an acquaintance.

Kendra shook the man's hand, putting on a smile and trying to hide the fact that she was nervous. "You are?"

"Archie! All of Archie's friends call him Archie!" he declared, then looked over at Mike and shook his hand as well.

Mike smiled. "I am sure the pleasure is all mine." Although he was polite, thoughts raced through his mind. *A fucking Russian. I knew I should have called Lucky. This is not good at all.* Kendra spoke up saying, "I love your accent, Archie. Is that Russian?"

"Yes, yes, I am from old country. I come here to America when I was boy. Learn the business from my poppa. Now I run a business." His demeanor remained friendly, always jolly as he continued to chew on his cigar.

"Amazing," she replied, "well, we are the melting pot of the world."

"Yes, yes, one big melting pot. Gustav, I like this Kendra." Archie said, looking over at her with a big smile, "She reminds me of daughter."

"You're too sweet Archie. So, what is the big surprise?" As she asked, she was hoping they would have all of the tools necessary for her to do her work. Without her tools, all she could do was imagine and plan, and the trip would be useless, so she thought.

Archie looked over at the other man, who was standing quietly next to the crate. "Pavel, open container and show eh?" Pavel took the keys from Archie and unlocked the container and opened the door.

With the door opened, Gustav walked and turned on a switch just inside the wall, and the lights came on inside. The walls and floor were white. Made from a thick plastic, with a drain in the middle of the floor. Above the drain, a man sat in a chair. They handcuffed him to the chair. His mouth, bound with tape, and his eyes blindfolded. Blood seeped from under the tape, and he had several bruises all over his body. He was naked except for his pants.

Mike looked in and rolled his eyes."What the fuck is this, Gustav? This isn't what she signed up for!" he shouted, getting angry.

Kendra looked at the man and thought of her parents tied up in their basement. She was not too sure as to what Gustav wanted her to do, and now was seeing that this could be something that she did not sign up for. "What am I supposed to do with this?"

Gustav went and stood beside her and stretched his hand out towards the man. "This, my dear, is your canvas."

"I don't get it."

Just then Pavel wheeled a large box on a dolly up to the container and muscled it up and onto the floor. He opened the box and pulled out several sharp knives, all rolled up, and a grinder with a wheel on it, a blowtorch, a drill and a sawzall. Archie brought up a folding table and set it up, and they neatly placed the tools on the table.

Mike was pacing and having a hard time keeping his composure. "Do you mind telling us who this poor son of a bitch is?"

Gustav walked into the container and knelt down, placing his hand on the man's knee. "This, my good friend, is public enemy number one. This is Jackson Baker. Mr. Baker likes to kidnap children and sell them to the highest bidder. Mr. Baker made one enormous mistake and took the wrong child."

The man struggled, shaking his head 'no', that it was not true. Muffled 'no's' came from behind the tape.

Mike, scatching his head, looked over at Kendra. "So that is what this is? Vigilantism artwork?" she asked Gustav.

Kendra, taking another glance at Mike, walked into the container. Jackson was hyperventilating, and sweat beaded on his head. She stopped and looked at Gustav, asking him, "Is this true?"

"I am afraid it is. But this is only the first part of it." He answered, and started walking. "Come." he insisted.

She followed him and went outside the container. "Remember that spray on concrete I told you I invested in?"

"Yes, I remember."

"Well, guess what? Today you revolutionize sculpting!" he announced, with great confidence pointing to the hopper and compressor that Pavel was unloading off of the truck, along with a few 5 gallon buckets. "By the time you are done, he will look just like a statue!"

She looked at Gustav, pursing her lips. "Mike, I need a fucking cigarette. Please." she mumbled, walking over to him.

Walking over, he gave her one, and lit it. "Kendra, look at me." he said quietly, with her looking up at him, "You don't have to do this. We can walk away, it's just money. Think about this."

She took a few drags and looked at the machine and then back at Mike. "I know why he is doing this, baby. He thinks it is going to help me."

Gustav spoke up, agreeing with what he heard her say. "I promise you it will help you. You will get rid of so much rage, pain and hurt that they caused you. Plus, help rid society of one more sick bastard."

Pavel walked back to the truck and retrieved a jumpsuit and a safety mask for her face. He walked up and handed it to her without saying a word. She took the items and looked at them, then looked back up at Gustav. "So this is it. This is what you wanted me for." she stated, frankly.

"No. This just came up. I have far greater things for you to accomplish. Think about it Kendra, think about what they did to you." Gustav rationalized, "He did the same thing to many others that never got to have a chance. Never got to go home, to have closure. Stripped away from the ones that loved them. He did that!" he yelled, pointing at the container.

Kendra put on the coveralls and carried the mask, walking up to Mike. "If this is too much-" she started to say as Mike stopped her. "Do what you have to do, Kendra. Long haul, remember."

She kissed him and drew back. "This will not take long."

She walked to the container, leaving Mike behind. Mike leaned on the steel entrance to the container, as Pavel brought her the last piece of her outfit, some rubber boots. She took them and put them on along with her face mask, walking over to the table and picking up the cordless drill and pulling the trigger. The drill bit started spinning with the motor humming. She let go of the trigger and put it down. Beside it was a box that she opened, and pulled out a paddle bit that was inside, changing the bit in the drill.

Jackson was straining and pulling at the handcuffs, making his wrists bleed. Muffled screams were coming out of his mouth, still covered by the duct tape. She approached him, pressing the trigger and letting it go. Reaching up with her free hand, she ripped the tape from his mouth. He opened his mouth to scream, revealing his tongue removed. Kendra looked back and saw Archie standing in the doorway, next to Mike and Gustav. "It was necessary at time, Kendra. Forgive me." Archie said with a shrug.

Saying nothing, she turned back towards Jackson. His voice becoming hoarse, he choked and gagged on his own blood that was coming from what used to be his tongue.

She blinked a few times, with Her back to Mike, and he could see by how her shoulders moved, that her breathing had gotten deeper. "Oh, fuck." he said, as he lit a cigarette, and watched, feeling the tension build.

What are you waiting for, you worthless little shit? You have a universe handed to you, and you fuck that up too? Did Daddy not fuck you enough? Is that the problem?

She listened to the antagonizing, raspy voice in her head, feeling the rage build, like a pot of boiling oil over a flame, that boiled over and ignited.

Suddenly, her voice exploded. "Fuck you!" She screamed,grabbing Jackson by the back of his head and pulling the trigger on the drill. The bit spun and sank into his right eye, tearing the eyeball into pieces and ripping it out. Jackson's body convulsed as the bit spun, tearing out what once was his eyeball. An empty socket remained, bleeding and covering the right side of his face with blood.

She stepped around to his left side and sank the bit into his left eye. A gurgling sound muffled Jackson's screams. After she retracted the bit, Kendra stood in front of him and bent down looking at his head, which was now hanging. The drill had splattered blood all over the walls, running down in various places while Jackson's body twitched as he sank into shock. Standing up, she walked back to the table, replacing the drill. She looked over the tools for a moment and then picked up the grinder, depressing the power handle a few times. The torque from the motor moved her wrist as she depressed the handle, and watched the blade spin.

Mike stood speechless. *Of all the women in the world, I took a chance on her. Why in the hell did I have to pick her? You're on the clock Mike, this isn't her. Just do your job.* He told himself.

Gustav looked over at Mike. "This is really a sight to behold, isn't it?" he asked with a twinkle in his eye.

Mike looked over at him, taking the last pull off of the cigarette, and throwing it to the floor. "Don't mistake me for a fool, Gustav. I know you have seen this kind of shit before."

Gustav grinned with his eyes narrowing. "As have you, my friend. But you always were using the tools. Is that not true?"

"I don't know what you're talking about."

"Really?" Gustav continued to probe, "Looking at that bridge everyday doesn't bring back old memories?"

Mike was tensing up, getting tired of Gustav and his little shots that he was taking towards him. He'd had enough.

"Look mother fucker-"

The thought of Gustav using Kendra to do his dirty work weighed heavily on him. Perhaps just killing them all and moving on, would wind up being the best choice he could make, for himself, and for her.

Gustav put his hands up in a gesture for Mike to stay calm. "Mike, Mike, we are all friends here." he reasoned, "We are all here for her. Just watch the show, and when it's done, you both can go back home to your little love nest, $2,000,000 richer than you are right now."

Mike looked back up at Kendra, who was walking towards Jackson with the grinder, and thought to himself. *Let it go Mike, this is not the time or the place. Just let it go.*

She lifted the man's head back. His body was limp, but he was still breathing. Holding his head steady with her arm, she held onto the grinder with both hands. The blade cut into the skin, ripping the flesh from his cheekbone. Then, taking the grinder, she cut a deep incision from the bottom of his left eye to the top, deep into his skull. His body convulsed, then stopped as soon as the blade penetrated his brain. Pieces of bone and bloody flesh hit Kendra's mask as she pulled out the spinning blade.

Jackson's body stayed bound to the chair, lifeless, as Kendra made the last cut over his right eye, then stood back and looked at what she had done. She turned around and walked to the doorway.

"I need barbed wire."

Gustav made a motion to Pavel. A few minutes went by and returned with a roll of razor wire. The same kind that lines the top of the fence outside. "How much do you need, Kendra?"

She looked at the wire and back at Gustav. "Give me about

four feet of it. That will do. And I need some pliers."

Pavel pulled out some pliers from his back pocket and cut the wire. She leaned down as he handed the wire and pliers to her, then walked back to Jackson, and wrapped the wire around the back of his head, and in between his jaws, keeping his mouth open. The wire was tight, causing the razors to cut deep into his skin. She twisted the wire together and stood back, admiring her work on him. She circled Jackson, slowly walking around him. There was silence, except for blood dripping from his body, onto the pool on the floor, which was running down the drain.

Kendra pulled off her mask and set it on the table, and walked to the edge of the container to take off the boots and coveralls. She looked over at Gustav, with the same blank look on her face. "He shit himself." she said plainly, and walked past him. Gustav motioned to Pavel, who then started cleaning up and getting ready to spray Jackson's body down, and make him eternal.

"Bravo! Bravo! Such work Archie has never seen!"

Archie cheered and clapped his hands, chewing on his cigar and walking up to Kendra, but Mike stepped in his way.

"Back off. Give her a minute."

"Yes, Archie understands this." he said, understandingly, "Every artist has certain things about them. No?"

"Yeah, you could say that." he said as he turned his attention towards Kendra, addressing her, "Jesus Christ, are you alright? Look at me!"

She looked up into his eyes. Her pupils were blood red and her eyes bloodshot. She looked dazed and became half coherent.

"Gustav? She needs some air, man!"

Gustav pointed towards a door in the back, and Mike walked her outside. They sat down on the ground and Mike lit her a cigarette. They stayed in silence until Archie and Pavel finished. Mike looked into her eyes again. They were turning back to their normal hazel color. "How are you feeling?" he asked her in a calming voice, realizing that she was not herself yet.

Leaning her head back against the wall, she sighed, "I have a headache."

"Yeah, I bet. Can I ask you something?"

"Yeah what?"

"Do you remember any of what you just did?"

"Why?"

"Kendra, your eyes turn color when you lose it. The other night they turned black."

"Really? I didn't know. It is all kinda hazy."

She had grown tired and weak, her mind remained clouded and had a hard time speaking. It seemed like it was all she could do just to say a simple sentence.

"Yeah, that's kinda what I figured." he continued, "Today they turned blood red."

She rubbed her temples and looked at Mike. "Mike, I want to go home."

"We will soon. They got what they wanted. Can you handle going back in?"

"Can we just sit here a bit?" she asked, leaning her head on his shoulder.

"Yeah, we can sit here." Mike put his arm around her and they sat in silence.

Kendra fell asleep. A few hours went by and Gustav opened the door. "Is she okay, Mike?" he asked, looking down at them.

"Are you just now checking on her? Classy man, real fucking classy. She will be fine." he replied, with a disgusted tone attached to his voice.

Kendra opened her eyes and blinked a few times, looking up at Gustav and then at Mike. He helped her get to her feet, making sure she was steady enough to walk, and they walked inside, with Gustav leading the way back to the container.

"I must apologize for the way I have been this morning. This is a new thing, and there is a lot of money at stake on this. We weren't sure if it was going to even work." he said, then stopped and addressed Kendra directly, "I think you are going to be very pleased with the outcome."

They followed him to the container. Pavel was finishing the cleanup. She looked in, and there, in the middle of the floor, suspended in midair on a hoist with chains, hung a concrete statue of the man she just brutalized.

"What in hell?" she gasped, stepping up inside and walked up to the statue. It was dry and hardened. She looked all around it, sliding her hand across the smooth finish. "I never would have thought."

She was fascinated by how the creation had turned out. What once was a living, breathing human being, was now cast in concrete, with the appearance of finely carved stone.

Gustav joined her, along with Mike. "It is pretty astounding. Don't you think so?"

"Amazing doesn't even cover it." Kendra agreed, "Do you have any more of this stuff?"

Gustav laughed, and pointed to the walls, and the containers that lined them. "I have 50 unopened crates."

"Good." she replied.

Mike looked at her out of the side of his eyes, asking, "Kendra, what are you thinking?"

Looking back at the statue, her mind was getting made up on just what she should do with Mommy and Daddy.

"My masterpiece."

Chapter 12

I Need Backup

Kendra slept on the ride home. Mike kept his concentration on the road, as the traffic was getting heavy. Driving through the city, he passed the street that led straight to Lucky's house.

"I should really get my car from there."

She stirred at the sound of his voice. "What?" she asked, stretching her arms.

Looking over at her, he rubbed her shoulder lightly and gave her a smile. "You slept almost all the way home."

She sat up and rubbed her eyes and looked out the window and back at Mike. "Who were you talking to?"

"Nobody, just to myself. I have a car at my buddy Lucky's house. I was saying I should get it one day soon."

"Shit, baby." she yawned, "That never even dawned on me if you had a car or not. What kind of car is it?"

Mike grew an excited look on his face. He missed his car, and it had been a while since he had gotten to drive it. "It's a classic I got from my old man. '69 Camaro."

"Oh, that's sexy." she exclaimed, "What color?"

"Never fails. Guys ask what's under the hood, women always ask the color." he replied, laughing, "It's red with black interior. I don't like to drive it much, it's too noticeable. So, I keep it at Lucky's place with some of my other things. Kinda like a safe house if I need it."

"Well, aren't you Mr. Prepared?"

"Yeah, I try to be. Speaking of which, we may need to talk about Reggie."

"Reggie? Okay, what about him?"

"I don't like this situation at all, I'm sure you know this by now. Nothing in the world is telling me this deal is good and everything is telling me it's all gonna go South. I need to know he is going to be readily available."

"Well," she said looking at him, "he is your friend, right?"

"Yeah, no doubt." he replied, "But the fact is, he has his own shit going on. Man's gotta eat, ya know."

"So, what are you saying?" Kendra asked him, crossing her arms.

"I don't know. Maybe we could put him on the payroll?" he suggested, "I feel like I need another set of eyes."

"Do you really think that we need him that bad? I mean, I kinda like this thing we have, you know, just you and I type of deal."

"So do I," he said, "but honestly, my gut never ever lies to me. These are not your run-of-the-mill thugs and this fucker has ties all around the world, is my estimation. If I am going into this any deeper with you, I need to have my people on board."

"And what will they say when they find out what I have done?"

She looked worried, and was not sure she wanted other people knowing what she was doing with Gustav. But, the fact reamined, she trusted Mike and his judgment.

"'Where do we put the bodies'? That is what they will say."

Sighing, she grabbed Mike's hand, looking out the window. "Fine, call your friend over to play if you really want to." she said, turning back and looking at him with a smile, "But Momma says you're in by 10pm, Mr. No exceptions."

"Deal." he replied, and kissed her hand as they both laughed.

∞ ∞ ∞

Back at the Canvas, they went into Kendra's office, and she turned on the computer. Mike was standing by the door, looking around. "Hey baby? What's in that room there?" he asked, pointing to a door on the other side of the office, just past the safe. Kendra looked over. "That? Oh shit!" she shouted, "I'm sorry. I never showed you." She stood up and unlocked the door and opened it.

She turned on the lights inside to reveal its contents. "This is my studio." she started to explain, "This is where it all happens, well, where all that is in my mind gets transferred into reality, should I say."

Turning to look at Mike, she continued saying, "Nobody comes in here, ever. Michelle has never even been inside here. You're the first to see it. Gustav is to never set foot in here. Now come on, I'll show you around."

She walked Mike around the room, giving him the tour. There was a stereo with speakers mounted on all four walls. The room was enormous, with a section for sculpting, and a section for painting. She had shelves upon shelves of supplies, with canvases of all different sizes, and paints of every color, with some that she had mixed herself.

"Don't say a word about the mess. This is my world." she announced, "It's an organized chaos."

"I didn't say a word." He was doing his best in letting her know that he knew better than to say anything about her sacred area. At this point, Mike was getting the hang of separating the relationship status of boss, and lover when it came to her.

"Well, that's enough." she said, "I want to see if Gustav has transferred that money yet."

They left the room, and she locked the door. "Mike, do I need to say it?"

It was apparent to him that she needed some more assurance that he understood exactly what she had meant about her studio, and the privacy that she required.

He sat in the chair against the wall by the door and replied, "No. I get it. Your domain. No exceptions."

"Thank you. I hope you understand. I don't enjoy having any distractions while I am working.".

"No, you're good. I totally get it."

"Awesome, thanks. So, now let's check the bank account and see where we are." she said accessing her account and sure enough, there sat a transfer of $2,000000 from another account.

"Fuck!"

"What it's not there?"

"No, it's there, just dawned on me. I have to have Michelle redo my tax bullshit. I am horribly dumb with it." she admitted sheepishly.

"Michelle is good with money?"

"Oh, don't let the ditsy blonde look fool you." she replied, "She is a wizard with numbers."

"Damn, never would have suspected that."

"Yeah, she is a gold mine with finances."

"So, about what is going on with your parents and what happened this morning. Would you trust--" Mike tried to ask. But Kendra was quick to interrupt with a fearful reply.

"Oh, fuck no! Oh God, she can't ever know that! I love Michelle to death. I have been working with her for years. But she isn't that kind of person to handle that. I'm not sure I am, to be completely honest."

"Well, that answers that question."

"Yeah, and it was a good one. So, how are you handling all of this?" she asked, turning her chair to look at him.

"All of what?"

Waving her arms around in a circle, she explained, "This, us, my parents this morning. How are you doing with it?"

"Honestly, it was a bit to get back into this type of thing, but as far as that goes, another day at the office." he replied, sitting back in his chair.

"What about us?"

"Yeah, 'us' is a big word," he said, "there hasn't been an 'us' in my life in a long time."

"That doesn't tell me shit, Mike." she smirked.

"I know. Look. I like where it is going. I'm cool and would like it to go further." he said, explaining his thoughts on it to her, "That's one reason I want Reggie back rolling with me. I have to keep you safe. That is my job, remember?"

"I remember." she said, "Call him. Offer him the same deal I gave you. But I am off the table."

Then she stood up and straddled Mike's lap, and wrapped her arms around his neck. "I belong to the hit man." she said smiling, and kissed him.

As their lips met, the thought of what she had done earlier clouded Mike's mind, but in the same sense, made him desire her even more. This woman, so fragile, yet capable of such brutalities and barbarous actions, was stealing his heart. Something that he once thought had become impossible.

Now, she was on his lap, deeply kissing him and showing an equal desire for him. The more he thought about it, the tighter he held on to her, filling them both with passion.

"Upstairs?" he asked her.

"No, right here, and right now." she exclaimed, pulling off her shirt, and throwing it to the floor.

As they stood up, after removing their clothing frantically, Mike picked her up and sat her in the chair. Grabbing her hips, he slid her forward, draping her legs over his shoulders.

He ran a line of gentle kisses up the inside of her thigh as she grabbed his hair with both hands, pulling him forward.

Goddamn! I must be the luckiest man alive! He thought to himself as he momentarily gazed at her, slid forward in the chair and her eyes begging for him to taste her.

Not making her wait any longer, he let his tongue explore, sending her writhing and gripping his hair with one hand, and the arm of the chair with the other.

Being caught in the throes of the sensations traveling through her body, she looked down at him. All she could see was the top of his head, but she looked past that, and saw the man she was falling in love with doing everything possible to make her feel loved, protected, and cherished.

The sight pushed her even further as his fingers entered her. She grabbed her breasts and moaned his name, begging him not to stop.

She knew she was getting close, and now wanted him inside of her. She pulled his head up by his hair, and got out of the chair. Standing up and turning around, she bent over, and looked back at him with a drunken look of ecstasy written on her face.

With one hand steadying herself on the wall, she slid the other between her legs, to feel him gliding into her.

He grabbed her by her hair, pulling her head back as he thrust into her repeatedly.

The slaps from skin on skin filled the room and echoed through the gallery as his hips repeatedly met her backside. As sweat dripped from his body, down onto her back, she rapidly rubbed her swollen clit, driving her closer to her climax.

Mike could not hold back any longer, telling her he was about to explode.

That was enough to push her over her limits. She screamed as her insides pulsed around Mike, who could no longer wait.

As he pulled out of her, he lay on her back, covering it in his fluids, and gripping her shoulders, biting her neck.

After a moment of collecting their thoughts, they stood up, sweaty and dripping in each other's juices.

"Oh my God, that was fucking amazing." she exclaimed. "And you made a hell of a mess!" she added, giggling.

"Well, it seemed like the thing to do at the time," he said, laughing.

"Shower?"

"Yes, we definitely need a shower."

They gathered the clothing they had thrown onto the floor and went up to Kendra's apartment, and into the bathroom.

She turned on the water and let the shower run, as Mike was

looking in the mirror, and she took a place next to him. "You know, we make a sexy ass couple." he said.

"Yes, we do baby." Kendra agreed, "I hope we stay this way."

Mike turned to her and kissed her, then pulled back. "I didn't know what I was missing before I met you. And now? I never want to be without it."

"Are you saying that you love me Mike?"

"I am saying I am falling in love with you, all of you."

After their shower was finished, Mike took Kendra up on her offer and gave Reggie a call while she was busy going over the finances with Michelle. He went into the Grotto and sat on the couch and dialed Reggie's number.

"Yo, this is Reggie."

"What's up, bro.?"

"Mike? Shit, that was quick homie. I just got up a little while ago. That fool I knocked out last night had the fuckin cops come."

"You good man?"

"Shit, dog, you know it. So what's poppin? What you need?"

"Kendra and I were wondering if you could hop on over across the bridge, bro. Got something to shoot by you."

"You alright?"

"Yeah, I'm good, nothing I haven't dealt with before. What do you have going on?"

"Me? Nothin these days," replied Reggie. "Just bouncin at that shitty ass night club. Things been pretty quiet. Got heated, so I had to pump the brakes. Ya know how it goes."

"Yeah, I do. Look, I got an offer for ya. I'll send the address and you can come by."

"Alright, bet. What time? I got to be at the club by 8PM."

"Sooner the better bro."

"Shit, lemme get my kicks on, bro. I'm on my way."

"Hell ya! See ya soon." Mike said, as he put his phone away.

Mike met Kendra back in her office. She was just hanging up with Michelle. "Are we all good?" He asked as he stood behind her, placing his hands on her shoulders.

"Yeah, she will take care of everything," she replied. "What about Reggie? Did you talk to him?"

"Yeah, he is on his way over. I figured I'd pitch it to him, and you can play boss."

"Whatever you think is best. I'm sure we will convince him."

Mike leaned down and smiled, looking into her eyes. "We again. You like that, don't you?"

She smiled. "What? Does it bother you?"

"No. Not in the least.", he replied, "I'm just gonna start calling you Bonnie, that's all."

She started laughing. "You're an ass. You know that?"

Mike stood up, chuckling, "Yup, and you love it!"

Kendra focused back on her computer screen. "Yes I do, cowboy, I mean Clyde."

Giving her a wink, he returned to the Grotto to wait on Reggie, and let her focus on her business.

It wasn't too long before Reggie pulled up outside of the Gallery. Mike could hear his exhaust from inside. He walked outside to greet him. "Bro! What is up with you and Dodge trucks?"

"Hey you know, gotta roll with the big dogs!" They hugged and went inside. "What in the fuck is all this?" Reggie took off his shades and looked at all of Kendra's art on the walls and displayed in the aisles. "Man, this is some Freddy Krueger shit, bro."

"Yeah, this is her newest work. She just had a premier the other night. Do you like it?"

"I'm thinking bout gettin' some of this in ink, bro. Make some sick ass tattoo work." Reggie said, looking down his arms as he held them out.

"I'm sure she would consider it an honor. Come on bro, I'll show ya the Grotto."

"The what?"

"The fuckin bar bro!"

"Oh, that's what's up."

They walked into the Grotto and Mike poured Reggie a glass of whiskey. "Here, bro. You're gonna need this."

Reggie grabbed the glass of whiskey from Mike. "Nice, just how I like it. What, you ain't drinkin with me?"

"I'll have one, just for old times sake. I don't drink too much these days, brother. Gotta keep my head about me."

Reggie sat down in one of the chairs. "That bad?"

Mike finished pouring himself a drink. "It's a little sketchy, for sure."

"Alright then, hit me with it. What's goin on that you need to call the Reggie man in?"

Mike had started to explain when Kendra walked in. Reggie took sight of her, and respectfully stood up. "Kendra, right?"

"Yeah! Reggie, good to see you again." She looked at them both and frowned jokingly. "Oh, I see how it is. Don't get the crazy bitch a drink," walking to the bar. "Guess I'll just have to get it myself."

Mike stood up, not wanting her to have to get it herself. "No, sit down baby, I got it."

She looked at him and started laughing. "Shut up, you ain't seen him in a while. You're good." Mike sat on the couch and Kendra joined him, throwing her leg over his.

"So you're the one who did all of that art out there?" said Reggie, after setting his drink on the table.

"Yeah, I did. What ya think?" she asked, taking a drink.

"That some bad ass wicked lookin' shit. I was tellin' Mike I want to get some of that inked. What ya think? Sleeve my arms with it!" He held out both of his arms with his fists clenched.

"I think that would take a lot of ink. I'd draw up some original work for you. I mean, if you're serious."

"Hell yeah, I'm serious. I never been inked before. I'm kinda thinkin' it's time, ya know. Plus, I got the perfect guy to do it, too."

"Sure, we can work something up that I am sure you will like. So, did Mike tell you why we called you here?"

"No, we were about to get to that when you walked in," Reggie replied.

"Go ahead and tellem Mike," Kendra said, putting her hand on Mike's leg.

Mike told Reggie about the last few days. He told him about how they met, the trip to her parents and what they had done with them. He told him about Gustav and his suspicions and what Lucky had to say about it. Then he told him about that morning and what Kendra did to Jackson. Reggie never flinched. Not once. "So, what we want to know is, do you want to work with me on this? $200,000 salary, plus expenses a year. Money is in the bank waiting."

Reggie finished his whiskey, got up, and poured another. "So, you want me to run with you, driving her around, and basically put the band back together? That what you're sayin? For $200,000 a year?"

"Plus expenses."

"Shit, bro. I gotta know one thing, though."

"What's that?", asked Mike.

"Where we dumpin' the mutha fuckin' bodies?", he asked, shrugging and taking another drink.

Mike looked over at Kendra. "Told ya."

"That you did, my love, that you did."

"Told her what?" Reggie asked.

"I told her that's what you'd say. So I still got all the gear at Lucky's. Unless you picked your stuff up, yours should be there too."

Reggie shook his head. "Yeah, I called that fool after you two left the club last night. Had to see what was goin' on. He's ready to go when we are."

"Really?" Mike asked, taking a drink.

"Yeah, Reggie knows when shit's about to pop off. I feel that shit, bro. It's like lightning in the air!" He stood up, filled with excitement. "Been a long time Mike! Glad you got hold of me. Like the old days?"

Mike stood up and toasted him. "Like the old days."

Reggie looked down at Kendra, still sitting on the couch. "Baby girl, you ain't got shit to worry 'bout. You lookin' at the two baddest mutha fuckas on the planet!"

She stood up. "Well, Mike seems to think I'm in a lot of trouble with this Gustav guy." She wrapped her arm around Mike. "So far, he is making us rich. But a girl can't be too careful."

"True that. Besides, I know what Mike's talkin' 'bout with these Russians. These people don't play. If it's the same crowd we was watchin' years ago, we gonna have some issues to deal with."

"Yeah, and we will deal with them, too. So, you hitting the club tonight? Or are we gonna go out and raise some hell?"

She looked over at Reggie. "Oh, you're going out with us tonight. We are raising hell. Boss's orders."

Reggie smiled. "Shit, I was hatin' that place, anyway. Fuck it! Let's ride!"

Mike pulled out his phone. "Think I should call Lucky up and see if he wants to come out with us? I thought we would head over to the Block Party. They got live bands there all the time."

Kendra grabbed Mike's arm tight. "Oh, I love live bands! Are they metal? "

"Yeah, usually. Lot of local bands play there. I used to drop people off there all the time until Uber came out, that is."

Reggie finished his glass and put it on the bar. "You know damn well that old man ain't never goin' out. He never leaves his house, much less go to some club with a bunch of drunk ass metalheads."

Mike pulled up Lucky's number. "What, you don't like metal?" grinning.

"Oh don't you start with that 'It's because I'm black bullshit!' I'll fuck that entire mosh pit up!"

"Yup, I'm gonna leave you two boys to hash out your love

spat. I'm going to get dressed. If I'm going out to a metal club, I have to get my war paint on." She laughed and ran out of the room. Mike looked at Reggie with a grin. "She, uh, has to go get her war paint on."

Reggie laughed. "Bro. Call the old man, see if he gonna come out."

"It would be pretty fucking cool if he did, but you're more than likely right. He doesn't like leaving his house," Mike said, dialing Lucky's number.

"Ya Mike," Lucky answered.

"Hey, we are goin' to the Block Party tonight. Me, Reggie and Kendra. Wanted to know if you wanted to come and join us for a drink."

Lucky responded. "Now that's trouble lookin' to happen. No can do. I'm on the trail and can't get off it. Call ya in a few days, Mike," and he hung up.

"Well, that was a big no," Mike said, putting his phone away.

Reggie laughed. "Told ya so."

"Yeah, you did. Fuck it, we are going to have a blast anyway."

Chapter 13

Out With The Boys

The Block Party's neon lights cast a glow onto the street out front of the club. As they approached the door, they could hear music from a band playing inside. Kendra looked up at a sign on the outside to the left of the door.

Tonight! Necrotic Filth. Show starts at 8PM $10.00 Cover. 21 and up.

"Oh man, this sounds intense!" Kendra exclaimed.

Mike grinned. "Sounds like hell on earth is what it sounds like."

Reggie looked at the sign. "These guys played at the club I was bouncin' at a few weeks back. Real heavy shit. That Death Metal vibe."

Upon opening the door, two men greeted them, took their IDs and cover charges. Close to the entrance stood a merch booth with two women behind it selling stickers, hats, t-shirts and C.D.'s that the band members had signed.

"Mike, are you gonna get me a t-shirt?" Kendra asked, with her arm around him, wearing a big smile.

"Yeah, we can do that. What about you Reggie? You wear that shit like it's going out of style."

"I already got one from the last time I saw them. If I had known, I'd have worn it."

As they continued inside, they looked up front and saw the

band playing on a stage that had a large dance floor in front of it, filled with people moshing and moving in large circles. Bouncers stood on all sides, making sure nobody sustained injuries. Off to the side, behind the bar, there sat a room. It had red neon lights surrounding the ceiling with tables and chairs. A few people were there, but not too many. Topless waitresses gathered drinks from the bar and delivered them to patrons through the club.

Mike put his hand on Kendra's lower back and leaned down so she could hear him. "Let's go grab a table and have a drink. It's fuckin loud out here."

They entered the room and sat at a booth. A moment later, a blonde with no top on, a leather thong, fishnet stockings and thigh-high boots came up to the table.

"What would you all like to drink?"

Reggie started laughing and Mike kicked him under the table. "Behave ya animal!"

She sat down next to Reggie and put her arm around his neck. "Oh, he doesn't have to if he doesn't want to."

Reggie just smiled back at Mike and then looked at her. "Oh, be careful now baby, big bad wolf is out to play tonight."

"Then you can call me Little Red Riding Hood."

"Oh damn! Alright Little Red Riding Hood, I think we can do three double whiskeys straight up. And make it Jameson."

"A big sexy wolf, with taste." She stood up and rested her hands on the end of the table, squeezing her breasts together with her arms. "I'll be right back." With that, she turned and walked out of the room, with Reggie watching her as she left.

"Goddamned son! I need to come here more often!" Kendra looked over at Mike. "What about you? Do you need to come here more often?"

"Nah, you keep me plenty occupied."

"Really?" she asked with a perplexed look on her face.

"Because I'd fuck the shit out of her personally."

Reggie burst into laughter. "Oh, man, brother! You got your hands full with this one!"

All three were laughing. "You have no clue, bro."

The waitress came back with their drinks and set them on the table. She slid a piece of paper to Reggie. "My name is Tanya, and I have tomorrow off. Call me." She winked at him and turned around and left.

Mike chuckled. "Mother fucker. We ain't in here five minutes and you got women giving you their number already. Damn, bro. Ya know what? It's gotta be because--"

"Don't you say it mother fucker! Don't you say it!"

"Oh, I'm gonna say it!" Mike threatened as he laughed.

Kendra was laughing at their antics. "It's because you're black, Reggie!"

Reggie and Mike both had tears running out of their eyes from laughing so hard. "Oh no! She didn't!"

"Yeah bro! She got your ass!"

After laughing for a few solid minutes, they grabbed their glasses. Kendra stood and spoke up, raising her glass. "To my boys! Salt and Peppa!"

Again laughter exploded at the table. "Oh my God girl! Yo seriously though, I'm glad y'all called me. We rollin' again!"

"Yes, we are bro."

They drank their doubles down, slamming their glasses on the table. Kendra's phone was sitting on the table and vibrated. "Oh hell, not tonight." She opened it up, seeing a new message from Michelle. It was a photo selfie of her in a car, with Gustav driving. "That little slut!" She showed the picture to Mike.

"Uh oh, that can't be good." He said, as he looked at the picture. "I don't think he would be dumb enough to say anything to her about what's going on. Do you?"

"What's goin' on there?" Reggie asked.

She showed the picture to Reggie. "This is my friend Michelle. She takes care of my books, taxes and deliveries for me. The guy she is with, though, is Gustav. They met the other night. I didn't know they exchanged numbers."

"Shit. Should we go find her?"

"No, she is just trying to get laid. She will be alright."

Mike looked at the picture again. "I don't like it. Look at the background. Outside of the window, that's New York City, baby."

"Yeah, well, Michelle is a big girl. She can handle him, I'm sure."

"If you say so."

Tanya returned to the table. "Another round?" Mike slid his glass over to her. "I guess one more will do."

"What? I thought we were raisin' hell tonight, bro? You getting soft on me?"

"No man. I don't drink too much these days. Actually, I don't drink at all anymore. Tonight's just a small exception."

"I feel ya. Yeah, make it one more round."

"Awesome. Want me to bring the bill when I come back?"

Kendra reached into her bag. "What are we up to?"

Tonya added their drinks. "Let's see, six rounds of Jameson doubles. I'll make it singles because you guys fucking rock and this man here is excruciatingly sexy," as she motioned to Reggie. "Comes to ninety dollars even."

Kendra pulled out three fifties and handed them to her. "Keep the change, love."

"Oh my, I may have to give you my number as well," giving Kendra a wink. "I'll be back with your drinks in a second." She turned and left the table.

"I want to see the band after we drink these." Kendra said, nudging Mike.

"Yeah, we can do that."

Windows lined the room, so customers that didn't want to be in the crowds could still watch what was going on. The floor, filled with people, would be impossible to stand on. People lined the railings around the floor, banging their heads, throwing horns in the air and screaming until they had no voice left.

Tonya came back with their drinks and placed them on the table. "So, ya gonna call me tomorrow?"

Reggie looked up at her with a big grin on his face. "Well, I will have to see what the boss says. But if I'm free, expect that phone to ring."

She leaned down and whispered in his ear. "You won't regret it." After running her tongue around the outside of his ear, she stood up and left once more.

"Oh yeah, she gettin' a phone call fo' sho!"

Mike looked at his phone. "Kendra, we have to get to your parents tomorrow. Better do it early."

"Oh, my God! Why do they always have to ruin my fun?"

"What you gotta do there?" asked Reggie.

"Make sure they are still alive."

"Oh yeah, that. Hey Mike, remember my cousin that used to be our on call if things got bad?"

"Yeah, I remember her, Veronica, right?"

"Yeah her. She's a private duty nurse now. Got her RN and everything. Want I should call her up? She does some work out there in Cherry Hill, anyway. Ya know, that old money when that place used to be all uppity up."

"Is she still cool? I mean, you know the circumstances."

"Yeah, she straight. Ain't cheap, but she straight."

"Nice!" Mike replied.

Kendra piped in. "What am I missing here?"

"His cousin, okay, you heard all of that. But we could get her to check on them and keep them alive until you decide what to do with them."

"That is an idea. Can she meet us out there tomorrow?"

"I can call and see."

"Do that. That will save me from having to run over there all the time."

"Bet. I'll call her right now." Reggie got up and went outside to call his cousin.

"Think she will be cool with it?" Kendra asked Mike.

"Yeah, she is a nasty bitch to piss off. I saw her gut a guy one night for trying to rip off Reggie. She is a straight up beast."

"Damn! And a nurse?"

"Yup. She used to check on Lucky when he was sick. I don't

135

know if she still does or not. Bottom line is, though, we can trust her."

"Good, that's all that really matters."

Kendra's phone vibrated again. Another message from Michelle. "Now, what is this chick doing?" It was another picture. Another selfie. This time in a living room. A bear skin rug in front of a fireplace with a fire blazing in it. There were a few paintings on the wall behind her from what she could see.

Where are you?

I'm at Gustav's. This place is amazing!

Slut lol

Jealous?

Nope. Have fun, Chicky. Be safe.

"She is at fucking Gustav's place. Can you believe that?"

"I believe she doesn't know what she is into. That's what I believe. Better watch her the next few days."

"Oh, I know her pretty well. I'll be able to tell if anything is up."

Reggie returned to the table and sat down. "What time you want to meet her tomorrow?"

Kendra had a puzzled look on her face. "Shit like that? Um, is ten in the morning too early?"

"I'll text her and see."

Mike started laughing again. "Man, look at you with a phone and shit. I remember when they came out. 'I ain't never gettin one of those damned things. Gives ya brain cancer and shit!' Now see how you are."

"Hey gotta roll with the times, bro." Reggie sent the text and received one back a moment later. He put the phone away in his pocket.

"We're good."

"She knows what the deal is?" Asked Kendra.

"Yeah, she knows."

"Does she know why I did it?"

"Yeah, I told her."

"What did she say?"

"She asked if she could be there when you do 'em."

Kendra smiled. "Damn, I like her already. Shit, let's drink these and go see the band," she said as she raised her glass to drink her double of whiskey.

They downed their drinks and made their way out to the rails by the stage. The lead singer was swinging his hair in circles as the guitarists were banging their heads along with the bassist. There was a guy playing keyboards, and a drummer behind a huge drum kit. All of them had their faces painted white with their eyes blacked out. They adorned themselves in black leather and spikes. On both ends of the stage, nude women were on their hands and knees, chained by the neck to posts laden with skulls.

The crowd on the dance floor intensified as the circles of people went faster. Every so often, Kendra noticed someone fall and she would gasp, only to be relieved when everyone helped pick them back up to their feet. "Mike, have you ever seen anything like this?"

He strained to hear her. "No! I have never been to a show like this. I have to say, it is pretty bad ass though!"

Kendra pulled out her phone and took a selfie with all three of them in it and the band behind them. She sent it to Michelle and waited for a response. After waiting for over a minute, she gave up and put her phone back in her pocket. "I definitely want to get a shirt and a C.D. Of theirs!" She yelled to Mike.

"Yeah! For sure! Hell, I might get one as well!"

They watched the band until the show was over. There were no fights, nobody got hurt and everyone seemed to have a great time. The front door got quickly filled with people sweating and trying to leave. Kendra, Mike, and Reggie were quickly at the merch table to avoid a long line. The band was beside the table, signing autographs and taking pictures with fans as

Kendra stepped up and greeted them.

"I have to get a picture with all of you!"

"Yeah, sure thing, love." The lead singer said, smiling. Kendra joined them behind the booth and they all posed while Mike took a picture.

"Oh my God, thank you." She reached into her bag and pulled out a card. "Here, look me up. I'll give you a hella discount on my work."

"Really, what, you're an artist then?"

"Yeah, here." She pulled out her phone and showed them some of her paintings and sculptures.

"You did these?"

"Yeah, right here in town. I have a gallery close to here."

"Hey look, love, we are heading back to Oslo next week. We have a show in New York this weekend. Think we could get a private viewing of your gallery before we leave?"

"I will have the bar stocked and the doors locked for ya."

"Aye? Sounds awesome love. Count on us being there for sure. I'll call ya and let ya know when. Bloody fuckin' sick work!"

"Um, Thanks?"

The band laughed, as she looked at them a little confused as to just what they had meant. "Yeah love, it's a compliment. We will be there."

"Fuck yeah! Thank you!" she exclaimed as she went to the front of the merch booth and picked out one of everything on the table. Mike grabbed a shirt as well. They paid for the merchandise and made their way to the door.

"Man, that shit was fun as hell! Been a long time since I got to just enjoy a show without splittin' some fool in the head." Reggie exclaimed.

Mike nodded his head. "I bet, bro. That was pretty cool. I could go to more shows. It was different, ya know?"

Kendra put her arm around Mike. "I had a great time. A night out with my boys. Just what I needed."

They made their way out to the truck and got in. Traffic was a little backed up as people were pulling out of the parking lot, trying to get home. Police cars had been stationed around the area to make sure nothing nefarios was going on. The night went perfectly.

"Reggie, are you gonna go home tonight? I mean, you can crash in the Grotto." Kendra asked.

Reggie nodded. "That works." Kendra's phone went off again. There was a new picture. Michelle was in a gigantic bed, topless, and in the background, on a nightstand, laid a spoon, a lit candle, and a syringe filled with brown fluid.

Chapter 14

The Nurse

Reggie, Mike and Kendra sat in the Grotto, drinking morning coffee. The day had started with everyone getting up and getting coffee, so they could take care of what they needed to. "You sleep alright down here?" Mike asked.

"Yeah actually. Thanks for letting me crash. I don't like driving after I have had a few," replied Reggie.

Mike looked over at Kendra, who was busy catching up on her emails through her phone. "Hear anything more from Michelle last night?"

"Yeah, she sent me a picture of her in his bed." She scrolled through the text messages on her phone, and showed it to Mike.

Mike took the phone and looked at the picture. "Kendra, tell me you didn't see what I'm seeing." he said, holding up the phone to Kendra.

"What's that?"

"That fucking junky rig on the nightstand." he replied, pointing to the needle and spoon on the nightstand in the picture.

"What?" She snatched the phone from him and looked. "Oh my God, I didn't even notice that last night. What the fuck?!"

Reggie looked up, in question of what they were talking about. "What's the deal? She got mixed up with a lil' scag?"

She handed her phone to Reggie. As he looked at the picture, he sipped his coffee. "Does she like to get down?"

"No! She likes her wine and booze, maybe smoke a little pot here and there, and been known to do some ecstasy, but she doesn't fuck with any of that shit. I need to call her, like, now."

Kendra got her phone back and called Michelle. "Come on dammit, pick up." The phone rang until her voicemail answered and Kendra left a message. "Girl, you need to call me as soon as you get this!"

Kendra, filled now with worry, put her phone on the table. "Fuck. I hope she didn't do what I think she did.

Mike glanced at her, picking up his coffee and blowing away the steam. "Maybe you should call Gustav and see what's up."

"Oh, and say what Mike? 'Hey, did you get my friend all fucked on heroin last night?' I am sure that would go over well."

"Yeah, I get it. Just keep trying to get hold of her today. We need to get to your parent's house and meet up with Veronica though."

"I know. We should get going. Are you ready to do this, Reggie?"

"Yeah, I'm ready. I need to swing by my place and grab a bag, though. Seems like I better be ready to crash here if I need to."

"Yeah, definitely. We will talk about that on the ride to Cherry Hill. I have an idea." Kendra stood up with Mike and Reggie, and headed out to the garage and left.

After stopping for more coffee, they were on their way to Kendra's parents. With Mike driving and Reggie in the back seat, Kendra sat with her back to the door, so she could see them both as she talked.

"So I was thinking. Mike, you are living with me now, until we see what we are doing, and that still leaves the other two apartments upstairs empty. My idea is, after we get Veronica set up, we go by some furniture stores, and let you two pick out whatever you want, and have them deliver it to the apartment. That way, it's all set up for whoever, whenever. What do you think?"

"Yeah, I like that idea. I mean, true, I don't know what's going to happen to us. I mean, that's just being real. But I also don't know what's going to happen with Gustav and his group of whatever, either. So I could see that being a pretty sweet set up. Kinda like a kick pad."

Reggie sat forward and chimed in. "I'm down with that. I'm not too particular about where I live, anyway. My place is nice, but it ain't all that."

"Well, I have two open apartments. They are there if you want one and get out of Philly."

"Alright, I'll think about that a bit." Reggie said, as he looked at his phone. "Yup, Veronica is on her way."

"Good, we should meet up right on time. Got to take care of my boys today," Kendra smiled and giggled.

Mike looked over. "What's so funny?"

"Eh, kinda feel like some mob boss woman or something. I don't know, I just found it funny."

"Oh, now we got to call you Mamma K or some shit like that?"

"Shut up." she said, smacking Mike on the arm, laughing. "Asshole."

Reggie sat back, chuckling. "Man, you two are a trip. I swear."

They pulled into the driveway and around back. A few minutes later, a white BMW pulled in behind them. Veronica stepped out of her car and retrieved a bag from her trunk.

She wore a white dress and nursing shoes, but kept her top unbuttoned to show off her cleavage as she carried a good sized bosom. Her skin was smooth and tight on her frame, and she was a little taller than Kendra. She didn't wear a cap. Instead, she had her hair down and curled loosely.

Kendra walked up and introduced herself. "You must be Veronica. I'm Kendra Blake," she said, shaking her hand.

"Nice to meet you. Reggie told me you got a hell of a situation here." she said, looking up and seeing Mike. "Hey baby, I see you're still looking fine as hell. How's that bullet wound on your back treating ya?"

"It's good. Little sore with the weather change, but good. Nice to see ya, girl, been a few years."

"Yeah, when Reggie told me you two were at it again, I thought to myself, 'Oh lord, here we go again.' So what you two fools got yourself into now?"

"Nothing we can't handle for sure. Let's go inside and we will give ya the tour." They took Reggie and Veronica inside and down to the basement.

"I have them in there. They have some cuts and shit, but Mike bandaged them up. I have to warn you, it stinks in there." Kendra said, shrinking up her face and grabbing her nose.

"Girl, don't you worry. I have seen it all. People puking on me, throwing shit on me, everything. This ain't gonna be nothin."

Kendra opened the door and turned on the light. Veronica poked her head inside, then faced Kendra, and smiled gently. "This is where you step back and let me take over." She stepped away from the door and let Veronica enter.

They were weak, dehydrated and sitting in their own filth. Veronica approached them, setting her bag on the floor. "I am Nurse Veronica. You can, and will, refer to me as Ma'am. Do I make myself clear?"

William looked up at her, barely having enough strength to lift his head. "What are you doing here? We don't like your kind."

"Like my kind or not, I am here. Now you sit there and keep your trap shut, or I'll shoot you up, and knock you out and just make this easy on myself. Understood?"

He nodded his head yes. She turned around and faced Kendra. "They are going to need some care here. How comfortable you want them is up to you. But sitting in shit, they more than likely already have sores started. I have to clean them up and get them hydrated. I can give them an I.V. Drip and keep them alive until you choose otherwise. Have to tell ya sister, This is pretty sick shit you got going on in here. But I would have put a bullet in both their skulls from what Reggie told me. I got you, girl. Just let Veronica take care of this mess."

"Thank you. I'm glad Reggie called you. And don't worry about the bill. I'll pay whatever you need."

"After what you went through, this is on me. I come out here every damned day, anyway. I'll be here for a few hours this morning. After that, it's just maintenance. How long do you plan on keeping them like this?"

"I don't know, not long. I think I have figured out what I want to do with them."

"You just let me know, sugar." She looked over at Mike and Reggie. "You two owe me, not her."

"Don't worry, we will take care of you." Mike replied.

Veronica smirked. "Mm-hmm. Oh, I know I heard that one before."

"Nah, seriously, got you hooked up. Trust me."

"Yeah, I'll be calling in that favor and soon, you trust me." She turned and looked back at Kendra.

"Leave me a key. Y'all can go do whatever you need. I got this."

"If you say so, you sure?" Kendra asked.

"Yeah, I'm sure. They give me any issues. I got some good knock out drugs in this bag. Trust me, they ain't gonna be a problem."

"Fare enough, then."

Kendra handed her a key. "We are gonna take off and get some things taken care of. Reggie will give you my number in case you need anything. I mean anything, you call me."

"Good enough. Now go on, I have work to do."

Kendra smiled at her, thanking her again, and joined Reggie and Mike upstairs, so they could leave and get things for the apartment.

∞ ∞ ∞

After a few stores, they had everything from furniture to a full theater system picked out and scheduled for delivery that afternoon. They arrived back at the gallery early, which gave Kendra plenty of time to check her emails, and keep trying to get hold of Michelle.

"Mike, I am getting really worried about her. Still no answer."

"If she is tied into that shit, she is probably not feeling so hot right now, if she has never done it before."

"Listen, do me a favor and take Reggie upstairs and show him the apartments. Give him the tour and make sure he knows about my studio."

"I got ya. Are you gonna be alright with Michelle?"

"Yeah, I am. Just not so sure about Michelle."

Mike kissed her and took Reggie upstairs.

"Okay Bro. This is Kendra's place here, first door. Alley is on the left and apartments on the right. Pretty simple. We are filling the one on the end."

"What's in this second one here?"

"Honestly? I have no clue. Never been in it."

They reached the apartment at the end of the hall, and Mike opened the door. "You're gonna love this view, man."

They entered, and Reggie looked around. "I can dig this set up. Good view of Philly from here. Also, a good way to spot people coming and going."

"Yeah, one of my favorite things. You can put your bag over there in that room. It's going to be like the bedroom."

Reggie walked in and placed his bag next to Mike's trunk. "Ah, ya got your trunk. This must be serious."

"Yeah, I was supposed to move in here, but things went a little in another direction with Kendra, so you know how it goes."

"Hey man, what's up with that, anyway? I never knew you to be involved with anyone, especially someone you are working for."

"I don't know, bro." Mike shook his head, laughing. "I guess there's just something about her. You should see it though man, when she killed that guy in the warehouse, the color of her eyes went from hazel to blood red. And before that, when she went off on her dad, they turned pitch black. Almost like she became possessed or something."

As he explained her transformation to Reggie, Reggie's eyes grew wide and his face a turn of disbelief.

"Well, all I know is, her head starts spinnin', and she starts spittin' out green shit, this motha fucka dippin' out. That's what I know." Reggie stated.

They both started laughing. "Yeah, don't worry, I'll be right behind ya. Hey, are you still packing?"

"No man, all my shit's at Lucky's house. Like I said, things got a little hot, so I had to lie low, walk that line a bit."

"Alright, I got something for you in my chest. Hold on."

Mike went over to his chest and unlocked it. He pulled out one of the smaller black cases and handed it to Reggie. "Sig Sauer p320 45. This will do the trick for sure."

Reggie took the gun from him. "Damn, now this is nice. Not my style, but nice. Thanks, man. I'll get it back to ya after I stop at Lucky's and get my gear."

Downstairs, Kendra was having a time finding Michelle. "Come on, bitch. Dammit, Michelle, what have you done?" she asked aloud, still getting no answer from Michelle's phone.

She is not coming back, Kendra. Now Mike and Reggie will leave as well.

"Don't you fucking start!"

Oh, and just what are you going to do? Sic your boyfriend on me (laughter) No, there is nothing you can do. Even when... they die, I will be here. Always.

"Fuck!"she yelled, standing up, and went into the grotto. Grabbing a bottle of whiskey, she uncapped it, looked at it for a moment and set it back down and put the cap back on it. "No!" She turned around and stormed out. "You will not win! I'm not the scared little girl I used to be!"

But you are. You are still that pathetic, wretched little stain on the face of the earth that makes people cringe just knowing your foul existence.

Just then, her phone went off. It was ringing. She picked up her phone. "I don't know this number. Hello? This is Kendra."

"Kendra. This is Veronica. Everything is good back at your parent's house."

"Oh shit, thank you. It's been a day, I forgot already. Did it all go okay?"

"Yeah, everything's fine. They are sleeping like babies now. I don't know how you dealt with them for so long, girl. He is one mean old son of a bitch, I will tell you that. Thought he was gonna fuck around and call me a nigga bitch. No sir, not having that. So I knocked his old ass out. They should be out till tomorrow."

"Good for you! I put that gash on his head with a statue."

"Yeah, it looks like you got him good alright. Damn fool still ain't learned."

"No, he won't either. Time is almost up for him anyway. Hey if you go across the bridge, come by the gallery. Maybe we can grab a coffee."

"One day, I'm all tied up right now. But I'll make some time."

"Sounds good. See you soon."

Kendra hung the phone up. Suddenly, she heard the front door of the gallery open up. She walked out into the gallery and Gustav was standing at the doorway, walking inside.

"Oh, um, hey. I thought I had that door locked."

"I'm sorry. Did I startle you?"

"No, um, not at all. Just trying to find Michelle. You haven't spoken with her, have you this morning or today?"

"Oh, I dropped her off just before noon. She was not feeling too well. I think she went back to bed."

"I see. Sometimes she can get out of hand." Kendra started

fidgeting with some papers on a table along the wall.

"Are you sure you're alright? You look nervous, unsettled." He approached her and went to move some hair from her face, and she pulled back.

"I'm fine, just a lot going on."

"I see. Where did Mike run off to? I don't see him anywhere. Don't tell me the warehouse incident scared him away now."

"No, in fact, he is living with me, and right upstairs with Reggie." she replied, pointing up to the ceiling.

"Reggie?"

"Yes, an old friend of his."

Gustav reached into his coat pocket and put on his sunglasses. "Kendra, you must be careful who you let inside. People with money become targets."

"Kinda seems to me, people without money can become targets just as easily. So people with money pay people for protection."

"I see. I'll be in touch soon, Kendra Blake. We have work to do."

Gustav turned and left the gallery and drove away.

"Creepy bastard."

She turned towards the stairs and started shouting, "Mike! Mike, get down here!"

Mike and Reggie came running down the stairs. Both had their guns drawn, and ready to take action on whatever had disrupted her.

"What in hell is going on?!" Mike asked loudly.

"Gustav was just here. He just showed up acting all creepy and shit." she exclaimed, panicked.

"Did he touch you? Try anything?" Mike asked, infuriated and half worried for her.

"No, he said he dropped off Michelle earlier, and that she wasn't feeling too good."

"Yeah, I bet she wasn't. That's it! From now on, you're not alone, period. I am telling you, he is up to some bullshit!"

Reggie looked out of the front window and tucked his pistol

into his waist. "I think it is time to pay Lucky a visit, Mike. And I also think I'm gonna stay here for a while. If that's alright with you, Kendra."

"No, please, knock yourself out. That's what the room is for, well it is now. Thank you, Reggie."

Kendra's breaths came heavy. "Look, the stuff for that apartment will be here soon. Can you both take care of it? I am going upstairs to lie down a bit. I don't feel so good."

Mike put his gun away. "Yeah, we got this. Come on, I'll walk you up."

He walked her upstairs and tucked her in. She closed her eyes and fell fast asleep within minutes. Her phone went off again. Mike picked it up. It was Michelle.

Sorry I ghosted ya. Not feeling well. Talk soon.

He closed the screen and set the phone down on the table. "Damn, if this ain't some fucked up shit." He kissed Kendra on her forehead and went back downstairs.

Chapter 15

Gustav's Brother

With everything delivered, and the truck pulling away, Mike and Reggie stood in the gallery and watched them leave. "Wanna go see the setup?" Mike asked?

"Hell, you know it!" Reggie exclaimed, rubbing his hands together.

Like a couple of kids on Christmas morning, they ran up the stairs and down the hall to the last apartment door. Mike opened it up and turned on the lights. "Bang!"

"Hell yeah! Now this is what I call a pad!"

There was a black leather couch with a matching chair. A 75 inch flat screen T.V. Mounted on the wall, backed with neon lights that glowed on the wall behind it. A brand new throw rug that covered a significant part of the floor, that matched the couches and end tables. A marble coffee table and dark wooden end tables accented with black iron. And under the T.V., a stereo system with towering speakers on each side, along with a surround sound theater system. The bedroom contained a Queen size bed and full dressers. Even the bathroom had gotten a makeover, of red and black towels, with matching shower curtains and rugs.

"This place is a place for kings, bro. Now I can chill in here." Mike exclaimed, looking around and admiring the furniture and equipment they had picked out.

"Yeah, better than the Grotto I'd say. Besides, that's for guests. You think that band will come this week?"

"I don't know Reggie. I think she is more concerned about Michelle right now. She has been asleep for hours."

"Yeah, looks like Gustav shook her up. Wonder just what happened down there."

"Not sure, but I am getting cameras installed, I think. Just in case. Think you can set those up?"

"Hell yeah, just get me the--Ya know what? I'll go and get the system. I know just what set-up to get."

They sat on the new couches, admiring the way the apartment turned out and how good it looked. They turned on the T.V and flipped through the channel, stopping at the news.

"Today, police are investigating a missing person in the Philadelphia area.. This time, it's one of their own. Detective Jack Gower has not been seen, nor heard from since Friday of last week, when he was investigating a sex trafficking ring operating in the area. Jack Gower is one of the many officers dedicated to making our city a better place to live."

Mike turned the T.V. Off. "Shit, it is going to take way more than that to make this place any better. They might want to start by cleaning out the corruption they got in the fucking department."

"Ya, fo sho the damned truth there."

"Look, I'm gonna call Lucky and see about stopping over tomorrow. We better gear up just in case. I don't want surprises. Gustav likes to make plans and spring them on her."

"Sounds good. Hey, you think I can bring that Tonya girl up here tonight?"

"Uh oh, get it Reggie. Dog will hunt! Yeah, I don't think Kendra will mind. Just keep it in here, alright?"

"Oh yeah, yeah, bet it up."

Outside, on the corner of a connecting street, a Black Mercedes sat parked. The man inside peered through binoculars at the Gallery. He picked up his phone and dialed a number.

"This is Gustav."

"Looks like she has another guy there alright. He is a big black guy. They just had a bunch of stuff delivered to an apartment upstairs."

"I think Mike is becoming a problem. He never knew how to keep out of other people's business. Keep watch and let me know what goes on. If all goes as planned, we will all be across seas in a few weeks. Then I can finish this. We just can't let her get harmed. Understood?"

"Understood." He hung the phone up and continued watching the windows.

After having a beer with Reggie, Mike decided that he had better go and check on Kendra, who to his knowledge, was still asleep.

He walked into her apartment. Kendra was in the shower with music playing in the bathroom. "How are you feeling, baby?" Mike asked, opening the door and walking in.

"Just capital love. You're gonna join me?"

"Yeah, I can do that." Mike undressed and stepped into the shower. "So Reggie has Tonya coming over tonight? Is that cool?"

"He is going to break that new bed in?"

"Yeah, I think so."

"Be a doll and wash my back."

"No problem there. Look, tomorrow we need to go to Lucky's house. We need to get our gear. I don't want surprises."

"Baby? I'm wet, lathered up, and naked. We can talk about Lucky later."

"Enough said." He replied, and continued washing her back.

When they finished their shower, they got dressed and sat on the edge of the bed.

"So he really freaked you out this afternoon?"

Kendra looked down at the floor. "Yeah. I don't even know why he stopped by. Seemed like a pointless thing."

"Look baby, he is no fool. He knows that picture had been sent and what was in it. He is looking to see what impact it made. I am telling you, he is trying to declare ownership over you. That's what guys like him do."

"Ownership? Jesus, I slaughtered a mother fucker for him. Isn't that what he wants me for? My artistic twist on things?" she said solemnly, laying her head on Mike's shoulder.

"I don't really know. But I plan on finding out. Lucky has been looking into him. I am sure he will have plenty to tell us tomorrow. Just wait until you meet him and his wife."

"What are they like?"

Mike started laughing. "They can't even agree on something without arguing about how they agreed. You'll see. They are a riot. But, if you want to know anything, Lucky is the man to find it. He lives on the dark web."

"What's that?"

"You never heard of it? It's like the underground internet. Lot of nasty shit goes on there. But, it's where to find out all the darkest details the normal web keeps hidden. You will see."

Kendra looked up at Mike. She carried the weight of worry on her shoulders, and it showed heavily on her face.

"Mike?"

"Yeah?"

"Don't lie to me. Do I need to be scared? I know it sounds funny coming from me after what you have seen me do, but do I?"

Mike looked at her with a plain look on his face. "Yes."

∞ ∞ ∞

The next morning came early. Mike and Kendra were already

up and dressed by 8AM. He picked up his phone and called Lucky.

"Yeah, Mike."

"Hey old man. Reggie and I are stopping in this morning. We are going to have Kendra with us. That's cool?"

"Yeah Mike, you know it is."

"We need to arm up, I think. So we're grabbing our shit from the bunker."

"Yeah, that's a good idea, Mike. I did some more digging. You're heading into a major shit storm."

"I was afraid of that. Alright, well, at least we know. See you soon."

Hanging up, he put the phone in his back pocket. Kendra had headed downstairs to her office. "Better make sure Reggie is up." he said, and headed down the hallway. As he was reaching the end, the door to the apartment opened and out walked Tonya.

"Oh, and good morning to you."

Mike shook his head as she walked by. She had on tight black leather pants and boots, topped off with a leather jacket and a band shirt from the other night.

"Yeah, nice seeing you again." She walked to the end of the hall, stopping to give a smile and a wave, before going downstairs to leave. He walked inside as Reggie was putting on his boots. "So, you had fun last night?"

"Shit, you know I did. We didn't get too loud, did we?"

"No man, didn't hear a thing. Hey, we gotta get going. I called Lucky this morning. He is expecting us."

"Yeah, for the bet, let's roll. I'm ready when you are."

They went downstairs and met up with Kendra.She was sitting at her computer staring at the screen, resting her head on her hand.

"Are you ready to hit it?"

"Yeah, I just talked to Michelle. Mike, she doesn't sound right. Usually she is all loud and full of it. Now she just seems blah. I don't know. She said everything was fine and she and Gustav hit it off pretty good."

"Well, I can tell you now, that's not good at all. Come on, let's get everything locked up. Lucky is expecting us." They locked up the gallery and left.

As Mike pulled into traffic, the black Mercedes parked on the street across from the gallery followed, staying a few cars back. They continued a few blocks down and turned to the road that led away from the city, and straight to Lucky's. As they drove, Mike kept looking in the mirror.

"Reggie, get a look at that car way behind us. It's been following us since before we left the city." Mike said, looking in the mirror.

"Yeah, I see it. I don't recognize it."

Mike looked over at Kendra, as he pulled out his gun and set it on his seat, between his legs. "Put your seatbelt on and slide down into your seat."

Putting on her seatbelt, like Mike had asked, she slid down as far as the belt would let her go.

"Is this good?"

"Yeah, now hang on."

Mike hit the gas and sped up. A road came up and Mike hit the brakes, turning right and drove quickly down it, pulling into an abandoned barn, and parking behind it. Both he and Reggie got out and waited. Mike looked back at Kendra. "Stay down."

They waited a few minutes and then heard gravel under tires getting closer. The black Mercedes pulled in behind them and stopped. Reggie and Mike had their guns on the driver and ordered him out of the car. Reggie walked over and opened the door, pulling the man out, whose hands were up in the air. Mike placed the barrel of his 45 on the man's temple. "Now, who in the fuck are you?"

The man remained speechless, not saying a word.

"Reggie, get his phone."

Reggie searched the man and found his phone. He opened the screen and went to his contact list. "Nothin Mike, just numbers with no names."

Mike grabbed the phone from Reggie and looked. Well, let's just call the last person you called and see who answers. Mike dialed the number and put the phone up to his ear.

"This is Gustav."

"Uh, huh? I got your man here, Gus. You need to give me one good fucking reason I don't put a bullet in his brain right now."

"Well, I see you have not lost your touch Mike. Good. Now, if you were to kill him, that would be very unfortunate. I know Kendra hired you for protection, but I have to make sure for my peace of mind, that my investment is safe. If you would be so kind as to remove your gun from his head, as I imagine that is where it is. I would very much appreciate it."

"Gus, she does not need your protection. Keep your fucking people away from her."

"Mike, Mike, Mike, calm yourself. We are on the same side here. I know what is going on with you two. I get it. You care about her, and I care about my investment. Let my man go, Mike. We have a lot of work to be done. I want to see her tomorrow at the warehouse. Be there at 10Am."

"You better watch your ass, pal."

"That temper Mike. Ciao."

Mike slung the phone back into the man's car, grabbed him and placed him in the driver's seat, and pressed his gun tightly against his head. "If I fucking see you, or anyone that looks like you, If I even think you're around, I will kill you. Nod if you understand me."

The man had both hands on the steering wheel and nodded that he understood. "Now pull out of here, nice and calm, and drive the other way. First and last warning. Next time, you get a bullet."

He shut the door, and the car backed out, and drove off. Mike and Reggie returned to the truck and got in. "Is it over?" Kendra looked over at Mike.

"For now, do you know how to use a gun?"

"No," she replied sheepishly.

"Just power tools, but no guns. Go fucking figure." Mike

exclaimed. His adrenaline was rushing through his veins and his heart was pumping hard in his chest.

"Well, I learned from remodeling the studio. Buzz taught me."

"Who in the fuck is Buzz?"

"Eh, nobody, an old boyfriend. Nobody to worry about."

"Well, guess what? Today you're going to learn how to use a fucking gun!" he yelled. "I am not going to have you walk around unprotected in case something happens to me or Regie! Son of a bitch!" He slammed his fist on the steering wheel, highly angry at Gustav.

Mike put the truck in drive and floored the pedal. The truck spun sideways as he left the back of the bard, kicking up dust and spraying the side of the barn with gravel, returning to the road to Lucky's.

They were almost there and not a car was in sight. Kendra looked over at Mike. "Ya know, you don't have to yell at me."

"Wait, What? I wasn't yelling. I almost just blew a guy's head off because of that Gustav fucker. Sorry if I'm a little on edge, okay?"

Reggie was listening in the back seat. "Uh oh."

Kendra turned around. "No Reggie, there is no Uh oh. Mike is right. I'm sorry I got you two into all of this."

"Yeah, I know. It's not your fault. Bad thing is though, we don't even know what all of this is yet. Maybe Lucky will have some answers." Mike replied, "I'm sorry I yelled. We just have to get you strapped, that's all, then I will feel better."

They came to a dirt road and turned, going down it until they reached a gate with a code machine. He punched in the code and drove in. With cameras mounted in several places, there was no sneaking onto Lucky's property. Trees surrounded his house that was at the end of a long drive, through some remaining forest.

They parked in front of the house and walked up to the door. Mike looked up into the camera and heard the locks unlock. A voice came over an intercom system. "It's unlocked, Mike."

Opening the door, they went inside. An older woman stood

in the living room with an apron on, straightening some magazines on the table. "Mike and Reggie! Oh my God, it's been years!" She ran up to them and gave them each a big hug. "And who is this beautiful young lady you have with you?"

Mike put his arm around Kendra, smiling. "Margie, this is Kendra. Kendra, this is Lucky's wife Margie."

A voice came from a room on the other side of the living room. "Jesus Christ, Marge, stop yapping and send them in for fuck sakes!"

"You stifle yourself, you old coot! They will be in, in a second, you scowling old fuck!"

She turned back around and smiled. "It's so good to see you with somebody, Mike." She looked at Kendra and placed her hand on her cheek.

"You have a real winner here, sweetheart."

Kendra smiled. "I know."

"So, how did you meet?"

"Well, I hired him, seduced him and now he is in love with me," she answered confidently, grinning.

Mike smiled and agreed. "Yeah, basically what she said."

Margie turned around and yelled to Lucky. "Did you hear that? You mean old son of a bitch?! She knows how it is supposed to be!"

"Dammit women, you know what Lucky means!?"

"Yes, I do! It means you're lucky I haven't educated you upside the head with a skillet! That's what it means!"

"Oh, Jesus Christ! Will you send them in here?!"

She turned back and smiled. "Better go see what he is pissing around about. I don't want to aggravate his blood pressure."

They were all laughing at the mayhem. "It was good seeing you again, Margie." Reggie said as he passed by.

"You to Reggie."

They went into the room where Lucky was sitting in front of 4 computer screens. He had an array of monitors, computers and wires running all over the place. It reeked of cigarettes and had empty beer cans stacked on his desk. Lucky looked old, but was only in his early sixties. His gray stubble covered the wrinkles on his face and his skin appeared to be old leather. "Ah! 'Bout time you fuckers got here."

"Lucky! How are you doing, old man?"

"Well, I'm not dead yet. Those fuckers are trying, but they ain't gonna get me without a fight! I can promise you that!"

Reggie started laughing. "Same old Lucky! Mean, and nasty to the core."

"Damn right Reggie! Jesus Christ! Did you get bigger?"

"Yeah, I put on a few pounds. Got to keep the machine fed," Reggie replied, flexing his muscles.

Lucky looked over at Kendra and raised his eyebrows. "Dammit, son, how much did you have to pay her to be on your arm?"

Kendra started laughing. "I am afraid that's the other way around. I'm Kendra."

"Yeah, well, honey, you got ripped off. And that's a fact." Lucky started coughing and lit up a cigarette. "Dammit Margie! Will you bring me a fucking beer already?"

"You just hold your horses, you old coot!"

Mike grinned. "Well, it sure is nice to see that some things never change.

"That's a fact Mike. Ya know when your old man and I were in Nam-"

"Here we go again!" Margie scowled as she entered the room. "Back in the war... blah blah blah! Here! And don't choke to death on it!" Setting his beer down on his desk, she smiled and looked at Mike. "Would you all like something to drink? We have coffee, sweet tea, beer and water. Pick your poison."

Mike shook his head. "No Margie, we are good. Maybe soon."

"Well, you know where the kitchen is if you decide you want something. I have to go sit down. These damned bunions are killing me." She turned and hobbled out of the room.

"I'll tell you what's killing me! Yap, yap, yap! All Goddamn day long, that's what!" Lucky yelled as she left.

"Oh, blow it out your ass!"

"Yeah, fuck you."

Kendra was laughing hysterically. "Oh my God, baby, you were not kidding."

"No, and I am not kidding, either. Now look at this. I have been doing some snooping around. This fucker is all over the dark web." Lucky pointed at the screen closest to him. "He has his hands into everything from hot cars to mail-order brides."

"Just what am I looking at, old man?" Mike leaned down to look closer.

"Oh, Jesus Mike! Come on, it's a fucking money trail! That's what this is." Lucky waved at the monitor, getting cigarette ashes all over the desk. "Oh, fuck me!" he snapped as he swept his hand across, sending them to the floor.

Reggie looked at the monitor. "Holy fuck, Millions."

"Yes, Millions and more. He spun his chair around and faced Kendra. "Now honey, what do you know about this, Gustav?"

"Well, he is rich. I mean, we all know that. He has a tea shop called The Two Brothers he opened up and dedicated to his brother who died in Egypt."

"Bull shit! It's a front. He launders money through there. What was his brother's name?"

"Um, Frits."

Lucky punched a few keys on the computer and brought up a picture. "Guess again, sweetheart."

Kendra looked at the picture. "Wait a second, that's fucking Dante from the tea house! You mean to tell me Dante is Gustav's brother? He is not dead?"

"Christ, no, he isn't dead. He is hiding from what they did in Egypt two years ago. Apparently, they pissed off some sheik. Had to do with one of his daughters. They sold her to some cult."

"Cult?"

"Yeah, a cult. Some satanic organization dead set on global domination. They are not that big, but they have a lot of money. "

"Where are they from?"

"That I can't even find on the dark web. Very hush-hush shit."

"Fuck me, I was afraid this was going to be more than I wanted to deal with," Mike sighed.

"Eh, bullshit! Grow some balls! These people thrive on fear. Show them you're not scared and they fall. If I were you, I would keep your cool and see how far down the hole you can go. Your girl there is an asset. They won't hurt her, at least until they are done with her."

"Oh well, that's fucking nice!" Kendra bellowed.

"Ah, calm down. Don't get your cunt hairs tied up in knots. Mike and Reggie won't let nothing happen to you. Now listen. I have everything of yours down in the bunker out back. I added some goodies to it recently that you guys will find useful. And I don't need to tell you not to get caught with any of it."

"What did you add, Lucky?" Mike asked.

Lucky looked up and put a huge smile on his face. "C4. Plastic explosive. Got enough to level a fucking city block, so be careful."

"Jesus old man! Is there anything you can't get hold of?"

"At the moment, yes." He picked up his pack of cigarettes, finding it empty. "Margie! God Dammit, bring me a pack of smokes!"

"Margie, bring me a beer, Margie god dammit this, god dammit that! You old bastard!" She showed up at the doorway and hurled a pack of cigarettes at Lucky and missed him, sending the pack landing at his feet. Lucky started laughing. "You're gonna have to do better than that, you old bitch!"

"Oh, piss off!"

"Damn Lucky, you two have not changed an ounce since I can remember."

"Well Mike, it's too late for that now, anyway."

"What do you mean?"

"Cancer. Doctors tell me I have a few months left. Of course, that was 6 months ago."

"Shit man, come on, don't be fucking with me. For real?"

"Ya see? That's your Goddamned problem Mike! You're too

fucking gullible! No, I don't have cancer. Anymore. I beat it."
Lucky stood up. "Now come on. Let's go out back."

"God damn Lucky. Ornery old bastard. Hey, I was hoping to
teach Kendra how to shoot a bit. Got something that will fit
her?"

Lucky stopped and looked her up and down. "Don't know
how to shoot, huh? Well, I got just the ticket for ya. Come on.
You're gonna love this."

They walked to the back of the house and out of the sliding
back doors. There was a concrete building, tiny, with a door on
it that had a lock. Lucky opened it up and revealed a set of stairs
going down. He started down the stairs, and the rest followed.

Chapter 16

Common Ground

L ucky turned on the lights. All along the walls there were canned foods, barrels of potable water and enough overall supplies to last a few people a few years. There were two doors on each side. Lucky entered the room after opening the door. A large room, containing a shortwave radio set up, beds, a few tables, and a large map of the surrounding area with strategic points marked off and scattered about.

"This is the living quarters. Doesn't have all the amenities most people want these days, but it has enough to get the job done." Lucky opened another door. "Now here is my favorite room. The Armory." Lucky stood, arms crossed, smiling and looking at all he had on the walls.

Wall to wall rifles, pistols, an entire row of shotguns and bullet-proof vests. He had everything from semi automatic to full auto.

"Holy shit! I have seen nothing like this!" Kendra walked up to a table and looked at the 50 cal. BMG sitting upon it.

Mike stood beside her, admiring the rifle. "When did you get this one? I don't remember you having it before."

"Because I didn't. It's new. Kinda came with the C4. Best not to ask." Lefty walked over to a large square form on the floor with a tarp over it. He pulled the tarp off and exposed the two trunks underneath.

"Here you boys are. Now I have a couple more cases for you,

but first, you're gonna love this." He walked over and picked up two rifle bags and placed them on the table. "Go ahead, open it."

Mike walked over and opened the bag. "Damn!"

"You're damned right. HK 416. Fully loaded. Picked them up last year. Figured you boys might like to play with them."

"This is straight up the shit, old man." Reggie exclaimed, as he picked one up and aimed down the sights.
"Hell yeah. I think I'm about to say 'I do'"

Lefty walked over to the wall with all the pistols and took down a Springfield Hellcat. "Kendra, come here. Now wrap your hand around this and tell me how that feels."

She took the gun from him and held it up. "I like this! Can I shoot it?"

"Yeah, we will go out back in a bit to the range. Let you squeeze a few off. Now you have 11 rounds in there. That's 11 bullets to kill whatever is in front of you. Here, let me see that."

Lefty took the pistol from her and showed her how it operates. She watched intently as Mike and Reggie got ready to carry all of their gear up and to the truck. "We are gonna start taking this up to the truck, Lefty."

"Yeah, go on ahead. I'll take your girl here to the range for a minute. Let her get some trigger time."

Mike looked over at Kendra. "You're in for a treat, baby. You're fortunate. Not everybody gets lessons from the old man."

"Ah! I'm excited! Never shot a gun before."

Mike and Reggie started carrying the trunk upstairs. As they put the trunks into the SUV, they could hear the gunshots from the firing range. Pop! Pop! Pop!

Mike and Reggie both grinned as they listened to Kendra shout and yell, "Holy shit! I hit it Lucky! This is badass!"

After they finished loading up, they met Kendra and Lucky walking back to the house. She ran up to Mike and hugged him. "You should have seen me! Bang! Bang! Bang!" Holding her new pistol.

"Nice! Did you hit anything?"

Lucky smiled and put his hand on Kendra's back. "You got a

natural here, Mike. Not a bad cluster at 30 yards either. I think she will be just fine."

"Good. Hopefully, we don't have to find out, but just in case, I'm glad she knows now." Mike said.

"Always the best option, for sure."

Kendra put her gun in her bag and pulled out her phone. "New message." She opened it up and looked. It was a picture from Gustav of a fallen angel.

Do you think you can recreate this?

"What the fuck? Mike, look at this."

Mike took the phone from her and looked at the picture. "Ask him what he means." She texted him back.

Not sure what you mean. A new sculpture?

Yes

"It is a new sculpture he wants me to do. If that is what I think, I am going to need materials."

It will be tricky, but yes, I can do it.

Excellent. I will see you soon.

When?

This evening at your gallery 5pm sharp.

OK. I will be there.

Kendra put her phone away. "He wants to meet at the Gallery at 5."

"Who does?" Lucky inquired.

"Gustav."

"Yeah, well, you watch your 6. Keep it simple and keep your fucking ears open."

Margie met them outside by the truck. "I wish you boys could stay longer. It really was nice seeing you. And very nice to meet you, young lady."

"Awe, you're so sweet Margie. It really was all my pleasure."

They got in the truck and started it up. Lucky stood at the driver's window. "I'll keep lookin' Mike. Just be careful. These aren't some wanna be wiseguys. They are well connected, and connected to God knows what."

"Thanks old man. I'll be in touch."

They took off down the long drive through the forest and left. The ride back to the gallery remained uneventful. No cars following, and no disturbing messages.

After they unloaded and got all of their gear put away in the apartment, they stood at the window, looking out for anything that looked out of place. Mike noticed nothing out of the ordinary. As was scanning the street below. "I told Reggie I am going to put in a camera system. Tomorrow he is going to pick one up. I want these streets to be watched. Maybe a few in the gallery as well."

"If you think we should. I don't care." Kendra was looking at the picture Gustav sent her on her phone.

"I wonder who it is going to be this time."

"What?"

"Who Gustav is going to have me--you know."

"Don't know. I don't like how he picks people, though. I mean really, think about it. Do we really know who these people are?"

Reggie stood in the corner, looking out the window. "So this guy calls you in, you kill whoever he tells you, and he makes a statue out of it and sells it. Is that the basic idea of what I am hearing?"

"Yeah Reggie. That is basically how it worked last time."

Reggie shook his head. "I swear, rich people do the most fucked up shit."

"Yeah, they do, brother. No doubt they do."

Gustav arrived at the Gallery at 5Pm. Mike greeted him at the door and led him into the Grotto, where Kendra and Reggie were waiting. He took a seat on the couch.

"So, Mike, are we alright? Do we have an understanding?"

Mike stood behind Kendra and rested his hands on the back of her chair.

"I don't know Gus. Do we?"

"I am sure everything will work out just fine. Just know I have a lot of money tied up in her, and I plan on this being a success."

Kendra frowned. "I am sitting right here, you know. I am not some fucking commodity at everyone's disposal."

"I am sorry. I didn't mean it like that." Gustav said, apologetically.

"Look, Gustav, it's really simple. You want me to make human art? I make human art. But understand. You do NOT own Kendra Blake!"

Gustav sat up and forward, looking at Kendra. "Okay, I never claimed ownership over you. You are definitely your own person. I have to say, though, I am loving this burst of confidence I am seeing. Well done, young lady. Well done." he said, quietly clapping his hands together.

Kendra calmed down. "I just have to make sure you understand where I am coming from. Things have escalated quickly and honestly, I am trying to come to grips with all of it."

"Yes, I understand completely. So how are you feeling in your head?"

"What do you mean?"

"Your mentality. Your situation with your parent's. Have you come to any decisions?"

"Yes. Right now, I have a nurse taking care of them. I don't want them dead yet. But when the time comes, I will need you to come to their house. Should be soon."

"So, what are you planning?"

"That, Gustav, is something that I will reveal when I am

finished. But I am sure your friend in Finland will want them after I am done. I guarantee it."

"Yes, well, I am sure it will be amazing. Your last piece is in route to his estate now. Say, you mentioned you wanted to see Europe."

"Yes, I would love to see it. I would not know where to begin, though." she replied, with her eyes widened at the idea.

"Perhaps when you finish with 'Mom and Dad', we can all deliver them ourselves. I assume everyone has the proper paperwork, passports and such."

Mike looked over at Reggie. He was sitting quietly and looking for any sign of treachery from Gustav.

"Reggie and I both need passports. But it will not be a problem for sure."

She looked up at Mike. "What do you think, baby? Want to go to Finland?"

"We will see how things go."

Gustav looked up at Mike, who was staring at him. "I see you still have your concerns. Don't blame you. Tell you what. I promise you, Mike, keeping her safe and out of harm's way is all you. I'll trust that you will guard her close."

"There isn't anything Reggie and I can't handle ourselves."

Gustav looked over at Reggie. "Of that I am sure." He directed his attention towards Kendra. "Now, as far as tomorrow goes-"

Kendra opened her phone to the picture again. "Do you want me to add wings? Because if you do, it will take a few days to make them."

"Actually, no. But we will need to suspend the subject in the air, falling to the ground backwards. How that is done, is up to you."

"How about suspension hooks? That would look pretty sick."

"Now that is something I think Nirro would be interested in for sure."

"Run it by him and see. Just let me know. Maybe I will stop in and see my parents before I head over, you know, for inspiration."

Gustav stood up. "Yes, it's always good to have that, I suppose. Oh, and one more thing. Would you have an issue with streaming it live to Nirro? He wants to see you work."

Mike looked back at Reggie. "I don't know about that. How safe is it really? The last thing we need is Kendra butchering someone, and getting out on the web, dark or otherwise."

"I assure you we will stream it only to him. We have a highly secured network. Nobody, and I mean nobody, gets in that we do not want. Of course, he has generously offered a substantial amount of money on top of what he was going to pay for the sculpture as well."

"I don't want my face shown. I will do it, but I have no identity."

Reggie looked over at her. "Kendra, are you sure you want to go down this road? I mean, there are a lot of things that can go way south on this."

"No, it will be fine. I just realized it's not just my ass on the line here."

Gustav smiled. "You're correct. No, this is nothing any of us want out."

Kendra stood up. "Speaking of which. Why is Michelle acting so strange? I saw the party favors on the table, Gustav. She doesn't do that shit."

"Michelle will be fine. Everyone's first time is heavy."

"This is not alright Gus! I don't need her getting into any of this and strung out!"

"I think Michelle is a grown woman, Kendra. We all have choices to make, as well as sacrifices."

"What's that supposed to mean?"

"Exactly what I said. Don't make an issue out of this, Kendra. I must go now. I have things to get finished to be ready for tomorrow."

"Fine, but if you see Michelle, tell her there are some things she needs to get done for me."

"I will relay the message. See you all tomorrow."

Gustav left, leaving behind an upset Kendra.

Kendra paced the floor while Mike and Reggie looked on. "What in the actual fuck? What?! Does he think he is some kind of God or something?!"

Her anger grew as she yelled, "I swear to God! If anything happens to her, I will make him a project, Mike! I will kill him myself! Slowly! And that faggot brother of his as well!"

Mike stood still, afraid to upset her further, realizing she was closely at the brink of losing it again. "Kendra, I hate to say it, but he had a point. She is a grown woman."

"What?! Who's fucking side are you on?!"

"I am on your side. I'm just looking at this with another perspective."

Kendra continued to pace. "Another perspective. I got a fucking perspective for you alright."

See Kendra, even now he is undermining you. You know you can't trust him. Whatever will poor Michelle do? Gustav wants to keep her as his toy.

"Shut up!" Kendra grabbed her head and started shaking it no. "Stop it! You're not fucking real!"

Oh, they are going to have you locked away in a padded cell. Good job Kendra, always fucking everything up! Fucking everything up! Fucking everything up! The voice screamed louder and louder.

Kendra fell to her knees, holding her head. Mike got up and knelt down beside her. "Kendra! Snap out of it!"

"Goddamned bro! She needs a drink or something?"

"No Reggie. She needs help, that's what she needs!"

Laying down on the floor, she curled up in a fetal position, holding her head with her eyes tightly shut.

"Kendra! Open your eyes!" She didn't move at all. The only motion was her chest heaving from her breathing that was starting to make deep vocal sounds with every breath.

Mike rolled her onto her back and straddled her, pressing her legs to the floor. "Open your goddamned eyes, Kendra!"

Reggie jumped out of the chair and ran into the gallery, locking the door. "Man this is some fucked up shit. This has to be a white people thing." he exclaimed, running back to the Grotto.

When he got back into the room, Kendra had sat up, hyperventilating and looking up at Mike. Her eyes were bloodshot, and their color had turned to red. Mike was bent over with his hands on her shoulders. "Kendra, are you here?"

She looked up and sneered, "Kendra is away. You are all going to die!"

Her voice had turned raspy and hissed when she spoke. As she kept her eyes on Mike, she slowly began to get up, then sat back down.

Mike stood up and backed away. "Okay, this is new."

Kendra sat and watched him back away, rocking back and forth. Then she stopped, and looked down at the floor, staying still and silent.

Mike and Reggie watched her for a few minutes, then she stood up, holding her head. "Goddamned it all. My head is killing me!" she wailed.

Mike walked over to her and looked her in the eyes. "Okay, you're back." Her irises turned back to hazel and remained bloodshot.

"I didn't go anywhere."

"No, not physically, but you went somewhere."

"What do you mean?"

Reggie went to the bar and poured a drink. "You said we were all going to die. That's where you went."

She walked over to the couch and sat down. "Fuck. Why does this keep happening?"

Mike sat next to her. "My guess is it is a form of PTSD. I have seen it before, but never like this."

"I don't remember shit. I know Gustav left, and he pissed me off about Michelle. Then it gets all cloudy."

"Yeah, that happened at the warehouse as well. It's like you black out and become something different. This time your voice changed."

"Shit. I'm sorry." She looked up at Reggie. "I'm sorry Reggie. I didn't mean to freak you out."

Reggie smiled. "No, I'm good. I have seen no one do that before, though. Hate to tell you boss lady, but you got issues."

She slightly laughed, "Yeah, you could say that." Then asked Mike to put her to bed.

Mike put his arm around her. "Yeah, I got you." He stood up and helped her to her feet. "Reggie, I'll meet up with you soon."

Reggie was finishing his drink at the bar. "Yeah fo' sho'. Handle your business, bro."

Chapter 17

The Fallen "Angel"

Kendra rose from her bed early. Standing over Mike, who was still sleeping, she watched him. His hair covered half of his face and moved every time he exhaled. She whisked the hair away and sat gently on the bed beside him. "What will I do without you? I can't expect you to stay around. You deserve so much better." She leaned down and kissed him, then went into the bathroom and shut the door.

She looked at her phone. 6AM. Then, looking in the mirror, she noticed her eyes were still slightly bloodshot from the night before.

"Good morning, bitch." she said with half of a smile.

"Well, good morning to you as well." She giggled at herself and turned on the faucet to wash her face. When she finished, she put some eyedrops in her eyes, blinked a few times, and wiped away the excess. "Ah, now that is better." Pleased at the way she felt, she left the bathroom and went into the kitchen to make coffee.

She sat at the table, drinking her coffee and scrolling through her phone. As she went through her email, noticing one she had not seen before. The band she had met a few nights before had contacted her.

Kendra. Sorry, but we cannot see your gallery, because of illness within the band. They have cut our tour short, and we must return to Oslo. We have looked at your website, and would like to know if you would be interested in designing our next album cover. Your work is genuine and represents many of the things our music expresses. We look forward to hearing from you. Necrotic Filth.

"Wow! That is kick ass!" She became busy emailing back to them.

Yes, of course! It would delight me to design anything you would like. Send me your ideas and I shall work something up for you as soon as I am available. The Daunting Canvas, Kendra Blake.

She looked out the window of her small dining area and watched the rain as it covered the ground, while light flashes came randomly in the sky with lightning hidden within the clouds. "Nice. I love a solid storm." Thunder sounded in the distance, rumbling off into nothing. She opened the window so she could hear the rain and sat in her chair with her knees propped against the table, enjoying the storm, until her phone ringing interrupted her solitude. "Shit. Who is bugging me this early?" She looked at the caller's name, Gustav. "Dammit!"
"Hello."
"Good morning Kendra. Glad to see that you are up and about early."
"I got up a short while ago. Are we still on for this morning?"
"Yes. In fact, today is going to be very special."
"Care to elaborate on it? Or is this another one of your surprises?"
"Let me ask you, do you read the bible Kendra? Are you a religious person?"
"No, and no. I have never even been to a church. Why?"
"No matter. I was just curious. Did you know the Vatican holds many secrets hidden deep within?"
"You mean like the Pope?"
"Yes, like the Pope. I'll see you soon, Kendra. Ciao."
She put her phone down on the table. "Fucking weirdo."

She stood up and stretched. "Fuck this, Mike's getting up." She walked over to the foot of the bed. Mike was still asleep. She looked down at him and smiled. Kendra removed her nightshirt and lifted the blanket, crawling underneath. "Time to get up, baby."

Mike stirred for a moment, then lifted the blanket to see the top of her head. "Oh man, now that's how you say good-morning."

She lifted her head, taking him out of her mouth, and smiled at him. "Just lay back and relax. This is all about you this morning."

Mike put his arms behind his head and smiled. "No problem."

In a matter of seconds, she had him fully erect and took him in deeply. He could hear the sounds of her slurping as she worked vigorously to provide him with as much pleasure as she could give.

As she continued, Mike threw the blanket from on top of her, off to the bed and watched her as he held the top of her head.

"Jesus fuck! Where did you learn that?!" he panted as she intensified the motion she was doing with her tongue and mouth.

Stopping momentarily, and replacing her mouth with her hand, she looked up at him with a smile. "I am full of surprises for you my love."

"Well, this is definitely one I like."

She continued her oral exploration of him as his hips thrust into her. "Baby, I am about to..."

She dove even harder at hearing his voice. He reached down to pull her head away, but she resisted.

"Holy fuck!" He exclaimed as he released, gripping her hair.

She didn't break her stride, but continued until he was drained, and too sensitive to handle anymore.

She stared at his manhood a second and patted it, smiling. "Good boy." she said as she climbed in beside him and curled up. "Now that's breakfast in bed." She said, then kissed him on his head.

"Yeah." Mike panted, still catching his breath. "I am definitely not letting you go, for anything."

∞ ∞ ∞

The windshield wipers beat the rain away as they headed towards the warehouse. The sky remained dark as the storm raged on. Sirens from an ambulance sounded out as Mike pulled over to let it pass. "Fuck, I hope there isn't a wreck by where we are going. We don't need that at all."

He pulled back onto the road and continued. The ambulance disappeared in the distance, hidden by the dense rain. "Jesus, it's coming down."

"So Gustav called me this morning before I woke you up."

"Really. What did he want?"

"He asked if I read the bible, or was religious. Babbled on about the Vatican holding secrets and weird shit like that."

Reggie pulled himself forward in the seat. "What he want to know that for? What, he want to go to church or somethin'?"

"No, that fucker definitely is not going to no church. Look, I have a plan."

"What's that?" Kendra replied.

"I am going to play it cool with Gustav. Lucky told me I should go down the rabbit hole, so I am. Just know, whatever I say to Gustav, it's an act. Keep your enemies closer, kind of deal."

"Do you think he will buy it?"

Reggie started laughing. "Yeah, he gonna buy it alright. We invented that game. You know how many times we had to play that back in the day?"

"Seriously Kendra. So, when I am being all cool with this dick, just know I'm setting him up for the kill."

"Are you going to kill him?"

"I don't know. But this is only going to end one way. Lucky

is following the trails and seeing what we can do. We have to have something on him to bargain with."

"Bargain with? Okay, this is above my pay-grade. I have no clue what you two are talking about." she said, admitting she was mentally lost in the conversation.

"I know. Just do what you do, and we will take care of the rest. We just have to be patient and see where this leads."

"Okay baby, you lead and I will follow."

It took them longer than before to reach Gustav's warehouse on account of the weather, but soon, they found themselves at the gate. As they pulled up to it, the gate opened, then shut behind them as they pulled into the parking lot and drove down to the warehouse. Gustav opened the door for them, as they got out of the truck and ran inside to keep from getting soaked by the rain.

"Well, I am glad we didn't have to send a rescue boat." Gustav smiled as they got inside and shut the door.

"For real. I haven't seen this much rain in a while." Mike brushed the water from his sleeves, looking into the warehouse. "What you got going on over there, man?"

There was a small building next to the shipping container they used before. They constructed it of wood and painted it white, with a cross above the door.

"I thought it would be a fitting addition. Considering who Kendra's subject is today. "

They all walked up to the door and opened it. Archie and Pavel were standing off to the side, setting up a camera and a laptop. On the stage, up in front of the tiny little church, lay a priest, strapped to a table.

Kendra looked around, seeing the stained glass windows and even a few pews that they set in place. Above the priest, in the ceiling, hung pulleys with steel cables running through attached to hooks.

"You really went all out on this, didn't you?"

"Indeed. Nirro is paying a lot of money for this show. I would like to give him his money's worth."

"So, what's the deal with the priest?" Reggie asked.

Gustav walked over and stood over the priest. "Do you remember a few years back, when there were several accusations against the Catholic church in Philadelphia of sexual misconduct from the priests on children?"

Reggie and Mike walked over and joined him. Reggie cracked his knuckles. "I remember that shit, so does my nephew. He was only seven years old. But by the time it all got out, and we heard about it, the ones who did it were long gone. This one of them mutha fuckas?"

"This is Bishop McPherson. No, he was not the one in that church. He is the one that held the broom to sweep it all away and under the Vatican carpet. So, he is just as guilty, if not worse."

McPherson kept his eyes focused on the ceiling. "Our Father, who art in heaven, hallowed be thy name-"

Kendra walked over to the table and examined the Bishop as he prayed.

"Gustav?"

"Yes?"

"Do you have the mask I asked for?"

"I have something even better." He walked over to Archie and retrieved an altar boy's robe out of a bag, and a white hood, with the eyes cut out.

She walked over to him and grabbed it. "Mike will hold on to this for a second?" She asked, handing it to him, and walked back over to the Bishop. He wore a crucifix made of gold around his neck. She grabbed it and ripped it free from him. "You won't need this where you are going, father."

Walking back over to Mike, she got undressed, completely naked, and grabbed the hood from him, putting it on. Looking over at Gustav, she grabbed the robe and threw it to the floor. "If he wants a show, he is going to get a show."

Gustav cocked his head to the side. "As you wish." He connected with Nirro on the laptop and secured the stream. "Can you see everything, Nirro?"

"Yes, this looks like it is going to be perfect."

"Good." He looked at Kendra and made sure Mike and Reggie were out of the way. "Then let the games begin."

Reggie nudged Mike and whispered. "Hey, I don't know if you noticed, but your girl ain't got no clothes on."

"Ya fuckin think?"

Kendra walked up to the table and circled it, with the Bishop still praying and keeping his eyes fixed on the ceiling. "Yea, I walk through the valley of death. I shall fear no evil--"

Kendra grabbed the priest's face and turned it towards her. "What's the matter, father? Too grown for you? Maybe I am not the right sex? What was it? Little boys, or little girls?"

What are you waiting for, Kendra? You know what you want to do to him. Do it! You cowardly whore!

Kendra backed away. "I am not a whore!"

Mike leaned over to Reggie. "This is the part where she flips shit."

"Do you hear me?! I am not a fucking whore!"

The Bishop looked over at her. "You are a defiled creature of Satan! You scarlet clad whore of Babylon! The fire of hell will consume you and you will suffer for all eternity with the rest of your minions!"

Reggie looked on. "I think he just seriously fucked up."

She knelt down to the floor, with her back turned. Her back heaved with every breath, as the Bishop carried on, cursing her and fueling her rage.

Do it Kendra! Send him straight to hell! We have been waiting for him!

She stood up quickly, spinning around hissing at the Bishop, "There is no hell you fuck!"

Her eyes had turned again from hazel to red as she grabbed the Bishop's coat and ripped it open, along with his shirt. McPherson looked up into her face and saw her eyes, with his skin turning pale with fear.

"No! No this is not supposed to happen! Get away from me you lapdog of Satan!"

Grabbing his throat with both hands, she pulled his head towards hers.

"This is happening! Your God won't save you now!" her voice hissed. She reached up and pulled one hook down, and sank it deep in his pectoral muscle. The Bishop screamed in agony as she reached for another, sinking it deep into gut, and forcing it through.

He writhed on the table, screaming to God for mercy as Kendra jumped on top of the it and over to the other side. "Oh, come now Father, we are just starting to have fun!" She pulled another hook down and pushed it through his other pectoral muscle.

"Look at you, Father! Bleeding like a sacrificial lamb!" She stood back for a moment, then bent over and whispered in his ear. "I have a secret to tell you."

The Bishop turned his head away, with his face wincing in pain and blood starting to seep from the holes the hooks had made.

"What secret?"

Grabbing a handful of his hair, she yanked his head towards her. "You're going to fucking die today!"

She stood in front of him, at his feet, and raised her hands in the air. Archie grabbed a switch box next to him and activated a winch. After the cables became tight, he turned it off. Kendra walked over and held out her hand to Mike. "Knife!" she demanded, with her voice hissing demonically. Doing as he was told, he pulled out his knife and gave it to her. Turning around, she started back towards the bishop.

His screams intensified, "God forgive me for my trespasses! Prepare for me a seat at your-"

His words turned to screams of agony as his body lifted off the table, when she cut away the straps. She raised her arms again, and the cables lifted him higher into the air. His arms swung, trying to free himself, as she reached up and cut his clothing free, letting let them fall to the floor below. With a push, she slid the table out from underneath the Bishop, and looked through her hood, at his body hanging in the air.

Reggie hid his eyes. "Oh no, no, nooooo. I can't see this-"

Kendra grabbed the Bishop's penis tightly and pulled. "You won't be needing this either!" she yelled, making a swift slice, and it released from the Bishops body, sending blood pouring onto Kendra. The severed penis was in her hand as she turned around, looking down at the bloody member she held.

"Pathetic! No wonder you like children. Too small for a real woman."

She dropped it to the floor along with the knife and spread her arms out straight, looking directly at the camera, addressing Nirro.

Her eyes were black, and her white hood was turning red from the severed stub in between McPherson's legs.

"Into your hands, I command this spirit!"

The Bishop's scream faded, his body stopped twitching and turned pale as all the blood ran from his body and onto Kendra, who was now on her hands and knees, still looking into the camera, and snarling.

Mike had seen enough, looked over at Gustav. and ended it. "Hey, the show is over, man."

He could hear Nirro clapping and applauding. "Yes! I have to get her here to my estate!"

Gustav shut off the feed and shut the laptop. Mike grabbed the robe laying on the floor and walked over, covering her up.

Reggie opened his eyes back up. "Is it over?" he asked, looking at the dead bishop hanging in the air. "Sweet Jesus!"

Mike helped her to her feet. "Look at me, baby. Look at me!" He reached and turned her head. "Are you in there?"

Kendra blinked a few times. "Yeah, I'm here." She looked around and looked back up at McPherson, then down at all the blood on the floor. "Good riddance." Her voice had gone back to normal. Looking over at Mike. "Baby, I need a shower."

She walked out of the small makeshift church with Mike as if nothing had happened.

Gustav followed. "Kendra." She stopped walking turned to look at him.

"Are you alright? There is a shower in the room over there on the side."

She smiled at him. "I'm fine." She replied laughing, and looked at Mike. "Come on, you can help me clean up."

Mike looked at her with concern. "Your head doesn't hurt? You don't feel tired, or faint, or anything?"

"No. Not a bit. Maybe I am getting better, like Gustav said I would."

"Or worse. Come on, let's get you cleaned up."

Reggie stood outside of the church with Gustav. "That was some crazy ass shit!"

"It was brilliant! What a performance!"

"And your boy saw that shit all the way over-- To where?"

"Finland. He has an estate by the lake of Bodom. Will you be going with us when we fly over there?"

"You're damned right. I ain't never been out of the country. Much less somewhere like that. Sounds like a good time."

"It will be the best, I assure you."

"Well, if Kendra and Mike are going, you know I will be there, too."

"Fantastic. you never know, you may not want to come back."

"My cousin should come. She a nurse."

"Really? LPN or RN?"

"RN, private duty."

"Well, the more the merrier, I always say."

After a short time, Mike and Kendra came out of the room, all cleaned up from the mess she had made. "Is he happy, Gustav?"

Gustav clapped his hands. "He is thrilled! Cannot wait for us to join him in Finland. We should start making the arrangements soon."

Mike lit a cigarette. "We still have to get our papers and shit. Shouldn't be a problem, though."

"If not, do not worry about it. I have a private jet at my access, and we pay the guards at the airport off there. We have a lot of business that runs in and out of that airport. So we have to make sure security is in our pockets."

"Sounds like you got a brilliant operation, Gus. I have to say, I am impressed."

"Thank you Mike. Hopefully, we can have a lucrative business relationship both here and there as well."

"Sounds great. So, are we all finished up here, then?"

"Yes, the money should be in her account within the hour. He must really love your work."

"Why is that?" Kendra asked.

"Because he is paying all four million for this. Not the three, he originally said. He only does that when he plans on doing more."

Kendra looked over at Mike and Reggie. "We are rich boys. Well, Mike and I are."

Reggie cocked an eyebrow. "Oh, just diss the black guy. I see how you rollin'."

Kendra laughed. "Nonsense. You can have the extra Million. We are family."

"What? You serious right now? I was just playin'."

"Sure. Why not? I think we are all going to be together for a while. Trust me guys, this is just the beginning."

"Damn. Now I see why you dig this crazy shawty, Mike. She straight as straight can be."

"Yeah, she is, my brother." Mike agreed.

"Look Gus, we have to go. I really need to check on Michelle. I'm not out to fuck anything up between you two. But she has not been acting right at all. Can you at least level with me about all of the heroin?"

"She likes it. Truth is, I have used it for years, and I am fine. It's pure. No fentanyl."

"Just please don't let her O.D. She has been my best friend for a while."

"She will be fine, I promise. Besides, we don't need her asking too many questions now, do we?"

"You have a point there. Well, we have to go. I'll talk to you soon."

They turned to leave and heard Archie call from the church. "Kendra! Come and see! Yes, come!" He was waving them back over to the church.

They walked over and entered.

"Damn!" Reggie exclaimed. "Is that shit for real?"

Kendra smiled. "Yes, it is. Looks like stone, doesn't it?"

"He is in there?" He walked up to what used to be the Bishop. "Can I touch it?"

Archie stood in the back. "Sure! You touch! Pavel do great job with Bishop!"

Reggie ran his hand along the Bishop's leg and looked at his groin. "Oh God, no." He turned away. "That's where Reggie draws the line. No way."

He walked back to Mike and Kendra. "We gotta get outta here."

"Great job, guys. Really looks amazing!" Kendra said as they turned and left the church.

They pulled out of the parking lot and headed home.   "Did you catch what that asshole said?"

Mike looked over. "About what?"

"Keeping Michelle quiet. That's why he has her on drugs! That fucker!"

Reggie added in to it, "The good thing is, it is pure. Believe me, that is less of a problem. It's still fucked. But less dangerous if she doesn't do too much. At least we don't have to worry about fentanyl being in it."

"So he says. I'm gonna kill him before this is over." Kendra boasted.

Mike looked in the mirror. "You got a good point man, but we gotta get her off of it, before she gets full blown hooked." Mike's phone rang, and he picked it up. "Oh shit, it's Lucky."

"Hey old man."

"Mike, listen. I found out who the guy in Egypt is. His name is

Tafeef Badawi. He has more money than all of congress. Big in the diamond trade."

"Shit, that is awesome news!"

"Yeah, yeah, now shut up and listen."

"Okay, Okay. What?"

"This Gustav character, he is only part of it, Mike. Find the head of the snake and cut it off."

"I think we did. It's Nirro."

"Like hell it is. Nirro is a spoiled ass playboy, living off his mommy and daddy's money. He is a major player, but not the head. Be careful, Mike. I got some friends I am getting hold of. Keep me posted."

"Sure thing Lucky… Lucky? God dammit, I hate it when he does that!" He put his phone down on the center console. "He fuckin' hung up."

Kendra laughed. "At least he had good news." Mike looked in the mirror. "Ready to go to war, brother?"

Reggie sat forward. "Is that what's goin' on? We goin' to war?"

Mike looked over at Kendra. "We better get some things settled, baby. This is about to get really interesting."

Chapter 18

The Fortress

Another day had gone by, and Kendra still heard nothing from Michelle. Reggie stood on a ladder, installing cameras in the gallery.

"How many cameras are you putting up?" Kendra asked, as she looked up, watching Reggie on the ladder.

Sinking in the last screw, Reggie climbed down. "That right there is the last of them. I put the two outside, three in here, One in the Grotto and in the Garage. Then I have two out back in the alley. Oh yeah, and one covering the street upstairs. Mouse ain't gonna be able to move and we won't see it."

"Damn! So how do I look at it? I mean, what are they showing?"

"That's the simple part. There is an app for your phone, and a website for your computer. Everything they record goes straight to your drive. Come into the office and I will show you."

Kendra and Reggie went to the office, and she opened her laptop. She stood up. "Here, sit here and do what you got to do."

Reggie sat down and pulled up the website. "Ok, here is your login. I wrote your password down, but you can change it. Mike and I have access to it as it is right now."

"No, that's fine. This is more your territory, anyway."

"Can't be too careful. Not when you're dealin' with these

clowns, anyway."

"True. So I think I am going to find Michelle today. It has been a few days. Haven't heard from her, or Gustav."

"Yeah, you better check up on her. I have lost a few people to that shit."

Mike walked into the office. "Are we all good and set up?"

Reggie stood up. "Yeah, we are good. Check that out." Pointing to the screen.

"Damn! Nice job man. This is great. And it records everything?"

"Yup, straight to the hard drive, bro."

"Perfect." Mike pulled out his phone, looked up the app, and installed it. "Baby, lemme see your phone so I can get you the app." She handed him her phone and a few moments later, he finished.

"There you go. Now we can all see what's going on whenever we want."

"Well, that is gonna fuck up getting laid in the Grotto and in my office!"

Reggie started laughing, "You can disable cameras on the app anytime."

"Good. Now I am happy." Kendra put on a dramatic smile and giggled. She walked out of the office and looked at the cameras in the gallery.

"Mike?"

"Yeah, what's up?"

"I want to go over to Michelle's. I need to understand why she isn't calling or answering her phone."

"We can go now. We are all finished with this."

Reggie was picking up the tools. "I'm gonna hang unless you want me to go with. I got some shit to take care of here."

"That's cool. Hopefully, we won't be too long," Kendra said, as they walked out of the Grotto and into the garage.

∞∞∞

Mike parked in front of Michelle's house. It was older. White, two stories with an old fence around the yard, made of wood with white paint that was fading and peeling. Parked out on the street, Kendra's work van sat and in the driveway, there was a blue BMW convertible. "Damn. You must pay her pretty damned good. That car goes for around eighty grand."

"I don't pay her that good baby. Must be one of Gustav's cars. I hope he isn't here."

They approached the front door, and Kendra knocked. Not hearing an answer, she knocked again. "Fuck this." Kendra tried to open the door, but Michelle locked it.

"More than one way to skin a cat." Kendra reached into her bag and pulled out a set of keys. A moment later, she opened the door.

"Michelle?!" she called out as they walked inside. The house seemed well kept, orderly. "Maybe she is in bed. Lemme go up and check, stay here."

Mike sat on the couch as Kendra went upstairs to Michelle's room. She opened the door, and there she was laying in her bed, asleep. Kendra sat on the edge of her bed and nudged her awake. "Hey, Chicky. Time to get up."

Michelle stirred and sat up, letting the cover fall off. "What time is it?"

"It's about 11AM. I haven't heard from you and I was worried."

"Yeah, sorry. I was taking some time."

Kendra looked on the nightstand and saw a used needle and a burnt spoon.

"Time, huh?"

"Yeah." she replied, rubbing her eyes. "Gimme a minute and I'll be down. Alright?"

"Sure Chicky baby. Hurry, Mike is downstairs waiting."

Kendra went back downstairs and joined Mike on the couch.

"Well?" Mike asked.

"She is using alright. Used rig up on her nightstand."

"Fuck. How does she look?"

"Honestly, not that bad. Just tired looking. She said she was taking some time."

"Yeah, I bet."

Michelle walked down the stairs and went into the living room, wearing only a long sleeve denim shirt, loosely buttoned. She sat next to Kendra and curled up next to her, resting her head on her shoulder. "I think I fucked up."

"What's going on?"

"I should not have hooked up with Gustav. He was fun at first, even let me drive the car out front."

"We saw that. Figured it was his."

"It is. But now he is always bringing me this shit, and I keep putting it in my veins."

"Can you stop?"

"I haven't tried yet. He comes over, we fix, fuck, then he leaves. I feel like an expensive hooker."

Mike was listening and trying not to notice Michelle exposing herself.

"I hate to say it, but that is exactly how he sees you. I don't think anyone that guy knows is safe. Everything, and everyone around him, is a commodity. Get what I mean?" Mike asked, trying not to stare in between Michelle's open legs.

"Yeah, I know. He brags a lot about how many people he has control over. Even you." Pointing at Kendra.

"Really. He has a major surprise coming to him." Kendra exclaimed.

"How so?"

"Because we already knew that. We know his game. So basically, we are just using him for the time being and playing along. He has made me a lot of money in the last two weeks."

"Yeah, about that. You need an offshore account. I can set it up for you if you want to go that route."

Mike looked over at Kendra. "That's a good idea. Lucky has something like that. He is too paranoid to keep all of his money in banks here in the states."

Michelle sat up and stretched. "I don't blame him."

Kendra laughed. "Michelle, do me a favor."

"Yeah what?"

"Go get dressed. Your tits are hanging out, and I have a clear shot of your snatch. So does my boyfriend. Nice shave job, by the way."

Michelle smiled. "Sorry. Let me go get some clothes on, then I'll go to the Canvas with you. Sounds good?"

"That sounds great. And Michelle?"

"Yeah?"

"Don't bring any of that shit with you. Not in my place."

"No, I am out anyway. We did it all last night."

Michelle went back upstairs. Mike nudged Kendra on her arm. "Now, why did you have to say that? I was getting a nice little show going on there!"

Kendra smacked him back on his arm and laughed. "Fucker! You better not have been looking!"

"Oh no, I swear. Scout's honor," Mike said sarcastically, grinning.

"I'm just playing. You can look. Just not touch."

"Did you?"

"What?"

"Did you ever sleep with her?"

"Really, Mike? Really?"

"Yes, really. I wanna know."

Kendra shook her head. "You're an asshole. You know that?" she asked, trying to avoid answering the question.

"Yup. I do know that for a fact. So, did you or not?"

"Okay, once. It was a while ago and I was drunk and on ecstasy."

"I knew it!" he laughed.

"Happy now? Jesus. What do you want, a list of who I have slept with? Because it's real fucking short!"

"No, I just wanted to know about that one," he said with a satisfied grin.

"Oh, so now you want her with the package?" Kendra asked, grinning.

"Now I didn't say that. Just a hot idea. What can I say? I'm a guy."

"Yeah, you're my guy, and I don't want to share."

"Good." Mike leaned over and kissed her. "I want you all to myself."

"Trust me, you have me completely to yourself."

"I know. Still think you're bat shit crazy though."

They both laughed and Michelle reappeared in the living room. "Alright, I am as ready as I can be, I guess."

"Are you going to drive? Or can you drive, should I say?" asked Kendra.

"Yeah, I'm good. I'll follow you back. How many deliveries do you have?"

"We already took care of it."

"Fuck, I'm sorry. I know I have been slacking. I'll get back on track again."

"That would be nice. I miss having you come by. I want my Michelle back."

Kendra walked over and hugged her. "Take more time if you need. I got my boys. Just get better, Okay Chicky?"

"I am. I promise. Let's get going. I am sure everyone has shit to do."

"Yeah, wait till you see the camera system they installed! It's fucking awesome!"

"I'm sure."

They all left and headed back to Kendra's studio.

Mike kept an eye in the mirror, making sure Michelle was good to drive as she had said. Satisfied, he figured it would be a good time to talk to Kendra about some of his own plans for the day.

"Do you think you will be fine with Reggie this afternoon? I have something I have to take care of."

"And I can't go?"

"Technically, yes you could. But I would rather you not."

Kendra crossed her arms and shot him a dirty look. "Well, that's fucked!"

Mike laughed at her aggravation, "Trust me, you will be happier if you don't. I won't be long."

Kendra looked out the window. "Fine, I have to get working on that band's cover, anyway."

"Oh? Did you settle on something?"

"Yeah, I pitched them the idea, and they seemed like they liked it. They sent me a grand as a down payment. So I guess it's legit."

"Baby! That's bad ass! Looks like you're going to be bigger than ever now. Never know, you could start designing album covers for a lot of bands."

"Yeah, I could. But really, it's not my thing."

"So, how are you feeling? You know, with the voices and all, you got over that spell really quick with the priest."

"I did. Don't know, really. I know I'm happy. Maybe Gustav is right. Maybe this is going to help me get over all of it. Then we can live a normal life."

"Normal?"

"Yeah, you know. Normal. I can do my art and we can buy a house in the mountains. You can look sexy all summer chopping wood without a shirt—Normal."

Mike started laughing. "That is your idea of normal?"

"Yeah. What? That isn't funny. I think it's nice."

"It sounds nice. Maybe a cabin with a creek. We can have Reggie get property next to us. Have cookouts, hunt in the winter…"

Kendra smiled and held Mike's hand. "That sounds like heaven. If there was a heaven, that would be it for me."

"Maybe after Finland?"

She looked over at him. "Maybe. Actually, yes, after Finland."

"Really? You're serious?"

"I am."

"Fuck. Alright then. The mountains it is."

They parked in front of the gallery and walked inside. Kendra looked at the door and examined the lock. "Did Reggie say something about putting in new locks?"

"No, he mentioned nothing to me."

"Hmm. Reggie?!"

Reggie came out of the Grotto, still wearing a tool belt. "Yeah, what's up?"

"You put new locks on the door?"

"Yeah, and one leading to the garage, too. Now you got a fortress up in here."

"What was wrong with the locks I had?"

"Because it took me thirty seconds to get past them. That's what was wrong with them. These are hard as fuck to get into. Plus, if anyone does, an alarm comes on."

"Damn! You really did a lot here."

"Yeah well, it's nothin'. My old man was a locksmith. So I learned at a young age how to pick open any lock out there."

Mike looked at the lock. "Yeah, these are some serious setups right here. I told ya baby, Reggie knows his shit with this."

"Thank you Reggie. Should increase the value when I sell it." Kendra said, as she looked around at the camera's in approval.

"Sell it?"

"Yeah, after Finland, we are all moving to the mountains."

"We are, huh? Me and Mike gonna be mountain men or some shit?"

"Something like that. Sure why not?"

They all laughed except for Michelle. "What? You're going to leave me behind?"

Kendra looked over at her. "Oh shit. I'm sorry. Reggie, this is Michelle."

Reggie shook her hand. "Nice to meet you. Heard a lot about you the last few days. You got this girl worried."

"So you are the infamous Reggie." She looked over at Kendra. "How do you keep getting these hotties, girl?"

Reggie and Mike started laughing. "Alright, look, I am going to take care of that thing I got. I'll be back real soon. Is that cool?"

Kendra walked up and hugged him, and gave him a kiss. "Fine. Don't be too long."

"I won't be."

Mike left, and Kendra walked into her office and sat down. Michelle and Reggie stood at the door. "I have some work I have to do. You guys can chill upstairs or in the Grotto and get acquainted. When I am done, we can go over the finances and see about that offshore account."

"Sounds good." She looked at Reggie. "You have a beer?"

He laughed, "Yeah, come on upstairs. I keep the place pretty stocked up. That way, Kendra can get her work done."

Michelle and Reggie went upstairs, and Kendra disappeared into her studio.

Reggie and Michelle walked down the hall to the apartment. Unlocking the door, Reggie walked in, followed by Michelle.

"Holy shit! You guys really made this place look amazing? So what, are you living in this one now?"

"Thanks, yeah basically. I just crash here mainly. I have a place in Philly, but I am here most of the time." Reggie reached into the fridge and pulled out a couple of beers. "Hear ya go. Nice and cold," he said as he handed her the beer and they went and sat on the couch.

"So you have known Mike for a while, huh?"

"Yeah, ever since high school. Been through a lot of shit with him."

"Good shit, I hope."

"Good, bad, ugly. Just ya know, shit. How long have you known Kendra?"

"For about six years now. We met at this nightclub and hit it off. Wound up partying all night. She was just opening up this place and dating this real asshole. The guy was seriously awesome for remodel jobs, but a real dick."

"Yeah, that happens. I have known my fair share of those, always boils down to just Mike and I, back to back."

"Kendra and I used to be like that. I think she is a little pissed at me, though."

"Kendra? Nah. She ain't pissed. Just worried. Pull up your sleeves. Lemme see your arms."

"You're joking right?"

"No, I ain't joking. Relax, I know what's up."

Michelle pulled her sleeves up and showed Reggie the track marks. "Well, you haven't been using it for long. At least you got good veins. If you want to keep them that way, you'll stop using that shit before you lose yourself to it."

"It sounds like you know a thing or two about it."

"Unfortunately, I do. Lost a few people like that, and some family. I never fucked with the hard shit. Not once. Now I may smoke a little weed now and then," Reggie was laughing.

"But I don't enjoy getting too fucked up. Besides, I never know when I gotta be on point."

"On point?"

"Means I don't let my guard down. You girls are involved with some shady characters."

"You may be right. Look, would you mind if I stayed here tonight? I can sleep on the couch." Michelle asked with a worried look on her face.

"I don't mind. Why? What's going on?"

"Gustav comes by every night. We do heroin that he brings, we sleep together, more like fuck, and then he takes off. I mean, he gave me that BMW to drive and all, but I don't think I want to do this anymore." She held up her arm.

Reggie looked at her and could plainly see that Michelle was in trouble. This beautiful blonde woman that sat in front of him was sinking. Pity took him over and his heart sank at the thought of such a person turning into a junky. Especially one of Kendra's closest friends.

"I got you girl. Stay here as long as you need. I'm sure Kendra will be square with it. One condition, though. Stay off that shit."

"I will. Thanks. I don't know what I am going to tell Gustav, though."

"I don't think he is going to care that much. No offense. I

195

think he is just using you as a mistress or some shit. You know, keep you high, you'll do what he wants."

"Yeah, I get that. I think you're right. Look, would you mind if I take a shower? I really feel like shit."

"Go on ahead. We will get you straightened out. If you have any detox, I can call my cousin. She a nurse. She will get you all fixed up in no time."

"Thanks Reggie."

Michelle went into the bathroom and shut the door. Reggie heard the shower run. "Oh fuck! The damned trunk."

Reggie got up and went into the bedroom and picked up Mike's trunk and carried it down to Kendra's, putting it inside. Pulling out his phone, he texted Mike.

Put your trunk in Kendra's Apt. Michelle is staying a day or two to get cleaned up.

Good deal. That will make Kendra happy. Need you to occupy Michelle tonight if you can. I'm taking Kendra out.

I got you.

"Ooh Mike gonna get him some tonight! My dog!"

He walked back to the apartment, noticing Michelle was still in the bathroom. "Yo! You good there?"

"Yeah, I'm good. I feel way better now that I have had a shower." She opened the door, wrapped in a towel and was drying her hair. "Goddamn, I can't believe I let myself go like this."

"You are lucky. Some people never quit. At least you are stopping before it gets real bad. You feeling Okay? I mean, no pain or anything?"

"No, I'm tired, and I could use another beer and 48 hours of sleep. But I feel alright."

"I can help you with that." Reggie walked into the kitchen. "Mike is taking Kendra out tonight. Wanna hang low and watch a movie or something? I can order some food. I know a great place that has the best pizza in the world."

"Yeah, that sounds amazing, actually. I haven't eaten in a few days."

"I figured. Have no fear, Reggie is here!"

Michelle laughed. "Kendra is lucky to have you guys. Really. I am glad. She hasn't had it too easy."

He walked back to the couch and sat down, handing Michelle her beer. "No, from what I understand she hasn't."

"What did she tell you? She never talks about her childhood. Just that it sucked."

"That's about what she told me. I found out something a long time ago. When people don't want to talk about something, there is a good reason. If they want to, they will. If not though, best to leave that shit alone."

"Yeah, I think that's a pretty good policy to have."

Mike pulled into the garage and shut the door. *She is going to love this.* He thought to himself. He walked into the Grotto, and into the office where Kendra and Michelle were going over finances and bank accounts. "Hey baby. Want to come see something?"

Kendra looked up. "Sure, what ya got?"

"Come on and I'll show you. It's in the garage."

She followed him out to the garage, and he opened the door to the truck for her to get in. He walked around and got into the driver's seat, and started the truck up. She looked down at the console, with a surprized look on her face "Holy shit! You got a new stereo?"

"Yup, and check this out." He pulled out the remote for it and put it on Sirius XM. "Now you can listen to whatever you want." He reached into the back seat and pulled out a box, and gave it to her. "I got you one for your studio too."

"Oh, my God! You see? This is why I love you!" She wrapped her arms around his neck and kissed him.

"Glad you like it. And tonight I am taking you out."

"Really? Where?"

"Just a place I know. I already made reservations. But we have to leave soon."

"Why?"

"It's in New York City."

Kendra's face lit up and her smile expressed the excitement she had welled up inside her.

"Ooh! Shit! I guess I can wrap up with Michelle and get ready. She is staying tonight anyway. Is that alright with you?"

"It's your place. If you say it's fine, it's fine."

"No, it's not my place Mike. This is our place. All ours!"

"I don't work for you anymore. Do I?"

She stopped for a moment and looked at the floor. Then she looked up at Mike. "No. You don't. And you're never going to work again, baby."

Mike smiled and kissed her. They got out of the truck and went back inside. Michelle sat at the computer working on the banking situation. "I think I have figured it out, babes."

Kendra stood behind her, looking at the screen. "Can you fill me in tomorrow? Mike is taking me to New York City tonight!"

Michelle looked up and over at Mike. "Well, aren't you just Romeo?"

Kendra started laughing as Mike smiled. "No, he is Clyde, and I'm Bonnie."

Michelle giggled. "Well, that will explain a lot. You guys have fun. I'm going to have pizza and movies with Reggie. He really is a special kind of cool."

Kendra kissed her on top of her head. "You behave tonight, tramp."

Michelle laughed. "I will. Maybe."

Chapter 19

Times Square

Mike and Kendra sped down the highway, headed to the big city. She had the stereo turned up, the window down and her feet on the dash. Mike looked over at her and smiled. She looked happy and free. "So I have a bit of a surprise for you."

She sat up and turned the stereo down. "Another one?"

"Yeah, we are spending the night in the city. I booked us a hotel in Times Square."

"Are you serious?!"

"As a heart attack."

"Wow! I can't wait to get there. You know what?"

"What's that?"

"I have only been to New York once in my life."

"Really?" he asked, looking over at her, shocked. "I mean we are not far at all. Why?"

"Always busy with my work and the gallery."

"You sure missed out on a lot huh?"

"Yeah, I did. But I got you now. You make it worth it."

"Don't kid yourself baby, nothing and nobody is worth what they did to you."

"I'm not kidding myself at all. I mean, that's just how I feel. Like maybe life is going my way for once."

"About that. I wanted to talk to you about your parents."

"What about them?"

"Can we make them the last?"

"You mean the stuff I do for Gustav?"

"Yeah. Mountains right?"

"You don't like me doing this, do you?"

"Honestly? No. I get why you're doing it, though. Do you know how many people I have put under ground?"

"No. I bet it's not that many."

"17."

"What?"

"I have done 17 hits. And that was all in a year's time. I am the reason they found the bodies in the river."

"That was you?"

"Yeah. It was me. Reggie was there. But like I told you before, we were into other shit as well."

"My point is, the more you do it, the less you feel. You become callused. You are so beautiful inside and out, I don't want to lose you to that."

"You will not lose me Mike. Never." She reached over and grabbed his hand, looking at him with a serious face. "Never."

"So after your parents, then?"

"They are the last, baby. I promise."

Reggie walked into the apartment carrying a large pizza box and set it on the counter. "Dinner is served!"

Michelle got up and looked at it after he opened it up. "That looks so good!"

"You're gonna love this shit! Best pizza in the world right here."

He grabbed down two plates from the cupboards, and a couple of paper towels. After they put a few slices on their plates, they sat in the living room in front of the T.V. Reggie flipped through the channels, stopping on the news.

"Looks like the storms are over for a while."

"Yeah, I am glad too. I hate storms."

They sat, eating their pizza and watching the news. "Oh, look at this shit. This will piss Kendra off for sure." Michelle said as she grabbed the remote and turned the volume up on the T.V. The anchor women on the news channel shuffled through papers as she covered another story.

"Local religious groups in Camden County say they are cracking down on immorality. They have hit the streets and are targeting all establishments that carry pornography, violent and debaucherous material. This is what one of their members had to say."

The screen changed to a woman talking to a reporter outside of an adult bookstore downtown. "Shit, that's only a few blocks away." Michelle exclaimed.

"Here we are standing across the street from one of the many adult oriented storefronts in the area. With us today is Karen Schlems with the Church of Fundamentals of Jesus. Karen, from what we understand, you have taken to the streets in a movement against these types of establishments. What exactly is your main mission, and do you think you will accomplish your goals?"

"Yes, and thank you. Our mission is simple. We are going to rid our neighborhoods of this filth once and for all. Too many of our young women and men fall short to the sexual temptations offered by these disgusting places. Drugs have riddled our streets, crime is rampant, and places like these are the core root of the problem. We will not stop until every store is closed down."

"I see, but don't you think that will trample the rights given to citizens by our very constitution?"

"These people do not deserve rights! We have the right to live in a drug and perversion free society. Everywhere we look, pornography, adult cinemas with prostitution, galleries that contain horrid acts of violence. It all ends now!"

"I see you are taking this seriously. Do you have a large

following to help you with your campaign?"

"We have the Bible!" she belted, and held up a Bible, waving it in the air. "This is our weapon! God will put an end to this modern day Sodom and Gomorrah! You hear me? He will end it!"

"Well, there you have it, folks. Looks like Karen has come to town, and she means business. Back to you Sally." The screen cut back to the newsroom.

"Looks like we are going to have a holy war going on in the streets. Better Bible verses than bullets."

Reggie turned the channel. "I feel bad for that bitch if she shows up here. Kendra will beat the shit out of her."

"No doubt. She is asking for it, always has to be someone running their mouth about something nowadays."

"For sure. You ready for some more?"

"No, I'm good. But you're right. That is the best pizza I have ever had."

∞∞∞

Kendra and Mike had parked the SUV in the parking garage of the hotel, checked in, and headed for dinner, wading through the busy Times Square.

After sailing through the sea of people,they had reached the restaurant. A small, fine dining place tucked away in the middle of all of the thighs and hustle of the square. On the front window, there was writing in gold letters the name, *Keith's*

"You're going to love this place. I have known the owner for a long time. He doesn't know I am coming, though."

"I thought you made a reservation?"

"I did. Can't eat here without one."

Mike opened the door for Kendra, and they walked in. A man

wearing a tuxedo greeted them at the door.

"Yeah, I have a reservation for 7PM. Mike Langley."

The man looked at him and got a disturbed look on his face. "I am sorry, but we have a dress code here. You cannot dine here wearing that."

Kendra gripped Mike's hand tightly. Mike looked at her, giving her a look that said 'Stay calm, I got this'.

"Is Keith in the kitchen?" he asked the snooty man that greeted them.

"Keith Loften? The owner?"

"Yeah. Be a good little asshole and go tell him Mike Langley is here."

Kendra restrained herself from laughing. The facial muscles clenched tightly as a grin formed on her face.

The man turned and walked away, disappearing into the kitchen. "Don't worry, he used to go to school with Reggie and I."

"Did you see the look on that dicks face? Now that was priceless."

A moment later, a short guy came out of the kitchen wearing a chef's uniform. He saw Mike and smiled.

"Mike Langley? Man, I thought you were dead!"

Mike gave him a hug. "Close man, but no. Your guy there in the penguin suit says we can't eat here dressed like this."

"Ah, don't worry about him. Scott is an asshole."

"Anyway, Keith, this is Kendra, my significant other."

"Well, very nice to meet you. I'll get you both seated and have a bottle of my finest wine sent over. On the house."

"You're awesome man. Great to see ya."

"Oh for sure. You too Mike. Look I'm busy, but I'll come and catch up for a minute before you leave."

"Sounds good."

Scott forced a smile and grabbed two menus. "Right this way."

They sat at a small table in the back, inside a dimly lit room. There were a few other tables occupied, but they mostly had a nice secluded spot to enjoy their dinner . A few moments later, a man approached their table with a bottle of wine.

"I am Andre, and I will be your waiter this evening. This is a Nth Degree Still Red Cabernet from 2015. It is one of our favorite wines here. I am sure you will find its taste more than satisfactory."

Andre opened the bottle and poured them each a glass, then set the bottle on the table, wrapped in a white cloth. She sat and watched, smiling, then picked up her glass, putting it up to her nose and taking in the aroma. "I have to get some of this for my premiers!"

"This bottle retails at about $123.00 American."

She looked up at him and grinned. "Well then I should order an entire case of it."

"If you like, I can give you the name of the place we ordered it from. I am sure they would always like more customers. You said premiers. If you don't mind me asking, what for?"

"I have an art gallery in Gloucester City in New Jersey. Every six months I have a premiere."

"Outstanding. Well, I hope you enjoy the wine, and I will be back soon to take your order. Keith tells me you are old friends, so anything you need, please do not hesitate to ask."

"Thank you Andre."

Andre gave a slight bow and walked away., leaving Mike and Kendra to start their evening.

"So, how do you like it so far?"

She sipped her wine and set it down. "I could get used to this."

"I was hoping you would enjoy it. I brought you here for a reason tonight."

"I don't know if I can handle anymore, baby. This has already been the best day I have had in a while."

Mike reached into his leather jacket and pulled out a small black box, and set it on the table.

"Well, do you think you can handle this?"

Kendra's eyes widened. "Is that what I think it is?"

"I don't know. Open it and find out."

She skeptically reached down and opened the box. She let out a scream when she saw the ring inside, quickly covering her mouth with her hand and looking at the other customers. Who were now looking over at them, most of them catching on to what just happened.

"Are you asking me to?" she asked quietly with the expression of excitement tainting her voice.

"Yes, will you marry me?"

All the people in the dining room looked on. There were whispers among them and pointing over at Mike and Kendra.

"I think he just proposed."

"Oh, that is so wonderful!"

Kendra jumped out of her seat and flew into Mike's lap. "Yes! Yes! Fucking yes!"

Every person eating in the dining room stopped and watched what was going on. One gentleman stood up and started clapping, and the rest followed. Quickly, they had become the center of everyone's attention.

Kendra sat back down and put her ring on, holding it out and looking at it. She looked over at all the people staring and smiling about the occasion. "And you all are invited to the wedding!"

The onlookers loved this, again giving approvals and comments of 'Congratulations' to her.

"Now, I am the happiest girl in the world. So, is this what you were doing today?"

"Yeah. look. I don't know what's going to happen. There are a lot of things happening. I just know whatever is going to happen. I want it to happen with you and I, 'us'."

Kendra pulled out her phone and took a picture of her ring and sent it to Michelle. She looked up at Mike. "The mountains baby."

"The Mountains."

Michelle and Reggie were sitting in the living room still, drinking beer and watching a movie. Her phone vibrated, and she picked it up. "Oh my God?! Did you know about this?"

"About what?"

She lifted her phone to him, showing him the picture Kendra had sent her of her engagement ring.

"What?! No, I didn't know anything about that. Damn, I knew Mike was into her, but damn!"

"Oh my God, I have to call her!" Michelle exclaimed, starting to call Kendra's phone, but was instantly stopped by Reggie.

"No, just let them be tonight. They don't need us all up in their business right now."

She put her phone back on the table. "I guess you're right. But damn! This is like—How long have they known each other anyway?"

"I don't know, like three weeks or something." Reggie said as he finished his beer.

"Hey, do you have any booze up here? We should do a shot!"

"You don't have to tell me twice."

Reggie got up and walked into the kitchen, pulling a bottle of Bourbon out of the cabinet and two shot glasses. He set them down on the table and poured them. After picking up their shot glasses, he toasted, "To Mike and Kendra."

She smiled. "To Mike and Kendra," and drank her shot down, setting the glass on the table next to the bottle.

"Damn. That's some smooth shit right there." she exclaimed, still admiring the flavor that lingered in her mouth.

"Yeah, I don't be fuckin with the cheap shit. If it's worth drinking, it's worth paying for."

"Makes sense to me."

"So you still feelin' alright?"

"Yeah, I feel fine, a little buzzed, but fine."

"You're lucky. Lot of people don't feel so good for a while. Glad you didn't get all hooked and shit."

"Yeah, really we only did it at night. And it didn't look like he put a lot in there. But damn, that first time really rocked my ass."

"I bet. It will do that for sure."

Michelle picked up the bottle, pouring another round for them and glancing over to Reggie.

"So, is there a Mrs. Reggie in your life?"

Reggie started laughing. "Hell no. No, Reggie don't get caught up in that. Next thing ya know there's little Reggie's runnin' all over the place. Nope, not for me."

Michelle laughed. "That's understandable. People like to have their freedom. I have had no one steady in a while. Kinda thought maybe Gustav, but that isn't turning out so well."

"No, it doesn't look like it." he agreed, "What you gonna do about him?"

"Ugh, another shot, that's what."

"Hell yeah, now you're talkin'. Fuck that fool anyway."

"I did that already. Truth be known? He wasn't even that good."

"Damn girl. You need another shot, then." Reggie grabbed the two she had poured and handed Michelle hers. He raised his glass up. "To brighter days and better lays!"

"Fuck! I'll drink to that!"

∞ ∞ ∞

Mike and Kendra were just finishing up their dinner, and Keith walked up to their table. "How was everything?"

"Fucking great man! You haven't lost your touch."

"It was wonderful, thank you. Best night ever!"

"I heard, congratulations. I am seriously glad you chose my place Mike. It really is an honor."

"No problem. I'm glad I did as well. So, what time are you out of here?"

"Oh I will be here till around midnight as usual. Why? What are you two doing tonight?"

"I know what we are doing tonight." Kendra said with a grin.

"I don't know, maybe check out Times Square , then hit the hotel. We have to get back in the morning."

"Oh Andre said he would give the place where to order this wine from. I'd like to order a case of it."

"Yes, he didn't forget. He will bring it out shortly. And don't worry about tonight. Let this be a wedding gift for you both."

"Come on Keith. That's poor business."

"Oh trust me, it's not. I have done pretty well for myself in this place. Besides, I still owe ya from years ago."

"If you insist, man. Your waiter is getting a hell of a tip tonight then."

"I am sure he will appreciate that."

Mike looked at his watch. "Fuck. We gotta get going."

"Why the rush baby?"

"I got one more little surprise for you."

Andre walked out with the card so Kendra could order the wine. "Ah, here he is now. Mike, I have to get back in the Kitchen. It was great seeing you again."

"Absolutely. Come and check out her gallery when you get some time. The Daunting Canvas. It will blow your mind bro."

"I will. Nice meeting you, Kendra, and congratulations again."

"Thank you Keith, it was a wonderful evening."

"Here is the place we ordered from." Andre said, showing them the illustrated catalog, and pointing to the name. "I am sure they will take good care of you."

"Thank you Andre."

Mike stood up. "Yes, thank you. And here." Mike pulled out three one hundred-dollar bills and gave it to Andre. This is for you man. Great service. Keith is fortunate to have you."

"Oh f- I mean thank you so much."

Mike started laughing. "You don't have to put on the act for us. But seriously, when we come back, you're gonna be here, I hope."

"I have been here for three years now. Keith is a great guy to work for."

"Yeah, he is a great guy period. Have a good night Andre."

They walked out of the restaurant and headed into Times Square, with Mike looking at his phone.

"Damn, those billboards are bright!" he exclaimed, pointing to all of them lit up, flashing and blinking.

Kendra looked up at all the lights, and signs changing colors and displaying advertisements. She rested her head on Mike's arm and looked up at him.

"Thank you baby."

He pointed to one particular billboard across from them. "I like that one there."

Kendra looked up at the sign he was pointing at. It read, *I love you Kendra Blake* and turned into a heart then changed again.

"No, you didn't!"

"Too corny?"

"Get your ass up in that room cowboy!"

Reggie and Michelle had turned the T.V.. off and put on the stereo. "I bet they are having the time of their lives tonight!"

"Yeah, if I know Mike, he did it right."

"I hope so. I am thrilled for her. She deserves this in her life."

"So does he. I'm kinda shocked. I had never seen him fall in love before. Glad for him and her. Hell, I'm just glad, period."

"How glad?"

"Glad-glad."

"Like super glad?"

"Real super glad!"

They both started laughing and Reggie poured another shot. "Damn girl, we gonna finish this fucker off tonight."

"That's okay." she said, standing up. "Uh oh."

"What's that?"

"I think I am just a little fucked up."

"You ain't gonna be sick are ya?"

"Me? No. But I got to piss. So look out!"

She made her way past Reggie and into the bathroom.

"Damn Michelle. You are on a trip. I should drink with you more often." Reggie exclaimed, laughing.

She shouted from the bathroom. "We can do that!"

Reggie laughed and slammed another shot. "I bet we can girl, I bet we can."

She came out of the bathroom and sat back down on the couch. "Hey."

"Hey. How you doin?"

"I'm doin pretty damned good. You ever do a navel shot?"

"A what?"

"A navel shot. You pour some booze into my belly button and drink it."

"I can't say I have ever done that," he replied, looking down at her stomach.

"Here." She lifted her shirt and laid back. "Now pour some in there." she said, pointing to her belly.

"You white people do some of the craziest shit. If you say so."

Reggie poured some in and went down to drink it. As he did, she lifted her shirt the rest of the way up. "Now I got you." And laughed.

He glanced up with his eyes. "Oh, hell! Yeah, I think I like these navel shots!"

Chapter 20

Eradicate The Stain

Intoxicated in the afterglow of their previous evening, Mike and Kendra enjoyed the drive back to the Canvas. The sun blazed a brilliant pattern in the clouds and warmed the world below. She didn't once turn on the stereo. With the window down, she let the wind do what it wished with her hair, feeling at peace.

"Mike?"

"Yeah?"

"Do you think we will make it out of this?"

"Out of what? This shit with Gustav?"

"Yeah. I don't know if I want to go to Finland anymore." she said, with a content look on her face.

"No? Why not?"

She rolled up the window and pulled down the visor, looking in the mirror and fixing her hair. "I just keep thinking about us, sitting in front of a fireplace, in a huge cabin, with snow falling outside. No drama, no killing, no Gustav. Just us. Reggie coming over for Christmas, maybe a garden in the spring and summer."

"We don't have to go, ya know. We can leave and disappear."

"Maybe I'll write a book. This would make a hell of a story. Don't ya think?"

Mike started laughing. "Better label it fiction."

Kendra laughed, "Yeah, you have a valid point there. I don't know. All I know is, I am happy, and I don't want to risk anything fucking this up."

Mike looked over at her and grabbed her hand. "Whatever you want to do, I'm with you. You want to go to Finland? We go. You want to blow outta here and escape, then that's what we do. The choice is yours. We have to finish the game though. That I know for a fact."

They turned onto the street, running along her gallery. "What in the fuck is that?" she asked, looking at the front of the gallery.

Kendra sat up in her seat, pointing at the small crowd of people that had gathered, carrying signs and yelling chants at her storefront. One woman had a bullhorn and was screaming into it.

"This looks like bullshit. Where in the fuck is Reggie?" Mike picked up his phone and called Reggie as he pulled into the garage.

"Ya Mike."

"What in the fuck is going on outside?"

"Bunch of church people. Protesting the gallery, it looks like. They just showed up about five minutes ago."

Mike hung the phone up and got out of the truck. They flew through the Grotto and out into the Gallery. Reggie and Michelle were standing at the window, watching the people outside.

"What in the hell are they doing?!" Kendra yelled.

Michelle pointed at the woman with the horn. "Reggie and I saw her on the news last night. She is some church bitch that is harassing adult stores and places that promote sex and violence. She said something about galleries, but I didn't think she meant this one."

Infuriated, Kendra opened the front door. "Do you mind explaining to me just what in the fuck you're doing in front of my gallery? Leave!"

Karen yelled through the bullhorn. "We have the right to live in a society, free of this smut you call art! Free of the sinful nature of people like you!" Karen shook a Bible at her and kept yelling through the bullhorn. "We are going to eradicate the filth in our city once and for all!"

The people gathered with her kept chanting and holding up their signs. "Eradicate the filth! Eradicate the filth!"

Kendra went back inside and slammed the door. "That fucking cunt! The most perfect night of my life, and I have to come home to this!"

"The bitch about it is, I don't think we can touch them. It will land us in jail for bullshit."

Reggie stood in the doorway, staring at the woman. "Mike has a point. But, if she were to come in here uninvited, asked to leave and didn't, well then she gets what she gets. I have an idea."

Kendra stood by Reggie, glaring at Karen who was still bellowing. "What's your idea? I'm up for a chainsaw and gasoline right about now."

"We already have a closed sign in the window. Let's put more of your work in the window. Then we will open the door. Tell her to leave because we are closed. This bitch think she entitled."

"I like it." They got busy moving her most grotesque pieces into the storefront in plain sight. Kendra opened the door and propped it open. She pulled out her phone and showed it to Karen. "I'm gonna call the cops!"

"We are under the authority of God! You're going to hell for the sickness that you spread in our community!" Karen bellowed back.

An older man standing next to her rambled off insults. "You will reap what you have sown. For you are a disgusting harlot that plagues this land, and its people. No forgiveness will be shown to you on the great day of judgment!"

Kendra started backing away from the door, and the woman kept approaching. Soon, just as Reggie predicted, she was inside, filling the air with her voice of opinion about who she thought Kendra was.

"We are closed!" Kendra yelled. "You need to leave now! This is the only warning you are going to get, you psychotic bitch!" After her warning, it was obvious that the woman would not leave. So Kendra grabbed her phone, smiling as she showed it to the lady, and dialed the police.

"911, what is your emergency?"

"Yes, this is Kendra Blake at The Daunting Canvas. I have a church group outside my building screaming threats. We are closed. A woman is inside, as you can hear. I told her to leave and she will not."

"Are you in immediate danger?"

Kendra changed the tone of her voice.

"She keeps holding up her bull horn like she is going to hit me with it. There are four of us here, but we don't want to get in trouble. I think she is on some kind of drug. Please send someone to get her out of here, quickly!"

"We are sending units to your location. They should be there in a few seconds."

Mike looked over at her, grinning, and mouthed out the words. "Well played."

A few moments later, two squad cars pulled up with their lights on. Four officers got out of the cars and walked to the crowd, with their hands on their guns. "Back up! Right now! All of you!"

The older man pleaded with the officer. "We have the right to a peaceful protest!"

The young officer pulled out his Taser. "You are about to have the right to remain silent! Now stand against the window or I will light you up in front of God and everybody!"

Another officer went inside, yelling at Karen. "Drop the bullhorn now!"

Kendra, Mike, Reggie, and Michelle backed up and let the officers handle the situation. Karen would not listen and kept screaming into the horn. "In front of truth! The devil will run! You sodomites will be forever cursed to damnation for the-"

She threw her Bible at Kendra, striking her in her chest.

"You Fucking-" Mike quickly grabbed her and kept her from attacking Karen.

The officer grabbed the bullhorn from her and threw it to the floor. "Yup! Alright, that is assault!" He grabbed Karen and put her face to the wall. Putting her hands behind her back, reading her her rights. All the while, Karen kept yelling.

"This is persecution! Only the righteous will inherit the kingdom of God! You cannot silence His Word!"

The officer walked her outside. "Too bad you don't know His Word, lady."

The other officers had the rest of the group against the wall, keeping them restrained.

"Arrest them all for disturbing the peace."

After he placed Karen in the back seat of his squad car, he called into the station. "We are going to need another unit. We have six people in custody. Situation resolved."

He walked back into the Gallery. Mike let go of Kendra. "Do you need me to call an ambulance? Are you injured?" the officer asked Kendra.

"No, I am fine. Just pissed the fuck off."

The officer laughed. "I cannot say that I blame you. I am sorry that you had to go through that this morning. Do you want to press any charges?"

"No, I don't need to do that. I mean, you saw what she did right?"

"Yeah, she is going downtown for processing. After I saw the news last night, I figured I would have to deal with them eventually. Better now before someone kills them."

"Well, we would not want that, now would we?" she responded sarcastically.

The officer looked around at her artwork. "Are you the owner? Is this your work?"

"Yes. I own this building, and yes, this is my work. I am Kendra Blake, and soon to be Mrs. Kendra Langley." she said proudly, showing him her ring.

"Well congratulations. I have to admit, these are some pretty disturbing images. My brother would love one of these. How much for one of your paintings?"

"They run in the range of around $500.00. But for an officer? I'll cut it in half, especially if you make sure they never come back."

"I'll keep that in mind. You have a nice day Ms. Blake."

"Thank you, officer?"

"Stevens. Officer Stevens."

He walked out and assisted the rest of the officers in getting the group into the squad cars. Moments later, they all pulled away, and left.

Kendra walked over and shut the door, locking it. "Jesus fucking Christ what was that?"

Mike looked out the window. "That was unneeded attention is what that was."

"He's right. We don't need that around here."

Michelle looked over at Reggie, perplexed. "Why? The cops did their jobs. We did nothing wrong. What's the problem?"

"It's just you know. This is an art gallery. High rollin people come in here. Kendra doesn't need the drama and this kind of publicity. That's all I'm sayin'."

"I guess you're right. I didn't think of it that way."

Mike and Kendra looked at each other. She figured changing the subject was a good idea as she turned and faced Michelle. "So, how was your night? Feeling better?"

"I am, I have to admit, a little hung over. Reggie and I had a little head splitter last night."

Mike looked over at him. "Guess you guys got along alright then."

Reggie shrugged and grinned.

"Uh huh." Mike chuckled, "A pimp is a pimp.".

"We had pizza and polished off a fifth of Bourbon." Michelle said, holding her head. "And now I need aspirin. Lots of aspirin."

Kendra, hearing a car pulling up, looked out the window.

"You're going to need more than that. Gustav is here. Fuck me! What next?!" She walked over and unlocked the door, opening it for him.

"You just missed all the action!" she exclaimed as he walked in.

"Thank you. How so?"

"Some nosy church radicals came and protested my gallery. They all went away in cuffs."

"The police were here?"

"Yes, I called them. Seemed the best way to deal with it, at the time."

"Well, it seems I missed out on what sounds like a good time."

"For sure."

He looked over at Michelle. "I thought I might find you here. I dropped by last night and you weren't home."

"Sorry, I crashed here last night. Had a little too much to drink, so I figured crashing here would be the best option."

"I see. One can't be too careful these days. You never know what you are going to run into. So tonight then?"

Michelle started getting nervous. "No, um, I have some things I have to take care of. I'll have to take a rain check."

"A raincheck. I understand. Well, let's not drag this out then. Keep the car. I can't have someone representing Kendra driving a van."

"What do you mean?"

"Exactly what I said. It was fun."

Mike looked at Gustav. He saw the anger in his eyes. The way his face contorted. Gustav didn't like being told 'no', and in a sense, that is what Michelle was doing. Kendra intervened, trying to break the ice that now covered the room. "So I have some news Gus!"

"And what would that be?"

She walked over and held out her hand, showing him the ring Mike had given her. "Mike and I are getting married!"

Gustav smiled. "Now that is something. I am happy for both

of you. I think you will make a wonderful couple. Do you have a date set?"

Mike interjected. "No, not yet. I am thinking soon though."

"You will have to keep me posted. I love a good wedding. If there is anything you need, just ask."

"Thank you Gus. You really are too kind."

"You might think about having the wedding on Lake Bodom. It is quite astonishing."

Michelle looked over at Gustav. "What is Lake Bodom? I have never heard of it."

"It is a lake in Finland. I have some very close family there. It is famous for some murders that took place, quite some time ago. I believe it was around 1960."

"That's just creepy."

"Have you fucking looked around here Michelle? I think it is quite fitting, if you ask me." Kendra said, looking at her like she had lost her mind.

"I can have it all arranged if you like. We can have the ceremony when we go to Finland in a few weeks."

"Wait. You're all going to Finland?" Michelle asked, with a surprised look.

"Yes. Kendra has been doing some fabulous work for one of my closest associates there. He has spent a good deal of money on it and would love to meet the artist."

"Why didn't you tell me Kendra? That sounds like a really fun trip."

"Oh sorry, I thought you would want to stay here and run things while I was gone."

"Come on! I wanna go!" Michelle pleaded.

Kendra looked over at Gustav and lowered her brow, replacing it with a smile and focusing back on Michelle. "Sure I guess we can all go. Besides, I'll need you to be my bridesmaid."

"Yes! When do we leave?"

Gustav smiled. "I will let you know. No harm in getting ready though. I am thinking in a few weeks, maybe sooner. But for now, I must be going."

Michelle walked Gustav out to his car. "Look, I'm sorry that-" Gustav cut her off.

"There are no sorry's in this world Michelle. Only experiences. I have, what some would say, a very extraordinary life. It's not for everyone."

"So, you're not mad?" She had a look of concern on her face.

"Of course not. It was a fun experience. I enjoyed our few days."

"Alright, I guess that's better than what I expected."

"And you expected what? A rich boy's tantrum? For me to throw a fit, take the car back? Yell and scream?"

"Well, something."

"There is a much bigger picture to see here Michelle. I must be going. I will see you all soon."

Gustav got into his car and pulled away, and Michelle went back inside, scratching her head. "Well, that was just odd as fuck."

"What's that Michelle?" Kendra asked, as she put her paintings back in their perspective places.

"His reaction. He just gives me a BMW like it's nothing. He isn't even mad. Said something about a bigger picture."

Mike helped Kendra set the last painting back. "Well Michelle, he lives in a much bigger world than we do. He is wealthy for a reason. He doesn't sweat the small shit. To him, this is nothing."

"That's kind of a dickhead way to be Mike."

"Yes, it is. But that's the way it is."

"I hate to break this all up, but I have to get home and see what I am going to bring. Besides, I have to make sure there are no needles or anything left lying around. I'd just as soon forget all of that."

"Are you sure you are going to be okay Michelle?"

"I'll be fine, Chicky baby. You just try to enjoy being engaged. I'll see you guys soon."

Michelle left and drove away, with Kendra watching her drive off. After Michelle was gone, Kendra looked over at Reggie. "Did you seriously fuck her last night?"

Reggie got a sheepish look on his face. "Um, yes?"

Mike started laughing. She looked over at him. "And you, this isn't funny."

"What? They are both adults. So they hooked up."

"Because Michelle likes to ask questions. Bad enough, she was banging Gustav. I don't need her around here more, because she wants Reggie's dick."

"In my defense, we were drunk, and she pulled her shirt up, when I was doing a um, navel shot." He hung his head down and Kendra started laughing.

"She totally got you, man. You're not the first she has nailed with that one. She has a magnificent set of tits though."

"That is true. They are a very nice set of tits," Mike agreed.

Kendra looked over at Mike. "Are you trying to get your ass kicked today?"

He shrugged his shoulders. "I'm just saying."

"Uh huh. Well, no harm, no foul. At least she is done with the needle. I hope she isn't blowing smoke up my ass about that."

"No, she was pretty serious about not liking it last night. I think she will be good."

"So what now? You and Michelle gonna hook up or some shit?"

"Hell no. Reggie don't lay down roots like that. Reggie is a free man and is stayin' a free man."

"Good."

Gustav walked into the Two Brothers, to see Dante behind the counter, reading orders on a computer. Looking up, he greeted Gustav. "Gus. Your usual?"

"No, not today. I don't have the time."

"How are we looking?"

"Everything is going better than expected. We should be ready to head across seas soon."

"And what about Michelle? Do I need to take care of her?"

"No, she will travel with us. I think she is going to prove very useful." Gustav replied.

"Useful?"

"Yes, I believe she will be the last piece of the puzzle."

"But she is clearly a whore." Dante arrogantly pointed out.

"Nevermind that. Have you spoken with Nirro?"

"Yes. He is making preparations for our arrival. They have taken care of securing us an airstrip close to his estate. Everything is falling into place."

"Good. I have our plane on standby. No customs to deal with."

"Excellent. And what about the return trip back to the states?"

"None of them will return."

"What about Archie?" Dante asked.

"Well, I guess we will have to get on without him. Total clean up Dante. Then we can continue with phase two."

"As you wish Gustav."

Gustav bid Dante farewell and left. As he drove down the street, away from the Two Brothers, he called Nirro through a video chat. Nirro appeared on Gustav's phone.

"Nice to see you again my brother." Nirro sat in a large leather chair, in front of a window surrounded by stone. His voice was deep and menacing. His long black hair flowed from his head, down around his shoulders, covering his chest.

"Yes, it is. Is everything set in place?? Gustav asked.

"We are right on schedule."

"Good, good. We have the final missing piece. I will let you know when we are leaving."

"This is good to hear. I am looking forward to seeing more from this Kendra Blake. I believe she is going to be very instrumental in what we are going to achieve."

"I agree." replied Gustav, "I believe she is the one we have been searching for."

Chapter 21

Lucky?

The morning had come and gone. Kendra, busy in her studio, finishing the album cover for Necrotic Filth had her own little world all to herself. The band's music played over the speakers and motivated her creative vibe.

Sitting high upon their thrones, corpses lay on piles of bones. Your minds twist with sweetened words. As sheep, you blend in with the herds.

"God dammit I love this fucking group!" Kendra danced in place, banging her head to the guttural vocals and driving guitar riffs that flowed through the air. "Fuck! I have to hook up with these guys if we go to Finland."

The image took form before her eyes. A cloven hoof, crushing bodies beneath, all dressed in suits and fancy attire. Blood sprayed from their bodies as their pillars lay in waste. A true vision of apocalyptic nature for the higher elites in power.

Mike and Reggie stood in the window of the apartment upstairs, peering at the street below. Passers would stop occasionally to look in the window. Some would try to open the door and enter but Kendra had locked it before she went into her studio, as usual.

"I wonder how many customers she loses this way?"

"I don't think she cares, Reggie. She enjoys being in her own little world when she is in her studio. That is her space and hers alone."

"I feel that. Gotta have that place to call your own, so you can get everyone else out of the way in your mind. I totally get that."

As they talked and looked out of the window, a car pulled up front. The lights in the rear shut off, and the doors opened. Lucky stepped out of the passenger seat in the rear and shut the door. The driver got out of the car and opened the passenger door up front. A man dressed in a suit got out and looked at the building.

"Holy shit! What in the hell is he doing out and about?"

Reggie shook his head. "I have no clue. We better get down there." he exclaimed, rushing downstairs and unlocking the door for Lucky and the other two men.

Lucky came in first, followed by the two other men. "Mike, just the son of a bitch I am looking for." He looked over at Reggie. "You too. And where is that little girl of yours Mike? She is gonna want to hear this."

"Well, good to see you as well, old man. Kendra is in her studio, locked away. She's doing an album cover for a band."

"Well, have her undo it. This is Dakarai Badawi, the son of Tafeef Badawi. Do you see the urgency here? Or do I have to spell it out for you?"

Mike shook the man's hand. "And this is?"

Dakarai introduced the man next to him. "This is my brother, Zahur." He shook Mike's hand and remained silent. "Your friend Lucky, tells me you have valid information on the location of Gustav Olsen. It is most vital that we know immediately."

Reggie shook both men's hands. "Let's go into the Grotto and sit. We can talk about all of this in there and away from the storefront."

"That's a great idea. You don't have a beer,do you?"

Mike laughed. "We have an entire bar in there. We got you, old man. Come on."

They all walked into the Grotto and sat down except for Mike. "I'm going to get Kendra. She is definitely going to want to hear this."

Mike knocked on the door to Kendra's studio. She opened the door with a provoked look on her face.

"Baby, I hope to fuck this is important. I am damned near finished."

"Very, Lucky is here with some men from Egypt. They are looking for Gustav."

"Oh, fuck!" she exclaimed, turning off the stereo.

"Yeah, oh fuck. Come on, they are in the Grotto."

Kendra and Mike joined the others in the Grotto. They sat drinking and discussing Gustav. Lucky looked up and noticed them walking in. "Ah-ha! There she is. Come and sit down missy. There is a shit storm of bullshit you have to know about your friend Gustav."

Kendra took a seat next to Lucky. She looked around nervously at the two men. "I'm Kendra Blake. I take it you would like to know where Gustav is?"

Dakarai set his drink on the table. "I will get straight to the point. Mr. Olsen, and his brother, took our sister away a few years ago. They sold her in to the sex trafficking business. We came very close to finding her, but lost her somewhere in Europe. The trail went dead, quiet. It was like there was never any trail at all. Now, this Gustav, he disappears as well. Again, we spent the last two years searching for him. Believing his brother to be dead. Now your friend Lucky tells me you are in business with them?"

Kendra looked up at Mike who was standing next to her. "Baby, be a doll and fix me a whiskey. Strong and straight." She looked back at the two men sitting on her couch while Mike made her a drink. Taking the drink from Mike,she drank half of it, then set it on the table.

"This 'business', I am in with Gustav, is a little complicated. He has invested a few million dollars in me and my artwork. He has me do special, custom pieces for a friend of his in Finland. For that, I also get paid millions. That is our business. But as far as him and I being friends, you're mistaken."

Dakarai laughed. "Millions. My father is a very wealthy man, and willing to pay a sizable sum for the head of this Gustav. You said Finland, yes?"

"Yes, we are supposed to go there in a few weeks, maybe sooner. The buyer wishes to meet me."

Dakarai leaned over and spoke to Zahur in Arabic, then leaned back.

"Okay, change of plans."

Mike looked at Lucky and then back at the two men. "What's a change of plans? I don't recall us making any plans at all."

Dakarai smiled. "Mike, is it?"

"Yeah, that's me."

"Your friend Lucky tells us you and your friend, Reggie? Correct?"

Reggie nodded. "Right again."

"Lucky tells us you both are very capable men, able to handle yourselves in certain situations when they arise."

"Damn right. Mike and I can throw down with the best of them fools." Reggie exclaimed with a gloating smile on his face.

"Yes, we admire men with confidence, as well as the ability to back it up. We wish you to make this trip to Finland. It was so close to Finland when we lost the scent of my sister's trail. If she may be, where you are going, we need to know. If we kill him now, we may never find out. Do you understand what we are asking?"

Kendra finished her drink and handed the empty glass to Mike. "Another, my love."

Lucky started laughing. "Jesus fucking Christ she has you whipped son!"

Kendra smiled and held out her hand. "And engaged, old man."

Lucky laughed even harder. "You poor, poor young lady! God dammit Mike, it's about time you settled down!"

Mike laughed. "I guess so, Lucky. I thought it was time, myself."

Kendra laughed. "If he didn't ask me, I was about to make him my next piece of art."

Dakarai looked at her, confused. "I'm sorry. Maybe I misunderstood the joke. Another piece of art? He is a man. You mean to paint him?"

She looked up at Mike. "Should I tell them?"

Mike grabbed another beer for Lucky and made himself a drink. "Gustav has Kendra come to a warehouse. So far it has been twice. The first one was a guy that was kidnapping children, and selling them, like Gustav sold your sister. The second was a priest. He helped sweep everything under the rug when it came out that local priests were molesting the kids in their churches."

"Did you paint these men? I do not understand the art of what you are talking about."

Kendra slammed her whiskey and slammed the glass down on the table.

"No! I fucking killed them. Then sprayed them down with a liquid that turned them into stone sculptures. They are sitting in Finland now."

Lucky took a drink of his beer. "What were their names, girl?"

Kendra looked over at Lucky. "Why? What does it matter? Two more sickos off the street, just like I'm going to do to those fucks that adopted me."

Lucky looked perplexed at her answer. "Oh no. Don't tell me they--"

"Yes. Yes, they did Lucky. We have them tied up in their basement. Don't we baby?"

Mike nodded his head. "They really did a number on her

Lucky. They have it coming."

Zahur finally spoke up. "This makes no sense to me. We understand, eh, sometimes, people need to die. Yes? But why would Gustav have you kill these men, when he himself has sold hundreds of young ones to slavery? This confuses me."

Mike spoke up, realizing that Kendra would not be able to explain the situation. "We didn't find out until right before the priest. So we figured we would play along and see how far this goes. I don't know, maybe take out the entire organization."

Lucky set his beer on the table. "Kendra, I need the names of the two you killed for him. I could give two fucks about your parents, send them to hell. But I have a bad feeling about those other two."

"Okay Lucky. The first one, his name was Jackson Baker. The priest was Bishop McPherson. At least, that's what he told us."

"And you just went right along and believed him. God dammit you kids are dumb as shit!"

"What do you mean?" Mike asked.

"What I mean is, you more than likely killed two people that were trying to expose the fucking ring! That's what I mean!" he yelled in response. "Ah fuck! It ain't your fault. I'd have done the same thing if I was in your shoes. But mark my words, don't kill for him again!"

Kendra shook her head and grabbed her forehead. "Fuck me! Oh my God. I'm going to kill that mother fucker I swear!"

Dakarai looked over at her. "I would have never guessed you to take another life. Then again, I see your artwork out there, and can see that you must have been deeply tormented by these people that adopted you. Yes, this makes complete sense to me now. Ms. Kendra, will you and your men here help us find my sister? If she is still alive. I will richly reward you, I assure you. My Father has sent me, with an offer of twenty million dollars for his head. I am sure it will be much more if you find my sister."

She, with full attention, looked up at him. "For that, I will gladly deliver Gustav to you. When we reach Finland. As far as your sister goes, we want nothing in return if we find her, and I hope we do. Nobody should have to pay to end suffering like that."

Dakarai and Zahur both smiled and stood up. "We thank you. My Father will be most pleased. May we trouble you for another drink? We rarely get to enjoy, what is it, American whiskey?"

"Of course. It is our pleasure. It's kind of like having royalty here. I will tell you what. Pick out something you like from my gallery, and take it with you as a gift for your Father. Tell him, we will do our best."

"Yes, you are too kind."

They sat back down and received their drinks. As Lucky opened another beer, he looked over at the two men on the couch. "Now look. I am going to need very specific detail from everyone here, if we are going to handle this. Do you two have any support you can offer when they land? We don't know what they are going to run into over there. I have raised Mike since he was a kid. I'm not ready to send him off to a death sentence in a foreign land. We lost enough to that goddamned war as it is. And every other fucking thing they got us involved with."

Dakarai agreed. "Yes, we have a good amount of men we can send. But we must know where and when. You have my word. They will have backup when it's time."

Reggie spoke up. "How about this? It's gonna go from us, to Lucky and then to you. When we get to Finland though, we gonna need to get a hold of you. Ain't no way the old man is going over there."

"Don't you tell me what the fuck I'm going to do and not do. Don't you forget, I still have a cargo plane and a landing strip. I can get past customs there. Which reminds me." he said, pulling out a cigarette and lighting it. "You all need to come over to my place tomorrow. I have passports ready for you all. I bet you will get in there without them, but you won't be able to leave. He isn't planning on bringing any of you back. That's a fact!"

"Yeah, that's a good point, Lucky," Mike responded.

"And another thing, have you met anyone else that he is with?"

Kendra piped up. "Yeah, he has that Russian Archie and this guy Pavel. I think Archie delivers for him. He sends the stuff to Finland I know, for a fact."

Lucky started coughing. "Yeah that's Archie Orlov. His whole family is involved in smuggling. Never people though. Guns, stolen merchandise, shit like that. If you have to get past customs, they are the ones to do it. That's good news!"

"Why is that good news, Lucky?" Mike asked.

"You just let me and these two fellas work that out. I have an idea. By the time we are all finished, they will all be pushing up daisies."

Kendra stood up and walked to the bar and poured herself another. "This is fucking great!" she exclaimed when she turned back around. "I can't wait to see the look on his fucking face when we blow the roof off of this shit!"

Zahur laughed. "Why would you blow the roof off of this place? This is your home, right? You Americans have some strange customs."

Everyone laughed. Reggie walked over to him. "No bro. It's a saying. It means we are going to kick their ass! That's what it means."

"Ah yes! Ass kicking! This I understand. Let's kick some ass!"

Kendra had gotten caught up in the excitement, and a thought rushed into her head. *What if we don't make it out of this? Fuck that! We are getting married. Today!*

Kendra looked at her phone. "Fuck! Mike, what time does the courthouse close?"

Mike looked confused. "I don't know, I think five."

"Let's get married. Right Now!"

"Wait what? We are kinda planning a war. I mean, we can, but-"

"Yeah but! But what if we die over there? Or we all go to jail. Or whatever. What then?"

Mike looked at her and smiled. "Alright. Let's go. If we hurry, we will make it."

Kendra jumped up and hugged him. "Oh, I love this man!" She looked at Lucky and the two on the couch. "Want to go to a quick wedding?"

Lucky started shaking his head. "Jesus fucking Christ. What in the hell do I need to do that for?"

"Because you, 'you old coot', as your wife would say, are going to give me away! I insist!"

Lucky looked up at Mike and winked. "Alright, young lady. Let's go get you two hitched." He looked over at Dakarai and Zahur. "You guys coming or what?"

Dakarai raised his glass. "Yes! Weddings are a big deal in our land. We have nothing with us to offer though."

Mike laughed. "It's just the legal part. The ceremony will be after we survive Finland. Besides, we got all we are going to need right here. I got Lucky, two well-dressed guys, my best man, and my soon to be wife. Let's roll!"

Kendra, ecstatic, ran and grabbed her bag. She ran back into the Grotto where they were all getting ready to leave. "Lucky? Can I ask you a question? It's okay if you don't want to tell me."

Lucky looked over at her and finished his beer. "What on your mind, girl?"

"Why do they call you Lucky?"

Mike looked at the floor. "Oh, shit."

"I got that name back in the war. A bullet came along and zipped off my left nut."

"What the hell? How in the fuck is that lucky?"

"Because another inch would have taken off the other along with my dick! That's why. So they called me Lucky. Satisfied?"

"Wow! I bet that hurt like hell!"

"Yeah it did. But the VC had some pretty goddamned good grass over there! Now enough of that. Let's go get you hitched. We still have a lot to do tonight before these two head back."

"Shit!" Mike yelled out. "Fucking birth certificates!"

"I have mine upstairs. Please tell me you have one."

"Yeah it's in my trunk. Let's grab them real quick and we will head out."

$$\infty \infty \infty$$

Not long after, they entered the courthouse. Kendra ran up to the desk. An older lady was there in front of a computer. "Can we get married here? Right now?" Her face carried all the excitement she was feeling.

The lady looked up at her and smiled. "Why yes dear, if you hurry. Go up to the second floor. Ask for Claire. She will have-- you know what?"

"What?"

"Let me call her really quick so she will have the paperwork sorted out for you." She picked up the phone and hit a number.

"Yes Claire?"

"We have a young couple coming up to get married. Do they have time?"

She hung the phone up a few moments later. "Hurry, she is getting your license ready." As she pointed to the staircase that led up to the second floor.

"Thank you! Want to come?"

"Oh, I'm afraid I have to watch the desk. But congratulations!"

They all ran up the stairs and met Claire at the desk. After filling out the paperwork and showing their birth certificates along with ID's, there was a small ceremony.

"Now do you have rings?"

"Uh oh. Dammit! Sorry, we were in a rush." Mike answered.

"Well, that's alright, not to worry. They are not mandatory." Claire said.

Reggie reached into his pocket. "Hold up!" He rolled up two twenty-dollar bills and gave them to Mike. "This will work! Wrap it around yalls fingers."

"What the hell, bro?"

"Saw it in a movie," Reggie answered, shrugging with a grin.

They did as Reggie said, wrapping the bills around their fingers, and after their "I do's" Claire announced to them saying, "I now pronounce you man and wife." Mike and Kendra both wore big smiles and looked at each other. "You may kiss the bride."

After a deep kiss, finalizing their marriage, Mike picked up the marriage license and handed it to Reggie. "Do me a solid and hold on to this for a minute." Reggie took the license. "I am so happy for you, man. I mean it brother. "

"Thanks bro. Now, I have a bride to take home."

Mike turned around and picked Kendra up. "Let's go home, baby!"

He then carried her all the way downstairs, and out of the courthouse, to the SUV. Lucky and the two men from Egypt stood by, congratulating them. "Hey, you all want to come back and celebrate with us for a little while?"

"Araid not son. We got things we have to get done. Besides, now I have to change your wife's passport. You kids are always fucking things up!"

Kendra looked out of the window. "Sorry, Lucky!"

Lucky chuckled. "No, I am just fucking with you. Seriously though, come by tomorrow. There are some things I want to show you. See if they ring a bell."

"You got it, old man. We will see you tomorrow." Mike looked at Dakarai and Zahur. "Nice to meet you both. We are looking forward to working with you. If she is alive, we will find your sister."

They both shook Mike's hand. "Father will be most pleased with this. May this be the beginning of a long and prosperous friendship. May I speak to your wife for a moment?"

"Oh yeah, sure, of course."

Dakarai walked up to the window. "Congratulations. I will make sure to give my father your generous gift."

"Oh, thank you Dakarai. And thank you so much for coming.

I know you do things differently in your country, so do we. But, under the circumstances. I didn't even notice. What painting did you pick?"

"The man that was Blood Eagled. I believe it was Viking way of torture. Yes?"

"Impressive! Yes, you are correct. That is one of my favorites."

"Yes, maybe we blood eagle this Gustav. No?"

"It would be my pleasure! I'll even come to Egypt and do it!"

"Maybe! But first, Finland."

"Yes, Dakarai, first Finland. I'll see you there."

Mike and Reggie got into the truck and started back to the gallery. After they got back, they made sure they locked everything up and all the lights were off, then headed upstairs. "Well, I am going to leave you two to go enjoy your wedding night. Damn! Not even a honeymoon?"

Kendra smiled and gave Reggie a hug. "No, he gave it to me in New York. Now I'm going to introduce to him some of my other hidden talents."

Mike looked at Reggie. "I'm scared."

Reggie laughed. "You better be brother. That's all you, Dog!"

Reggie laughed as he went down the hall to the apartment. Mike picked Kendra up again. "What are you doing? Or do you just like carrying me?"

Mike looked down at her and unlocked the door. "Tradition, Love. Gotta carry you over the threshold. Remember?"

Kendra kept her arms around his neck tightly. "I love you, Mike." He shut the door with his foot. "I love you as well, Mrs. Kendra Langley.

Chapter 22

The Nightmares Live

As she slept, her dreams turned to nightmares. Memories that used to replay in her head, came back to visit her in her sleep.

Walking down to her parent's basement, the light from inside the infamous room, peered through the bottom of the door. She heard the cries of an innocent little girl from behind the door. As she rushed to open the door, she froze.

As much as she tried, she could not reach out and open the door. She could only stand there and listen, helplessly.

"Now it is time for your lesson in obedience! How many times has your Mother told you?! How many times?!" she heard a man yell.

Kendra stood stiffly, recognizing the voice to be Williams. "No. No! Leave her alone! She has done nothing! She is just a little girl!" Kendra screamed.

There would be no response. She screamed louder, "Stop it! You're hurting her!" as she heard the cries of the little girl get louder.

Suddenly, with no warning, the door flew open. William stood there, in front of the little girl who had tears rolling down her face. His head turned towards Kendra. "There is room for you as well. Do you wish to play a game with us?" His voice, menacing and diabolical.

All Kendra could do was stand, screaming to let the girl go. William started laughing at her. Louder and louder, the laughter came, penetrating Kendra's ears until they bled.

The light turned off and a red spotlight shone on William. "Look! Yes, come and see the 8th wonder of the world! The little artist that never could!" he announced as blood began to run from his eyes, and out of his mouth.

The little girl, tied to the chair, naked, screamed and wailed. "Why are you just standing there?! Why won't you help me!?"

Kendra strained and pushed against the invisible force that held her in place. "God, I'm trying! I'm trying!" No matter how hard she tried, she could not move. Only watch in horror as William tortured the poor little girl, as he did her, for all of those years.

"Even now you are useless Kendra! Look! Look at what your father does to you! And you just stand there. Poor, poor, helpless little Kendra!" shrieked a voice from behind her.

Kendra turned to see Francine creeping down the stairs, pointing at her and speaking in the same voice that haunted her thoughts. Still, she tried to move, to stop the madness, but nothing.

"I'll kill you! You evil, twisted bitch! I'll butcher you both while you sleep! While you eat! While you breathe!" Kendra yelled.

Francine's laughter filled the air. Kendra closed her eyes and yelled.

"Just wake up! Please Kendra, just wake up! Make it go away!" But she didn't wake up. She opened her eyes, and she was tied, sitting in the chair. William and Francine both had their faces in hers, laughing viciously and taunting her, dancing circled around her singing, "Poor little Kendra, poor little Kendra, the artist that never made it, the artist that never made it."

When she awoke from her horror laden sleep, sweat dripped from her body and soaked the nightshirt she had worn to bed. She looked left and right then wrapped her arms tightly around herself, bunching up her legs and sat in a ball, rocking back and forth. She looked over at Mike, who remained asleep, not stirring once. Desperately, she fought the urge to wake him. "Just wake him up. He will make it all go away." She whispered to herself. But she resisted the notion.

Returning, and striking at just the opportune moment, the evil crept up and spoke again.

Look at little Kendra. All terrified. Poor, poor little girl. Whatever shall you do? Cut yourself away from everyone?

Getting out of bed, she started walking to the kitchen, holding her head. "No, not tonight! Please, not tonight!" she argued, trying to quiet the voice inside of her.

She walked into the kitchen and opened one drawer. Pulling out a large chef's knife, she held it up, looking at the glare the moon cast upon it through the window. The gleam called out to her as she ran her fingers up the flat of the blade, it's cold steel comforted her to an extent, but did not quiet the voice.

That's it. This is the answer you have been looking for. This is what you need Kendra! Look at yourself! You're a girl who has everything! Haven't you!? Just put yourself out of everyone's misery!

Kendra dropped her arm so the side with the blade coming down, and slicing a gash into her leg. She looked down, as blood ran down her leg. Slowly, she turned and started walking to the bathroom, leaving drops of blood on the floor as she walked. Looking in the bathroom mirror, she reached over to turn on the light. She brought her face in close, looking almost within herself, trying to see the being behind the voice. Her eyes were turning. The hazel slowly dissipated and turned to red as she watched without blinking.

You wanted to get rid of me! This is the only way it happens! Do it you coward! Take the knife Kendra. And slice your throat!

She tried to yell, but could barely whisper. "Help! Mike, please wake up!" Something constricted her voice as her arm gradually lifted. The knife in her hand shook violently as she strained to fight it.

You weakling pathetic tramp! You're a child and no match for me. Never will you best me!

Shaking, with tears rolling down her face, she put the knife up to her neck. "I'm sorry Mike. I'm so sorry." The blade made an indention on her skin as she applied more pressure.

"What in the unholy fuck!?" Mike exclaimed, storming into the bathroom, grabbing her wrist and pulling the knife away from her neck. Kendra dropped the knife onto the counter and it rattled off into the sink. "Baby! What in the fuck are you doing?!"

Kendra's legs gave out, and she sank to the floor, sobbing uncontrollably. "I can't do this anymore! I can't stand it! It won't leave me alone Mike, it won't leave me alone!"

He held her tightly as they sat on the floor, rocking back and forth.

"What? What can't you do? Whatever it is, just don't do it."

"It lives in me, talks to me, tells me things, lies!"

"What does? The voice you keep hearing?!"

"Yes! The nightmares are still there! They will never let me be happy! Never!"

Kendra sobbed and sobbed, still bleeding on the floor from her leg. Mike looked down and saw the deep cut on her leg. "Oh fuck! We need to take care of that quickly." he yelled, letting go of her.

"No! Please don't!" she begged.

"I will only be a second." He grabbed the knife from the sink and threw it under the bed on his way to opening his trunk. Pulling out a black box, he rushed back into the bathroom.

Kendra sat against the wall, staring up at the ceiling, still rocking from left to right. Mike knelt down and pulled her leg out.

"Jesus, you really did a number on yourself. We are going

to have to call Veronica over here tomorrow. You may need stitches."

Opening the box, he pulled out some gauze and some iodine. "This is going to sting love." Pouring the iodine over the cut, Kendra didn't make a sound or move. Making sure it had been cleansed, he grabbed some butterfly stitches and sealed the wound as best he could, putting super glue over the incision. He grabbed a fresh gauze pad, placing it on the cut, and taping it down to her leg.

"That's the best I can do, baby." he sighed, standing up and helping her to her feet. She raised her arms to him, and he picked her up, carrying her back to bed. He laid her down and covered her up, climbing in next to her and holding her tight. Kendra closed her eyes and slept soundly for the rest of the night, not moving at all.

Daylight made its way into the window. Mike turned over and saw that the morning had arrived. Sounds of early traffic filled the air with honking horns and revving motors. He looked back at Kendra to make sure she was still asleep. Pulling the covers back, he examined her leg carefully. "No blood. Old trick always works."

Placing the covers back, he got out of bed and stretched, then walked to the kitchen to make coffee. "Holy shit." he exclaimed, looking down.

There were bloodstains on the floor and a trail leading to the bathroom where he had found Kendra. "Fuck, I'll start the coffee first."

Mike started the coffee and then started cleaning up the blood on the floor, trying to hurry and get it done before Kendra awoke and had to relive the night all over again. Finally, making it to the bathroom after cleaning up the last drops and smears of blood, he poured the bloody water that was in the bucket he used, down the drain in the tub. He sat the bucket down on the counter and looked in the mirror. "What do I need to sleep for?"

He grabbed the bucket and returned to the kitchen, putting it away and grabbing his coffee cup, sitting down at the table, opening his phone to check for messages.

"Mother fucker!" He heard Kendra yell from the bedroom.

"Guess the leg hurts." Mike got up and went into the bedroom and found Kendra sitting on the edge, holding her leg. "You alright baby?"

"What in the fuck?!"

"I think that's what I should ask you. Is being married to me so bad you had to do that last night?"

"Do what?! What in the fuck happened?" she asked, looking down at the bandage on her leg and holding the wound with both hands.

"You really don't remember?"

"Oh God, what did I do?" she asked, looking up at him with sorrowful eyes.

He sat next to her on the bed. "I woke up and saw the light in the bathroom on. I saw you standing there with a God damned knife to your throat. Your eyes were red again, and you were bawling. If I had been a second later, well, we would not be sitting here right now. I can tell you that."

"Oh my God, I am so sorry. What knife?"

He reached down under the bed, and pulled out the knife, still stained with her blood. "I threw it under here last night when I ran to get bandages."

He lifted it to show her, and she looked away. "I don't want to see it."

He took it into the kitchen and washed it off in the sink before putting it away. Grabbing her favorite cup out of the cabinet and pouring her a cup of coffee, he returned to her. "Here. Just made it a few minutes ago." He gave it to her and sat back down on the bed.

"Thank you." She took a drink and set it on her nightstand, then lay her head on his shoulder. "I'm sorry I ruined our wedding night."

"Nonsense. You ruined nothing. You don't think I knew what I was signing up for with you? I knew there would be times like this. Just kind of surprised. Seems like this only happens when something triggers you. What happened last night?"

"I don't know. I can't remember. Wait--" She paused for a moment, looking up at the corner of the room.

"There was a little girl asking me for help."

"Okay, that's good. What else?"

"I'm trying to think, there was a light, and-- the basement! Oh fuck! William had a girl tied up in the basement. But I couldn't move. Now I remember!"

"Good! This is good. Then what happened?"

"Francine came down and was yelling at me and laughing. William kept laughing at me and the little girl kept screaming for help. They had her tied to the chair. Then it was me, all tied up, and they had their faces in mine just laughing."

"Jesus Christ. Baby, that's horrible."

"Then I woke up, and she started talking to me again. But I don't remember any of it. Just sitting in bed, soaked in sweat."

She looked down at her shirt. It was still damp and had blood stains on it from her leg. "Jesus, I need to get cleaned up."

"You don't need to get that bandage wet. Come on, I'll draw you a bath."

Mike stood up and helped her walk to the bathroom. "My leg is a little pissed off at me I think."

"Well, yeah, you cut the shit out of it last night." She leaned against the counter and Mike took her shirt off, and threw it on the floor. "Let me run a shallow bath for you. Just don't get your leg wet."

He let the water warm up and then filled the tub part way. Carefully, he helped Kendra into the bathtub and sat her down.

"Did you get any sleep last night?"

"No, a little until I woke up to you trying to pull an Alfred

Hitchcock on yourself." Mike replied as he washed her back.

"Haha, you're not funny Ace."

"I'm not being funny. You scared the shit out of me last night."

"I know. This needs to stop. I really am the happiest I have ever been. I just want to get past Finland, then I feel like we can finally start our lives together. You know?"

"I know. I hate to say it, but maybe Gustav is right about some things. Maybe when you 'off' your parents, that voice will die with them. I will bet that is where it stems from. How long have you had it?"

"I don't know, a few years. I think it started not long after I moved here. So, yeah. Think you're probably right. I should call Gustav and tell him to get Archie ready. I'm ready for this to be over."

She sat up and lay back in the tub.

"That's good, my back is done."

"Yeah and?"

"Come on, finish the rest. Crazy or not, it is still our honeymoon." She looked up and smiled.

Mike and Reggie got into the truck, with Kendra in the backseat. "You sure you don't want me to call my cousin? She got some good pills and can stitch you right up, good as new."

"I will be fine Reggie, thank you though."

"We will keep an eye out on it. If it looks like it is getting infected though, we are calling her." Mike added, looking at her in the rear-view mirror.

Soon after, they pulled up to Lucky's house. Margie met them at the front door. "Come in! Come in! Oh it's always good to see you! And you!" She pointed to Kendra and grabbed her for a hug. "I am so happy for you and Mike!" She turned and gave Mike a hug as well.

"Thank you Margie. Sorry you weren't there. It was kind of spur-of-the-moment."

Margie put her hand over her mouth and smiled. "That is always the romantic way. Running off in the middle of the night reminds me of Marlon Brando..."

"Oh, Jesus Christ! Will you shut the fuck up with the consent prattle and let them come in here?!"

"I will prattle you! You old crone of a son of a bitch!" she yelled back at Lucky, shaking her fist. Turning back around, she faced Mike, smiling. "Right this way, Lucky is having a cranky day. Better get in there."

Mike started laughing. "When ain't that old fart not having a cranky day?!"

Walking into Lucky's computer room, the smoke was thick in the air from his cigarettes. He sat at his desk, catching sight of them as they entered, and also noticing Kendra's limp, as she walked. "What in the fuck did you do last night Mike? Fuck her leg to death or something?"

"No, I slipped with a kitchen knife and dropped it, landed on my leg, but Mike stitched me up," Kendra interjected.

"Yeah, well, you better make sure that you don't get infected. Here." he advised, as he handed each of them their passports. "These will get you anywhere in the world. Memorize the names, and whatever story you all have to go wherever you go. You know how to play the game Mike."

"Yeah, I got it. Shouldn't be an issue. We won't need them to get into Finland."

Lucky laughed. "If it all works out, you will not need them to get out. I'm coming over there."

Reggie's eyes widened. "You're shittin' me!"

"Fuck no, I ain't shittin' ya. You're my favorite piece of shit ya son of a bitch! I got one good round left in this old carcass, and I will be Goddamned if I use it sitting around here waiting to die! Besides, her nagging is driving me nuts. 'You smoke too much. What did the doctor say? You should cut back on your beer.' Fuck that! What's the use in livin' if you're not gonna live?!"

Lucky started coughing and slamming his fist on the desk.

"If you say so, old man. Got to admit, I will feel better knowing you have our six on this. We appreciate it," Mike added.

"Good, because I decided, and now you don't have a say in it. Now, this unfinished business you have with your mom and dad. When are you going to handle that?"

Kendra looked over at Mike. "Soon, I need to call Gustav today. I think I am going to set it up for tomorrow."

"Maybe like? What in the hell is that?! Either tomorrow or the next day, next Sunday... I don't give a fuck when you do it, just decide so I can continue planning this shit!"

"Fuck me old man, you are cranky as hell today." Mike laughed, as Lucky shot him a dirty look.

"Fine! They die tomorrow." Kendra said sternly. "Let me call Gustav and clarify. I need to make sure his team is ready." She pulled out her phone and dialed Gustav's number.

"This is Gustav."

"Hey Gus, It's Kendra."

"Yes. What can I do for you?"

"I need you and Archie to meet me at my parent's house tomorrow, let's say noon."

"Excellent. Do we need to bring the full set up?"

"Enough for two statues. And these will be expensive."

"I see. Do you know what you are doing yet?"

"Let me ask you a question? Nirro strikes me as a kingly type of guy. Does he have a throne, by any chance?"

Gustav started laughing. "As a matter of fact, he does, and sits in it often. Why do you ask?"

"You will see when it's completed. I promise he will be more than willing to pay whatever you ask."

"You seem quite confident in your idea. I like that. You are coming a long way Kendra."

"One more thing."

"And what is that?"

"These will be the last. You have made your money off of

me and so have I. After Finland, Mike and I are vanishing and living the rest of our lives together in peace."

"Well, I couldn't agree more that you have definitely earned it Kendra. If that is your wish, my dear, consider it granted."

"Thank you Gustav. I will text you the address."

"Ciao."

Kendra put her phone away. "It is all set for tomorrow. How ya like the way I handled that?"

"You're a spunky little bitch, I give ya that. You're a lucky bastard, Mike." Lucky stated, as he started coughing again.

"Yes, I am. So, we should know soon when we leave the states. As soon as we hear, we will let you know."

"How much do you want to bet, I know before you?"

"How in the fuck?" Reggie asked. Lucky looked upwards and just smiled.

"I have little birdies all over the place my boy, all over the place. There ain't much I can't find out these days. I'll call our friends in Egypt tomorrow. When this is all over, we will all be fat and happy."

Chapter 23

Better Call the Nurse

A s they left Lucky and Margie behind, and returned to the gallery, a silence came over all of them. The next day would be the end, at least all of them hoped. The end of the voice that haunted Kendra, the end of the nightmares that plagued her dreams, and the end of her parents. Finally, in her mind, she would be free.

They had made it more than halfway back when Kendra's phone went off. A new message from Michelle came up on the screen.

Hey Chicky baby! I'm dropping in on ya in a few.

"Great. Not the best time. She is gonna be pissed she was not at the wedding."

"Who's that? Michelle?"

"Yeah baby. She says she is dropping by soon."

Reggie looked over at Mike, then turned to look at Kendra. "This ain't exactly the night to be partying. I mean, we got some serious shit to handle tomorrow."

"I know. I'll figure something out."

Mike looked back through the mirror. "How is that leg of yours feeling?"

"It's okay. Sore as all hell, but okay."

"Just let me know if it gets bad. We need to get it stitched up before any infection starts. I still say we have Veronica come by and look at it."

"If you really think it's necessary. I guess I don't want to be in the middle of everything with an infection. Hell, we could be in Finland next week this time."

"Yeah, let my cousin come over tonight. I'm gonna call her now. She will set you up right. Have no fear." Reggie said, pulling out his phone and calling her.

"Yeah Reggie. What's happening?"

"Hey, any chance I can get you to come over to Kendra's place tonight? Kendra gashed her leg pretty deep. May need some stitches."

"Oh hell! What she do?"

"She slipped with a knife."

Kendra yelled from the back seat, tapping Reggie on the shoulder. "No, you can tell her!"

"Okay then, I'll tell er' if you don't care." he replied, looking back at her. "Well she had a nightmare, and those voices got to her. Mike saved her just in time from slicing her own throat."

"That poor child! You tell her I'm on my way. How much longer am I gonna have to babysit those old fools anyway?"

"Tomorrow the bell tolls on them both cuz."

"Oh? You know I ain't missin that!"

"Alright, bet. See you soon. Oh Yeah! If a blonde is there, her name is Michelle. Keep her in the dark at all costs."

"I got you, mum's the word. See ya soon cuz."

Reggie put his phone away. "She gonna come and take care of that leg baby girl. Don't you worry about that."

"Your cousin is a rockstar."

Not long after, they pulled into the garage, back at the Canvas. Exiting the vehicle, Kendra yelled when she stepped down on her leg. "Fuck!"

Reggie reached out and steadied her as she tried to get her balance. "You okay there?"

"This fucking thing is sore. I think I'm glad Veronica is coming over. I have a feeling I cut it pretty deep."

"That knife you got ain't no joke baby. I just hope you don't have any muscle damage. Let's get you into the Grotto." Mike stated, opening the door so they could go inside.

Reggie and Mike got her into the Grotto and sat her down onto the couch so she could put her foot up on the table and rest her leg. "Hey baby, we have an issue."

Mike, looked down at her, thinking perhaps she needed ice, or something for swelling. "What's that?"

"How is she going to look at my leg with pants on?"

"Good point. I'll run upstairs and grab you something. Do you have any shorts?"

"Yeah, look in my bottom drawer. Get me my black ones."

"Gotcha."

Mike left to retrieve Kendra's shorts for her. Reggie stood over by the bar for a moment. "You want me to make you a drink? You might need it."

"I could use one."

"Double, straight up?"

"You're awesome."

Reggie gave her the drink and Mike returned with her shorts. "Here you go, let's get you up and changed."

"Ya I'm gonna just step into the gallery for a minute."

"Oh, shut up Reggie. Ain't nothin' you ain't seen before."

Standing up, she took her pants off with a little trouble and a lot of pain. "God dammit this is really hurting."

"I was afraid of that." Mike responded. Let's get your shorts on and I will take the bandage off and look at it."

Helping her get her shorts put on, and sat her back down on the couch, she propped her leg up on the table and sank back, getting comfortable so Mike could check her wound.

"Can you hand me my drink?"

"Yeah here, now let's look at that cut." Mike handed her the glass and carefully removed the bandage. The cut was getting red around the wound, but still sealed.

"I don't know. I'm glad Veronica is coming. This could be getting infected already. I'm not a doctor though."

"I'm gonna unlock the front door. My cousin should be here soon," Reggie exclaimed, walking out to the gallery. He made it to the front door to unlock it and Michelle pulled up. She got out of the car wearing a skimpy top with no bra, and a tight mini-skirt. He opened the door for her and she walked inside. "Hey sexy!" she exclaimed.

Reggie looked at her and grinned.

"She is in the Grotto."

"Oh, it's like that?"

"We got a situation goin' on right now."

"What's going on?"

"Kendra's leg is fucked up. You'll see, she cut it pretty bad."

Michelle walked into the Grotto and sat next to Kendra. "What the hell did you do Chicky baby?"

Kendra faked a smile. "I was washing the dishes, and the knife dropped out of my hand. Came down and cut my leg open."

Michelle looked over at Mike, with a distinguishable disapointed look. "See that? Making your fiance do the dishes and see what happens. She is an artist, she doesn't need to do dishes." Michelle exclaimed, having a slight attitude.

Mike grabbed the bottle of whiskey and poured himself a drink. "Well, excuse the fuck out of me." he sneered, giving her a dirty look out of the corner of his eyes.

Kendra got an irritated at Michelle's scolding, and was in no mood to put up with it. "First off Michelle, he is not my fiance, he is my husband. Second, it's not his fault. And third, he is the one that bandaged and cleaned me up. So don't jump to conclusions like you like to."

"Wait a minute, you said, husband? What did I miss?"

"We went and got married yesterday. Sorry I didn't call you. It was a spur-of-the-moment thing."

"You bitch! What happened to Finland and me being your bridesmaid?" Michelle shouted, placing her arms crossed in front of her, like a child that didn't get their way.

Kendra looked up at Mike and laughed. "Told you it would piss her off."

"Yeah I'm pissed off. What the fuck?!"

Kendra finished her drink and handed the glass to Mike. "Calm down. We are still going to Finland, and there is still going to be a ceremony. That means you will still get to be the bridesmaid. Happy?"

Michelle got up and made herself a drink. "I guess. It's not like you left me much of a choice in the matter."

"Do I hear a bunch of arguing in here?" Veronica exclaimed, walking into the Grotto. She still had her uniform on from work and carried a bag with her.

Reggie smiled. "The doctor is in the house! What's up cuz?"

"You know, same ol' shit. Dealin' with crabby old people that are just waitin' to die." She sat next to Kendra where Michelle had sat. "Okay baby, let's look at that leg."

"Thanks for coming out, Veronica. Mike did his best to stitch me up with what he had. But he thought it best to call you."

Veronica got closer to the wound and felt the outside. "Mmhm. And it's a good thing you did. What did you use to clean this out with?"

"I poured iodine on it."

"Oh shit, bet that hurt like a mutha fucka! Well, it's a little hot, and that's to be expected. I'm gonna give you a local, and clean what I imagine is super glue?" She looked at Mike in question.

"You guessed it. Never fails to seal a wound."

"Well, if that's all you had. You should have called me when it happened. You know I got you." She opened her bag and pulled out a new syringe and a vial containing a clear liquid. "Sorry baby, this is gonna sting a little, but it won't last long."

She injected Kendra's leg a few times around the wound., making her wince and grab the arm of the couch. "Mother fucker! Whoa, that shit sucks!" she exclaimed, gritting her teeth and trying to hold her breath.

"Almost done." She hit a few more spots. "Should be numb now."

Kendra let her breath out. "Yeah, it doesn't sting anymore. Glad that shit is over."

"Now let's clean that out. Are you allergic to anything at all that you can think of?"

"Not that I know of. I don't think I have ever had allergies at all, come to think about it."

She pulled out a bottle from her bag. "Take one of these. Wait, did you eat anything recently? And no, whiskey doesn't count."

"Yeah, we ate earlier."

"Good. Eat before you take these. It's an antibiotic. If you take it on an empty stomach, it could make you sick. Not always, but it's a good habit to be in with these."

She handed the bottle to Kendra. "Take one now, then 3 times a day with food. There should be enough there for a week. If that leg is getting infected at all, this will knock it out."

"Sweet! Now what?"

"Now, to get that glue off and put some proper stitches in."

Michelle looked on at Veronica tending to Kendra's leg. "Yeah, I can't watch this. I'm gonna be sick if I do." she admitted, then turned her attention to Reggie.

"Want to go chill upstairs for a while until they are done?"

Reggie looked over to Kendra, and she motioned to him to take her. "Yeah, we can do that. Got some new shit on T.V. I wanted to check out anyway."

Reggie walked with her out of the Grotto and upstairs. Kendra listened for them and could hear them walking down the hallway to Reggie's room.

"Good. She was getting on my last good nerve anyway."

Mike sat in the chair across from her. "Yeah she was being a little annoying."

Kendra laughed. "She sure pissed you off quick. Fucking with my husband like that. What is she thinking?"

"What? You two got married? When?"

"Yesterday. Last-minute kind of thing, you know."

"I didn't even know you were engaged."

Mike laughed a little and confessed, "That was the other night."

"Well damn! I'm happy for both of you. I think. Why the rush?"

"You want to tell her or should I baby?"

Mike finished his glass and set it on the table. "I guess I will tell her."

Veronica threaded the needle and started putting in the stitches. Mike looked over at her. "So this guy, Gustav, that one that invested all that money into Kendra. He has been sending her work over to Finland. Come to find out he is part of a big sex trafficking ring hooked to some cult out there."

"You have got to be shittin' me."

"No, I wish I was. Anyway, he wants us all to go to Finland after we finish her Mom and Dad. We are pretty sure he is planning on it being a one-way trip for us. So, in case something like that happens, we got married."

"That's sweet and all, but what you guys gonna do when you get there and they sacrifice you to a goat or some crazy ass devil shit?"

"Not gonna happen. We got it all arranged. Reggie and I got people. Actually, we have a small army from Egypt meeting us there. Even Lucky is going."

"That old fool? Damn, this must be serious."

Kendra spoke up. "It is very serious. I really did not know what I was getting into until Mike stepped in. Thanks to him, Reggie, and Lucky, we may just get out of this alive."

Veronica put on the last stitch. "Sounds like you guys are in for a terrible time. You're in excellent hands though. If anyone can pull it off, those three can."

Kendra pulled out her pistol from her bag. "I am not such a bad shot either, come to find out."

"Damn sista! Packin' some heat. Hey that's a nice piece, lemme see that." Veronica said, holding out her hand.

Kendra handed it over to her, with great pride, knowing that it was nice gun. Veronica aimed it at the wall, looking down the barrel. She dropped the magazine and unchambered the round. The bullet flew from the gun and she caught it mid-air. Kendra looked wide eyed at her. "Holy fuck! You got to teach me how to do that!"

"That's what you got a husband for. Who do you think taught me?"

Mike smiled, clapping his hands. "You haven't lost your touch girl. Still packin' that Glock we got you?"

"Shit. You know it. Never go anywhere without it."

She put Kendra's gun back together and handed it back to her. "Mike, I want one of these."

"Lucky gave her that. It was the only one I saw on his wall. But that doesn't mean he doesn't have more. You know how he is with his guns."

"Mmhm, I know. That man is a walkin' armory. He still tellin' those old war stories?"

"Yup, and Margie is still tellin' him to shut the fuck up about it." They all three laughed.

"There you go lady." Veronica said, applying a fresh bandage. "You are all finished. Here, I got these for you too." She reached into her bag and pulled out another bottle. "These are Vicodin. Don't overdo it, they will kick your ass. Only take three a day as needed for pain. You're pretty tiny, so one should do you just fine. Anything else happens, call me immediately. I don't care what time it is. You call."

"Thanks Veronica. You're amazing. Listen, it's cool if you want to be there tomorrow. But be careful. Gustav and his goons are going to be there as well. The whole thing is getting streamed to this guy Nirro in Finland that is buying the sculptures."

"Sculptures?"

"Yeah it's pretty fucking kick ass actually. When I am done, they get sprayed down and they turn to stone. It's amazing."

"So, you have done this before?"

"Twice." Kendra held up two fingers.

"God damn Mike, better watch out for this one. She is about a brutal bitch." she suggested, laughing.

Mike shook his head. "She can be, when provoked. I think I am safe though."

"Yeah baby, you're definitely safe." She looked over at Veronica. "Look, you have been really great to me. I want to give you some money."

"No baby. You don't worry about me. Just watching them get what's coming to them will be enough payment."

"You sure? I mean, like fifty grand I think would come in handy."

"Yeah, that kind of cash always does. But the thing is, I can piss fifty grand in a heartbeat. I had an old man I took care of for a few years. He left his entire fortune to me. He didn't have anyone else."

"Oh hell! So you're ballin' then?"

"Baby, I only work cause I enjoy what I do. Plus, ya never know, somebody might try cuttin' their leg off one night."

Kendra started laughing. "Yeah, no shit. Well, thank you anyway. When we get back from Finland, we have to hook up and hit the town. I mean you know, do it up right."

"Oh count on it, baby. You're family now. You know damn well we gonna fuck with some people."

Mike stood up. "I wonder how long he is gonna keep her occupied up there?"

"Shit! Knowing my cousin he already fuckin' that."

"He already has one time already!" Kendra interjected.

"Don't surprise me. He a male ho. Always with someone different."

"You two need to stop. Let that man have his fun." Mike chuckled.

Veronica grabbed her bag up. "Yeah, you're right. Besides, I got to get. I got my own plans with a man tonight."

"Uh oh. Nurse gonna get her some good-good?" Kendra asked, smiling.

"You know, girlfriend. He ain't had nothing till he got this black ass thrown on him." Veronica turned around and stuck her behind out, slapping it.

Kendra held her stomach, laughing and admiring her backside. "You have a nice ass that's for sure! Have fun girl. We will see you tomorrow."

"Bye Mike." She walked out and left.

Mike went and sat next to Kendra. "So she has a nice ass huh?"

"Well, not as nice as yours baby." She giggled and put her hand on his face.

"Yeah, yeah. Want to go upstairs and call it a day? Might want to take one of them pills. It will help you sleep tonight."

"I guess you're pretty tired huh? You were up with me all night."

"I am. Come on, I'll carry you up."

She smiled and held up her arms. "You must love doing that. You're always carrying me everywhere."

"Yeah well, I do kinda like it."

Mike picked her up and carried her upstairs, laying her gently on the bed, before he went to the kitchen to get her some water. "You need some water to take that pill with?"

"Yeah baby. Thank you. Hey! Is Reggie going to lock up?"

"I am going to see." He handed her the water. "I'll be right back."

"Hurry dammit!" He looked back. She was sitting up with her arms folded, grinning.

Mike walked to the end of the hall and knocked on the door, with Reggie almost immediately opening it, as if he was waiting for him to knock. "What you knockin' for, bro?"

"Didn't know if the house was rockin' or not."

"Nah bro, we just chillin'."

"Cool man. We are calling it a day. We have a lot to do tomorrow. You gonna lock up downstairs after she leaves?"

Michelle yelled out. "Oh, what I gotta leave now?"

Mike looked at Reggie with an annoyed look and mouthed out. "What the fuck?"

Reggie shrugged his shoulders and rolled his eyes. "Ain't nobody said that." he said, before answering Mike, "I got you man. I'll make sure everything is locked up tight."

"Thanks brother. I'll see you in the AM."

Mike walked back down the hall and into their apartment, closing the door. Kendra was still laying in bed, with her clothes on the floor, and her eyes closed. He walked up to the front of the bed and undressed, letting his clothes land in pile on the floor, and crawled under the covers, separating Kendra's legs.

"Oh my God!" she exclaimed, placing her hands on his head, and moving his hair out of his way.

Mike's only reply was muffled.

"Mhmm."

Mike awoke to the smell of coffee coming out of the kitchen. After getting out of bed, he got dressed, and walked into the kitchen to see Kendra pouring a cup of coffee for him. He wrapped his arms around her waist. "Good morning you beautiful little vixen."

She set the cup down on the counter and turned around, holding his sides. "Good morning, my love."

They grabbed their coffee and sat down at the table. "How's your leg feeling this morning?"

"I'm a little sore, but better. I already ate something and took that pill. Did you get enough sleep?"

"Like a baby. You?"

"After that lashing you gave me last night? I slept like the dead!"

Mike laughed, giving a polite bow. "I am glad I could help. It really was my pleasure."

"I could argue that." she grinned, taking a sip of her coffee.

"You think Michelle left last night?"

"Yeah, she was being a real bitch. I think she was getting on Reggie's nerves."

"I knew she was going to be mad. Mike, what are we going to do with her when we go to Finland? She is going to find out everything."

"I know. I have been wondering about that, and honestly don't know. Last thing we need is to get back and then she goes running her mouth."

"I'll seriously fucking kill her myself."

"Seriously?"

"I won't let anyone stand in the way of us Mike. I mean nobody! I have always loved her, but there is a point I will not go beyond, and that one is it."

"Hope it doesn't come to that. But if it does, it will happen over there. I just know she is going to flip out."

"Well, if her bitchiness doesn't change, she won't be going."

"Speaking of going, we better get ready ourselves. It's already pushing ten o'clock."

"I know. Why don't you see if Reggie is up and about? And alone!"

"Gotcha baby. I'll be back."

Mike got up and walked down to Reggie's, and knocked on the door.

"Yo bro, are you up?"

"It's open," he heard Reggie holler from inside. He opened the door and walked in, to see Reggie sitting on the couch watching the news. "No, Michelle?"

"Hell no! That crazy bitch complained all fuckin night. Bitchin' about Kendra, about how you are always around. About how her and Kendra ain't tight anymore and she didn't get invited to the wedding. I finally told her she had to go, that I was exhausted."

"Jesus man. I'm sorry you had to deal with that shit, but thanks brother. I owe ya one."

"Nah, we straight bro. I don't think she is gonna come back knockin' on my door again though. I don't mind tellin' you, I'm glad. Ain't no pussy worth that headache."

"I hear ya man. Kendra and I were talking about her this morning. She is going to flip when she finds everything out. You know damned well she is going to when we get to Finland."

"Yeah, I know. What did Kendra say about it?"

"Nothing good for Michelle, that's for sure. She said if she runs off at the trap she is gonna kill her herself."

"I came close to it last night." Reggie said, shaking his head and chuckling. "So what? Are we ready to do this thing?"

"Yeah, just about. I don't think we will need them, but just in case, bring the rifles."

"Damn right."

It was 11AM when they headed out to go to her parent's house. Kendra remained silent and just stared out of the window the entire ride there. They pulled in and parked in the back, behind Veronica's car, who was already there. Soon, Gustav and Archie would be arriving. This was it. This is the day Kendra dreamed about. The day she sets herself free.

Chapter 24

Day of Reckoning

All of them gathered downstairs in the basement. Veronica had just walked out of the room that contained her parents and shut the door. Kendra could hear William yelling from inside. "How long do you plan on keeping us here, you bitch?!" As Veronica shut the door.

"Not much longer, you old bastard." She looked and saw Kendra and the boys standing at the foot of the stairs.

"So today is it?"

Kendra looked at the shut door, with a disgusted grimace on her face. "Yes. I see he has learned nothing about humility."

"No. I took the liberty of making sure they were wide awake for this. I would not want them drugged up for the experience."

"Good call. Thanks again for all that you have done Veronica. I really appreciate it."

"Not a problem girl. You just do what you gotta do."

"Give me a few minutes. I want to talk to them alone." Kendra said to Mike and Reggie, as she reached for the door.

"You sure that's what you want to do baby?"

"I will be fine."

She opened the door to the room and shut it behind her. She stood in front of them with her arms crossed and shaking her head. "Just look at the both of you." She looked closely at where she had inflicted wounds on them. "I see she did a good job of healing you up. No matter. You will be out of here soon enough."

William looked at her, his eyes narrowed, hatred radiating from his glare. "So, this was all a big lesson was it? You're gonna show us! Well, I hope you're happy! They are going to lock you away Kendra. Lock you away and throw away the key! That's what they'll do!"

Francine stared at Kendra, with her breathing heavy, and her face reddened with anger. "Your mother's womb must have been rotted to the core, Kendra. To spawn off and give birth to such a disgusting individual as yourself. What gives you the right to do these things to us? What?!"

"You are both fools. You gave me that right when I was a little girl." she said with a dominant smile.

She looked over at William, pointing a finger at him. "You, with your little knots, and your visits to me. You gave me that right when you stuck your pathetic wrinkled up old dick in me."

She turned and looked at Francine, now pointing her finger at her. "And you? You gave me that right when you let him. What? Your old crotch was too dried up? Or maybe you got off on it. Let me ask you something, Francine. Did it make you feel superior when you beat me?"

"You had everything you got coming to you! Your behavior was intolerable! Nobody should be forced to raise such a monster! You were constantly an embarrassment to us! We had no choice." Francine scowled.

"No choice. I see." Kendra rested her chin on her fist and paced back and forth in front of them almost like a lawyer in a court scene, in an intence crime show. "So you had no choice. I guess sending me back so they could find me another home was out of the question. Because, as you stated, you had no choice. I guess sending me off to a school was out of the question as well, because, you know, you had no choice. Is this what you are telling me? Because I am really trying to understand here," Kendra stated. As her voice got louder, with anger taking control.

"You appreciated nothing Kendra!" William yelled, "You needed discipline! Even then you rebelled with your constant whining and sniveling." he sated, turning his head from her, then rasing his voice and shouting to her, "Fed to wolves! That's what should have come of you! Fed to wild animals!"

Kendra stopped pacing and stood in front of William, leaning down into his face. "I was." Her voice was calm, collected, and steady. She stood up and opened the door, and left the room. After she closed the door, she addressed Mike and Reggie, still waiting at the stairs. She knew exactly what she wanted them to do, to help her prepare.

"I will need both of you to drag them in their chairs, down to the end room. I have some work I have to do, before this even starts."

"Yeah, we can do that. Gustav will be here in a few minutes. You said noon right?"

"Yes, I did. Make sure they stay out here until I am ready."

"Okay," Mike replied, looking over at Reggie. "Let's get 'em in there."

Mike and Reggie went inside and started dragging William and Francine to the end room. "What are you doing? You had better be letting us go!" William ranted.

"You just don't get it, do you?"

Francine screamed at Reggie, "You brute bastard! Stop it this instant! I am Francine Blake! I will not tolerate this, not for a second."

Reggie stopped dragging the chair and whispered into her ear. "I don't think tolerating or not tolerating is an option that is on the table right now. Just sit back and enjoy this short flight on *You're Fucked Airlines.*"

They got them into the room and placed them side by side in the middle, so to give Kendra plenty of room, that she would be needing. "Why are we here?! Kendra! Get your ass in here! Kendra! Get in here at once!" William yelled.

The door shut as Mike and Reggie left the room, leaving them tied to their chairs. William looked at Francine, angry and ready to start laying the blame on anyone, but himself. "This is entirely your doing! You just had to have another child!"

"How dare you?! It was you! We are where we are right now because of you and your perversions. You just had to have another one of your own! You just could not be satisfied with the prostitutes anymore! Could you?"

"I don't know what you are talking about. I had no such dealings with women like that." he denied, looking away, disgusted.

"Oh? All of those business trips to New York? I know what you were doing!"

"I was working! That's what I was doing!"

"Working?! Is that what you call it? How many times did I find women's clothes in the trunk of the car William?"

"What are you talking about?! I never had one in the trunk of our car!"

"Ah ha! So you admit it!" Francine glared at him.

"Admit what?! Your countless escapades with the help? I know what you were doing those nights I was gone! I have proof!"

"You have nothing, William! Nothing."

Kendra walked into the room and shut the door. "I see you two are getting along nicely. I will need those." she demanded, pointing to their clothes.

She pulled a knife from her pocket and cut away the medical garment they were wearing. Kendra stood back and looked at them both, and thought outloud. "Hmm, I'll be right back. I need some more rope."

She left the room briefly. "Now what is she going to do to us?"

Francine looked over at him. "It's over William. That is what she is going to do to us. This is how it all ends."

"You're out of your mind! She would not dare!"

"I think she would. You did."

Kendra returned with some rope. "Now you two behave, or there will be some serious consequences for your actions."

She went to work tying knots, wrapping rope around their bodies and fashioning designs. After hearing voices outside, she closed her mind. Kendra had to focus. This was going to be her greatest piece, her masterpiece.

Outside, and right on time, Gustav walked down the stairs. Mike and Reggie were there, as well as Veronica.

"Where is my favorite artist?"

Mike pointed to the room at the end. "She has them in there. Leave her be for now until she is finished."

"Finished? She hasn't already started has she?" Gustav asked, looking worried with disappointment.

"No, she is just getting them and herself ready."

Gustav noticed Veronica standing there, and asked with a suggestive smile, "And who is this lovely woman?"

Veronica smiled back, shaking his hand. "I am Veronica, and trust me, you can't afford this."

Gustav lost his smile, realizing his intent was denied. "How charming." he replied, then turning his attention to Mike. "I have everything needed. Archie can start bringing it in. Yes?"

"That's fine. Just gather it all over by the door. I don't think she will be too long."

"Capital." he replied, "Archie, can you and Pavel get the gear from outside? We have a show to put on."

"Yes! Yes, of course! Pavel, what are you waiting for? Let's get everything in here." he ordered, as he looked at everyone standing there. "Archie will be back in a minute." He turned and made his way back up the stairs.

Gustav stood, looking at his phone for a moment. "Do you think she is ready for this Mike?"

"She is ready. I think that this will finally free her."

"And how is that?"

"Well, the nightmares, the voices. I can bet that they all stem from these two."

"Just as I said before?"

"Exactly. I told her the other night that I think you had a very good point. This would definitely be the key to healing her. The thing I am thinking about though, when all of this is over, I don't want any loose ends at all."

Gustav smiled at Mike, putting his hand on his shoulder. "Trust me, there will be none."

"Yeah."

Archie and Pavel came back downstairs, carrying some equipment and a few bags. As they were setting the bags down, Kendra walked out of the room. "They are ready."

Gustav looked at her. "I have a mask for you. Will you be requiring anything else?"

"I need red lights. Sorry, an afterthought."

"Ah, well good thing we are prepared. Archie, we will need the lighting as well."

"Ah yes! Pavel, get the lights from the truck, and the stands." Pavel left and returned shortly with the lights, handing them to Kendra.

"Thank you Pavel." she said, turning around and going back into the room, closing the door.

She started setting up the lights and turning them on as William watched her. "What are you doing now?"

She looked down at him as she turned the last one on. "If there is hell, I want you to get a good look at it before you go. That is what I am doing."

"Before we go? What is this nonsense?"

Kendra squatted down in front of them and looked up at their faces. "Foolish old man. Today is not about nonsense. Today, Daddy dearest, is your day of reckoning."

Kendra left the room and returned to Gustav. "You can set up the camera now. Did you, by any chance, bring that grinder? I will need a cutting blade on it."

"Yes. I thought you may wish to use it again. I also brought something very special for you."

"And what would that be?"

Gustav walked over to one of the bags and pulled out a large knife.

"This is an ancient and very sharp knife. Nirro gifted it to me some many years ago. It had been in his family for centuries. It would be an honor if you used it today."

Kendra held up the knife and looked closely at its construction. The blade was all of eight inches, sharp and had engraving in it. Ancient symbols of a runic nature she did not understand or know the meaning of. The handle was wrapped in leather topped off with a crude skull. "This looks like it will work just fine for what I have in mind." She walked over to Mike and Reggie. "Are you going to come in with me? I need you in case, you know."

"I got you, love," Mike assured her. "I am sure after this you will feel a million times better."

Gustav looked over at Kendra, and let his eyes focus on her leg. "I noticed you have a limp. Is everything ok?"

"It turns out I have little luck with kitchen knives. Perhaps this one will serve me better." she replied, holding up the knife he had given her.

Veronica spoke up, haveing another suggestion for Kendra, in preparation. "Speaking of, I imagine it is going to get messy. I have a bandage for you so that it will stay protected. It's waterproof."

Kendra looked at the bandage that Veronica was holding out, for her to see. "Then we better put it on." She got undressed and Veronica applied the bandage. "It is looking better. I think it should heal just fine."

"I am sure it will."

Reggie looked over at Mike. "There she goes again, taking her clothes off. What's the deal with that?"

"She is an artist bro. I guess that's something I will have to get used to."

Everyone gathered in the room in front of her parents. They were tied to the chairs in shibari knots. Their hands tied to their legs, palms up. On their chests, the rope was wrapped and fashioned into an inverted pentagram.

Gustav's eyes widened, and his face beamed with delight. "Now this is something to behold. Nirro will be most pleased with this."

All the lights were off, except for the red ones. The room glowed red, and a menacing overtone filled the air, adding to the sadistic ambiance she had created. Kendra walked over to a small radio in the corner and turned it on. Classical music came bellowing out of the speakers., and played as she put on her mask, before walking up to Gustav. "You can start the stream."

Veronica stood in a corner next to Reggie, speaking to him quietly, "This shit is about to get real up in here. Mike's girl about to handle her business."

Reggie leaned his head over and whispered. "Just watch. This is the sickest thing you will ever see."

Nirro popped up on the stream, sitting in his chair, drinking a glass of wine. Kendra looked at him, pointing to her parents.

"These are for your throne room. They are what made me who I am. Enjoy."

"I like this already. Gustav, can I keep her?"

Gustav replied smugly. "All things are possible."

Mike clenched his fist, fighting the urge to beat Gustav to a pulp, and then feed him to his wife. But, he remained silent, assuring himself that Gustav would be dealt with soon enough. *Your time is coming, mother fucker. Oh, I can taste it now. I will enjoy watching you die*, He thought.

"Kendra! Now listen to me! You stop this at once!" Francine was panicking. Her voice shook. "Money! You can have all of it. We will go away forever!"

Kendra slowly circled Francine like a shark right before he rushed in for the kill. "Do you honestly think I need your money? You were always too blind to see what was right in front of you, Mother. Now, you will have a reason!"

Kendra grabbed her by the hair, pulling her head back, and sinking the tip of the blade into one of Francine's eyes, being careful not to rupture the eyeball itself. Francine screamed in agony, as the eyeball was pried from its socket. After a moment, her eyeball hung out, still attached.

"Now, see? Isn't that better?" Kendra asked her.

Francine wailed in pain, calling for William. "Do something William! She is killing me!"

"Kendra! You bitch! Leave her alone!" he yelled.

Kendra turned her head slowly to him. "You Daddy, I think you are just too angry. You need to smile more."

Walking calmly over to him, she took hold of his head , holding it tightly to her chest. "No licking my tits now Daddy, those belong to my husband!" She sank the knife into his face,right below his ear, making William howl, and cut deep, all the way to the edge of his mouth.

"Well, that is a good start. At least you have half of a smile now."

His skin and flesh from his face sagged and bled, exposing his teeth and gums along his jaw. His screams became garbled with blood as it ran down the side of this face and onto his body. Temporarily satisfied, she patted him on the head. "Sit tight. I'll be right back."Moving to Francine ,who was still screaming and straining to break free. Kendra knelt down before her and looked into her face. "Golly Gee mother. Looks like you're lopsided."

She reached up and flicked the hanging eye and let it swing causing Francine to scream again. "Well, we are just going to have to fix that." she giggled.

Grabbing Francine again, and yanking her head violently, she dug the blade under her other eye, causing it to come out like the first. Blood shot out and sprayed across Kendra's naked chest, and ran down to her abdomen, as she tightly held on to her mother's head, laughing.

Francine writhed and pulled while her screams became louder, and intensified. "Please stop this, Kendra! Please!"

Kendra laughed, still taunting her mother, "Oh, it's too late for that now!" As she grabbed William by the head again, she cut deeply into the other side of his face. His head moved back and forth, shaking from left to right as he tried to make the pain stop. His words became gibberish as he tried to speak.

Stepping back, she looked at them both, and then at Veronica, pointing the knife at her, making Veronica's face turn blank. "Oh, hell no."

"Nurse! I will need a needle and some thread. Our patients have had a minor mishap. No anesthetic required."

Veronica sighed and walked out to get her bag. "Thought that crazy bitch was gonna involve me in this carnival of chaos. Holy shit! Girl is demented!"

She brought back the needle and stitching for Kendra. Kendra walked up and grabbed it from her.

"You really thought I'd hurt you didn't you? Silly little hottie nurse." she said, giggling as she walked back to William.

Veronica shook her head, looking at Mike. "Damn son, where in the hell did you find this one?"

Mike shrugged, "Just lucky, I guess."

Kendra slowly circled William again, running her fingers through the splattered blood on her chest, then rubbing it in.

"Now, Mr. Blake, don't you worry. I'll have you better than new in a jiffy!"

She pulled the flesh back together and started stitching it back up, with William's head pulling away as she sank the needle in. "If you don't stop moving, it will be a botch job!" she yelling, striking him on the head. "Now fucking stay still!"

Continueing to stitch his face, until she got to his mouth, Kendra paused with a thought. "I don't think you're going to be needing this anymore." she stated, as she started stitching it closed.

William's eyes moved from left to right rapidly. His muffled screams had been silenced as she finished up the other side. Stepping back and looking at what she had done brought a great sensation of satisfaction to her.

"Perfect! Now you will always have a smile on your face." She looked over at Francine and peered into her hanging eyes. "I really don't know if there is anything I can do for you Mother. Think you're just going to have to stay just like that-- on second thought, I do have a wonderful idea." Kendra giggled.

She started to sew Francine's sockets closed, taking care to not rip the stem that still attached itself to her eyes.

Francine howled and cried out in pain and she put in the stitches, taking her time, making sure Francine did not have relief too quickly.

When she had finished, she stepped back and looked at her work, pleased with the outcome.

"I'm not even sure you can see!" she exclaimed, throwing the needle and thread onto the floor.

Kendra picked the knife back up. "I think I am going to have to do something with your hair though. She started shaving off the gray hair on William until he was bald, leaving a few scrapes and cuts that bled from his scalp. She then went over and shaved Francine's head, while she talked to her. "You know mother, they used to do this to women after they had slept with Nazis. You haven't been whoring around now have you?"

Francine sobbed with her body was becoming weak as she started slipping into shock. "It will all be over soon my beloved ones. Yes. all over soon."

I think now, it is time for the grinder, she thought to herself as she went over and picked it up. "Now William, it is of the utmost importance you do not move. Understand, because this is going to hurt."

She held William's head tightly once more, and started cutting into his head, through the flesh and into his skull, spraying blood and skull fragments into the air, and covering them both. His body started convulsing as his bladder released, and muffled noises came from his sewn mouth, that strained at the stitching and bled.

Half way around his head, his body went limp. She finished cutting and set the grinder down and picking the knife back up. She stuck it in the cut and pried the top of his skull completely off and set it in his hands, like a bowl.

"Now to get rid of that awe-full brain of yours."

Reggie stood next to Veronica, looking in disbelief. "Is she gonna? Oh, hell--"

Kendra started pulling and prying out his brain, cutting the spinal cord from it. Once it was out, she put it in the bowl on his lap. "There now! Now, my Daddy dearest, you can rest in hell, and while you're at it, have a nice bowl of 'go fuck yourself'."

She looked over at Francine, with her face containing an evil grin, and her voice carrying a sarcastic tone. "Oh Mommy?" she called, "Guess what time it is? I have the cure for all of your headaches you fucking cunt!"

Francine screamed, "No!" Kendra grabbed the grinder up again, and leaned Francine's head back, cutting into her skull. Bits of flesh and skull flew in every direction as the blade spun, and ground its way through her skull. As she cut through the veins on the side of her head, blood sprayed and landed on Kendra's body, adding to the red saturation that already had adorned her.

Moments after she started, Francine's body stopped moving as life left her, with her heart finally giving out and stopping.

Kendra finished taking the top of her skull off when she was done cutting it open, and just like William's, she placed her brain on the top of her skull on her lap. She stepped back and looked at them both, very pleased at the creation that she had made out of the both of them. Covered in blood, mutilated and still bleeding, they sat lifeless, still tied to the chairs. She turned back around to look at Nirro, who was still watching intently. "See you soon." she said, as she dropped the knife, and walked out of camera view, and out of the room.

Kendra stepped from the shower and was handed a towel by Mike. She had washed away the blood, bone fragments and memories of her parent's, and let them get sucked right down the drain.

"Your eyes didn't turn, baby."

She looked in the mirror, drying her hair. "I know. I am not sure if that scares me or not." She brushed her hair and stopped, setting the brush down on the counter. Staring into the mirror, deeply. "Do you think it is gone?"

"I hope so. I can guarantee your mom and dad are though."

"Yeah. They are. I'm not really sure how to feel about it. I thought it would feel, you know, different."

"Well, you can't really control how you feel. So, how you feel is just what you're feeling, and that's it. I am no psychologist or anything, but it makes sense to me."

"I'm just afraid that they are gone, but not really gone."

Mike turned to her and placed his hands on her shoulders, facing her towards him. "Look, whatever happens, we are almost there. We will get Finland over with, come back, and head out west. Deep in the mountains, outside of some small little town, and never have to think of this again."

Kendra smiled. "I know you will make it all alright. You always do."

She reached up and kissed him, then turned and got dressed. "But for now, I can't wait to see how they turned out!"

They left the bathroom and rejoined Reggie in the basement. Everything had been cleaned up. Gustav stood next to Reggie and had been discussing Finland with him. "I think that you're going to find Nirro's estate quite satisfying. If there is any pleasure in the world to have, you will find it there."

"How do you mean?"

"Nirro is-How can I describe this? Very eccentric? He is a collector, much like myself, wines, art, women and many luxuries. He enjoys the more carnal pleasures of this world."

"Sounds to me like the Devil's playground." Reggie said, chuckling.

Gustav looked at him plainly. "It is." Reggie stopped laughing, taking notice of Mike and Kendra coming back downstairs.

Gustav turned and greeted her as she came down, "There she is. Wait until you see the outcome. I have to say, Nirro is more than pleased."

Kendra glanced at Reggie, asking Gustav, "Are they still in the room?"

"Yes, come and see. You're going to love this."

They all walked to the end room. All the lights, blood and mess had been cleaned spotless. In the middle of the room, sat her parents. Two figures, tied to chairs and turned to black stone, with an almost marble complexion throughout the finish.

"This is amazing!" she shouted as she glided her hand along her mother's arm. "How did he get it to finish like marble?"

"It is something that he has been working on. He just perfected the process the other day. I think it adds a very exquisite finish to it. Don't you?"

"Yes. It is actually quite beautiful."

"I am happy that you are pleased. So, we shall depart for Nirro's in a few days. That will give you enough time to get your affairs in order."

"Affairs? How long do you think we will be gone?"

"Well, it all depends. We may be gone only a week, or you may decide you would like to stay longer. It is entirely up to you. Many who have visited, have decided that they never want to leave."

Mike laughed at what Gustav had to say about Nirro's estate. "So what? You're telling me he has an estate filled with people that just visited and stayed. Like they just live there now?"

"No, of course not. I simply mean many get infatuated with his life, and the surroundings of the area, and decide that is where they find their happiness. So they stay in Finland. It really is a land of mystery and ancient things."

Kendra put her arm around Mike, deciding to inform Gustav of her plans with her husband. "Well, that will not be us. We have plans. After Finland, and don't take this the wrong way, I doubt you will ever hear from us again."

"That is unfortunate, but understandable. When one finds what makes one happy, they usually never let that go. I am happy for you both."

"Well, we owe you a lot of thanks. After all, if it were not for you, I am not sure we would have ever met, or gotten together at all."

"I take no credit for what the universe has planned. Everything happens for a reason. I am just happy to have been able to invest in such a talented young lady, even if it was for only a short time. It was well worth it to me."

"I'm glad you feel that way. Truly I am. We need to get back and start packing. I have a million things to do before we leave."

Mike shook Gustav's hand. "Well done man. Look, will there be any issues bringing anything into the country that normally you can't bring?"

"Such as?"

"I don't go anywhere without a gun. You should know that by now."

"No, there will be no issues. I have everything arranged. I doubt you will need it where we are going. We are all friends here and over there. It's a very laid back atmosphere, unlike the city here."

"Sounds like a delightful break from the normal."

"I find it is, usually. Never-the-less, I'll let you take your leave. You have a lot to do."

"Thank you Gustav. We will see you in a few days." Kendra said, as she turned away from him, ready to leave.

Kendra and the boys headed upstairs, meeting Veronica who was standing next to her car, waiting for them. "Damn girl. I have seen some shit in my life, but I never seen anything like that. I don't mind saying, you one crazy ass white girl."

Kendra laughed, "Yeah, so I have heard," as she looked up at Mike. "Or wait, what was it you said baby?"

Mike looked down at her with a grin. "Bat shit crazy?"

"Yes, that's it! Bat shit crazy."

Veronica started to laugh, still enchanted by how they carried on. "I think you both off your rocker. So what you gonna do now?"

"I guess we are going to Finland in a couple of days. After that, we are all headed for the mountains for good. We could use a nurse if you want to go with us."

"What in the hell am I going to do in the mountains? I'm a city girl. I'm good right where I am. Besides, I'll probably get eaten by some bear or mountain lion. No thanks. This girl gonna stay in the crime riddled city where she is safe."

They all seeme dto find great humor in the irony of her statement. Reggie gave his cousin a hug. "We will see you when we get back, for sure. But if you ever change your mind about out West, lemme know. I got you, Cuz."

"Mhmm. And just what your black ass gonna do out there?"

"I dunno. Maybe start a garden. I hear it's legal to grow weed out there now."

"Oh, that's just what you need to do." Veronica replied, laughing. "Okay, I'm gonna bounce. You guys take care of yourselves, and I'll see you when you get back."

Kendra gave Veronica a hug. "Thank you, for everything."

"You just make sure that head of yours is straight. And take all of them pills I gave ya."

"I will."

∞ ∞ ∞

On the ride back to the Gallery, Mike kept looking over at Kendra, with Reggie staying quiet in the back seat, looking out the window and fidgeting on his phone.

"What baby? You keep looking at me. What's on your mind?"

"You really didn't feel anything?"

"No, not really. Nothing."

"I ain't gonna lie. That is scarier than what you did to them."

"Why?"

"Remember me telling you on the way to the city? About

becoming desensitized? It happens when you have killed too much."

"I haven't killed that many people, baby."

"No, but it is how you did it. That is the most brutal shit I know I have ever seen. And now you're just as calm as could be. Like nothing happened."

"So what? Now you want me to feel bad or something? Fuck them! I couldn't care less." She snapped back.

"No, you're missing my point baby. Even if they had it coming, you should at least feel something, but you don't. It's just an interesting observation, that's all."

"Yeah well, I haven't felt pity for many for a long time. Especially for those fucks. Good riddance."

"I get it. Maybe mountain air and a stress-free life will help. I know you probably feel better knowing that it's over, but honestly, you have a long way to go before you are healed from what they did to you."

She grabbed his hand, rubbing her thumb on it. "I know. At least I know I don't have to hide it from you."

"No, you're safe with me." Looking in the rear-view mirror, he asked Reggie, "Hey you good back there bro.?"

"Man, you know some women over there don't shave their armpits?! That is some caveman shit, if I ever heard," he said, looking at his phone.

Kendra and Mike started laughing. "What the fuck man? What brought all that up?"

"I was looking on the net bout' customs and shit. Over in Europe they don't shave. I mean I don't know. You guys are set, but this man gonna be hitting some shawtys while I'm there. Gustav was tellin me that Nirro cat always has women around. But I don't know about no hairy armpits. Not to mention a big ole bush to match! I be gettin' hair caught up in teeth and shit! What the fuck I 'sposed to do with that?"

Kendra was holding her stomach and bending over, laughing to the point she could not talk. Mike, trying to concentrate on the road and drive, looked in the mirror. "Better pack a few razors then bro. I honestly don't know what to tell you."

"I do! Shit, I'll get myself one of those Tarzan outfits. I'll be swingin' through the bush hollerin!" Reggie started beating his chest and yelling a Tarzan call.

"Oh my God! Reggie, stop! You're killing me!" Kendra exclaimed, laughing as tears formed in her eyes.

"Even Kendra, she gets it. She keeps that shit shaved."

Mike shook his head. "Oh, now we're gonna analyze my wife's pussy? Is that where this is goin?"

"I'm just sayin, I don't see you coughing up no hairballs! Even Michelle shaves that shit!"

"Bro! What the fuck is up with you today?!"

"I'm just saying I ain't down with hairy assed women. That's all."

Kendra caught her breath. "Good God Reggie, tell us how you really feel."

"I just did." Reggie crossed his arms and looked back out the window. "Nope, if she hairy? Get yo mutha fuckin' clothes on and get the fuck out!"

"Oh my God bro. Did Gustav give you some drugs or something?"

"No." Reggie said, laughing. "I'm just lettin' it be known how Reggie rolls."

"Alright then. Now we know. No hairy bush for Reggie." Mike looked over at Kendra. "You better write that down. We don't want to forget that."

"Oh, for fuck sakes. I don't think I'll forget." She said laughing, and then stopped. "You unbelievable bastard!" She turned around and looked at Reggie.

"What I do?"

"Now I'm gonna think about that every time I shave!"

Reggie laughed out loud. "Ha! They all think about Reggie! Then have Mike do it."

"No, I'll just think about it too."

Kendra sat back in her seat. "Can we just change the goddamned subject?!"

Reggie was laughing hard laying over in the seat. "Sure we can do that. What you wanna talk about?"

"I need to eat so I can take this God damned pill. And maybe give you one of the others and put you to sleep."

"Alright, I'll chill." Reggie sat back up and looked back out of the window, quietly beating his chest and doing another Tarzan call.

∞∞∞

Getting back, they all gathered in Reggie's apartment, with Reggie busy in the kitchen making burgers for lunch. "You ain't never had a burger 'til you had one of mine! This is what I call the Reggienator!"

He handed one to Mike and Kendra on a plate, with some oven baked potato wedges that were lightly seasoned. Kendra took hers and sat on the couch.

"Jesus Reggie!" she exclaimed, after she took a bite and swallowed it. "This is bloody awesome! What did you make this with?"

He stood at the counter drinking a beer. "No, I can't tell you that. Nobody knows how I make these and that's the way it's stayin'."

Mike sat eating. "I can't believe I never had one of these. After all these years I just found out you can cook? What the hell, man?"

"You should taste my ribs! I like to keep it a quiet hobby. Gotta feed this machine the good shit bro. You know how it goes." Reggie rubbed his stomach.

"Ya know, maybe when we go out West, you could open up a place? Ya know, like Reggie's BBQ or some shit like that. I think it would be packed if the rest of your stuff is this good."

Reggie grinned and looked across the room out of the window. "Yeah, my own little place. I like that. You really think

I should? I mean, it's gonna be kind of boring really out there. Only reason I'm going is because you guys are."

Kendra was still eating. "I think it's a great idea! And I can help you decorate the place! It will be kick ass!"

He looked over at her, like she was crazy. "Um yeah, no thanks."

"What?"

"I don't want people losing their appetite because some guy's dick had been cut off and staring them in the face."

Kendra started laughing. "You got me fucked. I'll do whatever you want man. But that would be a cool place, just saying."

"Yeah, well, maybe after we get out there I will look around and get a feel for the area. Maybe I will open a little BBQ joint."

"You should bro. Because this right here? This is a killer. I can see this becoming really popular, real quick."

"Thanks Mike. I seriously like the idea. We will see what happens."

Mike finished his burger, and his phone rang. He picked it up off of the table and opened it. "Ah! It's Lucky. Games on!"

"Yeah old man. What's the news?"

"The news is, you are leaving in two days. Now I need you to get over here pronto and help me get everything to the airstrip."

"When? Today?"

"No, early in the morning. Like, 8 AM. We got a bunch of stuff we have to bring."

"How is everything looking with our other friends?" Mike asked.

"I'll talk about that tomorrow. Don't worry about shit. We are looking good."

"OK, well I guess we will be there early then. I'll see you tomorrow."

"Later."

Kendra got up and put her plate in the sink. "Well? What did he say?"

"We have to be at his place at 8:00 am to help load the plane."

"I wish we could just fly over with him."

"Yeah, that would be ideal, but no can do."

"I know. Did he say anything else?"

"No, not really. He said everything is good to go and he will fill us in tomorrow on the details. He doesn't like talking on the phone much. Always thinks someone is listening in."

Reggie cleaned up the plates and put away the rest of the food. "Yeah, his paranoia has come in useful though. Truth is, we don't know what that crazy old man has his hands into."

"No kidding. Surprises me he is going with us really. I guess he expects there to be some pretty heavy shit going down."

Kendra grabbed a beer from the refrigerator and took her pill.

"Sounds like he can handle it though."

"That's for sure. If there is a war, you definitely want him on your side. He will make sure we all make it out in one piece. The Egyptian guys though, I can't speak on them."

Reggie walked over to the window, drinking his beer. "I know if it was my sister that got snatched up and sold, I would want to help whoever it was that was lookin for her. That's what I know."

"Yeah, I agree. If Lucky says it's cool, I'll go with that and not worry about it."

"Shit!" Kendra looked at her phone.

"It's Michelle. I better take this."

"Hey Chicky, what's happening?"

"That's what I was going to ask you. What are you up to?"

"Just finished eating and taking that pill."

"How is your leg feeling?"

"It's sore, but better. She did a good job on me, I think. I'll be healed up in no time."

"Good. So about our trip."

Kendra rolled her eyes. "Yeah, what about it?"

"Well, I was thinking we could do some shopping this afternoon. You know, get a bunch of new outfits to wear over there."

"Honey, I don't have the time. We are leaving the day after

tomorrow and I have a shitload of things to take care of before I go."

"Well, have Mike do it."

"No Michelle, he is my husband, not my step and fetch it."

"Fine!" Michelle snapped. "Well, when are we leaving?"

"I am not sure yet, but I will let you know. We can pick you up on the way to the airfield if you want."

"I guess." Michelle sighed. "You know, we don't have any time to chill anymore Kendra. I was kinda hoping to hang out today."

"You can come by if you want. Like I said, I have a shitload of things to do. A lot is changing Michelle, something you're going to have to get used to."

"God! Whatever!"

"Hello? Michelle?" She threw her phone onto the couch. "What a spoiled little bitch! She hung up on me!"

Mike shook his head. "I have a feeling she doesn't need to be going with us. I'm just saying, she is a major liability. We are not going over there to play games."

"I know, baby. I don't know what to tell her though. Who knows? She may get over there and decide she likes it and stays."

Mike stood up and faced her. "Listen to me baby. By the time we are finished over there,there will be no one left to stay with. You understand?"

"Do you think it is going to be that bad?"

"Worse. Let me explain something to you. If Lucky is arming up like this, we will not go set them down for a stern talking to. We are going over there to annihilate some terrible fucking people."

"So we are just gonna go in with guns blazing and blow them all up?"

"I wish. That would be easy. No, don't forget, we have to find the sister. If we go crazy, we won't get most of them. They will scatter like rats and disappear. We don't want that."

Kendra sat back down on the couch and wondered, "Have you

ever done anything like this before?"

Reggie turned around and looked at them both. "No lies. This kind of thing is new to us too. This ain't no joke. Like Mike said, if Lucky is involved, we in for some shit."

"I feel like we will not come back. Like we will never see our cabin in the mountains." Kendra said, solemnly.

Mike got up and grabbed a beer and opened it, taking a drink. "Not gonna happen! You just get those thoughts right out of your head. I need you focused and your head secured. As much as it can be anyway."

"What? You worried I am gonna flip out over there?"

"I am not worried about that. But I think they are going to want you to. You put on a hell of a show for that sadistic fuck. What makes you think he will not want to see that live? Or worse?"

"You think so? Are they really that twisted?"

"Yeah baby, they are really that twisted."

"Well then, I guess it is what it is. Fuck it. We better head downstairs. I want to put everything up in my studio and close all the curtains. Just in case we are gone for a while."

"That's a good idea. I got some top of the line security goin' on up in here, but you don't want fools getting any ideas while you're gone."

Kendra looked over at Reggie. "Thanks. I really don't know what I would do without the both of you."

"I got you lil sis. Let's go close this bitch up."

Kendra got up and headed downstairs, as Mike stayed back with Reggie.

"Hey baby? We will meet you down there in a minute. I need to go over some shit with Reggie real quick." Mike hollered to her.

"Ok. Don't be too long though."

"I won't. We will be down in a minute."

Kendra left and went downstairs. Reggie opened another beer and handed one to Mike. "What's on your mind?"

"Remember that idea I had?"

"Yeah, I remember. Go out with a bang right?"

"Yeah. I need ya to take care of that tonight. Send me the phone number when you're done, so it's all set."

"Hell yeah! She gonna love this!"

"I know. Alright, let's get down there."

"Bet."

Mike and Reggie got downstairs and Kendra was taking her painting down. She carefully started stacking them against the wall. "God, it's going to look so empty in here."

"Where do you want to put them?"

"I don't know. I was thinking about my studio, but I really would rather not."

"Shit, why don't we put them in that empty apartment upstairs next to mine?"

"I thought of that. Good idea Reggie. If you guys don't mind?"

"No baby, we got it. You need to rest that leg as much as you can. Why don't you take care of your emails and let us handle this? We will be careful."

She smiled at Mike. "Okay. Love you."

"Love you"

She went into her office and sat at her computer, scrolling through emails. "Shit, I better update my website and let people know all orders will be put on hold for a bit." She though for a monent, then started updating her site and writing a letter to all of her customers.

To all of my wonderful customers. First, let me thank you for all of your support and for coming on this amazing adventure with me. It truly is a pleasure working with all of you and an honor to have my work displayed in all of your homes and businesses. For the next few weeks, all orders will be put on hold as I am traveling out of town. Upon my return, it will be business as usual. It is my regret that my gallery will be closed while I am away, but fear not! Kendra Blake will return with new ideas and concepts! Yours truly, Kendra Blake.

"There. That should be good enough. Now let's check the bank account. She opened her account up on her computer and signed in.

"Wow! Baby! Come in here!"

Mike came into the office. "What's going on?"

She pointed to the screen. "Ya think he liked mommy and daddy?"

"Jesus Christ! How much money does this mother fucker have anyway?"

"I don't know. Gustav said his pockets are endless."

"Fuck, if I didn't believe in what we are doing, I'd say fuck Finland."

"I know. The thought crossed my mind." She turned her chair and faced Mike. "Look, I went through literal hell on earth growing up. These fucks are doing the same thing to God knows how many people, baby. If we have a chance to actually do something good in this world, I don't want to pass that up. I hate thinking other people have to go through what I did."

"Then we go, and that's just it. Probably too late to back out now anyway."

She wrapped her arms around him, hugging him tighly. "I'm glad it's you and Reggie. I'm not even nervous. Kinda feel like a superhero or something."

"It's going to be insane. But yeah, I kinda feel the same way." Their moment was interrupted by a shrill voice from the Gallery, as Michelle mad an obnoxious entrance.

"Where in the fuck is she at?" snapped Michelle.

"You better slow your roll with that lip Michelle. Don't think you gonna stomp your feet and get what you want around me!" Reggie snapped back.

Kendra got up and went out to the gallery. "What in the hell, Michelle?"

"Oh there you are." Michelle exclaimed with her hand on her hip. She looked around for a moment. "What in fuck are you doing in here anyway?"

"Trying to close up Michelle, I told you I have a lot to do before we leave."

"I told you, I have a lot to do before we leave." Michelle sneered back sarcastically.

Kendra rolled her eyes. "What is your major problem? I don't have time for this shit today!"

"You are my major problem right now! All I wanted to do was spend a few hours shopping but no, you just have to be stuck up his ass 24/7!" she yelled, pointing at Mike.

Mike glared at her, having enough of her mouth and her temper tantrums. "Well, as you can see, she isn't up my ass. She is standing right there."

"Oh haha! Yeah, you're hilarious. I seriously don't understand what the big deal is about Kendra. A few hours will not kill you."

Kendra looked at her straightforwardly and lowered her tone. "Michelle, you are my friend, alright? And I love you to death. Really, I do. But understand, my world does not revolve around your every whim and emotion. I have a lot of shit to do, and a very little time to do it in. Instead of throwing a fit, you should be asking to help! Like an assistant is supposed to do! Or did you forget you work for me?!"

"Oh really? Is that what I should do? Seems to me you have all the help you need right here."

"As a matter-of-fact Michelle, you're right. I have all the help I need. Right here!" Kendra yelled back.

"Fine! Stay here with your idiot husband!" she shouted pointing at Mike. "Oh, you are sexy! No doubt! But I highly think you have nothing in between those ears of yours!"

"What in the fuck is your problem?!" Mike yelled.

Kendra walked slowly up to Michelle, with her fists clenched at her sides. "I will tell you this one time, and one time only. If you ever talk to my husband like that again, or say anything about him like that again, I will split that pretty little face of yours wide open. Do you fucking understand me?"

Michelle's face went blank, and she backed away, looking at

Mike and Reggie, then back at Kendra. She stood silent for a moment, then her eyes narrowed. "Fine! You know what? Fuck you, and fuck you, and fuck you! I don't need this shit!" She screamed as she left the gallery.

Kendra threw her hands up in the air. "Whatever Michelle!"

Michelle went to get into her car, then stormed back into the gallery.

"And another thing! I'm not going to fucking Finland!" She turned and left again. Kendra made her way to the door and yelled at her, "Good! Because you're fucking fired! Bitch!"

Michelle started her car and sped away, while Kendra shut the door and locked it, then closed all the curtains in the storefront. "God damned jealous ass bitch! I swear to fucking God!"

"Is that what all of that is really about? Is she that jealous?"

"Yes baby! She is that damned jealous!"

"I mean I get it. You're not there all the time anymore, but damn!"

Kendra walked up to Mike and explained it a little further. "No baby. You don't get it. Remember, I told you I slept with her once?"

Reggie started rubbing his hands together. "Oh hell ya, this is gonna be good."

Kendra looked over at him, glaring and pointing a finger at him. "Shut up Reggie! Not now."

"Damn sorry."

"Anyway, I played it off like a night of fun and partying. She didn't. She has had a thing for me ever since."

"Oh hell. Yeah, now I get it." Mike pulled his hair back and put it up. "Way too much drama for me though. I guess we don't have to worry about her and Finland anymore."

Kendra looked back out at the door. "No, I guess not. She is just hurt. I'll fix it when and if we get back."

Mike hugged her, trying to be understanding. "Maybe she will get over it."

Kendra, saddened inside over the fight she had with

Michelle, wrapped her arms around his waist. "I hope so.

Chapter 25

Out With a Bang

They pulled into Lucky's right at eight. He was standing outside, waiting for them. Lucky was looking at his watch as they climbed out of the SUV. "Good! Right on time! Now come on, we have to hurry! I want the wheels up at 0600 hours tomorrow and we have a lot to do."

"Damn old man, you're fired up about this aren't you?" Mike asked, as he shut the door.

"You're goddamned right! I am! I got Mackie down at the hangar. He modified the old bird so I can make the flight nonstop. I will coast in on fumes, but I'll make it."

"Fumes?" Kendra ask, a little confused and laughing at the statement.

"Yeah! Fuckin fumes! I'll be close to being out of fuel. Now let's stop this jabbering and come on!"

Lucky took them back to the bunker and went inside, pointing to all of the equipment he had prepared. "Now I have everything all packed up and ready to load. I just need you guys to carry it all up for me."

Mike looked at all the crates Lucky was pointing to, astonished on just how much he wanted to bring. "Dammit man. Looks like you packed up everything."

"I have Mackie and you guys, plus the guys from Egypt. I want to be prepared! Besides, Mackie and I humped a lot of bush together in the Nam. So we are going in hot and ready to throw lead"

Mike shook his head, rubbing his shadow that was growing on his face. "Um Lucky, I ain't trying to be an asshole or anything, but you guys are like—"

"What?! Getting old?! You're damned right we are getting old and not getting any younger. Now get your asses moving! We don't have much time."

"If you say so." Mike bent down and picked up one of the crates. "Come on Reggie, let's load this shit up."

"Is there anything I can carry?"
Lucky pointed at some duffel bags over in the corner.

"You can manage those, I think. Don't drop any of them though! You'll blow us all to hell!"

As they were walking to Lucky's Jeep, carrying some of the gear Lucky had packed, thoughts ran through Mike's mind. "Fuck me! I ain't seen him like this in years."

"I know, make me wonder if he ain't havin' a flashback or some shit."

"Yeah Reggie, you just be quiet with all that noise. That's the last thing we need."

Reggie started laughing as he loaded up a trunk. "Remember that time he got all whacked and started shooting up his computers? Damn fool thought the VC were spyin' on his ass."

Mike, remembering the incident, burst into laughter. "Yeah, that was a trip. Margie was standing there yelling at him, and we were ducking for cover. That was fucking hilarious."

"I don't know. Maybe this will be good for the old man. Somethin' tells me he ain't plannin' on comin' back though."

"What? You mean like one last big hurrah?"

"Somethin' like that. He is all fired up in military mode. That's what I know."

"Yeah, he gets like that. Just not in a long while. We better get the rest of this shit."

"For real."

They walked back inside and Kendra was carrying the duffle bags up, still struggling with a sore leg. "You got that baby?"

"Yeah, I'm good. This is fun!"

"Yeah okay, just be careful with those. Alright?"

Mike and Reggie each grabbed the side of a large crate, and got ready to carry it to the jeep, and place it with the others. "Damn man, what the fuck you got in here?"

"Fireworks my boy! God damned beautiful fireworks!" he yelled, with a triumphant grin.

"Oh, God."

They carried the crate up and placed it in Lucky's jeep, that Kendra leaned against, rubbing her leg. "Just relax baby. Trust me, we got this. Only one crate left anyway."

"It's just sore, that's all."

"Yeah, well, I don't want you ripping those stitches out. We don't have Veronica where we are going."

"If you say so, love."

They went back down and got the last crate, and loaded it up, before Lucky locked up the bunker and went to his Jeep. "Come on, get in."

They got into the Jeep and left, taking an old dirt road for a few miles until it ended up in an enormous field. It took them right to the end of a runway, where there was a gate Lucky had to unlock. "Sit tight, this will only take a second."

He unlocked the gate, and they continued onto the airstrip, pointing to the buildings on the other side, and shouted to Kendra. "That's where we are going. My bird is in there."

Kendra looked over at the building. "My God! How big is it?"

"Big enough! It's an old C-47 we picked up a long time ago. Mackie rebuilt the whole damned thing!"

"Who is that anyway?"

"He owns this place with me. He collects old warbirds. You will see here in a minute."

Lucky pulled his Jeep into the hangar and under the wing of the C-47, and parked.

Kendra got out and looked up at it. "Holy fuck, it's huge!"

"Damn right she is!" Lucky agreed, getting out of the Jeep. "Hey Mackie! Where in the fuck are you?!"

A man stuck his head out of the door some roll-around stairs were attached to. "Up here! Just about finished with her, Lucky!"

Kendra looked at Mike and Reggie, motioning to the giant old plane. "You guys ever been here before?"

"Shit, this was one of our favorite places. We used to come here after school and hang out for a bit." Mike informed her, crossing his arms and grinning.

"Have you ever been up in this one?"

"Yeah, I can fly it too. Damn old rattling thing scares the shit out of me."

Lucky lowered his brow. "You stow that talk away! You're gonna piss her off and she won't want to go!"

"No, I'm fine." Kendra said.

"God Dammit! Not you, the fucking plane! She is sensitive." He looked up the stairs. "Now you boys get that gear up there and stow it away. I need a beer."

Lucky walked up into the plane and grabbed a beer out of the cooler that was on the floor. "How are we looking, Mackie?"

Mackie had grease on his blue coveralls and smelled like aviation fluid. He had a short trimmed beard and looked young for his age, even though his hair had turned gray. "We will get there with a few gallons to spare. So no bullshit, and no stops."

"Ah, so you decided to come along, did ya?"

"Well yeah, why wouldn't I? I needed a vacation anyway."

Mike and Reggie walked in with the first crate. "Where do you want this?"

"Mackie looked over at them. "Well, I'll be a son of a bitch! Ain't seen you boys in years!"

"Hey Mack. Got her all ready to go?"

"You bet. You can square that away down there." He pointed to an area a short distance away. "We made space for it all to fit and be secured."

"Gotcha."

Reggie and Mike set the crate down and went back down for the rest. They got back down to the Jeep and Kendra was looking up into the plane, and filled with curiosities as to what it was like inside. "You want to go up and see the inside?"

"Hell yeah! I have never been on a plane before."

"They don't make them like this anymore." Reggie stated.

"No, they don't bro. Thank God!"

They muscled the crates up the stairs with Kendra following. She stepped inside the aircraft and started chuckling. "Oh shit! This is huge!"

Mackie looked over at Lucky, after seeing Kendra. "She can fly with us!"

"This is Kendra, Mike's wife, ya fuckin' dumbass!"

Mackie stood up, wiping his hands on his coveralls. "I'm Mackie. I keep this old bucket of bolts in the air."

"Will you people stop trying to piss her off?! God Dammit! I got four-thousand miles to fly and I don't need her all pissy!"

"I think she is amazing, Lucky. Can I see upfront?"

"Sure kid, come on, I'll show ya."

Lucky and Kendra went into the cockpit. She sat in one of the seats, gazing at all the gauges, and controls. "You really fly this huh?"

"Yup. I have flown all around the country with her. Never this long of a trip though." He looked over at her, getting amusement of how she had her hands on the steering column. "You sure you're ready for what's about to happen?"

"No. But I am not worried, if that's what you want to know."

"Just stick close to Mike and Reggie. You will be fine. Look, I packed up an MP5 for you. It's in one of those cases back there."

"What's that?"

"It's a small assault rifle. Fully automatic too. The rest of my guns I'm afraid are too big for you to handle. This is nice and compact. You shouldn't have any trouble with it."

"Ooh can I see it?"

"When we meet up across the water." Lucky turned in his seat. "Look, if I don't make it out of this, you and Mike make a go of it when you get back ok? Get the fuck out of here and go make a family somewhere. He loves you, ya know?"

"I know, and what do you mean, don't make it out? You're going to be fine. Besides, you're too God damned ornery to die."

Lucky started to laugh, but it was taken by his coughing. "You got a good point there. Anyway, I better get you kids back. You guys have an early flight in the morning. Now, you're going to be there before me. So just hold tight and play the game. I'll let you know when wheels hit the ground."

"We don't even know what time we are leaving yet."

"Trust me, you're taking off at 7AM."

"If you say so. Then we better get going." She got up out of the chair and walked back to Mike and Reggie.

"Lucky says he is taking us back. Also said we are leaving at 7AM. Wonder why Gustav hasn't messaged me and told me?"

"I am sure he will, but if the old man says that's what time we are leaving, then I guess that's what time we are leaving."

They said their goodbyes to Mackie and headed downstairs. Kendra looked at a few of the planes that were also in the building. "Are these Mackie's? The ones you told me about?"

Lucky looked over. "Yeah. You got a P51 Mustang, an old Corsair that still doesn't run worth a shit, and a Hellcat. He has more in the other building."

"Damn! Does he still fly them?"

"Sure does. Every chance he gets. We better get going."

They left the airstrip and headed back to Lucky's house. Pulling up to the house, they saw Margie outside watering the flowerbed. "Oh Jesus! Her and her damned flowers are going to be the death of me!"

"Oh relax old man, they're just flowers."

Lucky threw his arms down. "Bah! Bullshit I say!"

Kendra walked up to Margie and looked at her flowers she had growing. "They look really pretty Margie. Looks like you have a green thumb."

"Thank you dear. One of the pleasures in life I really enjoy."

"Jesus God almighty! Don't encourage her!" Lucky yelled.

Margie turned around and snapped at him. "Oh, go and blow yourself up you old coot!"

"I'm gonna blow something up alright!"

Kendra got a chuckle out of their bickering, as Margie went back to watering her flowerbed, hiding the grin she had on her face.

"You two are a trip."

"Oh, we don't mean anything by it. We have been fussin' like this for decades. Keeps us young."

"So that's the secret huh?"

"Well, not for everybody."

They giggled, and she hugged Margie goodbye. "You take care of yourself Margie. We will see you when we get back."

Margie Hugged her back and looked at her for a moment. "Kendra?"

"Yeah Margie?"

"Kill one of those fuckers for me too will ya?"

"You got it Margie. Just for you!"

After their goodbyes, they got into the SUV and headed back to the gallery.

"Damn, Margie is a cool old lady baby!"

"Yeah, you have to be, to put up with Lucky for that long, I suppose."

"No shit right?! Do you think she will be OK until Lucky gets back? Or we get back?"

"What do you mean 'Or we get back'? And don't let old Margie fool ya. That old woman is as tough as they come."

"Just something he said when we were up in the airplane. He acts like he may not be coming back."

Mike shook his head. "It's just jitters. He knows damned well he will be back in a week or so."

"I hope so baby. I really like those two."

They pulled into that garage and went inside the Grotto. "I

don't know about you guys, but I could use a drink."

"Sure Reggie, but take it easy. We got to be on our toes from here on out."

"Yeah, I know. I'm good bro."

Kendra sat down on the couch and rubbed her leg. "Mike, I think I better go upstairs and change the bandage. Besides, I have to take another pill."

"Alright, let's go and get you taken care of baby." She went to stand up and her phone rang. She took it out of her pocket and looked at it. "It's Gus."

"Hello."

"Hi Kendra. How are you doing? How is that leg?"

"I am good, just getting the last touches on packing up and getting ready for this trip."

"Yes, about that. Archie will pick all of you up early in the morning at five-thirty. We are taking off at seven."

"Oh wow, that is early."

"Yes. well it is a very long flight."

"Yeah like what? Four thousand miles or so?"

"Very good. Yes, it's about that. Not to worry though. The jet is very comfortable. I am sure you will enjoy it."

"That sounds great! Have to admit, I am excited."

"As Nirro is excited as well. Tell me, is Michelle all ready to go?"

"Um we kind of got into it, and I kind of fired her."

"I see. Well, that is unfortunate. I think she would have enjoyed his hospitality."

Kendra motioned for Reggie to make her a drink. "Well, she will get over it. We have been friends for a long time."

"See that she does Kendra. Nirro has a thing for blonde haired women."

"Um, I'll do my best."

"Make sure you do. I hate disappointing. I will see you in the morning."

"Okay see you then."

She hung the phone up and put it away. "Fuck!"

"What's going on?" Reggie asked as he handed her a drink.

"He all but ordered me to bring Michelle! Just what I fucking need! To babysit her the whole fucking time."

"Did he give any specific reason?"

"No. Just that Nirro has a thing for blonde haired women. What the fuck ever that's supposed to mean?"

"This ain't cool. What ya gonna do sis?"

"I don't know Reggie. I guess I'll call her and try to make up. Fuck!"

Kendra pulled her phone back out and called Michelle.

"Yeah Kendra. What do you want?"

"I want you to stop being nasty, get over here and have a few drinks so we can all go to Finland in the morning."

"Really?"

"Yes really. You're like my best friend." Kendra stuck her finger down her throat, causing Reggie to laugh. "I really was looking forward to you coming with us. Come on Chicky, it's a trip of a lifetime."

"I know. I'm sorry I acted like such a shit. Drinks, huh?"

"And from what Gustav tells me, Nirro loves blondes. And he is seriously rich."

"Shit, fine! You talked me into it. I'll be over in a little while."

"Awesome! Make sure you bring everything. Someone is picking us up at Five-thirty in the morning. So we can't get overly hammered tonight."

"Damn that's early. Oh well. See you soon Chicky baby!"

"Bye."

Kendra sighed and finished her drink. "Do I need to tell you guys how bad that literally sucked?"

Mike grabbed her glass and refilled it. "No. Great performance. But I bet it sucked pretty bad. She is getting put in some serious danger, coming along and all."

Reggie took a drink. "As long as she keeps that trap shut. That woman has a mouth on her."

"I think she will be alright. She feels kinda bad, I believe."

Mike slammed the rest of the glass. "Let's go upstairs and I'll change that bandage out for you."

"Ok, Love."

Kendra sat on the bed after she took her jeans off. Mike took the old bandage off and threw it away. "It looks good. Still sore though huh?"

"Yeah. Feels way better than it did."

"I'll put some triple antibiotic ointment on it and bandage it back up, and then check it again tonight."

Kendra rested back on her elbow and took her other hand, placing it between her legs, pulling her panties over to the side. "I don't see what the big rush is."

Mike looked up. "Oh hell. So that's what's going on? Alright."

Reggie sat in the Grotto, looking at his phone, until he heard someone was knocking on the front door. "Oh shit. Bet, it's that crazy ass bitch."

He got up and walked to the front door and unlocked it. "You calm down now Michelle?"

"Yeah. I'm sorry Reggie. I know I can be a real bitch sometimes."

"It's all good. Let's not worry about it. Ya got all your shit packed up?"

"Yeah, it's in the car."

"Backseat?"

"No, I put it in the trunk."

"Alright let's go get it. Then we will have a drink. Sound good?"

"Hell yeah."

Reggie carried Michelle's bag into the Grotto and set it on the floor, while she strolled over at the bar and poured herself a glass of whiskey. "Where is Kendra and Mike?"

"Oh, yeah, they went upstairs about an hour or so ago. Mike wanted to change her bandage."

"She is lucky. Wish I could find someone like that."

"Well, ya never know. Might just be waitin' for ya over in Finland."

"Yeah! Maybe. At least it's something to hope for." She smiled and took a drink.

"There you go."

She sat on the couch. "So, you think you will ever settle down?"

"Who, me?" Reggie asked.

"Yes you. Walk that Mrs. Reggie down the aisle?"

"I highly doubt that. I like to keep things nice and simple. No headaches and no drama." Although he laughed at her question, he was being serious with her.

"I can see that. You don't seem like the type to stay locked down to one woman anyway."

"What can I say? I like variety!"

Michelle giggled and took a drink. "I will definitely drink to that!"

Mike and Kendra finally mad it into the Grotto, to join Reggie and Michelle.

Michelle stood up and gave Kendra a hug. "I'm sorry Chicky baby. I didn't mean to be such a bitch."

"It's cool. There is a lot going on. Everyone's life is changing."

She pulled away from Kendra. "Sorry Mike. You didn't deserve that. I didn't mean it. Honestly, I am happy for you both."

"Don't worry about it. Let's all have a drink and forget about it all."

"Sounds good." Kendra agreed.

They sat and had a few drinks, told jokes and laughed until dark. Realizing it was getting late, Kendra looked at her phone. "It's getting to be about that time. Everyone ready for tomorrow?"

Reggie finished his drink. "I guess I am as ready as I'll ever be."

He looked down at Michelle. "What about you?"

"Oh, I am ready. Not too sure about being ready for bed yet though. But I'm ready to get on that plane."

"You can come upstairs if you want. I'm sure we will find something to do."

Mike laughed, "You're a damned slut Reggie!"

"I'm not a slut. I'm a fuckin pimp!" He responded, striking a pose.

Michelle, standing up, grabbed Reggie by the arm. "Alright then pimp, let's go. I'll be your ho tonight."

Kendra shook her head and laughed. "Fucking shameless!"

Archie picked them up right at 5:30AM. They made their way to the small airport and pulled up next to the private jet that was waiting. Gustav was there, leaning up against a car, talking to Dante. "Ah good. They have arrived. Dante, let's get them loaded up."

Dante and Pavel took their baggage and put them away in the storage compartment, while Mike walked up to Gustav. "Good morning Mike. How's today treating you?"

"Good Gus. Damn good. Look, I need to ask you a small favor."

"Sure, I am sure I may be able to help in some small fashion."

Kendra, Michelle and Reggie went into the aircraft and took a seat.

"Holy shit this is frikkin' amazing!" Kendra exclaimed, as she sat down in one of the leather seats. "What is Mike talking to Gustav about, Reggie?"

"I don't know. Nothing probably. You're right though, I gotta get me one of these."

Mike and Gustav boarded the plane. As Gustav got aboard, he looked at how everyone was seated, and directed them, starting with Kendra. "Why don't you sit here? Mike, you can sit next to her, and Reggie, you and Michelle can sit over there. Or rather, you sit here, and I will sit on that side. Yes, that should work out nicely."

They all got up and sat where Gustav had suggested, and got comfortable in their seats. A few moments went by and Archie boarded the plane and took his seat. Gustav looked around. "Is everyone comfortable?"

"Yeah, Gus. I think we are good," Kendra responded. She looked across the aisle at Michelle. "You good Chicky?"

"I am. This is some badass shit I tell you! We are like rock stars!" she exclaimed, raising horns in the air with her hand."

Gustav smiled. "Excellent. Let me talk to my pilot for a moment, and we shall be on our way."

He walked to the front and opened the door to the cockpit, closing it behind him. A few moments later, he took a seat and buckled. Looking over at Mike, he nonchalantly gave a nod. "Ok, I think we are all set. We should be in the air in just a few minutes."

The jet taxied down the runway and made it to the end, turned around, and quickly sped up, lifting off of the ground.

"Oh, Holy shit! This is intense!" Kendra exclaimed, gabbing Mike by the arm. Mike looked over and grinned, remembering the first time he had gone up with Lucky.

Pulling out his phone, he looked at Kendra. "Look out the window." The jet went into a bank, and she could see straight to the ground.

"Wow! That is amazing!"

"I remember my first time. I thought the same thing." Mike said as he looked at the ground below. "Hey baby, look! I think that's your parents' neighborhood."

Kendra peered out the window. "Holy shit! You're right! There is their house! I can see it from here."

Mike handed her the phone. "Keep looking at it baby, and press call." Kendra grabbed the phone and looked at it. "Who is this?"

Mike grinned. "Just do it, and hurry."

Kendra found her parent's house again and pressed the call icon. As soon as she heard the first ring, fire flew out of the sides of her parent's house and it exploded in flames, sending smoke billowing up into the air. Her jaw dropped open, and she slowly looked over at Mike.

"You did that for me?" Mike smiled and took his phone back. Kendra unbuckled, and sat in his lap, wrapping her arms around his neck. "I love you more than anything baby."

Mike kissed her. "And I love you more. Now let's go to Finland."

Acknowledgement

There are so many I would like to thank for the support I have received and the belief they have had in me to finally do this.

First, I would like to thank my wife and children for affording me all of the tireless hours I spent writing and rewriting this story. Second, I would like to thank my wonderful friend, Laurie Leigh, for reading every day and coaching me with wonderful idea's as I went along. My long time friend Ron Arold for the the humor and creative feedback, and my friends Ronny and Marybeth Asterud. Mary spent many hours reading over and checking my work, plus gave me some wonderful idea's when I was blank, and coaching me on punctuation, that I am sure I still do not have correct.

Last but definately not least, my good friend, Linzi Gray, whome without, this story would not be what it is now. Her and I spent many hours, days and months in writing the original screenplay that this book is based on, and will continue to create more in the near future.

And finally, thank you for all of the readers that took the time out of their busy schedules to indulge in the story. May you all be blessed.

J. Alexander Paine.

Made in the USA
Thornton, CO
07/08/22 08:03:59

072b7e32-afbd-402c-92fc-f3a9cde233e8R02